HEROES' MIGHT

JAKE TYSON

THE VINDICATORS BOOK THREE

HEROES' MIGHT

AMBASSADOR INTERNATIONAL
GREENVILLE, SOUTH CAROLINA & BELFAST, NORTHERN IRELAND

www.ambassador-international.com

Heroes' Might

Hardcover ISBN: 978-1-64960-446-0
Paperback ISBN: 978-1-64960-313-5
eISBN: 978-1-64960-335-7
Library of Congress Control Number: 2022946960

Cover design by Hannah Linder Designs
Interior Typesetting by Dentelle Design
Edited by Maggie Platt

AMBASSADOR INTERNATIONAL
Emerald House
411 University Ridge, Suite B14
Greenville, SC 29601
United States
www.ambassador-international.com

AMBASSADOR BOOKS
The Mount
2 Woodstock Link
Belfast, BT6 8DD
Northern Ireland, United Kingdom
www.ambassadormedia.co.uk

The colophon is a trademark of Ambassador, a Christian publishing company.

For Shiloh Dani Arden Tyson.

We will see you in Heaven someday.

I can't wait to meet you.

ACKNOWLEDGMENTS

The *Vindicators* series could not have come together the way it has so far without help from so many people.

To Jessica, my wife, for always being there for me, listening to me, encouraging me, and being one of my first readers and my number one fan forever: thank you for falling in love with my characters as much as I have and for wanting the world to love them, too.

To my family—Dad, Mom, Zac, Hunter, and MaKayla—as well as my in-laws and my extended family, for always being supportive of my desire to write, encouraging me to do so, giving me feedback on my writing, letting me bounce ideas off you, asking questions about the writing process, and suggesting *Vigilante's Light* and *Freedom's Fight* to anyone who'll listen!

To all the members of the Realm Makers Consortium who helped me figure out things like character names, superpowers, motivation, costume design, and on and on.

To Ambassador International for continuing to publish this series! It's been a great journey so far, and I'm looking forward to what the future has in store. Thanks also to the editors (Daphne and Maggie), cover designer (Hannah), and others who helped make each book in this series the best it can be.

To my wonderful church family at Oak Park Baptist Church. I have such a solid support system, and so many of you have been eager to read and promote my books to others. Thank you for that!

Thank you to all the readers of *Vigilante's Light* and *Freedom's Fight*. I'm so glad that there are readers enjoying this world I've crafted. I hope that there are more of you out there than when this series got started! Keep reading—I've got plenty more stories in mind that I can't wait to share with you.

Most importantly, I couldn't have done this without the desire and the ability to write given to me by my Heavenly Father, and I couldn't have written anything honoring Him if He had not saved me through Christ. Thank you, God, for leading me to this opportunity and for giving me the idea to write the Vindicators!

TEAM ROSTERS

The Vindicators:

Carter Jonson/The Crusader—Son of Wyatt Jonson, the first Crusader, nineteen-year-old Carter has taken up his father's mantle and his mission to protect the Brooks.

Dean Sterling/Drifter—Billionaire heir to Sterling Enterprises, Dean has funded the mission of the Vindicators from day one. He uses his teleportation powers and an array of tech to fight crime as Drifter.

Gideon Turner/The Seraph—The hero who started it all, Gideon Turner became the Seraph after his captivity in Venezuela, where Dr. Jeremiah Ashcroft gave him light powers.

Patrick Omer/Spright—Eighteen-year-old Patrick received superspeed through a flu shot that was infused with the Nephilim serum. Patrick became Spright and joined the Vindicators under Gideon's tutelage.

Wesley Turner/Rampart—Wes Turner, Gideon's younger brother, has the power to transform his skin into any material.

Jolie Anderson—An honorary member of the Vindicators, Jolie is Gideon's fiancée and a detective for Sojourn P.D. at the twelfth precinct in the Brooks.

The Regency:

Alfonso Mendez/Backfire—The captain of the guerrilla force that captured Gideon Turner, Mendez has the power to detonate anything he touches.

Artemis Wayans/Somna—Artemis was a career politician before Dr. Ashcroft recruited her as his second-in-command. She has the power to control the minds of others.

Audrey Knight/Stormcry—Under the name Silver Siren, Audrey Knight was a famed pop star and model. When cancer ruined her life, she came to Ashcroft for help. In exchange for her loyalty to the Regency, Ashcroft cured her and gave her the power of flight and sonic manipulation.

Dr. Jeremiah Ashcroft—Founder and leader of the Regency, Ashcroft was determined to create superhumans. With the DNA of the Nephilim, he has succeeded.

Kenton Pierce/Tetra-Hazard—Kenton Pierce was a violent criminal before joining the Regency. Having the power to manipulate toxic materials only makes him more dangerous.

Melanie Davies/Deluge—A teenage runaway, Melanie has the ability to manipulate water.

Randal Quinn/Red Raider—A British war profiteer, Quinn was Ashcroft's first success. Crime lord Luca Serban brought him to Ashcroft while in Romania. Quinn has the power to control fire.

Vince Powers/Fragment—Powers was a lowly drug runner before climbing the ladder to drug lord, running the Shine trade in Sojourn City. Ashcroft gave Powers the ability to duplicate himself at will, creating an army of doppelgangers.

Zeke Norris/Torrent—Zeke Norris was a soldier in the U.S. Army. When he retired, he joined a mercenary force and later came to work for Ashcroft, who gave him super strength.

Others:

Arianna Serafin—One of Dean Sterling's best friends, Arianna is one half of the duo that helps the Vindicators with any tech issues they run into.

Hannah Lonestar/Brass Bison—A Native American vigilante, Hannah protects her people from traffickers and drug dealers.

Jarrett Mercer/Yeoman—Jarrett Mercer is a former member of U.S. Special Forces. He lives on a farm outside Wichita, Kansas, and protects that city as a crossbow-wielding vigilante.

Katrina Monahan/Lancet—Katrina Monahan is a deadly assassin who worked for Luca Serban and was responsible for the death of Wyatt Jonson, the first Crusader.

Luca Serban—Luca Serban was a Romanian crime lord. After coming to Sojourn City in the USA, he formed his own criminal empire and nearly toppled the city until the Seraph interfered and locked Serban away in Stone Gate Penitentiary.

Lucy Carmichael—Patrick's next-door neighbor and crush, Lucy invited Patrick to church, where he was saved. She supports his endeavors as Spright.

Maddox Odell—Arianna Serafin's partner, Maddox works at Sterling Labs and helps the Vindicators with their technological needs.

Samuel Whitlock/Solar Flare—The world's first superhero, Samuel's existence was hidden by the U.S. government after his descent into insanity.

PROLOGUE

The desert wind tousled a few loose strands of Hannah Lonestar's braided hair, blowing them up to tickle her nose and eyes. She tucked the black hairs under her beanie to clear her vision. She was perched on a ridge that overlooked the vast plain. The silver glow of the full moon lit the expanse, which was sparsely vegetated. In the distance, lights twinkled, signaling the comforting presence of a reservation belonging to the Apache tribe—her tribe.

She put a hand on the grip of one of her twin revolvers. Since reaching adulthood, Hannah had become something of a local legend in rural Arizona. Tired of the abuses heaped on her people, Hannah took up her father's prized guns, disguised herself with a black bandana over her nose and mouth, and set out to right those injustices. They called her Brass Bison, the vigilante who took out sex traffickers and drug dealers. Tonight, her prey was not the dregs of humanity. It was something else. Something feral.

Hannah pulled her red denim jacket tighter around her and brought its Sherpa collar closer to her neck. The early fall winds chilled her to the bone. Staying out past dark in the desert could be perilous, but Hannah had lived here for her whole life. She knew how to take precautions. She could not build a fire for fear of scaring off her prey, so she wore multiple layers. A battery-powered heating pad rested between her hoodie and flannel shirt. She had thick gloves and wore a beanie down around her ears, along with two pairs of socks under her heavy cowboy boots. If she died tonight, it would not be from the cold.

The beast she hunted had never been seen—not by anyone reliable, anyway. A town drunk told her he had seen it a few nights before. He regaled her with stories of an evil spirit made flesh. Even in the dark of night, he could tell the creature was a mass of knotted muscle under gray fur. Its head was round, with a gaping rictus of a mouth splitting it in half. Razor-sharp teeth jutted from behind its lips. Its arms alone were the length of a man, and its fingers were tipped with sword-like claws. The townspeople whispered fearfully the name of an ancient folk story: *wendigo.*

Hannah wasn't sure she believed all that. Some creature had been coming into town and killing people, yes; but it was just as likely to be a mountain lion, coyote, or bear, driven by hunger and emboldened by the sparse population on the edge of the reservation. This was not Hannah's typical hunt. Regardless, she had taken it upon herself to protect this reservation, and she was honor-bound to follow through. Criminals were not the only threat to her people.

She had been out in the cold for almost an hour, and there was no sign of any kind of creature. Hannah was ready to call it a night and head back for the warmth of her home to curl up under her blankets. She put her gloved palms on the dusty ground to push herself up.

The bushes off to her left rustled. Hannah drew her revolver in one fluid motion, the metal barrel scraping against the leather holster. She rested her left hand on its twin, ready to draw it, too. It could be nothing. A rabbit. A wild pig.

The creature that rose from the bushes was no rabbit. It was six feet tall, at least, but its hunched back hinted at an even greater height. Its arms dragged the ground as it trundled toward her, its clawed fingers digging furrows in the dirt. Moonlight reflected off its short, gray fur. Hannah's eyes widened, and she backed away. The hairs on the back of her neck stood up. *Impossible.* The creature growled. Its eyes were not visible in the dark, but she did see its long, sharp teeth. The beast resembled a wolf, but it had the gait of an upright beast, like a gorilla . . . or a man.

The old drunk had been right.

"Wendigo," Hannah whispered.

The creature roared, the sound terrifying and deafening. Hannah whipped out her second revolver and fired both weapons in tandem. The muscular beast roared as the bullets struck its hide. It charged. Hannah yelped and squeezed the triggers again—and again. Six rounds in each gun spent quickly, and the wendigo did not go down.

Hannah hurled herself aside as the beast bore down on her. It lashed out with one arm, smacking her on the back with the force of a speeding car. Hannah's feet left the ground, and she screamed as the cliff face below her gave way. She hung in the air, nothing between her and the ground far below.

But as she fell, something wrapped around her ankle. Hannah screamed. The creature jerked her back onto the ledge and threw her to the ground. She landed in a dry patch of foliage. Twigs cracked under her. The impact drove the breath from her lungs. As the creature loomed over her, growling deep in its throat, Hannah loaded her right-hand gun with more bullets. Her fingers shook as she slid the brass projectiles into the chamber.

She saw its eyes. They were tiny, recessed behind protruding brows. They were black, unfeeling, emotionless. This creature—the wendigo—was death.

The wendigo leaned down and pinned Hannah to the ground with its right arm. She struggled to free herself, but its grip was supernaturally strong. She wiggled an arm free and trained it on the beast's head. The wendigo lowered its head toward her, its wolf-like maw wide. Saliva dripped from its tongue and splashed on the ground beside her.

Hannah steadied her shaking hand. She had to shoot the beast before—

Its teeth sank into her left shoulder. Hannah screamed in pain, angled her right hand, and aimed at the wendigo's eye.

Bang.

The foul beast's bite and grip slackened. It let out a high-pitched whine and slumped over on top of Hannah. She wrestled her shoulder free of its teeth. Each movement sent a fresh wave of stabbing pain rolling down her arm. Tears stung her eyes. She pushed the wendigo's head aside and wiggled her way out from underneath it. She managed to scramble away from the dead creature and slump to the ground before she broke into sobs.

What was it? She had never thought the legends of the wendigo were true. Even if they were, the creatures were said to reside in the North, near the borders of Canada. What had brought this one down so far south?

She holstered her guns, stood, and walked back down the trail toward her motorcycle, her shoulder screaming with every too-hard impact of her feet on the stone path. It would take her a while to get back to the reservation. She needed to hurry before she lost too much blood.

As she mounted her bike, a deafening roar pierced the air. Hannah's heart stopped.

There's another one out there.

There was nothing she could do about that tonight. If she stayed, she would die. Her first priority was to patch up her wounds. She could worry about the second wendigo after she recovered. She gunned the engine and raced toward home, leaving the haunting cry far behind, echoing on the desert wind.

CHAPTER 1

Twenty years ago

Dr. Jeremiah Ashcroft juggled an armful of documents, research files, and his briefcase as he stumbled up the stairs toward the science wing of Stanford University. Papers shifted in his grip, and he struggled not to lose hold of them. Everything here was essential to the presentation he was about to make.

His father had left him a small fortune and the means to rebuild their company. But for what Ashcroft wanted to do, he needed help. A veritable think tank of the country's top scientists had come to Stanford. This was Ashcroft's chance to get a foot in the door. Maybe literally.

He clutched his things to his chest as tightly as he could and snapped his foot up to kick the handicap button with the heel of his sensible Oxford shoe. As the door obediently opened, Ashcroft ducked around it to enter the building. Air-conditioned coolness greeted him, a welcome relief from the intense summer heat outside.

Ashcroft poked his head over his stack of papers to see which way he needed to go. Taking the first hall on the left, Ashcroft moved toward the nearest conference room, where the think tank was to meet.

"Jeremiah!"

He peered around his stack. Mark Garvin, an up-and-coming scientist with more money from his family fortune than he knew what to do with, stood outside a door ahead and to the left. Garvin and Ashcroft had been roommates in college. Though they had since gone their separate ways, they remained in contact. Garvin was the one who had arranged this appointment for Ashcroft.

Ashcroft smiled at the sight of his friend and rushed over. Garvin pulled open the door, allowing Ashcroft entrance to the conference room.

"It's Doctor now, but thank you, Mark."

Garvin rolled his eyes. "Of course, *Doctor.*"

Ashcroft stepped into the conference room, found an empty seat at the table, and set his things down. He hurriedly organized them into a neat pile, glancing around the room as he did so. A dozen men and women, all nationally recognized for their brilliant achievements, occupied the room. *Dad should be here at the head of the table.* Many of these people had been Father's contemporaries. How they had laughed at him when he had presented his ideas. Ashcroft would get a different reaction.

"Ladies, gentlemen," Mark said, "this is Dr. Jeremiah Ashcroft, the man I was telling you about. He's a recent graduate of our doctorate program. Dr. Ashcroft and I go back a long time, and I can assure you that whatever he's put together, it's brilliant. He has one of the finest minds I've ever encountered."

The room's occupants greeted Ashcroft, who sheepishly smiled and nodded. *They don't even recognize me, do they*? They'd forgotten all about Father. Ashcroft bit the inside of his cheek, bringing himself back to reality. He had to focus; the presentation had to be flawless.

One of the men gestured to the front. "Let's begin, shall we?"

Ashcroft opened his briefcase. He had expected to have a few minutes to set up, but he must have run late. He would have to do this on the fly. Removing a dry erase marker from his briefcase, Ashcroft grabbed a stack of papers and moved to the front of the room. He set his papers on the lectern and cleared his throat.

"Ladies and gentlemen, what is the greatest crisis facing our nation today?"

Several of them exchanged glances, though none offered a response. Ashcroft furrowed his brow. He had expected someone to volunteer a guess. Fossil fuels, global warming, diminishing resources and growing population—anything. But he didn't receive so much as a raised hand. So be it. He would answer his own question.

"Security. Not so long ago, we watched helplessly as one of our finest cities was attacked. Countless people died, victims of enemies who wanted to instill fear. And we realized then that we are a target. Our country is hated by many the world over. We need protection. Since 9-11, our country has been focused on security by means of technology and weaponry. We increase security measures in airports and production of armaments for our soldiers. The problem has never been the weapons. It has been the people."

Still, he received no response. The man who had welcomed him—his name was Adler, if Ashcroft remembered correctly—shifted in his seat, crossing his legs and resting his head against one fist. Ashcroft spared a glance at Mark. His old friend's eyes were wide with concern. Mark made a *pick it up* gesture, twirling his index finger in a fast forward motion.

"I have a theory." Ashcroft scanned his papers and drew a timeline on the whiteboard. "Ancient records and religious texts indicate that at one time, this world was occupied by people of great power. Call them what you will. Titans. Demigods. The Hebrews called them *Nephilim*. I believe these legends are not just myths. They are history."

"What is this?" a woman exploded. "If you want to discuss religion, folklore, and history, you have chosen the wrong field, Doctor."

"Stay with me. This is science. You will see. Well, let's skip the rest of the intro, shall we? And get right to my pitch."

Adler cleared his throat. "I think that would be wise."

"As I said, our country does not need weaponry. It needs people." Ashcroft finished his timeline and circled the 1940s. "Super soldiers. During World War II, several world governments thought that super soldiers were the next phase of warfare. As far as we know, none of these experiments produced viable results, but they were not for nothing. In the sixties, a man named Samuel Whitlock invented a serum that gave him power beyond imagination. He called himself Solar Flare."

Ashcroft held up a black-and-white picture depicting a man in a uniform. He remembered the uniform with crystal clarity, the body yellow and the cape green. His father had worn it many times, protecting his community from harm. How did they thank him for it? Ashcroft struggled to keep his expression passive as he recalled watching American soldiers open fire on Solar Flare.

"Unfortunately, the world was not ready for someone like Solar Flare. He was deemed a pariah. I still believe super soldiers are the cure for our world's security problems. People of great ability could protect us from any who seek to do us harm. Imagine not needing x-ray machines at airports because the guards had x-ray vision! Think of the possibilities provided by FBI agents who could read minds. We could stop terrorists in their tracks. We do not need weapons. We need heroes. Modern-day Titans. New Nephilim. People who can take Solar Flare's legacy and transform it into what it always should have been."

Several in the audience jeered. Ashcroft wiped sweat from his brow and shook his head. A cold fist gripped his heart. This was what had happened with Father. They laughed at him, and when he succeeded, they killed him. Ashcroft would not let that happen again. After all the horrible events the world had seen in the past fifty years, how could they not be ready for superheroes?

"If my research receives funding, I guarantee I could come up with a viable way to create actual superhuman beings. I . . . I could perfect Dr. Whitlock's formula."

The woman who'd spoken earlier scoffed. "You're insane."

"This is all science fiction and speculation," Adler added. "Solar Flare is a myth. Who are you, son? Who are you really?"

Ashcroft stared down the man. It sounded more like a demand than a question. In that moment, Ashcroft saw the truth. Adler knew. He recognized Ashcroft, made the connection between his presentation and his identity. Ashcroft's eyes flared, and he straightened his back. *Well, if the facade was over . . .*

"I am Adrian Whitlock, son of Solar Flare." Ashcroft pounded his fists down on the table. "I was forced to change my name because you monsters drove my family from the scientific community. You crucified my father because you weren't ready for his brilliance."

"I'm sorry, Dr. Ashcroft." Adler rose from his seat. "Your father's achievements were brilliant, but he was driven mad by his serum. He had to be put down. Why do you think no one has replicated it in all these years? I am sorry, but your grant request is denied. You've brought nothing here for us to work with. Just words and bad memories."

Ashcroft cast a glance at Mark. His friend's wide eyes were hard now. Ashcroft realized he had made himself a fool, and in doing so, he had disgraced Mark. Mark leaned back in his seat and crossed his arms.

"You'll regret this." He shoved his papers back into his briefcase. "I will rebuild Regency Inc., and I will perfect my father's serum. You will pay for burying him, for killing him. All of you! One day, the name Jeremiah Ashcroft will be lauded, and you will all regret the treatment you gave my father. And me."

"Don't humiliate yourself further, son." There was some compassion in Adler's eyes, but it felt like pity to Ashcroft. "I think it's time for you to leave."

CHAPTER 2

Present Day

Audrey Knight's life was unrecognizable from the one she had lived two years ago. She had been one of the most famous celebrities in the world, an acclaimed popstar and supermodel, known and adored by millions. She had been called Silver Siren for the single streak of silver she kept dyed into her wavy brown hair. She had money, companionship, fame—everything a person could want and more.

And then, it had all come crumbling down. Audrey became too sick to perform. Her doctor confirmed her worst fears—*cancer.* She was too young, too carefree, to believe that she could ever be brought low by something like cancer. And yet, it had happened. And it had been terminal. Audrey's life was over. She had canceled all of her concerts and modeling gigs and thrown money at any promise of a cure. Nothing had worked. Certain she was going to die, Audrey had sunk into a bottomless pit of depression.

But then, the miracle happened. A woman came to her, offering a new chance at life.

Grasping at this last strand of hope, Audrey took her up on it. She would have been mad to reject any possibility. The woman, Artemis Wayans, had brought Audrey to her employer, a man named Jeremiah Ashcroft. He had told her that he had a way to heal her. It was an untested cure, but if it worked, it could completely rid her body of cancer.

Audrey had accepted.

Within hours, the cancer had eroded. Whatever drug Ashcroft had injected her with, it was eating away at the cancer, destroying it and restoring Audrey's body to the way it had once been. Audrey had wept for joy and promised Ashcroft that she would give him anything he asked for. All he asked for was her allegiance.

"The world needs this cure," he had said. "But there are those who would stand in my way, who believe my methods are madness."

Audrey had sworn her allegiance to his cause—to the Regency. The world needed this cure. She had assumed that Ashcroft would want to leverage her fame to tell the world about his creation, using her concerts and public appearances to promote his cure. But she had been mistaken. He did not allow her to leave his laboratory, saying it was not safe for her to leave. He did not even allow her to contact her parents, and Ashcroft had leaked the story of Audrey Knight's death to the tabloids. It wasn't long before Audrey understood why.

Ashcroft's serum was more than a cure for cancer. Something had changed within Audrey. She could manipulate and project soundwaves at will, mute the world around her, project sonic blasts from her hands, amplify her scream to deafening levels. She could even fly. Ashcroft had not just given her a cure. He gave her superpowers. And a new name.

Stormcry.

The other members of the Regency were not as idealistic as Audrey. Wayans seemed all right most of the time, but she was snobbish. There was Alfonso Mendez, a grumpy man from Venezuela with a penchant for blowing up things. He did not like Audrey. But he was better than Vince Powers, who liked Audrey very much and was not afraid to show it. Powers was a junkie with no sense of boundaries. Audrey didn't like being around him.

But those three were gone. Ashcroft had sent them on a mission, and they had been arrested by some so-called "superheroes." Audrey snorted. *Traitors.* Ashcroft had given them their gifts, too, and they repaid him by trying to stop him from doing the same for others. Audrey wanted to share her gift with the world.

She stood leaning against a wall in the training room deep in the Regency's base. Two of her fellow superhumans, Melanie Davies and Randal Quinn, squared off in a boxing ring. Melanie was the youngest member of Ashcroft's command structure at nineteen years old. Ashcroft had given her the power to manipulate water, and he called her Deluge. Quinn was an arrogant, prickly British man with a constant sneer on his face. He was called Red Raider. As Melanie could control water, Quinn had equal control over fire.

Melanie and Quinn sparred, exchanging punches, kicks, and fire and water blasts. It was fun to watch, but it caused the training room to fill with steam as fire and water mingled. Sweat soaked Audrey, plastering her dark hair to her forehead and her tank top and sweatpants to her body. Melanie didn't seem too bothered; the sweat and steam only fueled her. Quinn, in turn, was feeding off the heat.

The last two members of Ashcroft's superpowered chain of command, Zeke Norris and Kenton Pierce, sat at a table outside the training room, playing cards. Norris had super strength and went by Torrent, while Pierce went by the more colorful moniker of Tetra-Hazard. He could excrete four different deadly substances from his body: acid, poison gas, venom, and radiation waves. His attitude was as toxic as his powers.

It was rare for all of them to be in the same place at once. Most times, Ashcroft had them spread across the country, sometimes the world, completing small tasks that would benefit the ultimate mission.

When they were brought together, it was always because Ashcroft had a job for all of them.

The sound of hands clapping broke the relative silence of the training room. Ashcroft walked into the room. He wore his white lab coat, as usual, and his black hair stuck out in every direction.

Ashcroft clapped his hands twice. "Attention!"

Melanie and Quinn stopped sparring, and Pierce and Norris looked up from their card game.

"Red Raider, Deluge, I want you to suit up and scope out Stone Gate penitentiary."

Quinn stepped out of the boxing ring. "Finally! Time to spring Artemis and the gang?"

"Not quite yet." Ashcroft grabbed a strand of hair and tugged at it. "But the nephiloids have been discovered, and the serum gas bombs are wreaking havoc. Gideon Turner and his cohorts will have their hands full with their delusional attempts to save the world. With them distracted, it will be the ideal time to strike."

"What about the rest of us?" Audrey asked.

"I want you prepped to strike the Vindicators when they return from investigating the nephiloids." He released the strand of hair and stood with his hands awkwardly at his sides. "They must be brought down."

Audrey had never been in a fight before—not a real one, anyway. Stealing Sterling Enterprises' data on their prototype dispersal device had required her to take down a few guards, but no one so deadly as a superhero. But she had a lot of training. She could do this.

The question was, did she want to? The superheroes thought they were protecting the innocent. They shouldn't be enemies. If they only knew the truth, they could be allies.

Ashcroft had given an order, though, and she would obey.

"It will be done." Audrey nodded to the others. "You heard him! Everyone, let's move!"

Finally, it was time to show the world the gifts they'd been missing out on. The rebels, however "heroic" they thought themselves, couldn't stand in the way of that.

* * *

An explosion rocked the aluminum-sided building at the corner of a dusty intersection. A pair of cars parked curbside bounced with the shockwave, and a teenage couple standing on the opposite street corner cried out and took off in a full-bore sprint in the opposite direction. Gideon Turner, the Seraph, crossed his arms in front of him in an X, blocking the shockwave with his conjured shield of golden energy. His booted feet skidded across the pavement, and he stopped in a ready crouch in the middle of the street.

There was a flicker of green light, and his best friend, Dean Sterling—in his superhero guise, Drifter—stood next to Gideon.

"First Raven City, then Wichita and Juncture City, now Phoenix?" Drifter shook his head. "Ashcroft is upping his game."

The Seraph lowered his arms and shunted his gathered energy downward to create glowing spheres around his fists. "Any sign of other superhumans in the area, or is it just this guy?"

"Just him for now, but I'm sure Ashcroft didn't detonate a gas bomb just to transform one ex-con." Drifter flexed. Twin aionium shields spun out of his gauntlets. "We'll be hearing of more sooner or later."

The ex-con in question—the source of the explosion that had rocked the street—ripped his way out of the chain-link fence surrounding the aluminum building. Tall, muscular, and hyped up on the newness of his powers, the con had been rampaging through Phoenix's slums when Gideon and Dean arrived. The police frequency Dean had been monitoring identified this criminal as Russell Quaid.

"Right." Gideon stepped forward. "Let's get this over with."

Based on the few minutes Gideon and Dean had fought him, Ashcroft's newest superhuman had developed the ability to create shockwaves. Confronting him directly was a no-go, even if Gideon's aionium body armor was strong enough to take the brunt of the Quaid's attacks without bending. It was still too risky and was liable to end with more property damage than this guy had already caused.

"You don't want to fight, do you?" Gideon held up his hands in a steadying gesture. "You aren't doing yourself any favors by violating your parole like this. Stand down, and let us take you in. We'll testify to your compliance, and when you get out again, maybe you can use your powers for good."

Quaid sneered. "Why would I do that? I'm too strong for the cops now. Way I see it, I take you two out? I'm home free."

"It was worth a shot."

As the supervillain brought his hands together to form a shockwave, the Seraph launched into the air, flying out of range of the impending blast. He arced around the street and peppered Quaid with golden blasts of light. The man stumbled back one step, then two. He growled and clapped his hands together, and the air rippled as the kinetic blast split the sky to cannon toward the Seraph. The superhero dropped into a dive, dodged the shockwave, and hit Quaid with two more energy beams. Drifter teleported forward and brought one of his shields down on the criminal's back. The ex-con stumbled forward.

The Seraph slammed into him feet-first, knocking him to the ground. As he hit, the Seraph pressed down and pinned the bigger man, punching him across the jaw with a glowing fist. Drifter knelt and slapped a power-dampening cuff onto Quaid's right wrist.

"All right. That wasn't so—"

Roaring, the ex-con shoved himself upright. The Seraph tumbled back and cushioned his landing with an energy field. Quaid swung a meaty fist at Drifter, who barely teleported out of the way in time. The Seraph lurched forward and dropped into a crouch, snaking his left leg out to sweep Quaid's feet from under him. As the ex-con fell, the Seraph threw both hands forward and hit him with a full-force energy beam, hurling him back through the chain-link fence—creating a new hole in the process—and into the side of the aluminum building. He soared in after Quaid, dropped to the ground next to him, and brought the cuffs around to connect them to Quaid's wrist and activate the dampening field.

"No! Let me . . . go!"

Gideon rose, shook his head, and pulled back his hood. Dean stepped into the building after him, running a hand through his curly, brown hair. His green super suit was covered in dust. Gideon looked down at his own blue and gold uniform, finding it similarly dusty. They were lucky they weren't in worse shape.

"Teach me to underestimate someone." He folded his arms across his chest. "All right. Want to get this guy back to Phoenix P.D.?"

Dean nodded. "Will do. And then I'll get to work on looking for any other superhuman transformations. With any luck, some of them will be on the heroic side of things. What about you?"

"I'm going to take the Raptor back to Sojourn City." He grinned ruefully. "Jolie and I are taste-testing wedding cakes today."

"Oh, the danger-filled life of a superhero. Go on. Enjoy your day. I have things covered here. If we need help or we're ready to come home, we'll call."

Gideon reached out and clasped his best friend's forearm. "Thanks, buddy. Don't know how I'd do this without you."

"You wouldn't look nearly as fashionable, that's for sure." Dean winked as he hauled the ex-con to his feet. "All right. Get out of here, lover boy. I'll have Maddox prep the plane; he'll be ready for takeoff by the time you get there. I can handle taking Mr. Macho here back to jail."

Gideon turned away from the battlefield. The teenage couple he had spotted earlier peeked around from behind the corner of a nearby building. Gideon waved. He didn't enjoy being in the spotlight, but that was part of this life. He had accepted a few months ago that he was a superhero now, not a shadowy vigilante, so he had to play the part. Dean insisted that Gideon should put on a nice face around bystanders whenever he could.

He didn't mind doing that, but somewhere in the back of his mind, Gideon knew that smiles and publicity stunts would not keep popular opinion in their favor if incidents like this kept happening. They had to find Ashcroft and stop him soon. Otherwise, it would not be long before the world saw superhumans-at-large as a threat, rather than a force for good. When that happened, what would become of the Vindicators?

CHAPTER 3

Six hours later, full of cake samples and hoping to burn off the needless calories, Gideon stepped back and raised his left hand to block the blow that his fiancée, Jolie Anderson, aimed at his throat. He swiveled his left hand to grab her wrist and raised his right arm underneath. He grabbed her elbow and pivoted, tucked himself under Jolie's armpit, and lifted. Jolie yelped in surprise and flipped over Gideon's shoulder. A loud *smack* echoed through the training room as she landed flat on her back on the foam training mat.

He released her arm and took two steps back. He stayed in a ready stance so he could move at a moment's notice if she jumped up and lunged at him. Jolie rolled over and pushed herself to her feet.

"Ow . . ."

Gideon grinned. "Don't leave yourself open. Use quick, fluid strikes so your opponents don't have time to grab you."

"Jerk. I'm still full of chocolate frosting." Jolie bent her knees and raised her fists. "Is that any way to treat the woman you're going to marry?"

She stepped forward and swung her left fist at his jaw. Gideon blocked the blow. Jolie brought her right fist in lower, aiming at his gut. Gideon stepped out of the way and retreated to the other side of the mat.

"It is if I want to keep you safe." He shrugged. "I just want you to be ready for anything. Bad guys won't wait for your dessert to digest. And you're good, but hand-to-hand combat isn't exactly your specialty."

"Maybe because I usually walk around with a gun, taser, and nightstick."

"You can't depend on them always being there." Gideon didn't wait this time. He lunged, driving his fist straight for her nose. Jolie darted her head to the left and used her left palm to push his hand aside. "Good move!"

Jolie swung the back of her right hand and struck Gideon under the ribs. She stepped around behind him. Ignoring the shortness of breath caused by her blow, Gideon caught her wrist as she jabbed a punch at his kidneys. He jerked her forward, spun her around, and wrapped his right arm around her neck.

"Guns are good, but I have superpowers and still train in hand-to-hand combat. You never know when you might need it."

She grabbed his forearm with both hands and lifted her legs in the air. When she dropped them to the floor, she pulled on his arm with all her weight. Gideon anticipated the move, so when she flipped him over her head, he tucked himself into a ball, rolled, and came up in a crouch.

He nodded. "Good use of leverage."

"Thanks." Jolie stood. "Want to keep going?"

Gideon pushed himself to his feet and cringed as his stomach protested. "I think that's good for now."

Jolie stepped toward him, wrapped an arm around his waist, and rose on her tiptoes to kiss him on the cheek. Gideon pulled her closer to him. He could not wait to marry her. Sometimes, it felt like they'd been together forever. They had been through more as a couple than most experienced in their entire lives. They could finally start planning their future.

He stepped off the mat and picked up a towel. As he wiped himself clean of sweat, he looked out the window at Sojourn City. In the three months since the Sterling Enterprises maglev launched, the city had experienced a boom of prosperity. The wealthy residents of the Platform and Lakeside took the maglev connecting all parts of the city as a cue. They poured money into the Brooks—the city's slums—and cleaned them up, finally putting into practice the theory that Sojourn City was founded on. They had Dean to thank for that.

It had been three months since Gideon had encountered one of Ashcroft's supervillains—not the wannabes he was creating with these gas bombs but his actual command chain within the Regency. Three months since Gideon had proposed to Jolie. Three months since he had learned that his powers came from the blood of a Nephilim—ancient offspring of fallen angels and humans interbreeding. Three months since they had found even a trace of Dr. Jeremiah Ashcroft, the man who had given Gideon his powers. He had been looking, but Ashcroft knew how to not be found. The doctor had been leading them on a wild goose chase.

Gideon was tired of waiting. Ashcroft was out there, no doubt putting the finishing touches on his crazed, vengeance-fueled plan to spread Nephilim DNA across the entire world. While Gideon and his friends had been busy dealing with Artemis Wayans, some of the scientist's other followers stole intel on a prototype dispersal device from Sterling Labs. In San Francisco, Backfire had acquired a genetic splicer from Garvin Technologies. Ashcroft had three months to prepare the splicer for whatever he intended to use it for, and there was nothing Gideon could do about it. It was like Ashcroft didn't even exist. For all his technological smarts and nearly unlimited resources, even Dean could find no trace of the doctor or of the Regency. The imprisoned supervillains who worked for Ashcroft were not giving them anything to work with, either. The Vindicators were stuck chasing gas bombs, trying to stop the emergence of new superhumans as they happened, rather than cutting straight to the source.

In the past few months, the media had taken to referring to those with powers as amplified persons, "amps" for short. Gideon was not sure how he felt about the term, but it had caught on. Superheroes, supervillains, civilians with powers—they were all amps.

Gideon looked down at his left hand and generated a small pulse of light from his fingertips. The golden energy danced across his fingers. Even knowing that his powers came from evil creatures such as Nephilim, Gideon was confident that the powers themselves were not evil. God had allowed him to receive them for a purpose. They were part of him, and he could barely imagine life without them anymore.

But that didn't mean powers were for everyone. It was likely that there would be mass deaths if Ashcroft succeeded in spreading his serum across the world, as some people's bodies wouldn't adjust to their new homeostasis. The elderly and infants would especially be in peril. But they had no idea who would die and who would gain powers. The thought terrified Gideon. If Ashcroft's plan succeeded, which side of the coin would Jolie fall on? Would she die as foreign DNA invaded her body, leaving Gideon a widower before they were even wed? That would destroy him. If it happened, he feared he would snap and murder Ashcroft and his lackeys.

"Hey, Mr. Introspective." Jolie kissed him on the cheek. "Where are you?"

Gideon lowered his hand, allowing the light to dissipate. "Sorry. I was just thinking about everything. My powers, Ashcroft, our engagement . . ."

"You're going to catch him, you know."

"Am I?"

Jolie nodded. "You are. Because you are a superhero, and that's what you do. You stop the bad guys, and you save lives."

Just months ago, Gideon had protested the use of the term superhero. That wasn't what he set out to be when all of this had started. He had just been a vigilante, cleaning up his city with violence. He was no hero. But over time, he had come to accept his new role. God had given him these powers for a reason, and there had to be more to it than giving black eyes to street thugs. Gideon felt better about stopping a runaway train than he ever had about the number of bad guys he had given a beating.

"I guess you're right. Thanks." He kissed her. "I should check in on Patrick. He's got to be bored out of his mind, stuck here in the city."

Patrick had begged to go along with them to Phoenix, but he was still in high school. He couldn't just cut class to fly across the country with the rest of the team every time Ashcroft detonated a gas bomb. Too bad. His speedster powers were useful in a fight. Gideon was glad that the young man remained in Sojourn City instead of returning to San Francisco, even if the reason for it was heartbreaking.

"He'll get over it." Jolie smiled. "Just take him on patrol tonight or something. He's got a good head on his shoulders. He won't hold it against you."

"You're right." Gideon rolled his shoulders. "I'll see you later."

"See you later. I love you."

"I love you, too."

* * *

Patrick Omer shouldered his backpack and squeezed through the bustling halls of Sojourn High School. He grunted as a linebacker pushed past him, barely acknowledging his presence. It had been just over a month since Patrick had started school, and he still didn't feel like he belonged here. He was a senior, and he felt like a freshman.

He should have been in San Francisco, at school with Lucy and Asher, his best friends. Instead, he was here—alone. Making friends was not exactly a priority. As soon as classes were over, he rushed back to Lakeside Central Tower, where the Vindicators were based. He spent his days there, honing his powers and waiting to use them for good. And, of course, he tried to keep up with homework.

"Hey, Patrick!"

The speaker was a girl from his chemistry class—dark-skinned and curly, brown hair with blonde streaks. She also worked with Carter Jonson, the next youngest member of the Vindicators, at a grocery store in the Brooks. Her name was Raina, he thought. She weaved her way through the bustling hallway to his side.

"I noticed you've been keeping to yourself," Raina said. "I was wondering if you wanted someone to sit with at lunch. I've been a loner before. I know it's not much fun."

Patrick considered refusing. What good would it do him to make friends here that he was only going to lose once he moved back to San Francisco? But on the other hand, he didn't know how long he was staying here. He hoped that he would only have to stay in Sojourn for this semester before moving back to San Francisco for his last semester, but if things didn't work out that way, lonely wasn't a great way to spend a whole school year.

"Sounds good."

Raina smiled. "Great."

Patrick weaved away from her toward algebra class. He wondered why she had spoken to him out of the blue. *Not looking for a homecoming date, I hope.* He didn't want any girls getting any ideas. He only had feelings for Lucy, and being apart from her so soon after he'd confessed those feelings was really the worst.

But Raina seemed nice enough. It couldn't hurt to be friends with her. It would make his time here less isolated, at least. More than likely, she had only singled him out because she knew he was a friend of Carter's.

He walked into the classroom, dropped into his seat, and opened his algebra textbook. His superspeed allowed him to read at an accelerated rate, so there was no reason to wait for the teacher. He flipped the page and flitted his eyes back and forth, absorbing all the information in the chapter.

By the time the teacher was ten minutes into his lecture, Patrick had skimmed the entire book and gone over the first three chapters again. He focused on those early pages, committing the details to memory. What good was having superpowers if he couldn't use them to get through school?

After that, the lecture seemed to drag on. Patrick forced himself to stay still and resisted the urge to rhythmically tap his pencil on his desk. His goal at Sojourn High was to keep a low profile. He didn't need to get a bad rap with the teachers or the other students. The smaller the splash he made here, the better.

"Did you hear about the fight in Phoenix?" a guy behind him whispered.

Patrick's ears perked up. Phoenix? Gideon and Dean were there. If it weren't for school, he would've been there with them.

"Yeah," the girl next to him murmured. "What are *our* heroes doing there, anyway? Those cities need to get their own superheroes."

"For real."

"Ahem." The teacher cleared his throat. "Roy, Melissa, is there something you'd like to share with the whole class?"

"No, sir," Roy stammered.

Patrick bit his lip. If he wanted to get popular around here, he could always just spread the word that he knew the Seraph and Drifter personally. But that would only raise suspicions about him. There was no reason for him to do that. He returned his focus to the teacher as best he could for the rest of the lecture.

When the bell rang, Patrick slid his textbook into his backpack, slung the bag over his shoulder, and walked out the door. Lunch was next. It was time to see if he could make his way through the horde of ravening high schoolers and find Raina and her friends. Sojourn High's cafeteria was big, but it was nowhere near the size of his high school's back in San Francisco. He should be able to navigate it by now. He entered the line of students waiting for their food and scanned the room. Raina waved at him from one of the back tables.

Maybe it would be good for him to have friends here. He had to socialize outside of the base sometimes. He and Carter had hit it off but the two of them had only had so much time together since Patrick had school and Carter worked a lot. When they did get to hang out, it was usually at the Tower, which meant they were usually either training or getting ready to hit the streets. He hadn't realized how lonely he was until that moment. As much as he missed Lucy and Asher, he should make the most of his time in Sojourn City.

CHAPTER 4

Consciousness returned like a mule kick to the face. Hannah squeezed her eyes shut and wished herself back to sleep. Anything had to be better than the pain screaming at her. She had no idea it was possible to hurt this much. Unfortunately, her body remained stubbornly awake.

What had happened to her? She had been up on the ridge, keeping watch over the valley. It had been cold . . .

Wendigo.

The name crawled its way through her mind, sending shivers down her spine. That was what had happened. She had fought a wendigo. It had chomped down on her shoulder, piercing her flesh. She had killed the beast, but as she returned to the reservation, the ominous howling behind her warned of more of them.

Hannah opened her eyes. The sun shone through the window to her right, stabbing at her pupils. She rolled over and covered her head with her pillow. She should not have done that. The motion aggravated the wound on her left shoulder. She screamed into her pillow.

"Hannah?"

She quieted. It was Axel, her best friend. He ran backup for Hannah when she was out as the Brass Bison, updating her with locations of potential crimes. He had patched up her cuts and bruises more times than she could count. Had he patched her up last night, too? She lowered the pillow and pulled the hem of her shirt back. A white bandage wound around her shoulder, stained crusty red with dried blood.

"Are you all right?"

Axel's kind, dark eyes stared down at her. He was in his mid-twenties, a few years Hannah's junior. A kind soul, Axel had never met a stranger or a person unworthy of helping. He reached down and put a hand on her forehead. His palm was freezing. She recoiled from his touch.

"Come on, Axel, wear some gloves next time you go out!"

"I haven't been outside all day. You've had a fever since you came in last night, but I think it's breaking. You're much cooler than you were when you passed out."

She bit her lip and nodded. "I came here after that thing made a meal out of me. You patched me up?"

"Don't I always?" Axel smiled gently. "I'm glad you're on the mend. So, it's dead?"

Chomp. Scream. Bang.

"It's dead. I put a bullet through its eye. But . . . I do not think it was alone. I heard howling as I was making my way back here. I think there are more of them out there."

Axel's face fell, and he sat down in a chair next to Hannah's bed. That obviously hadn't been what he wanted to hear; this thing was something out of a horror story. She never wanted to see a dead one again, let alone a live one.

"What was it?" he asked.

"I don't know, I . . . I have never seen anything like it. But I think the legends must be true. Ax, I think it was a wendigo."

Axel pinched the bridge of his nose, shook his head, and moaned. Hannah understood. Wendigos were bad news. Native American tribes had whispered of them for centuries. They were among the most horrific creatures on earth. Anyone in their right mind would reject the tales as fantasy just for their own sanity. If wendigos were real, the world would be a much scarier place. Maybe it was.

"I'll just have to go kill the rest."

"Are you insane?" Axel put a hand on her good shoulder to keep her down. "Hannah, that thing nearly killed you. What if you run into more than one this time?"

"I know how to beat them now. The eyes are their weak spot. All I have to do is draw a bead on those ugly black voids and pull the trigger."

"At least wait until you're healed up."

"No." Hannah shook her head and sat up, pushing past his hand. "Every night I wait, those things could kill more people. I am the protector of this reservation, Axel. I am going to do my job."

She reached for her gun that was sitting on the bedside table behind Axel. It was too far away and blocked by a lamp. She stretched farther but couldn't reach it. Suddenly, a lasso of bronze energy whipped out from her palm, snagged the gun, and dragged it toward her, knocking over the lamp. The weapon slapped into her palm, and the energy vanished. Hannah blinked, her gaze going from the gun to the lamp and back again.

"Uh . . . " Asher stood slowly. "Hannah, what did you just do?"

She stared down at the gun. "I have no idea."

* * *

Wes Turner stood in the ops room, arms crossed, and stared at the reports rolling across the screen. Strange, unidentified creatures were cutting a swath through rural areas in Arizona and Kansas, killing people and animals. They left behind giant tooth and claw marks, but no one knew what they were. It was likely that the reports were exaggerated and that the only threats were bears or wolves—wildlife that animal control or the police could handle. But Ashcroft had detonated bombs in Wichita and Phoenix, and now these reports . . . Could that be a coincidence? Even if it was, people were dying. If it wasn't their responsibility to stop that, what was?

Jolie walked into the ops room, carrying a water bottle. Today must've been her day off; she wasn't usually there in the afternoons.

"What are you looking at?" she asked.

"Something out of a horror movie." Wes gestured to the screen. "Unidentified monsters prowling rural areas, killing people at random."

"Sounds pretty horrific to me. Is the team going to investigate?"

"I think we should. It might be nothing, but we know Ashcroft is a mad scientist. What if he's working on more than just a new race of Nephilim?"

"You think Ashcroft is creating monsters?"

"I'm not saying that, but it's worth a look. That madman's been off the radar for three months. You can't tell me he hasn't been working on something more than just a few isolated bombings."

"Fair enough." Jolie took a sip of water. "Gideon's at work right now, but you should show this to him when he gets back. I'm sure he'll agree it's worth looking into; and since Dean is still in Phoenix, he's in the perfect position to investigate that report."

"Right." Wes highlighted the reports and stored them in a folder for later use. "How is Carter doing?"

"Oh, as well as a teenage vigilante with a single mother can be." Jolie shrugged. "He wishes he could come here more."

"Maybe we can take him along if we decide to investigate . . . whatever these things are." Wes stepped away from the console. "He's as much a part of this team as anyone else. So are you, for that matter."

"Thanks. I'm going to go. There's still lots of wedding planning to do."

As Jolie left the room, Wes pulled up another page on one of the smaller screens—Juncture City School of Law's website. If things stayed as quiet in Sojourn City as they had been for the past three months, he was considering reapplying sooner than he had originally planned. When he had decided to defer his enrollment, he was sure that he and the others would be so busy working to stop Ashcroft that he would never have time for law school. That was fine with him. He had only just become a superhero, and he had all the time in the world to go to law school. It would still be there when Ashcroft was dealt with.

But in the past three months, Wes had hardly done anything. His powers weren't exactly suited for saving kittens from trees. As much as Wes loved being a hero, he was an underdog—an incredibly powerful underdog. There were a few too many superheroes in Sojourn City. Maybe it was time for him to find his place in the world away from the rest of them, to discover what he was capable of on his own. Sojourn City wasn't the only place that needed heroes. Juncture City might be more appreciative of his talents. And if he could go to law school and be a superhero at the same time, even better.

* * *

"I'm telling you, dude; Raina is into you." Patrick grinned. "She invited me to have lunch with her at school, but all she wanted to do was ask me about you."

Carter blinked. Of all the things Patrick could've brought up as the two of them rode the elevator up to the lair, he hadn't expected his love life to be one of them. Carter wasn't opposed to having a relationship, but he wasn't actively seeking one, either. Between working to provide for his mother, taking care of his siblings, and protecting the city at night, Carter's schedule was full. A girlfriend would be nice—a much-needed preoccupation, for sure. He just didn't know if he had the time.

He definitely had not expected the girl in question to be one of his coworkers. He did like Raina, but he had never considered asking her out. She was friendly and pretty, and she shared a lot of his life experiences. Maybe it was not such a bad idea.

"I'll think about it. But from watching Gideon and Jolie, dating with a secret identity isn't easy."

"I hadn't really thought about that. Maybe you should just tell her you're the Crusader."

"Right, and that won't make you look suspicious at all. 'Hey, I just happen to be friends with the guy you're crushing on, and he is a superhero. I'm new in town; but no, I'm totally not also a superhero, just a regular guy.' Yeah, right."

"It was just a thought."

The elevator chimed, and the door slid open. Carter gestured for Patrick to exit first and then followed his friend. Carter liked Patrick. He was a straight-laced, stand-up guy and loved to have fun, too. He was sometimes a little too timid, but maybe that was his way of adjusting to a new setting. He *had* just been kicked out by his parents.

The door to the lair was protected by a password-and-thumbprint keypad. Carter entered the code and scanned his thumb. The door slid open. The bottom floor of the lair—the common area and kitchen—was vacant. Carter walked over to the refrigerator and grabbed a Dr. Pepper, tossed it to Patrick, and took one for himself. Maybe sodas weren't the ideal drink for on-the-go vigilantes. He had lost count of the times Gideon had pressed him to "hydrate, and that means water, Carter." There was no harm in it, as far as Carter was concerned.

"I heard some guys talking about superheroes at school today. They didn't seem to know much about me or Wes." Patrick frowned. "I guess because we haven't had a lot of activity here in Sojourn."

"Don't worry. Give it enough time, and I'm sure you'll be as famous as Gideon. Only maybe not here. In San Francisco, maybe."

"I know. I'm not trying to be a glory hound."

"I get it, man." Carter patted his friend on the shoulder and walked toward the stairs. "Just give it time."

They walked upstairs to the ops room. Wes, Gideon, and Jolie were already inside. Carter checked his watch. It was after six o'clock already. He'd completely missed out on dinner to get there.

"What's up, guys?" Carter asked.

Gideon glanced back at them. "It looks like we may have a mission, but it's out of town."

"No problem," Patrick said. "It's Friday, so I've got a couple days before I have to be back in school again."

"And I have tomorrow off work," Carter added.

"Good." Gideon gestured for them to join him. "For the past week or so, mysterious creatures have been popping up in rural areas in Kansas and Arizona, killing people and disappearing. We don't know what they are. It may be nothing, but my gut tells me this is Ashcroft."

"Monsters, eh?" Carter nodded and took a sip of Dr. Pepper. "Sounds like the work of a mad scientist to me."

Wes scratched his chin. "I called Dean to tell him. He thinks they may be failed experiments of some kind, maybe animals that Ashcroft tested the serum on before he tried it on humans."

"Gross." Carter shivered. "Don't like the sound of that."

"Agreed," Gideon said. "And we definitely don't need anything like that on the loose. So, we're going to split up. Patrick, you come with me to Kansas. Carter and Wes, you'll go to Arizona and meet up with Dean. Our goal will be to locate and capture these creatures if possible so that we can study them and determine whether they're Ashcroft's or not."

Carter looked at Wes and Dean. He didn't know the two of them as well as Patrick and Gideon, but maybe that's why Gideon had arranged the teams like this. Even if the monsters were urban legends, at least it would be a good team-building exercise. And the two of them should be able to make up for any weaknesses Carter might bring to the fight.

"How will we get there?" Patrick asked. "We have only one Raptor, right?"

Wes nodded. "Dean upgraded the Raptor and added in an SR-71 Blackbird engine. My team can drop you and Gideon off in Kansas and get to Arizona in no time."

Now, that was cool. Carter lived for the tech he got to use as the Crusader. His staff, the adhesive beads that secured captured criminals, the concussion gauntlets that gave him a little extra *oomph* when he needed it—not to mention his awesome armor. Carter couldn't imagine a cooler life, except one in which his father was still alive.

Gideon headed for the door. "If you have anything you need to get in order, do it now. We leave first thing in the morning."

* * *

When Wes told Gideon about these so-called monster attacks, his first instinct was pure skepticism. But if someone had asked him two years ago if he thought superheroes were real, he would have said no. They could not leave any stone unturned when it came to what Ashcroft could do. Even if these monsters had nothing to do with him, people were dying. It was a worthy diversion if it saved lives.

He wished Jolie could come with them, but she was working a weekend shift at the precinct. Leaving her was never easy. Now that they were engaged, it was even harder to step out of her embrace and board the Raptor. These last three months had been incredible. Although he and Dean had been traveling in the wake of Ashcroft's attacks, there had still been plenty of time to spend in Sojourn City. Gideon and Jolie had spent that time going on dates, picking out wedding decorations, and forging a stronger bond as they neared the day of their wedding. And kissing. A lot of kissing.

"Don't get eaten," Jolie said.

Gideon laughed. "I'll try."

"I love you, Gideon."

"Love you, too. I'll be back soon."

He stepped back and looked down at her from the top of the ramp. The rest of the team climbed past him onto the plane. Gideon gave Jolie one last wave.

Maddox Odell, one of Dean's coworkers from Sterling Labs, sat in the pilot's seat. As far as Gideon was concerned, there was nothing that Maddox and his partner, Arianna Serafin, couldn't do.

Arianna was normally Maddox's copilot, but she was staying behind in Sojourn City this time. Mayor Crowe had recently contracted Sterling Labs to create superhuman-proof prison cells, a catchall solution whenever they had to lock up a villain. They had three in custody, and all of them had to be restrained differently. A cell that could dampen any power would be far superior. Arianna had volunteered to remain home to keep working on a solution. The power-dampening cuffs Gideon and Dean had used in Phoenix were the prototype.

Gideon sat down in one of the seats that lined the rear compartment of the Raptor. Wes, who stood in the doorway to the cockpit, stepped out toward him.

"Looks like the most recent attack in Kansas was just outside Wichita, in a small town called Goddard. We'll drop you and Patrick at the site and head off to Arizona."

Wes was the one who'd done the research on this, so Gideon let his younger brother take point. Wes had an unfortunate tendency to brood first and emote later, so seeing him take responsibility filled Gideon with pride. Wes had acted rashly in getting his powers, but the lessons he had learned from that situation were invaluable. Gideon was glad to call him a partner and friend, not just a biological brother.

"Anyone Patrick and I should speak to?" he asked.

"Maybe the sheriff? Everyone seems equally confused about these things. Animal control is trying to hand it off to the police, but the police are content to let animal control handle it."

"No one wants to fight a monster, or they don't really believe that's what it is. We knew this might not be easy."

Wes pursed his lips. "At least you'll have some city resources. The attacks in Arizona are out in the middle of nowhere. The only civilization nearby is a small Apache reservation."

"It doesn't make sense, does it?" Gideon scratched his chin. "Arizona and Kansas. They're hundreds of miles apart, but they're the only two places reporting these attacks. They're also places Ashcroft has detonated gas bombs. But these animals aren't showing up anywhere in the states in between."

"Makes it more likely that it's an intentional attack, rather than random occurrence. Maybe Ashcroft released them in those locations for a purpose. Even though it's near Wichita, Goddard is a little nothing town. Maybe Ashcroft chose it, and the reservation, because nobody would look into them too closely."

"Sure. For the Arizona attacks, they could chalk it up to Native American superstition. In Kansas, they can say the attacks are bears or bobcats or something. If some evidence indicates something else . . . Well, those hayseeds don't know what they're talking about, right?"

"Right. Ashcroft wants to test these creatures somewhere remote. We've stopped his gas bombs multiple times. Maybe these more subtle attacks are his way of trying a different tack. Or maybe he's using them as a distraction. Or . . . " Wes shrugged. "They actually are bobcat or bear attacks."

"That's entirely possible." Gideon buckled his restraints as the plane's engines hummed to life. "But people are dying, so we've got to risk it."

"I know. It's like Dean says: the burden of being a superhero is an unending need to help whoever you can."

Gideon was glad that he didn't have to bear that burden alone anymore. As the Seraph, he felt like he carried the weight of Sojourn City on his shoulders, even when Carter's father had been out there with him. That was a burden that no one should have to bear. Now that he had the Vindicators at his side, he didn't feel the burden so keenly—but it was still there. He suspected it always would be. It was one he was glad to carry.

CHAPTER 5

Team Arizona

"Uh . . . Hannah? You're not going to believe this."

Hannah ignored Axel for the moment. She couldn't break concentration. Her left hand was stretched out in front of her, fingers spread. She furrowed her brow and concentrated. Bronze-colored energy sparked from her fingertips, vanished, and reappeared again, finally taking the form of the whip she had created earlier. She tossed the whip across the room, wrapping it around the wicker basket in the corner. Hannah dragged the basket left, then right. She brought it toward the center of the room. The strand of pure energy obeyed her commands. It was tentative; it was shaky. But it was working. It should've been impossible. What else could she form out of this mystical energy?

Whatever venom was in the wendigo's teeth had changed her. It was probably best to keep it quiet and only use it when she really needed to. People around these parts were a superstitious lot. She had done just fine without this strange, new ability, and there was no sense in startling the locals. She could continue to manage without powers. Her twin revolvers were all she needed.

She dragged the basket back into the corner and released the whip—or tried. As it returned to her, the strand of energy slashed through the basket. She glanced quickly at Axel to see if he had noticed her mistake. He sat at the desk, his laptop in front of him, but he wasn't looking at it. His head was craned around to face her. His concerned statement returned to her, and she focused on him.

"What is it?" she asked.

"A dangerous-looking black plane landed in the valley to the north."

Hannah frowned. "Government?"

"Doesn't look like it, but what do I know? It's probably the CIA, coming to take the wendigos to Area 51 or something. Maybe you should stay here. If they find out about your power, they might take you, too."

"No. Whoever they are, I should probably go check it out."

"What?" Axel jumped out of his chair. "Are you crazy? That thing almost killed you. Your shoulder is nowhere near recovered yet."

"I'll be fine. I'm not planning on getting into a fight." She pulled on her gun belt, anyway, just in case. "And besides, it's just my left arm. My dominant hand is still fit to fire."

She walked toward the door, not waiting for Axel to protest further. He was a good friend, but he was a little too protective sometimes. She bundled up and walked outside, closed the screen door behind her, and mounted her motorcycle. If this jet was carrying government goons looking for the wendigos, she was going to get the credit for the one she killed, at least.

She didn't want the government here. Didn't need them here. They had never done Hannah any good. Even less so her people as a whole.

She roared down the road and to the north. Whoever they were, she hoped they had a good explanation for being here.

* * *

Dean climbed out of his rented jeep and into the desert. His feet crunched atop some desert foliage. Dean kicked it aside. *It is going to take a month to get the dirt and stickers out of my boot treads.* As Wes and Carter stepped off the Raptor to meet him, something howled in the distance. Dean shivered despite the sunshine. *Just a coyote—I hope.* No big deal. He was overreacting, spooked at the thought of these creatures. As nuts as Artemis Wayans had been, her boss had to be even more psycho. It wasn't outside the realm of possibility that he would create a Frankenstein half-angel straight out of a horror flick. If Dean knew anything about those, it was that the funny guy always died first.

"Hey, you hear that?" Wes asked.

"Yeah. Just an animal."

"No, not that." Wes put one hand on Dean's shoulder and pointed with the other. "There. Look. It's a motorcycle."

Dean followed Wes's finger. He was right. A small, gunmetal vehicle trundled across the desert in their direction. And now that he was paying attention, he heard the engine, too. Dean bit the inside of his lip.

"No time for tearful reunions." Dean stepped forward. "Be ready."

Carter removed his truncheons from his belt and snapped them together into a short *jo* staff. Wes kept one hand near his utility belt, which contained a dozen different materials that he could touch and transform his skin into at a moment's notice. Dean tightened his fists, ready to extend the aionium shields in his gauntlets.

The motorcycle drew closer. It had to be at least a couple decades old, judging by the design and the sputter of the engine. The driver was alone. No other vehicles appeared in the distance. Local authorities? An explorer or daredevil?

The rider slowed the bike to a halt and parked it. The driver was a woman, dark hair thrown over shoulders clad in a Sherpa-lined, red denim jacket. A black bandana wrapped around her nose and mouth hid most of her features. Two guns were tucked into low-hanging holsters at her hips. Her left arm hung limply at her side, but she kept her right thumb hooked in her belt as she approached.

Dean analyzed the guns at a glance. Revolvers, old style. The bullets they fired would not scratch the Kevlar weave of the Vindicators' armor.

Dean stepped toward her. "Hello."

"Who are you?"

No preamble. All right. "I'm Drifter. This is Rampart and Crusader. We're superheroes from Sojourn City, Michigan. We heard about the strange creatures you have living here, and we wanted to see if there was anything—"

"Superheroes?" The woman's eyes narrowed. "You mean you have . . . abilities?"

Dean nodded. "Want to demonstrate, Rampart?"

Wes reached down and touched a rubber tile on his belt. His skin shifted to the same color and texture as the rubber. In an instant, the woman's right hand snatched a pistol from its holster and trained the weapon on Wes.

"What is this?" she asked. "Did you bring the wendigos?"

"Wendigos?" Carter's brow furrowed. "What's that?"

Dean studied the woman. Her left arm still hung limp. Probably an injury. If she had been in a fight recently or had encountered the creature, it would explain why she was so agitated. She was not an enemy. She was a civilian in need of talking down. Luckily, Dean had a knack for that. He put on his best disarming smile.

Her gun didn't waver. "The creatures you mentioned. How did you know about them?"

"We heard on the news," Wes said. "We're just here to help."

Dean held up his hands and stepped forward. "Can you tell us anything about the creatures?"

"Do you work for the government?"

"No, we don't."

"How come I have never heard of you?"

"Michigan's a long way from Arizona." He took another step. "I've been operating in Phoenix this week, but it's possible that word just hasn't spread out here yet, or—"

"*Don't* come *any* closer!" She clicked back the hammer. "Stay right there."

The bullet was unlikely to do any harm to Dean or either of his companions. Gideon had taken three bullets to the chest from a higher-caliber gun and was only winded. Still, there was no point in moving closer and making an enemy of her. They had no idea who she was or what she was capable of. Maybe she could even be a help to them.

"I'm not moving. We just need to know about the creatures. Once we have the information we need, we'll be on our way."

"You mentioned wendigos." Wes stepped up next to Dean. "I've heard that name before. Mythical creatures that live in woods in the North. Is that what you think they are?"

"Think? I know. I killed one myself with this gun."

Impressive. If the creatures were as fierce as her choice of name indicated, it was shocking that she—or anyone—had been able to kill one alone.

"Who are you?" he asked.

"My people call me Brass Bison. I protect them from traffickers, dealers, and the like. Now I protect them from monsters, too."

She's a vigilante. That explained the disguise, however feeble it might be. Gideon's first getup had been similar. A ski mask and a blue jacket were his costume, and a pair of *eskrima* sticks were his only tools. It had worked for a while. Dean noted that she declined to use her real name. That was fair, considering he and his friends had introduced themselves by their superhero monikers.

"Well . . . uh, Brass Bison, could you show us this creature you killed?"

"Why? You want to study it?"

"In a manner of speaking, yes, but not—"

Her gun had slowly been lowering. Now, she snapped it back up. "You want to make more of them?"

"No, no! We want to find out who made them and put a stop to it before anyone else gets hurt."

Carter took a step forward holding his staff. That move must have been too aggressive for Brass Bison. She swiveled her gun to train it on him. Carter jumped in surprise and activated the electrified ends of his staff. The woman fired. Dean extended his shield and blocked the bullet.

That's enough. Someone was going to get hurt. Dean teleported, appearing to Bison's right. He grabbed her gun, jerked it away, and teleported back to his previous position.

"Are you deaf?" Dean let his exasperation show as he popped the gun open and emptied the bullets onto the dusty ground. "I said no one else needs to get hurt. Crusader, put your staff away."

Brass Bison scowled and extended her hand. A tentacle of energy shot out, snagged the gun from Dean, and pulled it back through the air to smack into her palm. Dean cried out in surprise. A moment later, five bullets followed the gun into her grip.

"You have powers?" Wes asked.

"Where did they come from? How long have you had them?" Dean added.

She did not respond as she slid the bullets back into the chamber with her left hand. The fingers on that hand were trembling. Bison slid the last bullet in, closed the chamber, and pressed her left hand against her thigh. *The injury, her hesitation, the powers*—the answer was obvious.

"Since you fought the wendigo?" Dean guessed.

Brass Bison narrowed her eyes "How did you know?"

"Let's just say we have some experience with this kind of thing. Like I said, we're here to stop it. We can help each other. No reason to be hostile." He reached up and removed his mask. "My name is Dean Sterling. This is Wes Turner and Carter Jonson."

She frowned deeply. Finally, she tugged the bandana down around her throat, revealing her face. "My name is Hannah Lonestar. If you wish to help me find the other wendigos, you may. I do not know how many there are, and I am injured. I will accept any help I can get."

"Great." Dean nodded. "Where should we start?"

"The mountains. I believe the wendigos are afraid of sunlight; they strike only at night. But that means they must have a hiding place—a cave, or something similar. We can start at the spot where I killed the first creature."

"Lead the way."

"Very well." Hannah mounted her bike. "But hurry. In case I'm wrong, it would not do to be caught unawares out here."

Comforting. Dean gestured for Carter and Wes to follow him to his Jeep. As they approached the vehicle, the memory of the howls that had pierced the air earlier replayed in Dean's mind, and he walked a little faster.

CHAPTER 6

Team Arizona

Hannah led Dean's team to a dirt road that climbed toward a ridge overlooking the valley where they'd landed earlier that day. As they approached the ridge, she slowed. Dean did the same, and when she parked, he pulled up next to her.

She pointed to an outcropping on the mountain. "I killed the wendigo up on that ridge. I do not know if the carcass is still there."

"Doesn't hurt to check."

Wendigo. It made sense that Hannah's people would correlate these creatures with their folklore. If the beast had shown up in Mexico, the locals probably would have called it a chupacabra. If it had shown up in European countries, it might have been compared to a goblin or demogorgon. Whatever it was, it wasn't native wildlife.

Dean dismounted his bike and looked at the others. Carter held his staff at his side. Wes touched the aionium tile on his belt, and his skin transformed into the shiny metal. The three of them followed Hannah as she climbed the ridge. Dean stayed alert, ready to re-engage his shields if they were attacked.

She made it to the top of the ridge and gestured for them to join her. Dean pulled himself up and looked out over the valley. It was a great view; the small reservation in the distance was the only thing that broke up the wild beauty of the untamed desert. Dean turned his attention away from the view to the scene before them. The signs of a struggle were evident—crushed brambles and plant life, footprints and other disturbances in the dirt, spent shell casings, even a few patches of dark sand that indicated dried blood. But he did not see the carcass of a large, monstrous creature.

"Did it get up and walk away?" Carter asked.

"No, it was dead." Hannah looked around. "I made sure of it. But it is possible that its mate came and retrieved the carcass."

Dean scratched his chin. If these creatures were creations of Dr. Ashcroft, they might be intelligent enough to know to recover a body—or specifically trained or programmed to do so. Either way, the body's disappearance might lend credence to the idea that these were engineered beasts.

Dean knelt next to one of the darkened patches of dirt. Was it possible to get DNA from this mess? Unlikely. It was just stained dirt. He reached down and ran his fingers through it, and a few short, gray hairs turned up. He lifted them carefully between his thumb and forefinger and removed a small plastic bag from his belt. Dropping the hairs inside, he returned them to his belt and stood, looking at Hannah.

"You must be right. They have to live somewhere nearby. Do you have any idea where to begin our search?"

"The mountains are relatively uncharted, but I have a few ideas."

"Wait, do we really want to go into a cave with one of these things?" Wes asked. "If we go to it on its home turf, we'll be at a huge disadvantage. Shouldn't we draw it out instead?"

"Scared?" Dean grinned. "You're the one with impenetrable skin, remember?"

"I'm more worried about the rest of you."

Carter shrugged. "I don't like it, either, but we've got to do what we've got to do, right?"

"You coming or not?" Hannah called.

Dean looked back toward her. She was already ascending the mountain trail. This woman was . . . intense. He gestured for Wes and Carter to follow her. They nodded and picked their way through the bushes toward the trail. And, Dean assumed, ever closer toward the monster.

* * *

The muscles in Wes's upper back tensed as they approached a cave. He rolled his shoulders to loosen them and kept a hand near his belt. They had been searching the mountain range for hours. The sun had gone down long ago, and they had found no sign of the "wendigos." Just as they had been ready to give up and return to Hannah's house for the night, they had come across an opening. Hannah had gestured to brownish-red streaks in the dirt, indicating that the wendigo's body, or some other bloody carcass, had likely been dragged across the area. Either way, it seemed likely the surviving wendigo—or, possibly, wendigos—was inside.

Hannah shone a flashlight into the cave, holding it in her still-healing left hand. With her right hand, she trained her weapon unwaveringly on the mouth of the cave. Dean flexed his arms, and his aionium shields spun out into position. Carter brought his staff up.

Here we go. Wes—Rampart—reminded himself that it had been his idea to investigate these creatures. He had no one to blame but himself for being in this position. He stepped in front of the Crusader. If the wendigo was inside, it would be safer for Rampart to go in before him.

The kid only had his armor to protect him, and they had no idea how well that would hold up against this beast. Rampart's metal skin was likely to be more durable.

Wes studied Hannah. He wasn't sure yet that they could trust her. Not that he believed she was working for Ashcroft, or anything, but she clearly didn't care about what they had planned. Her sole motive was killing these beasts to protect her home. That was fair. He would probably feel the same way if it was Sojourn City.

She was certainly an interesting woman. He had noticed that her speech pattern was very formal and precise, as was everything else she did. Her intensity reminded him of Gideon, and while a little intensity could be useful, he hoped she would play well enough with others that her goals didn't drive her to do something stupid.

Bison and Drifter went in side-by-side, watching the cave from different angles. Rampart stepped in after them, scanning the interior of the cave as Bison's light swept across it.

A shadow darted through the beam of light.

Rampart's heart pounded. Before he could move, Bison fired. The bullet pinged off the rock wall. The shadow vanished. The gunshot echoed through the cave for a moment. Then, there was only silence.

Drifter whistled. "It's fast. Stay alert."

Rampart glanced back at Carter. If the boy was nervous, he wasn't showing it. He had gone full Crusader. His jaw was set, his expression steely. He had a firm grip on his staff. Rampart took a deep breath and composed himself. If Carter could be calm in the face of this kind of danger, he could, too.

He stepped forward. He was Rampart—a wall of protection. He couldn't be cowardly. It was his job to protect the people who couldn't protect themselves. Although Dean, Hannah, and Carter were all more than capable of taking care of themselves, Wes still had a responsibility to watch out for them. This mission had been his idea. He would see it through. He shunted his fears aside and followed Bison and Drifter.

He pointed left. "Shine the light back that way."

Bison swung her light slowly to the left. It illuminated the brownish-red rock, and then . . . blackness. There was a tunnel leading farther back into the mountain, deep enough that her light couldn't pierce. Rampart stepped toward the tunnel. That had to be where the wendigo had gone. It—

"Rampart, look out!"

Something struck him with the force of a truck. He hurtled toward the wall, and then he was safely back near the mouth of the cave, behind the Crusader, with Drifter standing over him. *He teleported me.*

"Thanks."

Drifter rushed back toward the cave. Rampart rolled to his feet and followed him. The Crusader flourished his staff and stepped forward. *Bang-bang-bang.* Bison's revolver muzzle flashed as the gun fired. Something bellowed out an angry roar. Her light fell across the beast. Rampart's breaths came in shallow gasps, and his heart rate accelerated. He was looking at something out of a nightmare.

The gray-furred creature was all muscle. It was huge—almost as tall as Wes and Carter put together. Its claws were the length of one of the Crusader's truncheons, and its gaping mouth boasted teeth like swords. When that mouth went wide to roar, the sound it emitted reverberated off the cave walls, filling the narrow tunnel with a cacophony of subharmonic noise.

Drifter whistled again. "I think we found it."

Rampart rushed toward the beast as it bounded toward Hannah. By Rampart's count, Brass Bison only had two shots left before she had to reload. As he crossed the distance, she fired one of them. The wendigo raised its arm, its claws gleaming in the beam of Bison's flashlight. Rampart leaped.

As he jumped through the air, he saw Drifter appear at Brass Bison's side out of his peripheral vision. He grabbed her and teleported away as the wendigo's arm descended. Rampart completed his jump, landing right in front of the arm and raising his hands to meet the clawed appendage.

He grunted and buckled to his knees, but he managed to hold the descending hand up and keep it from crushing him. The wendigo pushed downward. Rampart wrapped his hands around the creature's fingers and pushed back. Slowly, his legs straightened as he rose from the floor. He pushed with all his might, struggling against the creature's grip. It was like trying to stop the descent of an industrial crusher. Even with amplified strength, the task was nearly impossible. He gritted his teeth and yelled.

Drifter appeared on the wendigo's back and brought his aionium shield down on the back of its skull. It howled in pain and reared back, releasing its grip on Rampart and trying to buck Drifter from its back.

"Adhesive beads!" Drifter shouted.

The Crusader rushed to Rampart's side. "On it!"

The younger vigilante grabbed a handful of the beads from his belt and hurled them. They exploded at the wendigo's feet, coating them with goo. Good idea. They had to restrain it, not kill it. He jumped up and grabbed the wendigo's right arm, pulling it back toward the ground with the full weight of his aionium-skinned body.

Wait. Aionium was a light metal. Rampart reached down with one hand and touched the stone tile on his belt. His skin shifted to stone, and he wrapped his arm once again around the wendigo's and tugged. The beast roared again, the deafening sound echoing off the cave walls. Three more projectiles struck the wendigo's chest. Bison must have reloaded. The Crusader fired his grappling hook at the creature's left wrist and pulled with all his might.

"Bison!" Rampart shouted. "Help him!"

She rushed to his side and grabbed the grappling hook. Even with heavy stone skin, Rampart was struggling to keep the beast down. He clenched his jaw and roared incoherently through his teeth, pulling against the creature's furry arm with all his might. There was no way the unpowered Crusader could hold the beast himself. But with Bison's help, maybe . . . maybe long enough for Drifter to inject the beast with the tranquilizer they'd brought.

Rampart looked up at Drifter. He was struggling to stay on the creature's back as it bucked. With his right hand, he reached down to his belt and withdrew the syringe holding the tranquilizer while he held onto the beast's nape with his left hand. The wendigo roared and fought back with renewed vigor. Rampart yelped as it pulled its arm back, and he punched it in the forearm several times.

Brass Bison stumbled to the ground and cradled her left arm. Rampart had forgotten about her injury. The creature's struggle must've aggravated it. The Crusader pulled at the line. The kid was determined to keep the wendigo down. Rampart was impressed, but he knew the Crusader wouldn't last much longer. He might be stronger than the average kid his age, but he was no amp.

Drifter brought the needle down.

The creature's right foot ripped free of the adhesive goo. Rampart cried out and fell from the wendigo's arm. He grunted as he hit the floor. The beast lunged, hurling Drifter off its back. The green-clad hero teleported just before he slammed into the wall and landed next to Rampart. The Crusader stumbled back, the grappling gun jerking free from his grip.

"It's smart," Drifter said. "It's like it knows what we're doing."

Bang. The wendigo wailed, dropped to its knees, and collapsed. The cavern shook with the impact of the creature's body. Rampart steadied himself against the tunnel wall and shifted back to his normal form. Blood rushed from the creature's left eye. Bison lowered her gun.

"There," she panted. "Now it does not know anything."

CHAPTER 7

Although she had visited Michigan multiple times, Audrey's singing career never brought her as far north as Sojourn City. The closest she'd ever come was Detroit. She had been in Sojourn City once before, three months earlier, to steal intel from Sterling Enterprises, but she had infiltrated and exfiltrated before getting to know the city. When she, Pierce, and Zeke had arrived this time, she hadn't known what to think of it. The longer she was there and the more she learned, the more impressed she was. No other city in the world built half its architecture on a floating platform in the middle of the lake, connecting that platform to land with a state-of-the-art maglev train.

The city had cleaned itself up a lot in the past year. It had gone from a crime hub to a glittering jewel. The slums still had a gang problem, but the police were driving it back with much more success than in the past. Sojourn City owed much of that to Gideon Turner, which simultaneously excited and disappointed Audrey. On one hand, it was proof of all the good that Ashcroft's superhumans could do for the world. On the other, Gideon was not a willing participant in Ashcroft's plan and was actively resisting it. Turner seemed like a good person. How could he resist a movement that would change the whole world for the better?

The only explanation Audrey could come up with was that he wanted to keep his gifts for himself. He did some good with them, but if everyone else had superpowers, Gideon wouldn't need to do much. Everyone would take care of themselves. Couldn't he see that? He was just out for glory. Maybe that was the reason he was the only one of his companions with a publicly known identity. He wanted the spotlight to himself. He wouldn't even share it with his own brother.

Worse, his followers didn't seem to realize it. They blindly served him while he made them believe they were a team—the Vindicators. It made sense that his brother would follow him. But an eighteen-year-old boy? A brilliant mind like Dean Sterling? It was a tragedy. How could people like that, who seemed so good on the outside, be so corrupt as to resist positive change? If Turner was taken out of the equation, would the rest of them see reason, or were they too far gone already?

She wished there was some way to make them see without violence, but if Artemis, the smooth-talker that she was, failed to convince Turner's rebels, it was hopeless for anyone else to try as long as Turner was still around. Even if peace was an option, Audrey was the only one who wanted that resolution. The others were angry about what had happened to Artemis, Powers, and Mendez, and they just wanted to fight—even young Melanie.

Audrey knew it was inevitable. She did not relish the thought of combat, but she would do what needed to be done.

"I'm hungry," Pierce grumbled.

Audrey, Pierce, and Zeke were in a hotel in Lakeside, an upscale neighborhood. They were only a few blocks from Lakeside Central Tower, where the heroes' base was located. Although Audrey had bided her time researching the city and the Vindicators, Pierce was showing signs of boredom. Even Zeke, who was former military, made a few sullen comments as he paced the hotel room.

Zeke crossed his arms. "Let's hit the town. Find some grub and scope out the local nightlife."

Pierce bobbed his head vigorously. "Yeah. If I don't eat something soon, I'm going to get angry."

"Better feed him. He'll start spitting poison if you don't."

Audrey rubbed her forehead. "Order room service. We shouldn't leave."

"Hotel food is the worst." Pierce stood and grabbed the car keys. "I'm going out. You with me?"

"I'm in!" Zeke jumped off the bed. "Come on, princess, what do you say? The heroes just left this morning. They're not coming back anytime soon. We won't miss anything."

"Okay." Audrey grabbed her jacket. "But no powers."

The world was still acclimating to the presence of superhumans—amps, as the media had taken to calling them. Although most were welcomed at least hesitantly as heroes, others were feared. Audrey did not want to cause fear. She wanted to inspire hope. Using her powers tonight wouldn't do that.

Pierce rolled his eyes. "Sure, princess. Whatever you say."

Audrey pulled her sky-blue jacket over her black-and-white striped blouse and ducked out the door behind the two men. She supposed going out wouldn't do any harm. As beautiful as Sojourn City was, it would be a shame to only see it from a hotel room window. They had a night of peace before the rebels returned.

Might as well make the most of it.

Audrey nursed her milkshake and looked around the quaint, fifties-style diner. She never visited places like this when she had been a popstar. Her managers and promoters had been afraid she would be mobbed by fans. Audrey had been willing to take the risk, but they insisted that she stay in her hotel or bus or trailer or wherever she happened to be in a given week. They would bring her back whatever she asked for. Sitting there now, she realized how much she had missed out on. The environment was lovely, and the food was fantastic. The owner, a kindly old man, greeted everyone who walked in the door.

Audrey sucked in a mouthful of the milkshake through her straw. The peanut butter and chocolate flavor exploded across Audrey's tongue. She smiled and sipped at the shake, relishing every delicious second.

Pierce shoved a handful of french fries into his mouth, smearing ketchup across his stubbly chin. "See? This is much better than sitting in that room."

"You're right." Audrey smiled at him. "Thanks for convincing me."

Pierce leaned back in his padded, red chair and crossed his arms. Audrey didn't understand him. The guy seemed to be in a permanently bad mood. Maybe that was why he got his specific powers. "Toxic" and "venomous" seemed apt descriptors. They were on the same side, and she still had a tough time liking him. He was better than Quinn, though. The self-important twerp never had anything nice to say. He took pride in being Ashcroft's first success. She pitied poor Melanie, staked out by herself with Quinn, watching the prison.

The chime above the door rang. A young woman with hair a few shades darker than Audrey's stepped into the diner. She wore sweatpants and a gray t-shirt. As she entered, the owner looked up and beamed.

"Miss Jolie! What are you doing out so late?"

"Couldn't sleep." The woman smiled. "Thought an ice cream sundae might be the cure I needed. For the road, please."

Audrey didn't intend to eavesdrop; but there were so few people in the restaurant at this time, and her powers gave her heightened hearing. It wasn't her fault; the words just seemed to float through the air and into her ears.

"Coming right up!" the owner said.

Zeke glanced up. "She's not bad."

"Hmm?" Audrey asked.

"The girl who just walked in. Not bad."

Audrey scowled. "Really, Zeke?"

"What? Just saying. Look at her. She's in great shape, definitely active. Nice face, too."

Pierce smirked. "You in love, Zeke? Why don't you go get her number?"

Audrey glanced at the woman. "She's wearing an engagement ring."

"But she's here, by herself, instead of with her fiancé." Zeke shrugged. "Could mean something."

"Could mean you're a pig if you go over there."

Zeke huffed. "I didn't say I was going to. Calm down! That was Pierce's idea. I was just commenting. I'm not actually going to go talk to her."

Audrey pursed her lips. Zeke was one of the steadier heads in the Regency. His military training might have a hand in that. If she had to choose a friend out of the male members of Ashcroft's regime, Zeke would be her first pick. At least, he didn't hit on her or goad her. Still, he had rough edges.

The owner returned with Jolie's sundae. "How's Gideon?"

Audrey raised her eyebrows at the name and refocused her attention on the newcomer. There were probably other men named Gideon in a city this big. Still, it was a coincidence that she would hear one mentioned. She wished she had Turner's dossier with her. She thought it referenced a girlfriend, but Audrey couldn't remember her name.

The woman shrugged. "He's out of town right now. Not the greatest timing, you know, with the wedding coming up. But it was urgent . . . "

"Hang in there." The owner handed her the heap of ice cream in a to-go container, and she gave him cash. "Have a good night, Miss Jolie."

Out of town. It was almost certainly her. Gideon had left that day to hunt down the nephiloids. Audrey watched the girl leave.

"—not going to ask her out!" Zeke exclaimed at Pierce.

"Will you two shut up?" Audrey hissed. "I think that woman is Gideon Turner's fiancée."

"You're kidding." Zeke straightened in his seat. "Want me to grab her?"

"What? No!" Audrey shook her head. "What good would that do? She's not a part of Ashcroft's plan."

"Not a p—" Pierce started.

"She's leverage, Audrey," Zeke said calmly.

Pierce shook his head and downed a few more fries. "You really are oblivious, aren't you, pop star?"

"Leave her 'lone." Zeke patted Pierce's shoulder and gestured with one hand between the two of them. "She's not like us. Sorry, princess, but Pierce is right. Strategically, it makes sense to nab the girl."

Audrey considered. They didn't have to hurt Jolie. They could hold onto her until Gideon returned and force him to surrender in exchange for her safe return. At least, it would be a way to deal with him without violence. But as far as she could tell, Jolie was an innocent bystander in all this. She didn't really need to be brought into it, did she? Once Ashcroft's plan was put into motion, Jolie would have powers, too.

Audrey was sure that the woman would understand once the whole world was stronger.

There was no reason to apprehend her, but Gideon might visit her when he came back to Sojourn City. Maybe they should at least watch her. But Pierce wasn't the man for that. He was too dangerous, too volatile. Zeke's strength was also dangerous, but he was a little more restrained.

"Zeke, follow her. Do not engage. Find out where she lives and come straight back to the hotel. If she sees you, leave. Repeat my orders back to me."

Zeke stared her in the eyes, all business. "Follow, but do not engage. Leave if she sees me. Find where she lives. Come back."

"Good. Go."

* * *

Jolie slung her purse over her left shoulder and used her key fob to lock her car while balancing her sundae in her right hand. The aging Camry chirped loudly as the lock engaged, breaking the relative silence of the parking lot. She rounded her car and walked up the steps to her apartment, using her left hand to fumble through the keyring for the key to her front door. She grasped the right one and reached for the lock.

Something moved in Jolie's peripheral vision. She froze and kept a firm grip on her keys. If anyone made a move on her, at least she could use them to stab her attacker while she dropped her ice cream to reach for her gun. *That would be a shame*. She had left her home late at night for an ice cream sundae. If she returned only to drop her prize all over the porch, she would be very unhappy.

Slowly, she scanned the parking lot and the street behind her. A man climbed into his car, and a couple kissed goodbye behind a truck. Nothing looked out of place. Maybe she had just seen movement in the window of a neighboring apartment or a bat passing in front of a streetlight. She watched the street for a moment longer to be sure before she inserted the key into the lock and turned it.

Whoosh. Jolie spun around, leaving the key in the door and dropping her purse so she could reach for her gun.

A silhouette topped the roof across the street. Jolie knelt next to her purse and drew her gun, setting her sundae carefully on the ground. *This is silly; it's probably just a chimney.*

The chimney moved.

Not a chimney.

Jolie tightened her grip on her gun, ready to fire if the shadow came down from the roof and approached her, but its movement was in the opposite direction. It leapt across to another rooftop, and another, crossing each with a single jump. It was out of sight in seconds. Jolie reached down to return her gun to her purse, her hands trembling, and knocked over her sundae.

"No!" she groaned.

She scooped it off the ground before more than a few drops of melting vanilla ice cream dribbled out. She shouldered her purse, unlocked the door, and darted into her apartment, locking the door behind her and latching the deadbolt. There was no reason to take any chances. She set her purse and sundae down on her small table and leaned against an armchair. Her hands were still shaking.

Someone had been watching her—someone who could bridge rooftops in a single jump. Gideon and the rest of the Vindicators were out of town, and none of them had a reason to watch her from afar. If this was someone else, they weren't around to help her fight a potential amplified opponent. She walked across her apartment to draw the blinds and curtain on the living room window. Then she dropped onto the couch and took a deep breath. *I can take care of myself.* Gideon had been teaching her hand-to-hand combat for just such an eventuality. Whoever had been watching her was gone, but it was better to stay armed until she was sure she was safe. She rose from the couch, rushed to her bed, and flopped down onto it.

God, please keep me safe. She took a few deep breaths, and a comforting peace washed over her. She sighed in relief, sat up, and placed her gun on her bedside table. There was no reason to stay up all night worrying. If they came for her, she would wake up as they broke in. It would give her time to at least grab her gun before they got to her.

She returned to the kitchen, grabbed her sundae, and took it to her bedroom. God was looking out for her. Even a supervillain couldn't do anything against Him. She would be fine.

* * *

"I'm pretty sure she saw me," Zeke said.

Maybe sending him after Jolie had been a bad idea, Audrey mused. Upon returning to the hotel, she had checked Gideon's dossier to confirm that Jolie was his fiancée. At least she hadn't sent Zeke after some poor, random woman. Maybe his surveillance would pay off somehow.

"Did she get a good look at your face?" Audrey asked.

"No." Zeke dropped down onto a bed. "I was on a rooftop across the street. If she saw anything, it was just a shadow."

"Should've sent me," Pierce grumbled. "She never would've seen me."

"Yeah, 'cause you would've blinded her with acid," Zeke snapped. "Look, she went into her house, and I left. I've got the address, and she didn't ID me. So, what's the problem?"

Audrey cut in. "No problem. You did what you were told. It's not your fault she saw you."

"Now what?" Pierce asked.

They were supposed to strike the rebels when they returned, but until then, they were in reserve. Melanie and Quinn would break the others out of prison when the guard shift changed at six a.m. Audrey and her team could run backup for them if things went wrong, but she doubted the two of them would have a problem. Once Artemis, Mendez, and Powers were able to use their abilities again, they would make short work of the guards.

"Get some sleep." Audrey looked out the window toward the rebels' tower. "It's going to be a long wait."

CHAPTER 8

Kansas Team

Eighteen hours earlier

As the Raptor descended toward Goddard, Patrick lowered his goggles. The lenses tinted his vision purple. He wiggled his arms and jogged in place to loosen his muscles. *Relax.* Whatever they faced out here, they could handle it. Gideon's powers were the strongest Patrick had ever seen. If anyone could go toe-to-toe with a monster, it was him. Patrick just hoped it wasn't some giant beast like the rancor monster from *Star Wars*. He wasn't ready for the nightmares something like that would bring.

"Setting down in five!" Maddox called. "And . . . three, two, one."

The plane barely jostled as it settled on the ground. The tech on this thing was amazing. As the ramp lowered, he looked at Carter. Carter grinned, nodded, and tossed Patrick a casual two-fingered salute.

"Good luck, buddy."

Patrick saluted back. "You, too."

The ramp touched the ground, and the world seemed to slow around Patrick. Outside, the tall grass blew gently in the morning breeze. Patrick took a deep breath. Hoisting his backpack over his shoulder, he ran.

He sprinted from the plane out into the middle of the field and did a quick recon of the area. He didn't see any sign of monsters—or anything, really. This place was barren. In the distance, he made out the uneven shapes of a cluster of buildings. He slowed down and stopped next to the ramp as Gideon stepped onto the grass.

"Nothing here." Patrick pointed at the horizon. "Town's that way."

"Let's go."

Gideon lifted into the air and soared toward Goddard. The world slowed down again, and Patrick rushed after Gideon, blasting down the road at nearly a hundred miles an hour to keep pace with his flying friend. As they neared the small town, Patrick slowed to a halt, and Gideon descended toward the ground. Better not to approach the city in all their glory. He wondered what they would look like to observers—a bright, golden light soaring through the sky and a purple blur keeping pace on the streets below. These poor farmers would probably think Gideon was a UFO or something.

"Are we sure it's a good idea to waltz into town decked out in our suits?" Patrick asked. "People around here probably aren't all that familiar with superheroes."

"The bomb that went off in Wichita a few weeks ago created some amps, but you're probably right." Gideon pointed to the west. "That barn over there looks abandoned. We'll change into plainclothes and walk into town."

Patrick removed his backpack, which held his and Gideon's street clothes, and unzipped it. The two heroes walked over to the dilapidated barn, slipped through the half-broken door, and swept the building to ensure they were alone. Patrick removed his mask. The place was as abandoned as Gideon had suspected.

Moving in a blur, Patrick changed into a pair of faded blue jeans, a gray flannel shirt, and a brown jacket. He stuffed his costume into his backpack. Gideon removed his gloves, boots, and armor plates but kept his bodysuit on, pulling his blue jeans, red Henley shirt, and black leather jacket over it. Patrick handed him his backpack, and Gideon carefully tucked the rest of his suit inside. It was a tight squeeze, but it all fit.

"All right." Gideon stepped out into the sun. "Let's hit the town and see what we can find out."

* * *

Hands tucked in his jacket pockets, Gideon stepped through the glass door into Goddard's small, city office building. A police officer in a blue uniform glanced up from his desk, pushed himself out of his chair, and sauntered over toward Gideon. The officer eyed him as he approached. He no doubt knew Gideon was not from Goddard, which would either intrigue him or set him on edge. Gideon probed him gently with his empathic powers. The officer didn't feel edgy—more bored than anything.

"How can I help you?"

Gideon extended his hand. "My name is Gideon Turner. I'm a scientist from Sterling Labs. I'm following up on reports of unidentified creature attacks in the area."

"Ah. Those." The officer shook Gideon's hand. Gideon sensed a new tension and unease rise in the officer. "I'm sorry to tell you, but there's nothing to those reports. Just old wives' tales popping up again because of an increase in bear attacks and the bombing in Wichita."

"Are you sure?"

"Look, I know people think supernatural happenings in small towns are the most interesting thing in the world, but unfortunately, reality is usually a whole lot more boring than folklore. I'm afraid we can't help you."

"Of course. Honestly, I didn't expect to find anything as exciting as a monster, but as a scientist, I had to do my due diligence."

"I understand. Have a good day."

Gideon backed out onto the street. Patrick stood nearby, reclining against a telephone pole. He straightened as Gideon exited the offices.

"Anything?"

Gideon shook his head. "They were adamant that it's just an upswing in bear attacks, but that could be a PR smokescreen. There was something off about the way he felt, like he was hiding something."

"What do we do?"

"Most of the attacks have been reported at night. Let's find a restaurant or something and wait for sunset. Once it's dark, we can investigate the spots that have already been attacked and see if we can find any clues. And hopefully, we can get this sorted out before the end of the day."

As the sun fell, Gideon and Patrick went into the fields outside of Goddard, where the previous attacks had been reported. The field was otherwise empty. If not for the police report, Gideon never would have suspected that anything had happened here at all. Ever. *Could these creatures have chosen a more boring place to hunt?* He scanned the field for evidence.

He and Patrick were back in their suits; the cover of night should be enough to keep the citizens of Goddard from getting too curious. Even if they did see Spright or the Seraph, there was nothing tying them to the out-of-towner scientist who'd shown up at the city offices earlier that day—at least, provided no one did their research and found that Gideon Turner and the Seraph were one and the same. On the off chance they did put the pieces together, the two of them should be gone by tomorrow.

"Over here!" Patrick called.

Gideon stepped over to the younger man's side. Patrick was kneeling in the middle of the field, shining a flashlight on the ground. As Gideon approached, Patrick flicked the light off, and Gideon lit up one of his hands, casting a brighter beam of golden light on the area. Patrick ran his hands over a trio of deep furrows in the grass.

"This could be something. These don't look like any animal tracks I'm familiar with. What do you think?"

Gideon knelt. The furrows vaguely resembled claw marks, but they could have been from a manmade blade. It was hard to tell without anything to compare them to.

"If this came from the creature, its claws are significantly longer than a bear's." Gideon stuck a finger in the furrow. It didn't come close to brushing the bottom. "This has to be six inches deep, at least. I don't know of any creature that has claws that long. If it is an animal, it's got to be mutated."

"Comforting." Patrick looked around. "Where do we go from—"

The night split with the wailing of police sirens. Gideon lowered his hand and extinguished the light pouring from it. Four police cruisers sped by on the interstate, their lights flashing and sirens blazing. Gideon looked at Patrick and nodded. The boy pulled his mask down over his head, dropped into a runner's crouch, and was gone, a breeze tugging at Gideon's hood in his wake.

The Seraph leapt into the air, soaring after Spright. He barely glimpsed him in the dark night, and he knew what to look for. Only someone watching for the speedster would have noticed him.

Police lights dotted the horizon. They had stopped. Whatever they'd been called to deal with, they'd reached their destination. The Seraph arced toward them. He wondered what they thought of him. He was a golden blur of light, speeding through the air. He hoped they didn't open fire. It wouldn't hurt him, but he would have to talk them down, which would take time—time that they could use to catch the beasts.

Luckily, no gunshots went off. A few officers swung toward the Seraph and raised their weapons as he approached, but they didn't fire. He landed in front of them and raised his hands in a placating gesture.

"Who are you?" one demanded.

"I'm the Seraph." Spright appeared at his side. "This is Spright. We heard about the monsters that have been terrorizing your town. We want to help."

"Monsters." The officer snorted. The Seraph recognized him as the man he had spoken to in the office that morning. "It's wildlife."

Gideon lowered his hood. "You told me that earlier today. You were no more convincing then."

The officer lowered his head. Gideon sensed his chagrin. If he had known Gideon was a superhero that afternoon, would he have answered the same way? His small-town practicality was out of place in front of a pair of superheroes. Gideon was used to it. Now that he had been reprimanded, he might be more helpful.

"Can't hurt for us to take a look," Spright said. "We'll be fast. And if it really *is* just wild animals, then there's nothing to worry about, right?"

The first officer lowered his gun. "All right. The animal's out in that cornfield. He got a hold of a cow and dragged him off."

"No one's been hurt?" the Seraph asked.

"Not tonight. But two have died since these things showed up, so the sooner they're gone, the better."

"We'll take a look."

The Seraph stepped toward the stalks of corn and dampened the light energy flowing from him. The last thing he wanted was to start a fire and burn the whole field to the ground. Spright stepped up beside him. The Seraph took a deep breath. He sensed Spright's nervousness and the officers' fear. He also sensed something . . . feral. And something else, too. Focused determination. The determination of a hunter.

"Someone's out there. Someone else is tracking the monsters."

"We need to hurry." Spright took a step forward. "We need that thing alive."

The Seraph walked into the field, clenching his fists. The wind rustled the stalks of corn around them. Would he be able to hear the beast coming? How would he know the difference between a moving creature and the wind? He sensed the feral hunger, but his powers didn't give him any indication of how far away the presence was.

He brushed through the stalks. Spright moved to the right, so the Seraph veered left. He shook his head. *What am I doing?* He could fly. If these creatures were big enough, he could see them from above. He lifted into the air, above the stalks, and looked down over the vast acres of farmland. The stalks to his right moved, indicative of Spright's presence. He looked out into the rest of the field.

There. The stalks on the other edge of the field moved, and a dark shadow appeared in the open plain behind it.

"Spright, clear the field!"

The field parted as the speedster burst through the cornfield to the plain. The Seraph flew after him and descended toward the dark shape. Whatever it was, it was no bear. It was too lean for that; its tall body was a mass of taut muscle. What was it? Spright came up on the thing's right flank.

The creature swung an arm roped with taut muscle. Spright sped around the arm, avoiding it. The Seraph descended toward the creature. Suddenly, a projectile lodged in the creature's shoulder. The Seraph hit the ground and searched for the attacker.

A man stood at the edge of the field. He wore a hunting vest and hat and held a crossbow at his shoulder. The Seraph felt the man's determination spike.

"Stand down!" the Seraph called. "We'll handle it!"

The man fired another arrow. It struck the creature's other shoulder. The beast howled. Spright skidded to a stop beside the Seraph.

"What is this thing?" Spright exclaimed.

The creature, covered in thick, gray fur, was tall, with arms the length of its body. It had beady, black eyes; and its mouth, shaped vaguely like a wolf's, was a wide rictus of jagged teeth. The Seraph had never seen anything like it.

"I don't know, but we need to sedate it now."

"Sedate it?" the hunter shouted. "We need to kill it!"

The creature roared and charged. The Seraph turned toward it, raised a light-charged fist, and swung at the beast. It swept its arm toward him, striking him with the force of a semi-truck. His feet left the ground, and he flew back toward the field. Spright circled around the creature, running too fast for the Seraph to see, boxing the monster in. The Seraph staggered to his feet, grimacing as his ribs ached in protest, and reached for the tranquilizer in his utility belt.

He hoped it would work on this beast. They were more likely to get information from a live specimen, rather than studying a dead one.

The beast lashed out and knocked Spright to the ground. The Seraph shook his head. How could it be that fast? The hunter fired another arrow, striking the creature square in the chest. It howled and bounded away. The Seraph rushed after it.

"Seraph!" Patrick lay on the ground, grasping his knee. The hunter dropped to the ground next to him. Gideon glanced over his shoulder and watched the creature scramble for the tree line. He let it go and joined the hunter at Patrick's side.

"I think . . . it's broken," Patrick gasped.

The man nodded. "He's right. We need to get this set."

Gideon clenched his jaw. At least, the creature hadn't killed anyone this time. "I'll carry him."

"Bring him back to my place. I was a field medic. I can patch him up."

"Who are you?"

"Jarrett Mercer, former Special Forces. And I'm the only man who's killed one of these beasts."

CHAPTER 9

Team Kansas

Gideon helped Patrick ease onto a couch in Jarrett Mercer's living room. Patrick hissed and clutched at his knee. The injury was severe, but the bone had not punctured skin. They could count their blessings for that, at least. Still, Gideon remembered the pain of his own broken bones keenly. He did not envy Patrick's condition. Gideon stepped back and looked at Jarrett.

"Do you need a hand? I was a surgeon before—"

"Before you started flying around in a blue suit of armor?" Jarrett nodded. "Thanks, but I can handle this. I've set more than my fair share of bones."

The man removed his bright orange vest and camouflage hat before searching through the kitchen cabinets. Gideon watched him as he worked. Mercer was only a few years older than Gideon. His brown hair, flattened and matted from hours under his hunting cap, was surprisingly long for someone who had been in the army. He wore a gray, long-sleeved shirt with dark blue jeans and a Glock tucked into his waistband at the small of his back. He looked tough, but Gideon sensed kindness in him. This man had not let his experiences turn him into a hard shell. Gideon probed him further. Underneath Mercer's determination was a soft side and a wry sense of humor. Gideon had the feeling that Mercer was an easy person to get along with.

"Here we go."

Mercer grabbed a first aid kit and knelt next to Patrick. Gideon lowered his hood, removed his armor plates, and set them down on the counter that divided the living room from the kitchen. Crossing the room, he eased down next to Mercer.

"Anything I can do to help, Mr. Mercer?"

"It's Jarrett." He shook his head. "And no. This'll just take a second."

He worked fast, setting Patrick's knee and wrapping it in a bandage. Patrick screamed as his bone cracked back into place, but the pain seemed to be receding. Gideon was impressed with them both.

"He's a speedster?" Jarrett asked.

"Yes."

"His metabolism probably works faster, too, and possibly his healing processes." Mercer rested a hand on Patrick's shoulder. "Stay on the couch until then, all right?"

"Yes, sir."

"No 'sirs.' I'm not an officer." Mercer packed up his first aid kit. "So, you boys are out hunting cryptids, eh?"

"Cryptids?" Gideon asked.

"Yeah. Scientific term for 'we don't know what they are.'" Jarrett carried the kit back to the cabinet. "My wife, Janet, is a biologist. She's in D.C. for some important conference. Great timing. Maybe she would be able to tell us what these things are. I've got a dead one in the cellar."

"You're kidding."

Mercer's deadpan expression didn't waver. "Yeah, I'm kidding."

Gideon chuckled. *Who is this guy?*

"I did kill one, but when I went back the next day to get the body, it had vanished. My guess is its packmates came and dragged it off.

They're not sapient, but they're very intelligent. It's like they knew we'd study the corpse."

"That's . . . unsettling."

"I call it creepy." Jarrett shrugged. "You're more than welcome to stay the night here and continue your hunt tomorrow. I'd like to tag along, if you don't mind. These things are a menace."

"Tomorrow? We need to find this thing now. We've already been away from Sojourn City for too long."

"I'm sure they can live without you for one more day."

Gideon clenched his jaw. Crime was down, but that wasn't why he wanted to be home. He missed Jolie already. The next day was Sunday, and he wanted to be in church, not out hunting some big beast. But without Patrick, he and Mercer were at a disadvantage if they ran into the beast that night. Reluctantly, he nodded.

"So, why hunt with a crossbow?" Gideon pointed at Mercer's belt. "You carry a gun. Why shoot it with arrows when bullets would do the job more effectively?"

"Not my style. I did guns in Special Forces, and I was really, really good with them. Too good. It felt impersonal for me. When you kill someone, it's not fair to be able to distance yourself from it. Death's not a joke. It's not meant to be cold or easy. Taking a life means something. It should affect you. If it doesn't, you're a psychopath. That's why I use a crossbow. Because it's more personal, more . . . real. A gun is a last resort for me."

"You sound like you've killed more than just monsters."

Jarrett ran a hand through his thick hair. "You're right about that. I try not to kill, but . . . Wichita's a big city. There aren't a lot of those around here, so any criminal element looking to get a foothold in this state is going to come here. It's gotten ugly and . . . "

"You decided to take it into your own hands. You're a vigilante."

"Yeah." Jarrett chopped his head in a short nod. "Like I said, I try not to kill. But I'm not perfect. Sometimes, an arrow meant to disable is a lot more lethal than intended, you know? And it's easier to make mistakes like that with a gun, so I try for the less lethal route."

Gideon understood. He had never intentionally killed during his time as the Seraph, but there was no way to know if any of the criminals he had beaten up in his first few months as a vigilante had died from their wounds. His light-amplified punches were powerful, and it had taken time to learn how to control them. It was possible that there were casualties out there about which Gideon had no idea, and he preferred to keep it that way. Gideon knew he had killed guerrillas in a life-or-death situation in Venezuela, and like Jarrett said, it had changed him. Gideon had no room to judge Jarrett for what he did.

"I get it. You have to do your part to protect your city."

"I'm glad you understand."

"What do they call you?"

"Yeoman."

"I'm the Seraph."

"Good to meet you, Seraph. If we're going to hunt that creature, we should get an early start. If you want any sleep, now's as good a time as any. Guest room's down the hall. If you need anything, let me know."

Gideon glanced at Patrick. The kid was already fast asleep. Jarrett was probably right; they should do the same.

"Thanks. See you bright and early."

* * *

Patrick was shocked by how quickly his knee healed. As the sun peeked through the thin curtains of Jarrett Mercer's living room, Patrick bent his leg and carefully lowered it to touch the floor. He pressed down on it and cringed in anticipation—nothing. It didn't hurt at all. It was like it had never been injured.

This was an aspect of his powers he had never considered before. Superspeed probably wouldn't help much if he got his leg blown off, but broken bones and bruises were virtually meaningless now. Patrick pushed himself to his feet and walked a few laps around the living room. *Awesome.*

Gideon stepped into the room. He rubbed his eyes and blinked a few times. At first, he didn't seem to realize the relevance of Patrick being up and about. Then, his eyes widened, and he laughed.

"Looks like Jarrett was right about your powers."

"It's great, isn't it?" Patrick grinned. "So, are we going to go out and hunt down that ugly dump truck or what?"

The front door squeaked open. Jarrett entered, once again wearing his bright orange vest and camo hat.

"Good, you're up." He walked toward the kitchen. "I was just doing a quick perimeter sweep. We're clear. How about some breakfast before we head out?"

Patrick's stomach rumbled. Breakfast sounded amazing. The curse of his powers was a much higher metabolism, meaning he had to consume truckloads more food than the average person. He hadn't eaten anything since before they encountered the . . . whatever it was. His body had worked overtime to heal his knee. It needed sustenance, or he was likely to pass out the next time he tried to use his powers.

"I know city folks expect us hicks to be able to cook bacon and eggs." Jarrett smirked. "Lucky for you, I can. Otherwise, we'd be eating dry cereal. I'm out of milk."

As Jarrett prepared their meal, Gideon and Patrick sat down at the small kitchen table. There were four chairs at the table but only two placemats. And based on the pictures on the walls, it appeared that Jarrett and his wife lived there alone.

"No kids?" Patrick asked.

"Not yet." Jarrett glanced up from the stove. "Someday. Between my deployment and Janet's studies, we haven't had time. We're still young, right? Kids will come."

He sounded hopeful. Patrick wondered if there was more to the story, but he didn't pry further. He barely knew the man, and he didn't want to be impolite, even though there was something about Jarrett that made him easy to talk to. Patrick settled back in his seat and waited.

Jarrett placed a carton of orange juice and three glasses on the table and stepped back to the stove. The sound and smell of bacon crackling made Patrick's stomach rumble again.

Jarrett studied them out of the corner of his eye. "You guys must've seen a lot of interesting stuff. Why did you come all the way out here for the cryptids?"

Patrick looked to Gideon, who took the lead. "Primarily, we wanted to stop the killing. But the reason they drew our attention in the first place is that they're . . . abnormal."

"They're not your average wildlife, you mean. No, I guess they don't fit in any known genus, do they?"

"No. And they've also shown up in Arizona, hundreds of miles from here. These attacks and appearances aren't random. We think they might be tests."

"Tests?"

Gideon nodded. "If we're right, these creatures were created by a man named Jeremiah Ashcroft. Patrick and I have these abilities because of him. We learned recently that he's planning to genetically modify everyone on the planet. He's been releasing gas bombs in cities around the U.S. These creatures may be a part of his plan."

Jarrett handed each of them a plate of bacon and eggs. Patrick grinned and dug into the food. The salty flavor spread like a shockwave through his mouth, and he sighed contentedly.

"Sounds way beyond my pay grade." Jarrett half-smiled. "But, hey, that's what guys like you are for, right?"

"I suppose so. Although, I used to be more of a guy like you than, well, a guy like me." Gideon took a bite of scrambled eggs. "Thank you."

Patrick had noticed that Gideon was coming to terms with being a superhero, not just a vigilante. For someone like Gideon, who had been exposed to the very dark, harsh realities of the world, being called a superhero must have seemed fantastical nonsense at first. But he had stopped protesting the use of the term since he had rescued a train full of people in Sojourn City. That was a good sign, as was his use of the phrase "used to be." He was accepting who he was.

"You're welcome." Jarrett dropped into a third chair and started in on his own breakfast. "So, once you're done with the cryptids, you'll head back home, I suppose?"

"That's right. We need to keep looking for Ashcroft. It's possible he released these creatures as a distraction while he works on something else."

"If you're aware that's a possibility, why would you still come after them?"

"Like I said, people are dying. We can't just sit around while that's happening."

Patrick didn't have Gideon's empathic powers, but he thought Jarrett was impressed. The man swallowed a mouthful of eggs and took a drink of orange juice.

"Any idea where we should look?" Patrick asked.

"My guess?" Jarrett pressed his lips together in a thin line. "Barns and other shelters. Far as I can tell, these cryptids don't like sunlight—or, at least, prefer to avoid it if possible. There aren't many caves or dense woods around here, so they'll make do with whatever shelter they can find."

Gideon nodded. "We should start at the field where we fought the creature last night and see if we can pick up a trail. If there are any barns or other empty buildings nearby, those would be the first to search."

Patrick finished his meal and settled back in his seat while the other two continued to eat. Five minutes later, they put their dishes in the sink, and Jarrett walked toward the door. He picked up his crossbow, checked the sights, and looked back at them.

"Let's get moving."

CHAPTER 10

Team Kansas

Gideon knelt next to a row of the cryptid's claw marks, identical to those Patrick had discovered the previous night. He looked back at the cornfield. Stalks were snapped in half, others knocked flat. Even if he hadn't seen the beast for himself, this evidence would have been enough to vouch for the creature's size.

Jarrett twirled a few blades of grass in his hands as he studied them. Gideon eyed the hunter. Mercer was an interesting man. Everything about him seemed trustworthy. He was open and straightforward, but the way he probed them at the breakfast table felt off. There was something the archer wasn't telling them. It probably wasn't anything sinister, but still, there was something.

Jarrett reached into his pocket and withdrew a plastic bag, dropping the blades of grass inside. *Was there evidence on them? Maybe the creature's blood?*

Patrick zipped into the field, a purple blur trailing him. "No sign of it in any of the barns or silos on any of the farms between here and Wichita."

Gideon cupped his chin in one hand and looked out at the tree line the cryptid had run toward. The woods were not dense enough to block out the sun entirely. There were only a handful of trees. Still, it had gone in that direction . . .

Gideon looked up at the tree line. Movement flickered in his peripheral vision. He opened his mouth to call out to Patrick and Jarrett.

But it was just a man. He stepped out of a lightly wooded area and looked straight at Gideon. Gideon frowned and approached him. The man wore all white—jeans, boots, shirt, and even a white leather jacket—and his dark brown skin contrasted dramatically with his wardrobe. Gideon stepped closer to the man, studying him as he walked. He looked familiar, somehow . . .

No, it was impossible.

As Gideon approached, the man backed away and stepped into the woods, gesturing for Gideon to follow.

"Hey!" Gideon picked up his pace and pushed through the trees, but the man was gone. Gideon reached out and probed the area, but the only emotions he felt were from Patrick and Jarrett behind him. He shook his head. Had he been imagining things?

"Gideon?"

Patrick stood at the edge of the field, a bewildered look on his face. Gideon looked back out through the trees.

"What's wrong?" Patrick asked.

"Nothing. I . . . " He shrugged. "I just thought I saw something. Come on, let's look this way. It's where the cryptid ran last night."

Maybe the beast can cause hallucinations. Gideon hadn't been cut by the cryptid's claws, but it had struck him. He wondered if there was a chemical in its skin that could mess with a human's brain chemistry. He hoped that was the case because he could think of no better explanation for what he had seen.

The man in white was Wyatt Jonson—Carter's father, the first Crusader. And Wyatt Jonson was dead.

Just focus on finding the cryptid. No need to think about anything else. Not right now.

He scanned the area around him. The small cluster of trees didn't run more than a few dozen feet. After that, it was open plains again. *Why would the cryptid run this way?* He stepped forward.

"Gideon, watch it!"

Gideon grunted as Patrick slammed him to the ground. His adrenaline pumped, and light flooded his body as he prepared to fight. Patrick rolled off him, stood, and extended a hand to help Gideon up. Gideon frowned and accepted his hand. He didn't see, or sense, any threats.

He looked down at his feet and understood. In the place where he had nearly stepped, a giant hole gaped, mostly concealed by foliage. If Gideon had stepped down, he would have tumbled straight through.

Jarrett knelt next to the hole and whistled. "Looks like an underground cave."

"Perfect hiding place for a creature that doesn't like light. I'll go down first."

Jarrett checked his crossbow. "Good idea. We don't have any idea how deep it is, but you can fly down to the bottom and let us know. Plus, your light powers might scare the cryptid—or at least spook it long enough for us to get down to help you."

Gideon looked down into the hole. It was too dark to see the bottom of the cave. He floated into the air, hovered over the opening, and nodded to Patrick and Jarrett.

"I'll let you know when I reach the bottom."

Jarrett pulled a bolt from his quiver. "I've got a grappling hook arrow. After you get down there and let us know how far it is, I'll fire it, and Patrick and I can descend the line."

Gideon floated through the hole. As he passed out of the sun's rays, he brightened the light pouring from his body, allowing it to illuminate the cave. The cavern was huge and just yards from a farm. It was incredible that it had not been discovered before.

"I make about seventy-five feet!" he called.

He didn't hear Jarrett's response. He floated the rest of the way to the cavern floor and settled onto the ground. Puddles of water pocked the cavern, and a larger pool occupied about a third of the floor to Gideon's right. Water dripped from the ceiling into the pool, echoing through the otherwise-silent cave. Gideon shuddered. It was cold—a good twenty degrees colder than on the surface, at least.

An arrow chinked into the ground next to Gideon. He stepped aside and looked up as Patrick and Jarrett descended. They were committed now. Wherever the beast was, they had entered its lair. It would only be a matter of time until they found it. He hoped they were ready for it this time.

* * *

Spright slid down the line and dropped into a crouch next to the Seraph. He pulled his mask up to cover his nose and mouth and lowered his goggles over his eyes. The purple-tinted lenses flashed as their night vision function kicked in. Dean spared no expense in designing the superhero suits. Anything they might need in an emergency, he had included. Boots thumped to the ground next to Spright, and Yeoman raised his crossbow.

A quick run through the cave would let Spright know whether the cryptid was there or not, but he wasn't inclined to do that. As fast as he had moved last night, the thing had still managed to knock him flat and break a bone. If Spright got knocked down while he was away from the Seraph and Yeoman, he might not be able to get away before the cryptid jumped on him. It might tear him apart before they ever reached him.

Yeoman clipped a flashlight to the end of his crossbow. "It's probably hiding. Punching through the brush covering the hole let the sunlight in. The cryptid will be on alert."

The Seraph nodded and stepped forward. Spright fell in line behind him. He really liked Jarrett, but in this case, Gideon was the safer person to stay close to. He had a suit that was nearly impenetrable, plus superpowers that were probably their best chance against the cryptid. His empathic abilities might be able to sense the creature's primal urges. Yeoman was skilled and had killed one before, but all he had was a crossbow. If it came down to the two of them, Patrick's money was on the Seraph.

There were several tunnels leading out of the main cavern. Odds were good that the cryptid was in one of them. Seraph headed for the one on the left. Spright looked around. There were claw marks in the stone walls, almost like the cryptid had marked its territory. It was a strange creature, whatever it was. If Ashcroft really had created this abomination, how had he managed it? Spright didn't like this. It was way too much like a horror movie.

Yeoman whistled sharply. "Over here. Blood."

The Seraph stopped. Spright glanced down at his feet. Yeoman stepped between them and pointed at a darkened spot on the stone floor. The hunter swept a finger through it.

"It's not fresh, but no older than a day." He looked around. "Could have come from my arrow, or the beast has a fresh kill. It's here."

Something rumbled. The sound echoed off the cave walls, making it difficult to detect the source. Spright suspected it was coming from the tunnel the Seraph was headed toward. He took an instinctive step backward. That subharmonic growl chilled him to his bones.

"We're close." The light emanating from the Seraph's fists brightened as he spoke. "Let's finish this. Remember, we want it alive, if possible."

Spright grabbed the syringe from his belt. His speed made him ideally suited to tranquilize the cryptid, but they had also given Yeoman a dose of the serum to place in an arrow with a needle tip. If it came down to it, Yeoman could fire the serum directly into the creature. Spright was still their best hope of taking it down fast.

"Here, monster." Yeoman clicked his tongue and whistled, as if calling for a dog. "Here, boy."

Spright grinned under his mask, and the Seraph snorted, but Yeoman didn't crack a smile. If Patrick hadn't known better, he would have said the guy was totally serious.

"Guess he's not housebroken." Yeoman shrugged. "Oh well."

They walked into the tunnel. Yeoman swept his flashlight back and forth while the Seraph's light radiated around them. The hairs on Spright's arms stood up, and the world around him slowed. A shadowy form moved ahead.

As the Seraph took a step forward, the cryptid howled and recoiled from his golden light. Spright darted forward, and the cryptid took a step back, raising its arms to shield its beady eyes. He slid under the cryptid's legs and jabbed the syringe into the base of its spine. He thumbed the depressor.

Reacting again with startling speed, the cryptid swiped its arm. The limb struck Spright in the chest. The air whooshed from his lungs, and the world sped up as Spright tumbled back and slammed into the wall. The cryptid stomped toward him and raised a clawed hand.

A blast of light knocked the creature aside. Spright stumbled to his feet and sped back to the Seraph's side. The syringe was still embedded in the cryptid's back. All he had to do was run to it and inject the tranquilizer.

He dropped into a runner's crouch. "Draw its attention."

The Seraph aimed an energy blast at the creature. "We're on it."

Spright drew in a breath and held it. The rest of the world, even the cryptid, slowed around him. He remembered training with Gideon—remembered learning to dodge the beams of light Gideon fired, which did not slow the same way the rest of the world did. If he could dodge those, he could dodge this lumbering beast. He only needed discipline and focus. He closed his eyes, feeling every molecule in his body vibrating individually.

Spright opened his eyes.

The cryptid crawled to its feet and stomped toward the trio. Its first step seemed to crawl by. Spright released the breath he had held, leaned forward, and ran. He passed the cryptid in a split second, circled around it, and palmed the injector. The cryptid howled as the tranquilizer flowed into its system. Spright didn't wait around to find out whether it would work. He sped away as the cryptid flailed. The Seraph and Yeoman fired at the beast, bombarding it with blasts of light energy and crossbow bolts. Spright zipped back over to their side, skidded to a halt, and turned to face the cryptid. The beast, now on its second step, barreled toward them.

"Move!"

Spright shoved the Seraph aside, grabbed Yeoman, and tackled him to the ground. The cryptid bounded over them, arms swinging wildly.

Its left hand caught the cave wall, and its claws carved deep slashes in the stone. Spright pushed himself to his feet, ready to move again. But the cryptid stumbled around drunkenly, arms waving like pinwheels.

Yeoman raised his crossbow and loaded the injector arrow, but he did not fire it. Spright's muscles clenched, ready to move if the cryptid came back around. If the cryptid's immune system diffused the tranquilizer, he hoped the second dose would knock it out.

It wasn't necessary. The cryptid dropped to its knees, whimpered like an injured animal, and collapsed. Jarrett lowered his crossbow.

"Is it still alive?" Patrick asked.

Gideon stepped forward. "Yes. I can sense it."

"Great, we did it!" Patrick grinned and looked at the two men. Then, he realized where they were. "Wait. How are we going to transport it?"

Gideon puffed out a breath. "We'll have to carry it somehow."

Jarrett pursed his lips and touched the tip of his nose. "Not it."

CHAPTER 11

Vince Powers was not a religious man. He didn't believe in anything beyond making himself rich and happy. Nor did he particularly care about anyone else. He had been burned too many times for that. He had learned at a young age that if anyone was going to make him happy, it would have to be himself. Everyone else was a disappointment.

The Shine business had been a good way to achieve happiness. He had started out as a buyer—a junkie who survived on the stuff. The brief highs the drug gave him were all he had to look forward to. Eventually, sitting at rock bottom, he was forced to decide whether to claw his way back up or die at the bottom. He had decided to become more. He became a dealer and rose through the ranks until he was at the very top of the Shine business. Even that had not brought true happiness.

Artemis Wayans had approached him with an offer—power. Power that could make him more than he was. Maybe it would make him happy at last. Despite his last name, Powers had never felt anything but powerless. Grasping at any opportunity to change that, Powers gratefully accepted her offer. Becoming a superhuman had been the closest to a religious experience he had ever felt—or ever expected to feel again. It was amazing. He could feel everything his doppelgangers felt, yet he was not them. He could be himself and many other people, all at the same time. For a while, he was as happy as he thought he could be. He committed himself to Artemis's and Ashcroft's cause. He had purpose.

But it had all been brought to nothing when he was sent after Wesley Turner. That boy, along with his brother and merry band of superpowered friends, had ruined everything. Now, Powers sat in a prison cell, unable to duplicate himself without being shocked. When he was outside his cell, he had to wear power-dampening cuffs made by the eggheads at Sterling Labs. It was miserable.

He never should have let himself get sucked in. If he ever got out of jail, he was done with Ashcroft and the Regency. He would go his own way, use his abilities to cut a profit. He could get rich in Vegas or something. Powers possessed a talent with limitless possibilities that he had not explored yet. It was time to fix that.

Of course, that all depended on getting out. As far as he could tell, there was no way to do that. Stone Gate was a maximum-security prison. Nobody got out. Even Luca Serban, the great crime lord from Romania who conquered the Brooks and nearly the rest of Sojourn City, was powerless to leave. Not to say he didn't have power *inside* Stone Gate. Serban had the biggest gang of prisoners in the whole place. He even had some guards on his payroll. But for all that, he was still stuck there. Powers supposed that meant Serban was no better than he. That made him feel a little bit better about himself, at least.

"Powers! On your feet."

As the guard approached, a buzzer sounded, and the cell doors opened. All but Powers's. He had to stick his hands out through the rectangular opening in the bars and let the guard put on the special cuffs first. Powers submitted, rolling his eyes. The guard snapped on the cuffs, stepped back, and slid the bars aside.

Powers fell in line with the rest of the prisoners heading to breakfast. The food was decent. Powers had eaten far worse in his day. But it wasn't enjoyable, either. It was just there for sustenance, plain and simple. No frills, nothing extra. They ate, and they went back to their cells, the yard, or one of the various prisoner work programs. That was it.

Across the cafeteria, which was divided in half by heavy, metal bars, the female prisoners lined up for their meal. Powers spotted Artemis in the line. Judging by the retinue of muscular women surrounding her, her persuasive skills worked even without her hypnotic superpower. She was just that charismatic. They had been behind bars for three months, and she all but ruled the female prisoners.

There was one standout. A tough-looking blonde constantly cast her eyes around the cafeteria, watching her own back. She kept her distance from Artemis. Powers recognized her from Serban's gang. She was an assassin named Katrina Monahan, codenamed Lancet. *Bad news, that one.*

A hand fell on Powers's shoulder. He spun around, hands automatically rising to protect his face, but it was just Alfonso Mendez—Backfire—the third member of Powers's and Artemis's superpowered gang that had been thrown in jail by the Turners.

"Look," Mendez rumbled.

Powers's eyes flicked upward to follow Mendez's gaze to the balcony overlooking the cafeteria. Eight guards always patrolled the balcony, ready to step in if there was a brawl or riot, but Mendez was focused on one guard. The wiry man was standing in a corner and leaning on the rail. What was Mendez getting at?

Powers recognized him suddenly. The sharp features, the arrogant half-smirk that constantly marked his smug face . . . The guard was Randal Quinn, another member of the Regency.

"Is he . . . "

"Be ready to move, *amigo*." Mendez nodded to Artemis. "When Red Raider makes his move, get to her."

The last thing Powers wanted was to be involved in Ashcroft's band again, but if it got him out of prison, he could endure it for a little longer. It was better than rotting here. He gave Mendez a thumbs-up, took a tray of food, and headed for a table. To his left, Serban and his top lieutenants sat together. The crime lord glowered at him. Powers looked away and then looked back. What if Serban could be used as a distraction? And if the Romanian just so happened to escape, too, Powers would be in his good graces. That might come in handy one day.

He changed direction, walking toward Serban's table. He heard Mendez call out, grunt, and move on. Powers kept his focus on Serban. Two of Serban's lackeys noticed Powers approaching and rose from their chairs. One had a shiv tucked in his left palm. Powers stopped at a distance, where they couldn't reach him without provoking the guards.

"What do you want?" one of the lackeys said.

"I have information for Mr. Serban."

"You can tell us."

"It . . . it involves one of the guards."

"You'll have to do better than—"

Serban held up a hand. "Let him come, Lionel. Leave us."

The rest of Serban's gang rose from the table and moved away. Powers dropped into the seat across from Serban and put his tray down, nudging aside the trays left behind by the other inmates.

"What's this about a guard?" Serban asked. "And make it good. I don't need my boys to kill you. I can do that myself."

Powers jerked his head to the right. "See that guard up there, on the balcony? He's not a guard. He's from my organization, and he's here to bust me and my companions out."

"Is he?" Serban's expression didn't flicker.

"He is. And he can do it."

"Ah." Now, Serban smirked. "Because he's a freak like you, huh? Yeah, I know who you are. I worked with Ashcroft. Brought him test subjects." Serban peered up at the balcony. "As a matter of fact, I brought him that fella up there. Ashcroft paid generously, but I didn't like him. His work was insane."

"Be that as it may, you know we can make it happen."

"Maybe. So, what are you here for?"

"I'm going to make you an offer." Powers leaned in close, so he could whisper. "This is the perfect opportunity for you and your boys to slip out, too. And the more prisoners trying to escape, the better."

"You want me to start a riot. Is that it?"

"Seize the opportunity. Get yourself and those you trust most out of here. You'd be back on the streets. You could have real power again."

"Real power? I run this place. I have all the power right here. You think some bars concern me?"

"Maybe not. But I know freedom's a whole lot sweeter. And out there? Out there, you can make an empire."

"I tried that. Didn't go over so well."

"Because of the Seraph?" Powers snorted. "Trust me. He's not going to be a problem much longer."

Serban chewed his lower lip. "What's the plan?"

"When Quinn makes his move, just have your boys make as much chaos as they can. Use that opportunity to slip out. We'll do the same. Bring Monahan, if you want."

"Monahan." Serban huffed. "That woman failed me one too many times."

Powers rose, leaving his tray behind. "Just think it over. We're getting out of here today. Up to you if you want to come with."

Powers walked over to Mendez and dropped down in the seat next to him. As he did, he glanced up at the balcony. Quinn was standing in a corner, rubbing his hands together. He was about to make a move. Powers tensed, ready to run. Until he was free of these cuffs, he had to keep his head down.

Quinn extended his hands to the left and right, angled so they were facing the balconies on either side of him. His hands reddened and glowed. Powers felt his heart rate spike. He looked over at Mendez, who nodded, and back to Quinn. Pillars of fire rushed from Quinn's hands, spreading across the balcony in either direction. Chaos broke loose in the cafeteria. The guards on the balconies screamed as the flames washed over them. The guards on the other two corners of the balcony that hadn't been consumed by fire raised their guns. Powers saw the thin line of Quinn's smug grin as he swept his hands toward them and engulfed them in a raging inferno. The guards on the ground reached for their weapons as prisoners shouted and leapt from their seats.

One guard approached Artemis's table. Powers kicked through the gate separating the men's side of the cafeteria from the women's.

Artemis leaned forward and grabbed the guard by his wrist, spun him around, and slammed him to the ground. Powers dropped to his haunches and slid to the floor next to the downed guard, searching for the key that would unlock the power-dampening cuffs. Artemis yanked the guard's gun from its holster and opened fire at the other guards.

"I knew he wouldn't leave us!" she said.

Sure, you did. Powers decided not to vocalize the thought. He yanked the key free and worked it into the lock between his wrists. It was difficult to turn it, but he managed. The cuffs made a soft *snap* as they came free. They fell to the floor, and Powers felt a rush of energy. He grinned and created two duplicates of himself.

"Artemis! Cuffs!"

She handed the gun to one of Powers's duplicates and extended her wrists.

The doppelganger took the gun and trained it on a guard across the room. He snapped off a shot, hitting the guard in the chest, and scanned the room for more guards.

Powers inserted the key and unlocked Artemis's cuffs.

"Thank you." She looked around. "Mendez?"

"I'll get him. You work on securing a way out of here."

He closed his eyes and saw through the eyes of his other duplicate.

He rushed back across the cafeteria to where Mendez had been. The burly man was wrestling with a guard, trying to yank his gun away. Powers's duplicate bashed the guard across the back of the head.

"I've got the key," Powers said.

Powers opened his eyes—his real eyes—and ran toward Mendez and the doppelganger. He spared a quick glance at the balcony above. Quinn had finished off the last of the guards. The fire alarm buzzed, and the automated sprinklers kicked in. Powers returned his attention to Mendez and extended the key.

"Good job, *amigo*." Mendez grinned. "Let's get out of here."

The door to the cafeteria swung open, and a dozen guards in riot gear rushed in. A few of Serban's gang had secured the weapons of fallen guards, and they opened fire on the riot squad. Water droplets splashed on Powers's head. He looked up at the sprinklers and saw a floating pool of liquid forming above the cafeteria. The water flowing from the sprinklers coalesced into a single, huge bulb. *Melanie!*

The water rushed down toward the riot squad like a tidal wave, knocking them back through the door. Powers grinned. Even if Melanie hadn't been there, he could have easily created more than a dozen copies of himself to overpower the guards. But now, that wasn't necessary.

"Fragment! Backfire!" Artemis called. "This way!"

She stood by the double doors that led to the areas of the prison accessible only to the guards. A large padlock was clasped between them. Powers and Mendez ran to her side. The bigger man grinned and wrapped a meaty hand around the padlock. Powers exchanged glances with Artemis and stepped back. The padlock reddened as Mendez's powers heated it. With a *pop*, the padlock exploded in the burly man's palm. Mendez kicked the doors open.

A rush of heat washed over them. Powers shielded his face. Quinn, slowing his fall with twin pillars of fire, dropped to the floor next to them and extended his palms toward the open doorway in an *after-you* gesture. A few other prisoners rushed past them through the doorway. Powers nodded and ran through with Artemis and Mendez.

"Where's Deluge?" Artemis asked.

"She's up top," Quinn replied. "Covering our escape. She'll join us outside."

Powers looked around at the other prisoners, wondering if Serban was among them. Had the crime lord decided to break free, or would he take his chances in prison? Powers didn't see him, but he did see Katrina Monahan, Serban's assassin-for-hire. She was just ahead of them, shoving her way through prisoners to reach the exit, a shiv in one hand and a guard's pistol in the other.

Powers pointed at Monahan. "Grab her."

Mendez frowned. "What?"

"She could be useful. Grab her. Not forcefully—just make her an offer."

"I'll do it," Artemis said. "Don't send a muscle-bound idiot to do a negotiator's job."

Less than five minutes out of prison, Artemis once again thought she was in charge. Powers rolled his eyes.

But he let her go. She was right; she was the best choice to persuade Monahan to come along. Powers rounded the corner, and Quinn pushed a barred door open. They stepped outside into the dawn. Goosebumps rose on Powers's arms, and he shivered. Powers envied Quinn's abilities. Flames licked the air around the man's body, keeping him warm in the cool morning air.

A lithe figure dropped to the ground next to them, water droplets floating around her in a halo. Unlike Quinn, who had been disguised out of necessity, she wore her garish super suit—a deep blue leotard and matching cape, light blue leggings, boots that matched her leotard and rose past her knees, and a masquerade-style mask that covered her face from the nose up. *Melanie.*

Quinn nodded. "Good work, kid. Load 'em up."

He rushed toward a black armored truck parked nearby. Melanie gestured to Powers and Mendez.

"You heard him."

Powers looked back into the prison. Artemis appeared a moment later, Monahan running right behind her. The two women rushed through the open doorway, past Powers, and toward the truck. Powers ran after them and jumped into the back of the truck. As he settled down in a seat next to Mendez, he closed his eyes and reached out to his duplicate back in the cafeteria.

Fires crackled on the balcony. Unconscious and dead guards lay in puddles of water, and someone nearby moaned in pain. Most of the prisoners had filtered out. A few lay motionless with the guards. Powers glanced around, looking for any sign of Serban.

One prisoner remained seated near the back of the cafeteria. He looked to be in his early fifties, and he had dark hair and a full beard. As far as Powers could tell, he hadn't moved a muscle since the rioting began. He picked at his food with a fork. Powers heard footsteps.

Serban walked back into the cafeteria, twirling a sharpened toothbrush in his right hand. His eyes were set on the other prisoner.

"You should've run," Serban said.

"I have no reason to run." The bearded man shrugged. "I will serve out the rest of my sentence. If I run now, I will only incriminate myself further."

Powers wondered if the bearded man was naïve or just resigned. As Serban approached, he stopped twirling the shiv and took it in a backhand grip, like he was holding an icepick.

"If you kill me, you will lose a great deal of your power in here," the man said.

"Will I?" Serban shrugged. "I don't see any guards. Lots of guys are lying around, dead. Who's to say I'm the one who shanked you? You could just be one more casualty of the riot."

The bearded man said nothing to that. Powers considered intervening. He was a bad guy—he'd freely admit that—but he'd never been a murderer. Watching Serban stab this guy would be unpleasant. But this was none of his business.

Serban hovered over the other man. "I could run. I could drive this shiv into your throat, run out those doors, and disappear."

"Then why don't you?"

"Oh, it would be satisfying. Believe me, there's nothing that would bring me more glee than to end the guy who's responsible for me being here. But . . . that would only end your suffering."

"True enough." The man shrugged. "I've got nothing to lose, and my faith assures me that if I die, I'll enter into paradise."

"Exactly." Serban tossed the knife onto the table between him and the man. "So, I'm going to let you rot here instead. Enjoy it, knowing that I'm going to be free. Knowing that I know the best way to get revenge on you is to find your son and gut him instead."

The bearded man shot to his feet. "Don't you dare!"

"Who's gonna stop me?" Serban strode toward the open double doors. "I know you won't."

The bearded man clenched his fists but didn't move to follow Serban. Powers shook his head. If that had been him, he would have grabbed the shiv from the table, jumped on Serban's back, and ripped him open from top to bottom.

But the man just sat back down. "Lord, protect my boy. Protect Dean."

Dean? *Powers blinked. As in, Dean Sterling? The pieces clicked into place. The man was Edgar Sterling, the man who'd brought Serban and his*

Romanian mob into Sojourn City in the first place. No wonder Serban had an axe to grind with him.

With Serban's disinterest in Powers's offer, Powers closed his eyes and allowed the last doppelganger to vanish.

He opened his eyes, and he was in the back of the armored truck again. The vehicle was moving, roaring down the road away from Stone Gate Penitentiary. Mendez sat to Powers's left, and Artemis and Monahan sat across from them. Quinn and Melanie were in the front.

Powers grinned. Forget Serban. Forget Sterling. He was free. That was all that mattered to him.

CHAPTER 12

Hannah crossed her arms and watched the heroes as they prepared to depart. Dean, dressed in plain clothes rather than his super suit, stood at the foot of their plane while Wes, Carter, and their pilot, Maddox, boarded it. After killing the wendigo in the cave, they had searched thoroughly and found the body of the first one Hannah had killed, but there was no sign of any other living creatures. Hannah was relieved that they had killed the last of the abominations, but Dean seemed disappointed. Puzzling. None of his friends had been harmed, and now the beasts would not endanger anyone else. He had knelt next to the carcass in the cave, using a small science kit to take samples. When they had returned to her home, she had let them stay until daybreak—although they had slept on the floor, as Axel had fallen asleep in Hannah's bed.

Hannah liked them. She wasn't a social person, and she preferred to work alone when she was Brass Bison. But they were good people—kind, reasonable, likable. That did not change that she worked alone, and she was glad they were leaving. She didn't need help defending the reservation, and having these three here would only draw more trouble. Working alone, she was inconspicuous.

She ran her fingers over one of the wendigo's teeth. She had pulled it from the beast's mouth as Dean studied it. As Dean stepped toward the airplane, he glanced down at the tooth.

"Why did you keep that?" he asked.

"You don't kill a creature like that without taking a trophy. Besides, it will be proof to my people that the wendigo truly is dead."

"Fair enough." Dean shuddered. "Remind me not to get on your bad side."

Hannah almost smiled. "Won't be a problem. I doubt we'll ever see each other again."

"Right." Dean paused. "Unless you want to come with us."

He must have been mad. Their city did not need another protector. Her reservation, her people, had no one outside of her. If she left, she doomed her people to the devices of the drug dealers and sex traffickers who would return once they knew that the Brass Bison was gone. It would be a disastrous venture.

"Your powers are new, and you're still learning to use them," Dean pressed. "We can teach you. Gideon thinks there will be a war between us and the Regency—the guy who probably created these creatures, plus his followers. If that's the case, we'll need all the superheroes on our side that we can get."

"I cannot leave. My people need me."

"It wouldn't be forever. You would be free to come back anytime you want."

"I'm not big on teams." Hannah looked over her shoulder to where the reservation was just visible in the distance. "I like working alone, and I like my home."

Something about what he said bothered her. If it was true and the wendigos were the creation of a man who was planning a war, it would be dangerous for her people if they were ever in the crossfire. A war like that was bound to spread. Perhaps, with her help, they could stop the war before it ever started.

Crime around the reservation was at an all-time low, thanks to her activities. Axel could watch over things until she returned. He wasn't a fighter like her, but he was a good observer. If anything happened while she was gone, he would notice. She could deal with the perpetrator when she returned. If it came down to it, anyone could shoot a gun. She would leave Axel one of her smaller quick-draw pistols for an emergency.

It would be easier to protect her people if she understood the power welling within her. Dean was right. She needed their help, as much as she hated to admit that.

She forced a smile. "All right. Let me return to my home, tell Axel where I am going, and get my things. I will meet you back here in an hour."

Dean grinned. "Good to have you aboard."

"I am not *aboard*." Hannah eyed him sternly. "I am doing this for my people's benefit, no more. I like you and your friends, Dean Sterling, but I owe you nothing."

"I understand. Any help is good help at this point. I'll see you in an hour."

"Very well."

Hannah mounted her motorcycle and headed home, hoping that she wasn't making a mistake.

* * *

Jolie pulled on her jacket as she stepped out of the bathroom, wishing her morning shower had cleared her drowsy brain a little more. Her night had been restless. Every sound woke her, and she felt an instant's panic, wondering if her watcher across the street had come for her. Then, she felt an inexplicable peace again and drifted off to sleep. It happened over and over again, all night long. When she gave up and got out of bed in the morning, she didn't feel rested.

She walked over to her bedside table and reached for her gun and phone. She paused before touching the gun. It was Sunday, and she was going to church, not to work. She doubted she would need her gun. She grabbed her phone and glanced at the screen. She had three missed calls—all from the precinct. That was never good. Maybe she would need the gun after all. Grabbing the weapon and tucking it into the holster on her hip, she crossed the living room.

She dialed as she walked out the door. "This is Detective Anderson. What's going on?"

"Anderson, it's Pulaski. There was a massive riot and prison break at Stone Gate this morning."

Jolie's blood went cold. "Who got out?"

"There are dozens of prisoners unaccounted for. Most notably, the amplified criminals escaped with the aid of two other amps who staged the attack. Katrina Monahan and Luca Serban are among the non-powered escapees."

"This just keeps getting better." Jolie slid into her car. "I'm on my way."

She hung up, started her car, and sped down the road toward the prison. It was bad enough that Artemis Wayans and her cohorts had escaped. But Serban? Jolie's stomach tied itself in knots. Serban was a madman and a criminal mastermind. He was not amplified, but he didn't need powers to be deadly. His planning had nearly led to the downfall of the city. If he was loose, all the work the police, not to mention the city's superheroes, had done to clean up the Brooks could be undone.

And of course, it happened when Gideon and the others were out of town. That couldn't be a coincidence. Pulaski said that two superhumans had aided in the escape. They must have known the Vindicators would be out of town and planned the prison break accordingly. She swallowed back a dry heave at the thought of the figure watching her last night and tightened her grip on the steering wheel. *So much for church.*

She took a deep breath. Once Gideon and the others got back, they could track down the supervillains. Jolie and the police could focus on finding Serban and Monahan. Her next step was to get to the prison and gather all the information she could. Sojourn City depended on her.

* * *

The Raptor rumbled as it soared through the upper atmosphere. Gideon paced around the tranquilized form of the cryptid. Just before Dean and the others from the Arizona team had arrived, Jolie had called him with terrible news. A prison break had allowed Artemis, Powers, and Mendez to escape Stone Gate, and Serban and Monahan were in the wind, too. All the work Gideon had done since he had returned from Venezuela had been undone in one morning. He had to catch them.

Dean was worried about his father, but Jolie assured him that Edgar had shown up alive and well as the remaining prisoners were rounded up. A few guards had testified that he refused to take part in the rioting. Dean was understandably relieved. Edgar may have committed a terrible crime, but he was still Dean's father.

Gideon was glad for him, but he was preoccupied with the thought that Ashcroft might have released his creatures as a means to distract the heroes. They had taken the Vindicators away from Sojourn City while his lackeys broke the other supervillains out of prison.

Gideon's eyes fell on Carter, sitting next to Patrick and talking quietly to the other boy. Monahan had murdered Carter's father. This had to be tearing him apart. Gideon probed the younger man and tumbled into a bottled-up fountain of rage and sadness inside. Carter would work relentlessly until he stopped Monahan, and the hairs on Gideon's neck rose as he sensed what Carter would do if he did.

But I just saw Wyatt this morning. Gideon couldn't reconcile the strange vision with reality. Wyatt Jonson was dead. Why had he seemed so real?

Carter wasn't the only one with a grudge to settle. Patrick and Wes had personal feuds with Mendez and Powers. They were carefully holding their emotions in check, but they had to be chomping at the bit to capture the escaped criminals. The flurry of anger and disappointment bouncing around the plane was almost too much for Gideon to handle.

"You should probably sit down," Dean said. "We'll be descending soon, and you really don't want to experience that if you're not strapped in."

Gideon dropped into the seat next to Dean. He probed the cryptid with his mind. It was still in a restful state, subdued by the sheer strength of the tranquilizer in its system. One thing was going right, at least.

Dean nudged Gideon's shoulder. "I told Arianna to deliver a containment cell to our lair. It's a portable prototype of the tech we're going to use to create power-dampening prison cells. With any luck, it should hold the wendigo."

At least, they didn't have to worry about it breaking loose while they searched for the escaped villains—one bright side in a mess of bad news. Gideon glanced across the plane to where Jarrett sat, fiddling with his crossbow. As the Vindicators reunited and loaded the slumbering cryptid onto the Raptor, Jarrett had approached Gideon.

"This Ashcroft guy sounds like trouble." Jarrett had hefted his crossbow. "I'm no superhero, but you guys need all the help you can get. If you'll have me, I'd like to come."

Gideon welcomed Jarrett's help. Having been in the army, the archer was more tactically minded than the rest of the team, and he would see past some of their blind spots. Plus, his skills with a crossbow couldn't be discounted. Having another ranged fighter on the team would help with opponents like Powers, who tended to hide his original form among throngs of doppelgangers.

Dean's team had brought a guest of their own. She stayed to herself in the far corner of the compartment, twirling a revolver around one finger. Dean had introduced her as Hannah Lonestar. Gideon wondered what her story was. The emotions radiating from her struck him with harsh edges. Hannah was all anger and stubbornness, almost the exact opposite of Jarrett's calm aloofness.

"Do you trust him?" Dean asked.

"I do." Gideon studied Jarrett. "I can tell he's keeping something secret, but I'm not sure what. I don't sense that he's dangerous, though."

"We all have secrets. If he helped you catch this thing, he can't be too bad, can he?"

"No. I think I like him. Patrick does, too. He's friendly, straightforward, and skilled. I just can't get a clear reading on him. I do believe he's on our side, at least."

"Good. At least, this gives me an excuse to design two more super suits, right?" Dean rapidly raised his eyebrows twice. "You know I love that."

"Coming in for a landing," Maddox called over the intercom. "Make sure that thing is restrained."

Gideon and Dean quickly checked each of the cryptid's restraints and returned to their seats. The plane arced downward toward Sojourn City. Gideon closed his eyes. It was hard to believe they had to deal with the same villains all over again. If Ashcroft needed all his people on deck, he might be on the precipice of his big move.

That would complicate things, but the Vindicators had grown more accustomed to their powers since the last time they had faced Artemis and her companions. This time, they had Jarrett and Hannah's help. And Gideon believed God wanted them to defeat Ashcroft. He was certain that he had been given his powers for that purpose. He didn't take that lightly.

* * *

Jolie picked her way through the cafeteria where the prison break originated. Puddles of water mingled with blood on the floor. Scorch marks blackened the walls. At least, the bodies had been removed. The M.E. and coroner would be very busy for the next few days.

She had been glad to hear that Edgar Sterling was all right and that he had chosen to remain in custody rather than attempt an escape. As much trouble as she had forgiving him for bringing the Romanian mob to Sojourn City, his motives had been to correct the injustices he perceived. Sterling was not a wicked man, but he was confused. He was one criminal Jolie truly hoped to see rehabilitated and free from prison one day.

She glanced at the warden. "You're telling me that the culprit was one of your guards?"

"Yes. A newly hired one. He had just completed his interview two days ago and started yesterday." The warden was a portly man, kind but stern. As Jolie spoke with him, he rubbed his forehead and squinted. "Everything checked out. I can't believe he could defeat all our checks, even a lie-detector test, so thoroughly."

"He's a professional, whoever he is." Jolie mounted the stairway to the balcony. "He was up here when the chaos started?"

"Yes." The warden followed her. "He fired two jets of flame down the balconies, murdering half the guards up here. Good men—men with families . . . I don't know if he had hidden flamethrowers on him, or . . . "

"Or he was amplified. That's more likely. Especially if, as you said, he was seen leaving with Mendez, Powers, and Wayans."

"He was. Along with Katrina Monahan and a teenage girl."

Jolie frowned. "Monahan went with them? What about Serban?"

"Serban left the prison much later than they did and snuck out alone. Our footage shows him leaving the prison grounds on foot, heading toward Sojourn City."

Great. Sojourn City was a big place. If Serban made it to the city, he could lie low until they lost his trail. He could even get out of the city on a boat or plane if he still had contacts at the docks or the airport. She looked down into the cafeteria, where a couple of FBI agents were sweeping the scene.

"The feds have jurisdiction here. I'm going to meet with the Seraph and his team. They can handle the search for the powered inmates."

"Feds may not like that. Mayor Crowe may have recognized the Seraph as a hero, but there are still those in the national government that feel he's nothing more than a glorified vigilante."

"Don't tell them." She nodded down at the FBI agents. "Besides, they may be more concerned with Serban's escape. The supervillains' activities aren't well-known. Serban's are."

That meant she needed a head start. She had nothing against the FBI, but she wanted to be the one to drag Serban back in handcuffs. She finished her examination on the balcony and walked downstairs to the cafeteria. One of the FBI agents, a pale man with dark hair slicked to the side, caught sight of her and approached, leaving his partner to continue his investigation.

"Detective Anderson?" he asked.

Jolie frowned. "That's right. Do I know you?"

"No, we've never met, but I've seen your file." He extended a hand, which Jolie shook. "Agent Timothy Ross. I was one of the agents who brought your boyfriend, Gideon, back from Venezuela."

"Ah." Jolie's eyebrows raised. "Quite a coincidence."

"Not really." He shrugged. "I'm stationed in Detroit now, and we're the closest Bureau office to Stone Gate. Anyway, I just wanted to let you know that we appreciate your assistance. If you find out anything about any of the escaped inmates, especially Luca Serban, please contact us."

He handed Jolie a business card. Jolie slid it into her jacket pocket and nodded. Ross seemed like a nice enough guy, and she owed him something for saving her fiancé's life. She had no reason to be hostile just because she didn't want him to get to Serban before she did.

"I will. Thank you, Agent Ross."

"You're welcome. See you around, Detective."

Jolie walked out the doors toward the exit. She hoped she would not need Ross's help. She was familiar with many of Serban's old haunts in Sojourn City, and if she played her cards right, she might be able to grab him before he found a way out of the city. But first, she needed to meet with Gideon and his team to coordinate a search for the supervillains.

Of the escapees, she wasn't sure who scared her more. As powerful as Wayans and her friends were, Serban had come far closer to bringing Sojourn City to its knees. And Jolie never wanted to see that again.

CHAPTER 13

Dean checked the restraints on the cryptid's holding cell. The last thing they needed was this wild beast rampaging through Sojourn City while he and the other heroes were out looking for the escaped criminals. He hoped Arianna's cell design was sound. Even if it was, there was no guarantee that the dampening field affected the cryptid in the same way as it did an amplified person. Unfortunately, right now, it was their only option.

The cell was set up in the middle of the lair's training room. Even if the cryptid—Dean liked the more scientific term better than "wendigo"—managed to break out of the cell, the training room's weapons might contain it. If they couldn't, at least they might delay it long enough for Dean and the others to return.

He stepped out of the cell. Maddox slammed the door shut, and Arianna typed in a command on the cell's keypad to activate its power dampeners. Now that the cryptid was taken care of, Dean could focus on the jailbreak.

Thank goodness his father was safe and that he hadn't tried to join the other convicts in fleeing Stone Gate. Dad had done some terrible things, but Dean felt that he was genuinely trying to make up for them. Hearing that he had willingly stayed behind while the other prisoners ran had only solidified that. Dean had already forgiven his father, but a new wave of peace swept over him, knowing that Dad really was trying to make a change.

Arianna eyed the cryptid. "We'll stay here and observe the creature. Go be a hero."

Dean nodded. "I'll call you when we've got word on the escapees."

Gideon, Patrick, and Carter had already headed for the prison to meet with Jolie. Wes, Hannah, and Jarrett had stayed behind with Dean. They were waiting downstairs in the common area. Despite being unfamiliar with the city, the two newcomers might be useful in the search. They were both unknown, so even if they were seen in public, no one would be able to identify them. He jogged down the steps. Wes was in the kitchen, while Hannah stared out the floor-to-ceiling windows. Jarrett lounged on the couch.

Jarrett sat up as Dean reached the living room. "So, you guys live in the world's fanciest attic."

"This view is amazing," Hannah said. "I've never seen so many skyscrapers, even when I visited Phoenix."

"Nothing quite compares to Sojourn City." Dean smiled. "Glad you like it. Come on. We've got some work to do."

Jarrett scooped up his crossbow. "Where to?"

"There are only a few places the escapees could go if they're looking to get out of town fast. They'd either try the pier or the airport. Gideon and the others went to meet with Detective Anderson. The rest of us should split up. I'll take Hannah and go to the pier. Wes, you take Jarrett to the airport."

Jarrett quirked an eyebrow. "Weren't we just at the airport?"

"Yes, but we had to get the cryptid back here before it woke up." Dean grabbed the doorknob. "Let's get moving. If we don't find anything, we'll start looking at places they might be hiding within the city."

"What about the interstate?" Jarrett asked. "Couldn't they just drive out of the city?"

"Cops set up checkpoints on every road out of town. Even if they switch vehicles, they won't get out. So—"

The door blew inward, the heavy wood striking Dean. He grunted in surprise and stumbled back into Wes's arms. Wes steadied him and stepped forward, his skin taking on a gunmetal shade as he tapped a panel on his belt. Jarrett's crossbow and Hannah's revolvers were trained on the door in a second. A tall, muscular man stepped through the gap. He wore a dark gray jumpsuit with black armor plates and a matching black mask.

"Hey, Vindicators. Name's Torrent. This is Tetra-Hazard. I think it's time we had a talk."

Torrent stepped aside, and another man entered. A light green, armored uniform with red slashes on the shoulders and knees framed a figure less imposing than Torrent's, albeit not by much, and a mask with the universal symbol for radiation emblazoned on the forehead covered him from forehead to nose. A faint aura of energy rippled the air around him.

Tetra-Hazard smirked. "Knock, knock."

Before Dean could react, a terrible screech ripped his eardrums. He cried out and dropped to his knees. The sound faded, and the door to the exterior terrace crashed open as a third newcomer flew in. She soared over their heads and landed in front of the two men who had come through the door.

She wore a black and white costume—a neck-to-toe bodysuit with blue decorative stripes across the torso; thigh-high, black boots; and bicep-length, black gloves. A subtle musical note emblazoned the buckle of her blue belt, and her opera-style mask was a matching shade of blue. Dark brown hair trailed over her shoulders, and a single lock of silver hung down over her mask and right eye.

Dean felt the sudden, inexplicable conviction that he knew her. That silver lock in her hair—he was sure he had seen her somewhere before. He shook his head and pushed himself to his feet. It was not the time to try to figure out his opponents' secret identities.

As the two men flanked the woman, she spoke. "We're here with a message from Ashcroft. Stand aside, or the Regency will bring its full wrath to bear on the Vindicators."

"Fat chance." Dean teleported behind Tetra-Hazard, jabbed his shield into the small of the man's back, and teleported back to where he'd been kneeling before. "Vindicators, move!"

Wes lunged into action as Jarrett and Hannah opened fire, and the entire penthouse filled with migraine-inducing supersonic sound.

* * *

Arianna dropped to her knees, clutching her head, which felt like it had just been split open with an axe. Maddox knelt next to her, grimacing and pressing his right hand against his ear. With his left hand, he grabbed Arianna by the shoulder and hoisted her to her feet. She staggered after him toward the ops room, barely able to keep her footing. The intense, shrill noise threatened to blast her into unconsciousness or at least destroy her inner ear and render her unable to find her balance. Maddox slid the ops room door shut behind them. The sheer force of the sound lessened.

Maddox gasped in relief. "Dean built dampeners into all the doors in case of a sonic attack. We'll be safe in here."

"But the others." Arianna ran to one of the computers and pulled up the security footage. "They'll need help!"

The monitor showed their friends struggling with a group of three intruders. They were severely hampered by the continued sonic attack, which appeared to be originating from the woman leading the newcomers. She was down on her haunches, her mouth spread wide in a constant scream.

Maddox rifled through a supply cabinet nearby. Arianna activated the security system's facial recognition and ran to help him. He pulled out a small box and handed it to her.

"Sonic dampening earplugs."

He inserted a pair into his ears and pulled out two snub-nosed rifles from the locker. Arianna finished inserting her earbuds and took one from him. They had designed these stun rifles based on the same technology as the Vindicators' shock beads. They delivered an electric charge to the neural pathway, rendering the victim instantly unconscious and temporarily paralyzed.

Arianna fumbled with the rifle. She never thought she would be the one to use it. She was tech support, not a fighter. But their friends were in danger, and from the look of things, they couldn't fight back properly until the sonic attacker was disabled. Since she and Maddox were the only two with the dampening earbuds, it was up to them.

"I'll call Gideon." Maddox pulled out his phone and dialed. "He and Patrick should be able to get here the quickest."

Arianna took a few more earbuds from the cabinet to give to the others, in case the stun rifles didn't immediately incapacitate the woman. They had no idea what these particular superhumans' physiologies were capable of withstanding. Sometimes, they had an enhanced durability that had no apparent relation to their other powers.

The footage showed Wes, who had shifted from steel to rubber, struggling with the green-clad man. Jarrett and Hannah were trying to line up a shot at the attackers, but every time they had an opening, the woman unleashed a more focused, directional sonic blast from her hands, knocking them back again. The gray-clad man was wrestling with Dean, keeping him from helping Wes or incapacitating the woman.

The monitor also showed increased levels of radiation in the room. Arianna activated a rad scanner. The discrepancy was emanating from the man locked in combat with Wes. No wonder Wes had transmuted to rubber; the radiation would have cooked him alive otherwise. *Stay away from the man in green, and check Wes for radiation poisoning as soon as the situation is under control.*

"Gideon's on his way." Maddox hung up the phone. "You ready?"

"As I'll ever be."

Maddox slid open the door and rushed out. Arianna followed him, clenching the rifle tightly. They came out onto the balcony overlooking the first floor. Maddox shouldered his rifle and aimed it downward. Arianna stepped up next to him and took aim herself. It would be hard to hit either of the male attackers with Wes and Dean locked in hand-to-hand combat with them, but the woman was in the middle of the room, several feet away from any of the others.

Arianna trained her rifle on the woman. She peered through the scope and rested her finger on the trigger. She hadn't fired a gun since . . . well, ever. But how hard could it be?

Maddox fired first. The woman jerked and spasmed, stumbling back as electricity coursed over her body. The gray-clad attacker shoved Dean aside and looked to his comrade.

"Stormcry!" he shouted.

Arianna fired. The man grunted as the stun bolt struck him. He took a step back, planted his feet, and clenched his jaw. His gaze rose to the balcony, and even through the small eye holes in his mask, Arianna could tell that his gaze was set on her and Maddox.

"Uh oh." She backed away from the railing. "Run!"

The man didn't bother with the stairs, leaping all the way up to the balcony. Arianna stumbled back as the man landed in front of her, grabbed her rifle, and jerked it away. Maddox stepped in and smashed the butt of his rifle against the man's skull. The rifle shattered, but the man didn't flinch. He swept his left arm at Maddox, knocking him through the air. Arianna shrieked and backed away. *Think, think, think.* The attacker stepped toward her, popping his knuckles.

A rush of wind blew in from the terrace, and a blue-and-yellow blur intercepted the attacker. *Gideon*! Arianna rushed to Maddox's side and helped him up. There was a gash on his forehead that was bleeding, but it wasn't bad. She wrapped her arm around his back and hoisted him to his feet.

"You all right?" she asked.

Maddox grunted. "This is why we're tech support."

* * *

The Seraph struck the attacker in gray and carried him across the balcony to hurl the man into the wall. His light-encased fist connected with the man's jaw with considerable force. The attacker barely flinched.

The Seraph blinked in surprise. That blow would have knocked anyone else out cold.

"I've wanted to face you for a long time now." The supervillain dropped into a ready stance. "Let's see if you live up to your reputation."

The villain slammed a fist into the Seraph's chest. It hit like a speeding train, a force Gideon knew all too well. He sailed backward and tumbled through the air, managing to catch himself and hover over the balcony.

He took a moment to scan the penthouse. Drifter and the others were below, dealing with the last conscious attacker. For some reason, none of them except Rampart were trying to get close to him. And as that attacker grappled with Rampart, he occasionally extended a hand and fired a greenish substance toward Drifter, Yeoman, and Brass Bison.

Anytime now, Spright.

The purple blur appeared in the doorway behind the green-clad attacker and tackled him. The Seraph nodded in satisfaction and turned back to his opponent.

The brute leaped into the air and crashed full force into the Seraph. He grunted in surprise and tumbled toward the ground. The villain landed on top of him, raised a fist, and brought it down into the Seraph's unprotected face. Pain exploded through his skull. The Seraph raised his hand and fired a blast of light into his opponent's chest. The villain stumbled back.

The Seraph rose to his feet. Droplets of blood ran down his lip and dripped to the ground. He shook his head and wiped his nose—*ouch, broken*—on the back of his glove, staining the blue material.

This supervillain was stronger than any of the other superhumans the Seraph had ever faced. He had taken an energy-powered punch to the face and a full-force blast to the chest, and he hardly looked winded. How could the Seraph take on someone like this?

Good thing I'm too stubborn to stop trying. He raised both hands and fired another blast of light energy as Torrent charged him.

* * *

Drifter stumbled away from Tetra-Hazard. The shimmering air around the villain was an aura of radiation. Any time Drifter tried to get close, he instantly felt woozy. Rampart, by transforming into rubber, was ignoring the energy and engaging the villain at close range, but Drifter felt helpless standing there and watching. To make matters worse, the villain kept firing globs of acid at them.

Spright's intervention had temporarily helped as he knocked the villain to the ground, but the speedster had been forced to back away as the radiation levels dizzied him, too. He stood next to Drifter, waiting for an opportunity to go back in. Crusader, who had been carried in by Spright, hunched next to Yeoman and twirled his staff.

Brass Bison growled. "I can't get a bead on him! Wes is in the way!"

"Rampart!" Drifter snapped. "Codenames only in the field, Bison!"

Yeoman raised his crossbow. "Go help the Seraph. We'll handle this guy."

Drifter nodded and looked up at the balcony. Flashes of light were punctuated by grunts and growls. Torrent and the Seraph were going at it hard. Drifter imagined himself standing on the balcony, and instantly, he was behind Torrent. The muscle-bound villain was wrestling with the Seraph, trying to pin his arms down.

Drifter stepped in and smashed his aionium shield between Torrent's shoulder blades. He might as well have struck the villain with a flyswatter. Torrent swung his left arm in a precise uppercut. Drifter raised his shield, and Torrent's fist battered the disk. The force of the blow knocked Drifter back.

"Enough!" the Seraph growled.

He held both hands together, gathering a ball of light. Drifter shielded his eyes. The powerful blast echoed through the room and was joined a moment later by the sound of a body crashing into metal. Drifter looked up. Torrent had flown into the training room and shattered—

Oh, no.

The villain's body had smashed the containment module holding the cryptid, destroying the door from the outside. The beast wailed and tugged at its restraints.

Gideon grimaced and pushed his hood off his head. "Oops."

Drifter climbed to his feet. "Not your fault. But we need to stop him. Now."

Torrent grabbed the containment module's door and tugged. It tore away from the module like a banana peel. The cryptid roared at the promise of freedom and struggled to free itself. Drifter put a finger to his earbud, activating the communicator.

"Spright!" Drifter called. "Get up here now!"

Spright appeared between Drifter and the Seraph. "What's—oh, boy."

The young speedster darted forward and shoulder-checked Torrent. The speed with which he moved must have delivered considerable force; the villain staggered back and released the hatch. Drifter teleported in and swung his shield into Torrent's face. A moment later, the Seraph joined them, hitting Torrent with a double-punch combo.

Torrent growled and unleashed a flurry of tight punches. Drifter ducked under a blow and smashed his right shield into Torrent's knee. Something popped, and Torrent howled in pain. The Seraph grabbed Torrent's arm and hovered in the air, gripping the limb with all his might.

"Arianna, Maddox!" Drifter called over the comms. "Get the tranquilizer and sedate the cryptid!"

He jabbed his left shield into Torrent's other knee, but the villain's foot was already rising to meet him. The heavy boot cracked into his chin. Drifter landed flat on his back and moaned. Stars filled his vision. *Stay conscious, Drifter.*

Spright whirled around Torrent, hitting him with rapid-fire punches and darting away again. Drifter pulled himself back and rested against the containment unit. Torrent struggled to free his right arm from the Seraph's grip. Finally, he reached up with his left hand, grabbed the Seraph's right wrist, and tugged down hard. The Seraph plunged onto the floor.

Arianna rushed in from the ops room, a syringe in her hand. She stopped at Drifter's side, and he shook his head and motioned for her to get the cryptid. She nodded and stepped into the module, careening out a moment later, screaming. Drifter's eyes widened. He teleported across the room, grabbed her, and teleported to the floor. He grunted as he landed, cradling her on top of him.

"You all right?"

Arianna's eyes were wide with fear. "It's loose."

CHAPTER 14

Brass Bison threw herself to the side to avoid a spray of acid from Tetra-Hazard. Torrent, the large powerhouse in gray, had disappeared upstairs, and the woman with the sonic powers was unconscious. That left Hannah free to focus on the acid-spitting man in green, who was tangling with Wes.

The problem was that her only options to take him out were to use her powers or to shoot him. She could not control her powers well enough to target the man when he was so close to Wes, nor could she draw a bead on him while he and Rampart were grappling so wildly.

"Bison, shoot!" Rampart shouted.

"I'll hit you!"

"I can take it! Shoot him!"

Was he insane? Brass Bison didn't believe his rubber skin could take a bullet. If he was in the form of steel or another strong material, maybe she would have risked it; but while he was rubber, she couldn't take the shot. Conversely, as long as Tetra-Hazard emitted radiation, Rampart had to remain in his current form, or he would be affected by the energy. The acid that Tetra-Hazard kept flinging at Yeoman and Bison wasn't helping matters, either.

Bison stepped to her left, angling for a clear shot at the man. As she did, the black-and-white-clad woman stirred. They didn't need her unleashing her sonic blast again. Bison trained her gun on the woman.

A powerful roar split the air. Brass Bison's eyes widened. The woman on the floor must have recognized the sound, too. As she rubbed her head, she looked up at the balcony.

"Fall back!" she shouted.

She leaped through the air, grabbed the green-clad man by the shoulders, and flew upstairs and out the balcony door to the terrace. Torrent bounded out the transparent door after them. For a moment, the room was silent.

The wendigo roared again.

Bison bit out a harsh word under her breath.

Yeoman shouldered his crossbow. "Upstairs. Upstairs, now!"

Rampart rushed past them, shifting from rubber to steel as he mounted the stairs. Bison was right behind him, her guns trained on the balcony. Yeoman kept pace with her, matching her step for step and keeping his crossbow up, too. The Crusader brought up the rear, the electric tips of his staff crackling. The wendigo stood in the hallway between the balcony and the training room with its back to Bison. It roared at the others, who were still inside the training room.

"We've got to disable it," Drifter called. "Don't kill it!"

"We may not have a choice," Bison snapped.

The beast looked back at them and roared again. She raised her revolvers and trained them on the wendigo's head. She had killed two of these monsters already. Why not drop a third? She understood that Dean wished to study the creature and understand its origins, but if it came down to studying it or letting it rampage through a city, Hannah knew which option she would prefer. Dean would have to study a carcass. She tightened her fingers around the triggers.

The wendigo rushed toward them. Bison and Yeoman fired as one, her bullets striking it in the chest and his arrow piercing its shoulder. But the wendigo did not slow. Brass Bison threw herself to the ground as it bounded past them. It charged across the balcony toward the terrace door. Bison emptied her guns into the wendigo, but the beast had scented freedom. Gathering itself, the wendigo leaped from the terrace, hovered over the city for a moment, and dropped toward the street.

Jarrett's crossbow lowered. "Oh, no."

"It's loose!" Rampart called.

Gideon pulled his hood up over his head. "We've got to stop it before it hurts civilians. Vindicators, move!"

* * *

Audrey descended toward the rooftop of a luxury hotel two blocks away from the Lakeside Central Tower and set Pierce down. A nauseating static fuzzed her brain. The inside of her mouth was dry, like she had chewed cotton. Whatever that woman had shot her with, it had been a doozy. Audrey wavered as her feet touched the roof, her stomach turning and threatening to release its contents onto the gravel beneath her boots. Audrey swallowed the rising bile. Now was not the time to lose it.

She looked back toward the tower. Zeke's burly form leaped from rooftop to rooftop, drawing ever closer to them. Audrey's focus was on the terrace door they used to exfiltrate. The nephiloid smashed through the door and leaped away from the building, falling out of sight toward the streets below. A monster had just been released on the citizens of Sojourn City, and Audrey and her partners bore the responsibility.

She straightened and walked toward the edge of the rooftop. "We've got to stop it."

"Are you insane?" Pierce laughed. "It's doing our job for us."

"No. Innocent people are going to get hurt; that was never part of the plan. If the nephiloid was trapped in their headquarters, that would be one thing. But if it's loose on the streets, it will cause mayhem."

"Grow up, princess." Pierce shook his head. "This is a war, and people die in wars, even innocents. This is all the Vindicators' fault, anyway. If they would've just submitted, there would be no war. Besides, the nephiloid will evolve anyone it bites into a superhuman, and isn't that what we want?"

"That's assuming it only bites them and leaves them alive. The nephiloids operate on pure instinct. If they feel threatened, they will kill everything in their path. This one is in the middle of a city in broad daylight. Its kill instinct is going to be dialed up to a hundred."

Zeke landed on the rooftop next to them. "What's going on?"

"Princess here wants to stop the nephiloid before it hurts anyone." Pierce sneered. "I'm trying to shake her out of her fantasy world."

"He's right, Stormcry. This is a good thing."

"People will die."

"Sorry, kid. That's one of the hard truths of war." Zeke shrugged, but his expression was not unsympathetic. "If that thing kills even one of the Vindicators, it's worth it to us."

Audrey couldn't believe their callousness. These people hadn't asked for this. They had no idea when they woke up that morning that their Sunday would be interrupted by a rampaging monster, that they might die because of it. Audrey and her friends had the ability to stop it—the ability and the responsibility. This was their fault. She took a step forward. Pierce put a hand on her shoulder and squeezed. Audrey pulled away and stared out at the tower and at the streets that the nephiloid would destroy.

Pierce jerked a thumb over his shoulder. "Let's go. Ashcroft will want our report."

He was right about one thing—their duty had been to take out the rebels. They had failed, but the nephiloid might still complete the task. By herself, how much difference would she make? The Vindicators could handle this on their own. She took off, picked up Pierce, and flew back toward the airport.

She hoped that one of the Vindicators would take out the nephiloid before they died. Turner and his friends might deserve what was coming to them, but the people of this city didn't. They should not pay for the Vindicators' crimes. Her only consolation was that the sunlight would weaken the nephiloid. Maybe the Vindicators would kill it quickly.

CHAPTER 15

The Seraph swooped out of the window, carrying Yeoman by his biceps. The cryptid stood in the street below. It swung its head back and forth as if seeking refuge, and it kept waving its arms in the air. *Sunlight*. It was standing in the shade of Lakeside's skyscrapers, but there was enough reflected light to send the creature into a frenzy.

That made it more dangerous, but it also gave them an advantage. As the Seraph dropped toward the ground, Yeoman fired at the cryptid with his crossbow. The creature raised its arm as the arrows rained down on it. The Seraph flew past and dropped Yeoman on the sidewalk. Spright appeared next to him, carrying the Crusader. Across the street, a green flash of light announced Drifter's presence. A quick glance confirmed that he had brought Rampart and Brass Bison with him.

The Seraph pointed at the cryptid. "Bring that thing back in—alive."

Cars screeched to a halt as the drivers noticed the cryptid and frantically tried to turn around. The beast was atop the vehicles in an instant, attacking with single-minded ferocity. The Seraph launched himself at the cryptid and barraged it with light blasts as he soared past. Spright's telltale purple streak zipped by, circled the cryptid, and darted away. The beast howled.

Gunshots cracked off to the Seraph's left. If Brass Bison wasn't careful, she would kill it. The cryptid's hide seemed tough enough to withstand her shots, but if its eyes were as weak as Drifter suggested, Bison might accidentally drop it with a stray shot. Or maybe that was what she was going for.

The Seraph fired another blast at the wendigo. The beast roared and swept an arm at him. He flew backward, out of reach of its clawed hands. A taxi screeched to a halt, barely avoiding the blow. The claws raked across the vehicle's hood, shredding it like paper. The Seraph landed next to the taxi and yanked the door open.

"Get out of here!" he yelled.

The driver nodded and scrambled out. The cryptid howled and brought its arms down on the cab, smashing the windshield. The Seraph fired a light blast into its face. The cryptid stumbled back, and Spright darted underneath its legs and jammed a syringe into its thigh. He sped away, leaving the needle protruding from gray-furred flesh.

If their experience in the cave proved anything, it was that one dose of the tranquilizer might take a moment to work. The Seraph lunged toward it and punched it across the jaw. The creature reeled back and swatted at him, and he barely ducked under the blow.

Bolts of electricity rippled across the wendigo's body. The Seraph glanced to his left. The Crusader and Rampart stood on the curb, flanking Yeoman, each wielding a shock rifle. They fired again and again. Yeoman trained his crossbow high, toward the cryptid's neck.

If Yeoman missed, he didn't have another tranquilizer arrow. They would have to go back to the tower to get more, which would cost them time. The shock rifles seemed to be slowing the beast, but they needed it to hold still. The way it was flailing about, spasming as jolts arced across its body, Yeoman would never get a clean shot.

"Bison!" the Seraph shouted. "Hold it in place!"

"I've never held something that big on my own before." She shook her head. "Especially not while it's struggling. No way I'll be able to hold on."

"Just try."

The Seraph soared toward the cryptid and grabbed one of its arms. The creature howled, reached up with its other arm, and grabbed his leg. The cryptid was a fast learner. It wouldn't fall for the same trick again. He jerked his leg, trying to free it from the wendigo's grip.

The creature hurled him down the street. The Seraph tumbled through the air and fought to get control of his fall. If he could just—

Pain exploded through every nerve in his back as he struck a car. He groaned and slumped forward. At least he hadn't hit his head. He put his palms on the ground and shoved himself to his feet. Dean was right. This aionium armor was impressive stuff. He probably would have sustained a severe spinal injury without it. He was not keen to experience that again.

He was several yards away from the cryptid. Spright ran circles around the beast, hitting it with rapid-fire punches and darting away before it could react. Although it was stumbling drowsily, the cryptid didn't go down. Maybe it had built up a tolerance to the tranquilizer. The single dose seemed to have affected it even less than the first dose had in the cave fight.

The Seraph glanced at Brass Bison. She had holstered both guns and had her palms extended toward the cryptid. Her eyes were squeezed shut, and the Seraph could sense her panic. She didn't believe she could do it. Drifter put a hand on her shoulder before teleporting away. A moment later, he appeared next to Yeoman, grabbed the tranquilizer arrow from his crossbow, and vanished. The next instant, he was on the cryptid's back, jamming the arrow deep into the cryptid's neck. The beast howled.

Get out of there, Dean! The Seraph raised a hand and fired a solid beam of light at the cryptid's chest. The cryptid roared and rushed toward the Seraph. Drifter vanished from the cryptid's back, leaving the arrow lodged in its neck. The Seraph kept up the burst of light, and the wendigo slowed but didn't stop. Seconds later, when the tranquilizer should've worked its way through the beast's system, it continued to trundle toward the Seraph, growling and reaching clawed arms toward him.

"It's not working!" the Crusader shouted.

He and Rampart opened fire with the shock rifles again, but the electricity only seemed to stoke the cryptid's rage. It renewed its charge toward the Seraph. Eyes wide, he cut off the stream of light and soared into the air, out of reach of the cryptid. The beast narrowly missed him and continued its charge down the street. It knocked a car aside as it loped along.

Someone screamed. The car was still occupied, a mother and a little boy in the back seat. She was struggling to free the child from his car seat. The cryptid spotted them, rumbled deep in its throat, and raised its arms.

"No!" the Seraph cried.

He raised his hand to fire a blast of light—and stopped. In the back seat with the mother was Wyatt Jonson, again dressed all in white. The Seraph blinked in surprise. *No, not now!* The cryptid brought its hands crashing down.

Drifter appeared next to the car, grabbed the mother and child, and teleported away. Both civilians disappeared, too. The cryptid's arms buckled the vehicle.

"That's enough."

The Seraph heard the words distinctly but could not make out the speaker. He sensed their resolve, though. A golden-white beam of light sheared through the air and through the cryptid's back, slicing clean through and blasting out of its chest. A moment later, a sharp crack sounded behind him. Blood spurted from the cryptid's left eye. An arrow sliced through the air and punctured the wendigo's right eye. The cryptid whimpered and fell atop the crushed car.

Hannah stepped forward. Her palm held a gun, but not one of her holstered revolvers. This gun was made of pure bronze energy. Hannah stared down at the gun, her eyes wide. The ephemeral weapon vanished from her grasp. Hannah recoiled and looked around.

"How did I . . . "

A hand touched Gideon's shoulder. Jarrett stood next to him, training his crossbow on the wendigo with his free hand. Gideon realized that his own right hand was still raised and glowing brightly. He lowered it.

Gideon pulled his hood back and shook his head. "You killed it."

"No, I think you did. But innocents would have died if you hadn't." Jarrett slung his crossbow across his back. "The tranquilizers and stun rifles weren't working. The angrier it got, the more durable it became."

Hannah nudged the cryptid with her boot. Gideon stared at the burning hole in the center of the cryptid's chest. Jarrett was right, but it would have helped to study a live specimen. How had he managed a blast powerful enough to shear through the beast's chest? He had never tested the upper limits of his powers, and he always kept them in check. To project a blast like that unintentionally . . .

Gideon stepped toward the car. Putting aside the thought for a moment, he focused on the apparition he had witnessed just before Dean had arrived.

Wyatt? He investigated the crushed back seat. There was no sign of a body, and yet he was sure he'd only seen Dean take the mother and child. This was the second time he'd seen the phantom image of the first Crusader, only for him to disappear without a trace. And the voice he heard, the resolute, "That's enough."

Gideon shuddered in realization. The voice and the resolve he had felt were his own, and he had fired a blast powerful enough to slice clean through the cryptid without realizing he was doing it.

What was going on with him?

* * *

Patrick's legs weighed him down like pillars of lead as he dragged himself through the door and back into the lair. Fighting the cryptid would have tired anyone out. Adding in a battle with a trio of new supervillains and the revelation that his grandfather's murderer had escaped prison dragged him to new lows. It had not been a fun day.

He slumped down on the couch as the others filtered in. Dean and Wes wrestled with the carcass of the cryptid, taking it upstairs to the shattered containment cell. Jarrett walked to the kitchen, and Hannah trailed behind him. The newcomers seemed to be sticking together, two fish out of water, bonding over their mutual distance from the team. Hannah still looked awed by the weapon she had formed out of thin air.

And then there was Gideon. He wandered around with a dazed, confused expression. He hadn't spoken to any of them. Patrick wondered if he should talk to him.

Carter plopped onto the couch next to Patrick. "I'm wiped."

"Same, dude." Patrick sighed. "I need a weekend to recover from this weekend."

"I feel that. I should probably get changed into my street clothes and go home. Mom's got to be worried about me."

Patrick slapped Carter on the shoulder. "Good work today. And don't think that I've forgotten about setting you up with Raina. It's still happening."

As Carter disappeared up the stairs, Patrick stared at the middle of the living room floor. Thinking about Raina only made him miss Lucy even more. He fished his cell phone out of his utility belt. After a day like today, he really needed to talk to someone. Maybe she would be willing to listen. He jumped off the couch, walked upstairs, and stepped onto the outdoor balcony, which was seldomly used and should be private enough.

He dialed Lucy's number. Where was he going to start? He hadn't talked to her since before he sat with Raina at lunch. Maybe starting small with "I made a new friend, and she has a crush on Carter" would be good, and he could lead up to the monsters and supervillains.

"Hello?" Her melodic voice melted Patrick's insides. "Patrick?"

He mentally facepalmed. *Use your words, idiot.* "Hey, Luce. Sorry I didn't call you yesterday. It's been busy around here."

"I want to hear all about it. What's going on in the life of Patrick 'Spright' Omer, super-speedster extraordinaire?"

He started at the beginning. She seemed thrilled that he'd made a friend; there was not a hint of jealousy in her voice. That was a relief. But as he detailed their encounters with the cryptids, the supervillain attack, and the prison break, she grew silent. He hoped he wasn't scaring her. But it was too late. The words poured out of their own volition, and he was not sure he could stop them if he wanted to.

“Wow. That’s . . . intense.”

“You’re telling me. I feel like I just lapped the whole world in a day.”

“I’m glad you’re okay. Wish I could be there to give you a big hug. There’s nothing like it to relieve stress.”

“That sounds great. I want to come back to San Francisco soon. I love it here, and I’m doing a lot of good, but . . . ”

“But it’s not home.”

“Right.” He knew she would understand. “I should probably go see if anyone needs help . . . you know, with the monster corpse. Or maybe the escaped prisoners.”

“Take care of yourself, speedster.”

“I will. You too, Luce. Bye.”

“Bye.”

Patrick stuffed his phone back into his utility belt and leaned forward, resting his forearms against the railing. Somewhere out in the city, a bunch of supervillains were gathering, planning who-knew-what. Patrick was young, and he was not sure about much. But this he knew: They were the good guys, and they were going to win.

CHAPTER 16

Gideon and Jolie sat on the floor of Jolie's living room, surrounded by a plethora of decorations and pictures. As much chaos as there was in the city right now, they still had a wedding to plan. As far as Gideon was concerned, sorting through all this was infinitely less stressful. He'd take this over fighting supervillains any day.

He looked up at Jolie. "You know, it's a crazy world we live in that we come home from a day of tracking escaped criminals and fighting monsters and can still plan a wedding in peace."

"Makes no sense. I'd feel a lot better about it if I'd been able to find any trace of Serban. He just vanished."

"He's been doing this for years." Gideon finished sorting a stack of pictures and put them in a Ziploc bag. "He's an expert. But even he will have to show his face eventually, and when he does, you'll be there, waiting for him."

As personal as Gideon's conflict with Serban had been, part of him was surprised that he didn't feel a primal urge to track the mobster down and drag him back to prison. He expected the brutal vigilante iteration of the Seraph to resurface, determined to bring Serban to justice again, but he still felt like himself. He trusted Jolie to catch Serban. He was much more concerned about the havoc that Artemis and her companions could wreak, especially if they were joined by this new trio of amps that had shown up at the lair today.

He wondered if the shadowy figure Jolie had noticed watching her last night was one of the trio. It was unsettling to know that Ashcroft's people knew where she lived, but when his identity had been made public, he knew that was inevitable. Artemis had already targeted so many of the people he loved. If only he could put his secret identity back in the box. Life would be so much easier if he could separate Gideon Turner from the Seraph.

Jolie smiled. "Let's not worry about any of that right now. We're just months away from saying 'I do.' Better get this thing planned now because I will not have chaos on that day."

"Yeah, the last thing we want is Detective Bridezilla jumping on the case."

She glared at him. "Take that back."

He sensed her amusement hidden behind the feigned outrage. He also felt how tired she was. Probably as tired as he was. She might not have to deal with phantom images of dead friends, or with shooting a lethal beam of light without realizing it, but she had her own stressors.

When he was with her, it was easier to forget. She held his heart, and being around her made the problems of the outside world fade away, even temporarily. It was relieving. One day, when all of this was over, maybe it would be like that forever. Gideon was looking forward to that day.

* * *

Audrey drummed her palms impatiently against her thighs. Their liberated comrades were supposed to have met them in this warehouse hours ago. She, Pierce, and Zeke had arrived on time and made sure the area was clear. They had been waiting ever since, and there was still no sign of Artemis, Powers, Mendez, or even Melanie and Quinn.

Half an hour ago, tired of waiting, she had gone out to walk around the docks. It was risky; the police would no doubt be prowling the docks for escapees looking for a ride on a ship. She had changed from her Kevlar-lined white-and-black suit into a black skirt, a flowy top, and her sky-blue leather jacket. It would be easy to look like she was out for a late-night stroll on the pier. It was distressingly easy for a pretty girl to dupe a police officer, she had found.

The Platform glistened across the water, a beacon of light in the middle of Lake Superior. Audrey admired the city for its ambition. She hoped it would make the changes to which its leaders aspired. It would be easier once Ashcroft's plan was complete.

By the time she returned to the warehouse, there was still no sign of the others. The warehouse reeked of fish and mildew, but it was only a temporary stop. Ashcroft had requisitioned a smuggler's boat to take them across the lake, where they would be outside Sojourn City's jurisdiction. The FBI could still follow, but they wouldn't know where to start. Twenty-four hours from now, they should be able to move on to the next phase of Ashcroft's plan.

Zeke kicked a pallet. "I'm about to crack open one of these crates and cook a fish. Where are they? Even the best-planned op can be ruined if the timing isn't right."

"They'll be here. Quinn will have relayed our instructions to Artemis, and she's nothing if not precise."

Audrey wished she was as confident as she sounded. If the authorities had cracked down harder than expected, maybe they had already located the escapees. They might be pinned down and battling police and FBI agents right now. They could go out and comb the city for their allies themselves. But if they did that, and Artemis and the others showed up at the warehouse, they would have no idea where Audrey, Zeke, and Pierce had gone. They would all end up running in circles. No, the best option was to wait there, however infuriating that might be.

"I don't think Ashcroft's going to take our failure too well," Pierce grumbled. "We should've kept fighting, even after the nephiloid got loose."

Audrey shook her head. "Too risky. The beasts aren't trained to differentiate between us and the Vindicators. Fighting it and them at the same time would have divided our focus."

And the longer the fighting went on, the more likely innocent people would've been killed. She didn't say it out loud. By now, they had established that they did not care or understand why she did. Someone on this team had to look out for the little guy. Otherwise, what was the point of it all?

Pierce snorted. "Yeah, well, they killed it, and none of them even got so much as a sprained pinky."

"You're exaggerating. We'll get another chance at the Vindicators soon enough. Even though we didn't kill them, we managed to keep them distracted while the others escaped, so I still count it as a success. I th—"

Cool metal touched Audrey's throat. She froze. She should have been able to sense someone approaching. Her attunement to soundwaves gave her exceptional hearing. Even the quietest tiptoe should have been detectable. But there she was, caught off-guard with a knife blade resting just beneath her jaw. She swallowed. Pierce and Zeke tensed. Audrey shook her head slightly. They weren't fast enough; whoever was holding her could open her throat before either man got close enough to help.

"Who are you?" It was a woman's voice.

"My name's Audrey. We're waiting for someone."

The knife pulled away. "Turn around."

Audrey spun on her heel. The woman in the warehouse entry was dressed in black jeans, a gray top, and a black leather jacket. Her blonde hair was tied back in a severe tail. Her expression was steely, and though she had lowered her knife, she kept it in a firm grip at her side.

"I've introduced myself," Audrey said. "Care to return the favor?"

"Katrina Monahan." She waved back toward the door. "It's clear!"

Quinn stepped through the door first, flames tickling his fingertips. He looked at Audrey, extinguished the flames, and nodded. Melanie walked in after him, followed by Artemis and Mendez. Powers came last, facing away from the group and training a gun on the pier. He grabbed the warehouse door and slid it shut.

"About time," Pierce said.

"What took so long?" Zeke asked.

Artemis offered a carefree shrug. "We had to find some clothes. We couldn't exactly wander around the city in prison uniforms, could we?"

"You were supposed to be here hours ago," Zeke pressed.

"Enough." Audrey stepped between them. "They're here now. Let's just get to the boat and get out of here. Ashcroft is waiting."

"Won't the feds be watching the docks?" Mendez asked. "What makes you think it's safe to leave this way?"

"The boat was requisitioned by Ashcroft." Audrey walked toward the door. "He paid off the dockmaster. No one will notice. Now, do you want to keep loitering in this fish-smelling hole, or do you want to go home?"

"She's right," Artemis said. "We should go."

Audrey felt a surge of pride. Artemis was Ashcroft's second-in-command, so having her support meant a lot. Audrey had looked up to the woman for a long time. She was a bit stern and stuck-up, but she was a great leader.

"Who's she?" Pierce asked, pointing at Monahan. "She's coming with us?"

Artemis nodded. "Her skills will be useful, and she's willing to undergo the Evolving."

Monahan sheathed her knife. "The world is changing. People like you are going to be everywhere. I might as well get a head start on them. A killer must adapt to her target."

Audrey shuddered. Monahan's tone and demeanor sent chills down her spine. This woman was an unrepentant murderer. Did they really want her on their side? Then again, Mendez was a violent warrior. Pierce was a murderer. Quinn was a profiteer. Not all of the people on Ashcroft's side were upstanding citizens.

"Are we all done now? We've all said our piece?" Artemis led the way toward the docks. "Good. Let's go. Ashcroft is waiting."

CHAPTER 17

A wicked grin spread across Jarrett's face as the archer faced down Hannah, Patrick, and Wes. The four of them stood in the training room, the containment cell that held the cryptid's body now pushed off to the side so the room could be used for its intended purpose. As Patrick and the two heroes on his side of the room spread out and prepared to face Jarrett, Patrick wiggled his fingers and bounced up and down on his heels.

Everything happened at once. Jarrett snapped his crossbow up to his shoulder and fired a training arrow at Wes. Patrick raced around the circumference of the room, making it two laps around before the arrow had crossed halfway between the two men. Hannah's hand raised, ever so slowly in Patrick's perception, and Wes reached down to touch his utility belt.

Patrick completed another lap around the room when four panels on the walls, equally spaced throughout the room, opened. He knew what was coming. Patrick slowed to a halt and dropped into a crouch. The panels slid aside, revealing two shock cannons and two projectile launchers. All four weapons were designed to detect movement, and now Patrick was not the fastest-moving person in the room.

Hannah's hand reached full extension, and she tugged Jarrett's arrow from the air with a lasso of energy. Wes's hand touched his belt, and his skin shifted to a burnished bronze. He lunged toward Jarrett as the archer fired again.

The shock cannons opened fire on Wes. The younger Turner turned his lunge into a forward roll as one of the electric blasts struck the ground where he had stood. A moment later, one of the projectile launchers fired, and a sphere of solid aionium shot across the room and struck Wes in the back. Jarrett trained his crossbow on Patrick. Patrick exploded into motion, the world slowing around him as he ran across the walls. The guns—their motion detectors alerted by Patrick's abrupt burst of speed—swiveled to track him.

This was when Patrick felt alive. When he was running, nothing stood in his way. It was just him and his speed and God, the rest of the world crawling around him. It was like he was on another plane of existence, one that only he could see. The aionium spheres and bolts of electricity were too slow to catch him. It was an amazing, euphoric experience. Grinning, he let out a whoop of excitement as he ran.

As he circled the room, he watched his teammates battle. Jarrett tried to keep his crossbow aimed at Patrick, but he couldn't tell where Patrick was. He certainly couldn't turn fast enough to track him. Hannah stretched her hands out to either side, her features scrunched in concentration; and a pair of hatchets formed from pure energy appeared in her palms. Since her accidental creation of an energy gun while fighting the nephiloid, she had learned to expand her powers—to create different objects, mostly weaponry, out of the energy fields she projected.

Patrick leaped off the wall and arced across the room as one of the stun blasts nearly reached him. He came down in a crouch and immediately pushed off again, running before Jarrett could draw a bead on him.

"Stand still!" the archer shouted, exasperated.

Jarrett grunted as a stun bolt struck him in the back. He stumbled forward and threw himself into a side roll as Hannah charged at him, hatchets swinging. He raised his crossbow and fired at Hannah, who dodged immediately. Patrick circled them, waiting for an opportunity to strike. Hannah, whose motion had alerted one of the projectile launchers, raised her hands to shield her face as an aionium sphere hurtled toward her, and her hatchets dissipated, replaced by a circular shield. The projectile struck the shield and tore through it, knocking Hannah flat as it hit her solar plexus. Jarrett and Wes made it to their feet at the same time.

Patrick circled around one of the projectile launchers and switched it off. By the time he reached the second one, the two shock cannons had turned to face Wes and Jarrett. The two men lunged at each other, and the shock cannons fired. One blast struck Wes, but his body's metal texture dispersed the jolt. Patrick switched off the second launcher and raced for the shock cannons. He switched both off in rapid succession. Then it was time to deal with Jarrett and Wes.

He lunged off the wall and raced toward them as Wes delivered an elbow strike to Jarrett's temple. The archer crumpled. Patrick rammed into Wes, leading with his shoulder. The joint protested as it hit the bronze form, but Wes collapsed, just the same. Patrick skidded to a halt and examined the room. His three companions lay on the floor, groaning and rubbing their bruises.

"Good match," Patrick said. "Want to go again?"

* * *

Wes dropped down on the couch and exhaled deeply. Even without the grueling training session he had just endured, his body was stretched thin. Arianna was concerned that traces of radiation from fighting the green-costumed villain the previous day remained in his system, causing his sickness. Even in his rubber form, Wes might have soaked up enough to affect him. Dean assured him it wouldn't cause permanent harm, but the headache pounding behind his eyes and the fever made it seem bad enough. He didn't want to know what full-blown radiation poisoning felt like.

He didn't have time to be sick. He wanted to help the rest of the Vindicators search for the runaway villains. Whatever they were planning, they wanted the heroes out of the way when they executed it.

The newly repaired front door—a heavy, metal slab rather than a normal wooden one—clicked as someone opened it. Wes did not open his eyes, but he grunted an incoherent greeting.

"You all right?" Gideon asked.

Wes peeked from behind his heavy lids. "I'll be fine. Just tell me when there's someone to punch. Until then, I'm going to sack out here."

"I'm going to go help Arianna and Maddox study the cryptid. They're smart, but their specialty is technology. This needs a doctor's touch."

Sometimes, Wes forgot that Gideon had been a surgeon. His medical expertise was the reason he had been in Venezuela in the first place. If not for that, he wouldn't have powers. But now, the Seraph was all Wes saw when he looked at his brother. It was amazing how quickly something could become the defining trait in a person's life.

Wes closed his eyes as Gideon walked up the stairs. *What is my defining trait?* Even outside of being the Seraph, Gideon was a doctor, a bio-analyst, and a great martial artist. *Who am I? Who is Wes Turner, besides Rampart? This is why I need law school.* Wes loved fighting crime, but when he took off the mask and costume, he still wanted to be useful. He thought his powers were what he wanted most in the world. He had them, and he still didn't feel as useful as he had hoped.

Law school had waited long enough. As soon as they dealt with Ashcroft and his forces, Wes was going to get on with his own life.

* * *

Gideon pulled on a pair of white latex gloves and stepped up next to the observation table that Arianna and Maddox had brought into the training room. The cryptid's giant body lay on the table, its arms dragging on the floor. Based on the unusual combination of physical traits, Gideon guessed that Ashcroft had, as Dean so colorfully put it, "Frankensteined the mess out of this thing." Its body resembled a large gorilla, but the fur and head were more reminiscent of a wolf. Two snake-like fangs stored its venom, a hundred-plus shark-like teeth lining the rest of its mouth.

He glanced up at Arianna and Maddox. The two scientists stood on the other side of the table and looked at the cryptid in horror. They probably hadn't seen many corpses in their time, and they certainly had never seen a giant, gray monster carcass. Of course, neither had he. Gideon took a scalpel. He had no idea where to begin or how to identify this creature.

"Take some blood samples," he said. "I'd like to see if its blood shows similar properties to a superhuman's."

After an hour of dissection and study, they were no closer to learning what the cryptid actually was. It was certainly not a natural creature of any kind. Gideon had found so many kinds of animal tissue that he wondered if Ashcroft had cut-and-pasted whatever looked like it fit. *He definitely "Frankensteined" it.* Maybe the creature's origin didn't matter. They only needed to verify that Ashcroft created it, and that seemed certain at this point. The blood did show similar properties to Gideon's. Gideon started to remove his gloves.

"Wait."

Gideon looked up at Arianna and Maddox.

"The fangs. We need to take samples of the venom in its fangs. The creature that bit Hannah transmitted powers to her."

Arianna took one of the teeth and pressed the tip into a beaker. A greenish venom oozed out. She swirled the liquid in a beaker and walked toward the workstation she'd set up. If that venom really did transmit superpowers, maybe they could figure out a way to stop Ashcroft from spreading the Nephilim DNA any further.

Gideon peeled off his gloves. "Let me know when you find something. See if you can work up an antidote, too."

"Will do."

Gideon walked out of the training room and onto the exterior balcony. He looked out at the city. *An antidote.* What if it were an antidote to more than the creature's venom? What if they could work up an antidote for Ashcroft's serum? Could they remove someone's superpowers? From the blood tests he had done on himself, Gideon suspected that the Nephilim DNA that Ashcroft used in his serum bonded with human genes, forming something altogether new. But in this case, blood tests might be insufficient. They might have to study this thing down to the last strand of DNA.

If Ashcroft managed to spread his "miracle" across the world, a cure would be a necessity. Every living person having access to superpowers was asking for trouble. If someone like Luca Serban ever received powers, there was no telling what he would do. And what about terrorist groups like al-Qaeda? Superhuman terrorists would be a nightmare. Innocents across the world would be in danger.

Gideon stared at his hands. He could hardly imagine life without his powers, and the rest of the Vindicators had put their abilities to good use. Plenty of other good people would do the same. But what if the only solution to stopping Ashcroft was to remove the possibility of superpowers entirely? Would the sacrifice be worth it?

That was a choice that was out of Gideon's hands. The idea of an antidote was purely theoretical. And even if one was created, that didn't mean everyone had to use it.

* * *

The annoying thing about masks was how difficult they made facial recognition. Of course, that was the point of wearing one in the first place, but when the bad guys did it, it was a whole new level of frustrating. Dean had given up trying to figure out the identities of Torrent and Tetra-Hazard, but he was determined to identify the woman in white. She had been so familiar to him, and he had no idea why.

Dean turned his attention back to the warning system he was programming. It would be a good idea for everyone on the team to have a way to send an emergency broadcast to the rest of the Vindicators at a moment's notice. When he broached the subject with Gideon, he eagerly agreed. Dean suspected it would be easy to rig up such a program, so he was working on it while also trying to find their assailants' identities. He also sewed a tracking device into each of the Vindicators' suits, so that if one of them was in trouble, the rest could find their location even if they couldn't send an alert.

He ran a hand through his waves of hair as he glanced back at the image of the woman. Was he imagining things? Maybe he only thought he recognized her. There were lots of people in the world who looked alike. She might have borne a passing resemblance to one of Dean's old schoolmates, or a distant cousin, or something. But . . . no. He couldn't shake the feeling that he knew her from somewhere. Even her voice had sounded familiar—her speaking voice, not the shrill, sonic cry she'd belted out.

Belted out . . .

Dean zoomed in on her face. The resemblance was there, but it wasn't possible. *Was it?* She even had the silver streak in her hair. Dean opened an internet browser and typed in the name "Silver Siren." The pop star and model had been dead for almost two years after a tragic battle with cancer. It couldn't be her.

The search results displayed an image that, if a mask were superimposed around the eyes, was the spitting image of the white-clad supervillain that had attacked them yesterday. Dean gaped at the screen.

"That's impossible."

He jumped from his chair and out to the balcony. Wes was resting on the couch; and Patrick, Hannah, and Jarrett were out of sight, their voices emanating from the kitchen. No time for the stairs. He teleported down into the kitchen, reappearing next to the refrigerator. Patrick jumped, and the other two spun around.

Patrick yelped. "Don't do that, Dean!"

"Sorry. I just got an ID on the woman who led the attack yesterday."

"Who is it?" Jarrett asked.

"You're not going to believe it. Do you remember Audrey Knight, the Silver Siren?"

Hannah nodded, and Patrick murmured, "Of course."

"The name sounds vaguely familiar," Jarrett said. "Who is she?"

"A pop star and supermodel," Patrick explained. "Extremely famous. Attractive."

"Very attractive," Dean agreed. The others stared at him. "Anyway . . . Apparently, she's not as dead as the media says she is because she was the woman who attacked us yesterday."

No one said anything for a moment. Hannah and Patrick exchanged bewildered glances, and Jarrett blinked.

"Well." Jarrett stared off into the distance. "Take that, cancer."

CHAPTER 18

Seven years ago

"Humanity is weak. Inferior." Ashcroft's vision blurred as his eyes struggled to focus on the walls of the dim corridor. "The product of flawed evolution—or a God Who failed."

Father had been religious—devoutly so—in church every Sunday, spreading the Good Word to his neighbors with a tract or a pocket Bible. He held onto that faith until the end, sure that God was guiding him to become Solar Flare. If that was true, God led Father astray. Solar Flare's early days were commendable; but his popularity had quickly waned, and the people he protected had denounced him. Ashcroft did not know if God was real, but if He was, He had betrayed Father. He had betrayed Ashcroft. It was time for Ashcroft to take destiny into his own hands. It was not that he was an atheist. Rather, he just hated the idea of God.

He shook his head. "Either way, humanity has come as far as we can on our own. We need a push."

The tunnel he stood in was among the reasons Ashcroft could not altogether disregard the existence of God. Ashcroft held his flashlight aloft as he rambled, shining it across the dirty, cobweb-covered catacomb walls. Years of research and calling in dozens of favors had led him here. The scientific community had all but abandoned him after his catastrophic presentation all those years before. Mark had cut ties with him altogether, their friendship dissolving after one disagreement. That stung, but it had only reinforced the truth that Ashcroft had begun to understand. *We don't have what it takes.* Even the world's brightest minds ridiculed the truth he brought to them. They wouldn't do what was necessary to make the world a safe, secure place for future generations. Ashcroft would show them.

"As you say, Doctor," his assistant, Roger, replied.

Roger had heard Ashcroft's ramblings hundreds of times before. With no outlet to express his frustration, words were Ashcroft's only option. Roger didn't mind. He had been Father's assistant before he became Ashcroft's. He even helped Father during his time as Solar Flare, acting as his tech support of sorts. He was loyal to Ashcroft's family and to Regency Inc.—recently rebranded as "the Regency" by Ashcroft. Roger would bear Ashcroft's words and remain by his side, no matter how many failures he endured.

Perhaps the winds of fortune were finally changing. Finding the catacombs had been a boon of luck. Every bit of research Ashcroft had done on the Nephilim indicated that they had been a hyper-advanced people for their time.

Half-angels, the legends said. Ashcroft believed they were more.

If his research was correct, these catacombs held the key to uncovering the truth. They had been discovered decades before but were believed to be empty. The language written on the walls was a mystery, potentially predating Egyptian hieroglyphs yet distinctly letter-based. Ashcroft believed that the catacombs had been an underground kingdom of Nephilim. The letters on the walls could be an ancient language that only the Nephilim had been able to put into writing. If the biblical accounts of the Great Flood were accurate, then the Nephilim had likely died there, drowned in their own halls.

But there was no evidence of the Nephilim in the tunnel, which meant that they must have had a secret place within the catacombs, a sanctuary. Had they survived the Flood? Unlikely, or they would have shown themselves to the world long before. But if the Nephilim really were the same as the Titans and the Demigods, perhaps some had survived, for those legends had arisen not long after the Flood.

If the legends were true, Ashcroft understood the Nephilim, identified with them. They came from a heritage that wanted to be free of God's control. With their power and his intelligence, maybe he could finally accomplish it. Maybe he could make the world what he wanted it to be.

"What now, Doctor?" Roger asked.

Ashcroft swept his light over the wall in front of them. There had to be some way forward. He hadn't come all this way for nothing; he would find answers. He was certain. History, linguistics, religion—he'd studied them all to get to this point. But it was science that would carry him through to his end goal. Ashcroft removed a scanner from his knapsack and ran it over the walls.

"There must be something. Something . . ."

He lowered his scanner to the floor, and the readings spiked. His eyes widened. There was some form of energy coming from beneath them. There must be a substructure far below. He removed his knapsack and handed the scanner to Roger.

"What does this mean?" Roger asked.

"We go down." Ashcroft knelt. "Our answer is below us. We just need to find it."

CHAPTER 19

Present Day

Powers crinkled his nose at the musty smell of Ashcroft's base. He had forgotten this particular odor; it had been a long time since he had cause to visit the base. It was no worse than the smell of prison, but no better either. Just a different kind of pungent. He fell in behind Artemis and kept his eyes on the floor. He hadn't forgotten his resolution to strike out on his own. He had been swept up in the escape, but he was still determined to get out from under Ashcroft's thumb. Being a part of this insane crusade had brought nothing but trouble to Powers's life.

With his duplication abilities, Powers could do anything. He could run his own criminal empire all by himself. He would never have to trust anyone else. His doppelgangers could do all the work. No one would be able to find the real him. Anytime it looked like he might be caught, he could leave a doppelganger behind and quietly steal away to a new hideout, even a new city.

But first, he had to get out of there. That wouldn't be easy. If Ashcroft caught wind of his plans, he could have Artemis hypnotize Powers and trap him there, enslaving him to Ashcroft without any hope of escape. He had to time his escape carefully.

He took steady breaths. No external tic would give away his plan.

When he left, he could even leave a duplicate behind. It would take longer for the others to realize he was gone. He nodded to himself.

Sneaking off in the night while the others slept, leaving a doppelganger in his bed to throw them all off—it was his best option. It was a pity the others were so blind. He liked some of them. Artemis was gorgeous, but he would never trust her to stay out of his head. Zeke was an all-right guy. Audrey was friendly and beautiful, too, and more trustworthy than Artemis. But she had made it clear she didn't care for Powers's advances.

He glanced up as Artemis turned the corner into the central planning room. Ashcroft was across the room, studying a monitor that displayed what looked to Powers like a shipping manifest. He lowered his head again and tried not to look at it. Best not to get too invested. He didn't care what Ashcroft was planning; he would not stick around long enough for it to matter to him.

"My prodigal children! It is so good to have you back safely."

Artemis inclined her head. "My lord."

Powers mentally rolled his eyes. What a suck-up. Ashcroft wasn't "lord" of anything. He was an insane scientist who had, against all odds, accomplished what he had set out to do. But he wasn't competent enough to be any kind of ruler. He was barely competent enough to be their employer. Powers wondered if the title was Artemis's way of playing to Ashcroft's ego or if it had been Ashcroft's idea.

"We beg your forgiveness for our failures," Artemis continued.

She nudged Powers. He grunted softly and inclined his head with her. It had already been down, anyway; but apparently, it hadn't been reverent enough for her tastes. To Powers's left, Mendez joined them and bowed his head, too.

"As do we," Audrey said. "We were unable to defeat the Vindicators."

Ashcroft snorted. "No matter. The next phase of my plan is upon us, and we must work in unison for it to be achieved."

Powers raised his head. *No, no, no.* If Ashcroft had a key role for each of them to play, he would keep a closer eye on them. That would make it even harder for Powers to sneak out.

"Sterling Labs has completed the prototype for their atmospheric dispersal unit." Ashcroft gestured at the screen behind him. "Thanks to the work of Red Raider and Stormcry in Sojourn City three months ago, we know the prototype is being shipped from the Washington, D.C., branch of Sterling Labs to the Pentagon for a demonstration to the government tomorrow morning."

Powers pressed his lips together. "You want us to steal the device."

Artemis snapped her head around and glared at him. Powers clenched his jaw and kept his gaze on Ashcroft, ignoring her. She might deify Ashcroft, but he did not. He would speak when he pleased.

"Yes. The route will be guarded. Torrent, you and your mercenaries will be my instrument for this mission. Somna and Stormcry, you will run backup, while the rest of you remain here to build toward the next phase of my plan."

"Even from as far away as Sojourn City, Turner and his cohorts may intervene," Artemis cautioned.

"Yes. That is why you must be swift, precise. I have chosen you all for this moment. I trust you will not fail me."

Powers bit the inside of his mouth. It would have been easier to slip away unnoticed if he went with the D.C. team. Here, he was surrounded by fanatics. But he wasn't ready to put his life on the line facing the Vindicators again. Better to lay low.

"Bring the device back here, and we will make plans to distribute the serum across the world." Ashcroft stepped away from the computer. "I leave you to plan the details of the mission."

"Wait." Monahan weaved her way to the front of the group. "I was promised powers if I joined you. I'd be an asset to this mission. I've fought Turner before, so I know his skill set. Give me powers, and I'm in."

"Katrina Monahan. I've heard of your exploits. Yes, you most recently worked with Luca Serban, who I have also had the distinct displeasure of working with before. He brought me a few of my first test subjects, including Quinn, here. If you are like Serban, why would I want you on my team?"

"I'm nothing like him." Monahan sneered. "I am a consummate professional. And besides that, I'm motivated. Turner—the Seraph—is the only person I've failed to close a contract on."

"Indeed?" Ashcroft chuckled. "Very well. Right this way, Ms. Monahan."

Powers watched her go and shook his head. Why would anyone willingly join this operation? Were they all so fooled by the promise of power that they couldn't see past Ashcroft's madness? Maybe so. Powers had been the same, once. Now, he was wiser.

The only person worth swearing allegiance to was himself. And that's the only way it ever should've been.

* * *

The Broken Glass was one of the last places Jolie ever expected to set foot in again. The bar had been one of Luca Serban's main hideouts when he ran his operation in the Brooks. Most of the regulars and even the bartender had been on his payroll. In the months since Serban's imprisonment, the Glass had been closed for repairs and subsequently reopened by a new—and hopefully less criminal—owner.

But maybe Serban didn't know that. It was possible he would try to find shelter in the bar, which made it worth investigating. Jolie reached down to ensure that her sidearm was ready to draw. Last time she was there, she and her former partner, Paul Jordan, ended up in a nasty scuffle with some of Serban's cronies. It was best to be prepared. Steeling herself for anything, Jolie stepped through the door.

Roughly a dozen people occupied the Broken Glass, many of them watching a football game on the TV that hung over the bar. Jolie scanned the room. Serban wasn't there—at least, not in the front room. None of the patrons looked like his typical goons, either. There were no leather jackets or skinny ties to speak of, no telltale signs of poorly concealed weaponry. That was a good start.

She stepped up to the bar. The tender was a woman in her mid-forties. She looked rough but not mean, like she had lived in the Brooks for a long time, was accustomed to life there, but had not let it corrupt her.

"How can I help you?" she asked.

Jolie held up her badge. "Detective Anderson, Sojourn PD. I'm looking for a criminal who escaped Stone Gate Penitentiary yesterday. He used to be a regular here. I thought he might come back."

"Haven't seen anyone in orange or gray. Sorry, Detective. I didn't start here until the reopening. Anyone who used to be a regular here was before my time."

Jolie handed her a picture of Serban. "This is the man I'm looking for. My phone number is written on the back of the photo. If you see him, call me. He's dangerous."

Jolie stepped away from the bar and glanced around one more time. No one had so much as raised a head to look at her. Maybe the new owner really did clean the place up. She stepped outside and pulled her jacket close. *Where else might Serban hide?* He had a foothold in almost every part of the Brooks at one point, and even in some parts of Sojourn outside of the slums. There were lots of warehouses or abandoned apartments where he might hole up.

This could take a while.

* * *

Hannah leaned against the kitchen counter and watched the people around her. Even aside from their powers, they all had quirks that made them different from anyone Hannah had met before. And in many ways, their powers proved to be quite opposite from the personality traits they held.

Patrick's speed implied a short attention span. Yet as she observed him, she realized that he thought deeply, and when he had a conversation with a person, he could focus intensely on them. And Dean. His powers suggested that he jumped from one thing to the next, but she had seen him zone in on the same project for hours at a time. Wes' powers indicated a strong, confident man, but she detected an air of uncertainty in him. He was struggling to find who he was.

Jarrett Mercer approached, opening the refrigerator. He caught her gaze and nodded to her. Mercer was an interesting man. He didn't speak much, but when he did, his words were either very meaningful or humorous. There seemed to be no in-between for him.

"Tell me about yourself."

Hannah blinked and looked up. "Me?"

"Yeah." Jarrett popped open a soda can and sipped. "We're both newbies. We've got to stick together, right?"

"There's not much to tell. I grew up on a reservation in northern Arizona. A few years ago, I got fed up with the sex trafficking and drug dealing going on around me. No one seemed able—or willing—to do anything about it. So, I did." She tapped one of her guns. "I took my father's revolvers, went out, and trained myself to shoot. Eventually, I started shooting traffickers instead of targets."

Jarrett nodded. "I don't blame you. That's got to be hard, especially in a place as isolated as a reservation."

"It was." Hannah clenched her fists. "I never intended to become a killer, not really. I just wanted to help people, but . . . "

"But to do that, you sometimes had to kill people. I've done the same thing. Before, when I was in the Special Forces, I killed all the time. And when I came home and saw the mess my city was in . . . When you're a Spec Force soldier, you've got a skill set that's ideally suited to stopping that kind of thing."

"I'm sure." Hannah studied him. "You use a crossbow, not a gun. A gun would be more efficient."

"What can I say? I was a big fan of Robin Hood as a kid, but bow and arrows are just too clunky." Jarrett smiled. "Simplicity of a gun, elegance of a bow. Crossbow's the best of both worlds."

"How can you do what you do and have such a sense of humor?"

"I have to." He shrugged and took another drink. "Keeps me sane. If I don't, it's a downward spiral into complete darkness. My wife worries for me, but . . . she keeps my feet on the ground. Protecting her is half of why I do this."

Hannah smiled. "I have never married. I suppose the closest person to me is my friend Axel. But that is all he is—my best friend."

"Hmm. Sometimes things like that can sneak up on you. And if you're not paying attention, they'll keep sneaking past, and you're never the wiser."

Ouch. It had been a long time since Hannah had given any thought to her personal life. She didn't want happiness to pass her by. Jarrett might have a point. But Axel? She doubted he would ever be more than a brother to her.

"Everyone to the ops room in five," Dean called.

Jarrett finished off his soda. "Good talking to you. Let's go see if we can get all this resolved. I don't know about you, but I don't plan on living in this tower forever."

Me, either. Hannah had come to Sojourn because protecting the world from Ashcroft's schemes would also protect her reservation. But there were other dangers still facing it, and she refused to leave it unguarded for long. If that meant letting Dean and his friends deal with the fallout of this villain's actions themselves, so be it.

CHAPTER 20

Gideon leaned against one wall in the ops room and watched as the others trickled in. Patrick and Carter entered first, talking quietly. Gideon was glad the two had struck up a friendship. Carter was certainly going to miss Patrick when the speedster returned to San Francisco. They had both needed a friend and had found one in each other.

Wes entered the room next. Gideon sensed turmoil and confusion in him. He made a note to speak to his brother later. When Wes had received his powers, Gideon thought his internal conflict would still. Instead, it only seemed more tumultuous.

Jarrett and Hannah entered last. Gideon couldn't get a good sense of Jarrett. He had a hidden darkness; Gideon knew that much. But was it just the haunted conscience of a man who'd killed too often, or was there something more? Hannah, on the other hand, was an open book. All she wanted was justice. Gideon liked them both. It was a shame they wouldn't be permanent additions to the Vindicators.

"Welcome, everyone," Dean said. "Our first order of business is for our newcomers. You can't keep fighting supervillains dressed like models."

Gideon smirked. Jarrett's brown leather jacket, dark gray shirt, and dark blue jeans with brown boots and matching belt and Hannah's ripped blue jeans, white top, and red, Sherpa-lined denim jacket certainly fit that description.

Jarrett looked down at his clothes and back up at Dean, one eyebrow raised.

"Thought I was the funny one."

Dean crossed his arms. "I've been here longer. I reign supreme."

"Fair enough."

"Anyway." Dean held up two cases. "These are for you. Our way of saying thank you for helping out the team."

They took the cases and popped them open. Jarrett withdrew his suit. It was a sleeveless brown jumpsuit with matching bracers and boots. The cuffs were lined with cobalt blue stripes. A matching quiver and a pair of blue-tinted goggles rounded out the ensemble.

"It's a Kevlar weave," Dean said. "And the goggles have a built-in heads-up display including a rangefinder."

"Nice." Jarrett examined the suit. "Always wanted to show off my biceps while fighting crime."

Hannah's suit was burnt orange and had a black bison's head emblazoned on the chest. A black domino mask, gloves, boots, and belt tied her uniform together. A pair of silver vambraces clasped over the gloves and held several rolls of ammo reloads for her revolvers.

Dean pointed to Hannah's waist. "I didn't add holsters because I figured you would wear your own gun belt over it. Along with the vambraces, the belt can hold extra ammo—up to four reloads for each gun."

Hannah gave a rare smile. "Thank you."

Gideon pressed his lips together. He didn't much like the idea of Hannah running around strapped up with lethal weaponry. It went against Gideon's—and by extension, the Vindicators'—code of no killing. However, she was not a permanent member of the team, so he had no place to order her around. Hopefully, she would keep her kill shots to a minimum.

"One more thing," Dean continued. "I've installed trackers into each of our suits. They can be traced from the central computer here in the Tower or—if you'll each check your phones—from the app I've just sent you. That app will serve as an alert system for the team. If you're in trouble, hit the button. It'll ping everyone else's phones. We can track one another's phones and suit trackers." Dean glanced at Gideon. "I've also sent Jolie a link to the app, even though she doesn't have a suit."

"Thank you."

When Dean had thought up the idea for the trackers, Gideon was quick to agree. Whoever had been watching Jolie the other night could come back. If they did, at least she had a way to call for help in a hurry.

"Now that we're all up to date on our fashion . . . " Dean gestured to a monitor. "As you all know, earlier today, I discovered that the woman who led our attackers is Audrey Knight, also known as Silver Siren. This brought about much conflict because I am simultaneously elated that she is alive and devastated because she's evil."

"Dean had a huge crush on Audrey when we were teenagers," Gideon explained.

"It's not fair. All the gorgeous ones are secretly evil." Dean huffed. "Anyway, sorry. This discovery led me to put her image through Sojourn City's traffic cameras and CCTV footage, and I found images of her with her two companions from the night before the attack, which means we now have full-face shots of both men. Without further ado, meet your attackers."

The screen blinked, and three images appeared. Knight's image was in the center. She looked about like Gideon remembered her—soft features, piercing blue eyes, and dark hair with a silver streak. The man on the left was muscular, with a square jaw and a blond crew cut. The other man was bald and burly, with a scruffy, blond beard and a mean look in his eye.

"The man on the left is named Zeke Norris," Dean said. "Former U.S. Navy. After he came home from his tour, he got involved in a private security force that went bad. We're not sure how he joined up with Dr. Ashcroft. He's the one who identified himself as Torrent."

Jarrett clenched his jaw. "I've heard of security forces like that. Guys come home from war and don't know what to do with their skills. Recruiters from these forces offer them a way to feel useful. Sometimes, the jobs are innocent—bodyguarding the rich and foolish—but other times, they end up robbing banks, shipping drugs, things like that. Could've been me, but I decided to shoot the bad guys instead of becoming one."

Jarrett spoke lightly, but Gideon sensed a trace of sorrow beneath the words. In a way, Norris was a kindred spirit to Jarrett. They both had similar experiences and were only a knife's edge away from ending up the same way.

Dean nodded. "The man on the right, Tetra-Hazard, is Kenton Pierce. Much less flattering record. Pierce committed his first murder at eighteen. For the past twenty years, he's been in and out of prison and part of half-a-dozen gangs. He's a messed-up guy; it's no wonder he ended up with Ashcroft."

"Have we identified Pierce's powers?" Gideon asked.

"We don't know the full extent of them. He exudes low-level radiation from his body and excretes acid from his fingers. But beyond that? We're not sure. His name hints that he has at least four dangerous abilities. We're lucky he spent most of the fight going up against Wes. The radiation he absorbed would've put anyone else in the hospital."

Wes rubbed his head. "Glad to be of service."

"So, stay as far from Pierce as we can," Gideon said. "We'll need to take him out from a distance next time we go up against him."

"Right. Or drop him by surprise before he has a chance to put up a radiation field." Dean tapped the keyboard. "I've got a facial recognition algorithm running. It's unlikely they're still in Sojourn City, but if they do turn up, we'll know about it. That's all I had to say, so you're dismissed, ladies and gents."

Gideon stared at the three faces. Three more lives caught up in Ashcroft's scheme. Was there hope for any of them?

* * *

Ashcroft watched the splicer fuse the blood of each Nephilim, combined with a cocktail of other drugs and chemicals he had used to perfect his serum. Each Nephilim's blood had a different effect. One had given each recipient different nature-manipulation powers, such as pyrokinesis and hydro-kinesis, and even Sterling's teleportation. Another gave the sound- and light-projection powers that Stormcry and Turner had received, and another provided Backfire with his explosive touch. The exact nature of the Nephilim's powers was a mystery, but Ashcroft could only imagine what would become of the man who had combined them all into one formula.

He was about to find out. Backfire had stolen the splicer from Garvin Technologies in San Francisco. *One way or another, Mark ended up helping me.* After months of reprogramming the splicer and running simulations on the formulae to ensure they would work, Ashcroft was finally ready. Much of the Nephilim blood had gone into the splicer. His stores were all but drained now, the last of that ancient line of mythical beings nearly gone. He had left just enough of their blood to create a synthetic counterpart for the prototype dispersal unit. Ashcroft and his creations would carry on the legacy and name of the Nephilim into the future. He had considered what he would call himself once he had become a god. Jeremiah Ashcroft was a good name, but it had always been a temporary one, taken to hide his relation to Solar Flare. He was about to become so much more than that. It seemed fitting to take a name that would honor the source of his power.

Father had not had the Nephilim DNA. He only had the scientific brilliance that his mind had concocted. With that formula spliced with Ashcroft's, his power would be nearly unlimited.

The red light on the splicer flashed three times and blipped out. A moment later, a green light glowed in its place. Ashcroft grinned and stepped toward the splicer. Somna shifted behind him, no doubt eager to observe the next step in her master's evolution. It would be glorious. Ashcroft opened the splicer, revealing a vial of liquid. It was not all that impressive, but its appearance belied its power. He removed the vial, inserted a syringe into it, and sucked the serum into the needle.

Ashcroft looked at Somna. "My ascension is at hand."

"I await it eagerly."

"Gather the others." Ashcroft studied the syringe. "They, too, must bear witness."

Somna nodded and departed the lab. Moments later, she returned with the others—all of Ashcroft's faithful lieutenants. Even Lancet, the newest member of their retinue, joined them in the lab. She crossed her arms and leaned against a workbench. Fragment seemed the tensest of all of them, but he had returned from Sojourn City rather than attempting to flee in the prison break. His loyalty had been proven.

Ashcroft spread his arms to his congregants. "Behold your lord."

This is for you, Father.

He inserted the needle into his arm and pressed down on the syringe. The serum rushed into his bloodstream, instantly chilling him. He shuddered as gooseflesh rose across his arm, onto his back, and down his whole body. *So . . . cold . . .* He dropped to his knees. Agony ripped through his insides, but he bit back a scream. The pain was necessary. The serum was altering his body on a molecular level.

"Oh, my . . . " Fragment gasped.

Something that felt like spikes drove through his shoulder blades from the inside out. Ashcroft did scream now, through gritted teeth, and struggled to remain on his hands and knees. His flesh rippled, and his mind seemed to crack open and encapsulate more than he could've ever imagined. Wisps of black smoke drifted from his fingertips.

"What's happening to him?" Stormcry demanded.

"Stay back!" Somna growled.

"I am being . . . reborn . . . " Ashcroft gasped.

An explosion detonated in Ashcroft's gut and washed through his chest and upper arms. His breath whooshed from his lungs, and he collapsed to the ground. The pain left, replaced by a dull, relentless ache.

Is this how it felt for you, Father? Is this the feeling that drove you to madness?

The thought chased away the last vestiges of Ashcroft's consciousness, and he saw only blackness.

* * *

Powers looked at the thing Ashcroft had become with a mixture of fascination and horror. It almost served him right after all the evil he had done that his "godlike" form would be something so horrific and ugly, but Powers wouldn't have wished this on his worst enemy.

The mad scientist was barely human anymore. He still had normal human appendages, but that was where the similarities ended. Full, leathery wings had sprouted from his shoulder blades and were splayed over his body like a horrific blanket. His fingernails were long, black talons. His thin frame had become grotesquely muscular, so much so that his arms and chest had ripped through his lab coat and shirt, and his feet and clawed toes had shredded his socks and shoes. His wild, black hair was even stringier, hanging limply into his face. His skin had darkened to a sickly orange. Wisps of black smoke floated around his hands. Ashcroft had been unconscious since the transformation. The only evidence that he was alive was the shallow breaths that disturbed the black smoke.

"This is . . . " Audrey started. She didn't finish.

Powers was having trouble finding words himself. He had already been planning to leave Ashcroft when he had just been a mad scientist. But this thing? It looked like Ashcroft had achieved his goal; he had become more than human. There was no way Powers was sticking around for whatever Ashcroft would do next.

Artemis was the first to move. "We need to get him to a bed."

"*How?*" Powers exclaimed. "Look at him. He's like the Hulk. We'll never be able to carry him. And even if we could, how do you suggest we lay him on a bed when he's got those wings poking out?"

"I'll do it."

Zeke stepped forward, knelt, and scooped Ashcroft up in his arms. The super-strong man lumbered out of the lab, carrying their transformed employer.

"Stormcry, Lancet, get ready to move," Artemis said. "Ashcroft's last orders still stand. The two of you, Torrent, and I will hit the Sterling Labs convoy."

As Audrey stormed from the room, Powers backed into the shadows. He only had to bide his time. Maybe with the others distracted with the mission or after, when the others were celebrating, he could slip out unnoticed. But one thing was for sure: Powers couldn't root for Ashcroft in good conscience. The man had become a monster. As much as he hated the Turners and their super friends, Powers hoped they could beat Ashcroft. He didn't want to live in a world where a monster like this was running things.

CHAPTER 21

The early morning sun rested just above the curve of the Washington, D.C., Sterling Labs' domed façade. It created a beautiful, double-domed illusion too bright to look at. Still, Audrey let her gaze linger just below it a moment longer. She needed to see beauty after the horror she had witnessed the previous day. Ashcroft was a monster, the most hideous thing she could have imagined. Doubt filled her mind, and she questioned whether she had been wrong about him all along. If his new form was a sign of the ugliness inside him, he was not the man she had imagined. But it was too late now. She was too far into this to back out.

Audrey dropped her eyes to the loading dock on the back of the building. Security was tight. Six guards armed with automatic rifles stood on the dock while a crew loaded the dispersal unit aboard an armored truck. Two U.S. military Humvees were positioned to escort the package, each one occupied by four soldiers. Two more private security guards rode shotgun in the armored truck with the package.

The Regency's team had to wait until the truck left the dock to make their move, when the six guards with the disperser would be in the back of the truck and the convoy would be away from the lab. Every advantage helped. On the road, reinforcements would not be as readily available.

Artemis and Monahan lay in wait two miles down the road, and Zeke's mercenaries would close the trap in front of them. It was up to Audrey and Zeke to come from behind and complete the circle.

Zeke's professional tones broke the silence. "Package is in the truck."

He was the most experienced member of the team, which was why Ashcroft had chosen him and his mercs for this job. He'd pulled off dozens of heists like this in his time. Quinn and Mendez were the only two who could really compare, and even they had deferred to Zeke—albeit reluctantly, in Quinn's case. So, while Artemis was in charge of the mission, Zeke was the tactician giving them play-by-play instructions.

"The doors are closed." Zeke straightened. "The package is moving."

Zeke and Audrey each straddled a motorcycle. They would ride in behind the convoy, and Audrey would hit the rear Humvee with sonic blasts to knock it out. Zeke said the key to getting the package quickly was taking out the military escort first.

The lead Humvee rolled by. Audrey ducked behind the bushes to ensure she wasn't spotted. A moment later, the other two vehicles rumbled past. Audrey's pulse hammered. If she and Zeke were spotted now, the whole mission could be a bust. They couldn't leave without the device, so they would have to fight. Things would get ugly—uglier.

The troupe passed without incident. Audrey glanced up at Zeke, who nodded and gunned his engines.

"They're on the move." He peeled out. "Strike team, go!"

Audrey sped after him, and they fell into a holding pattern half a block back from the convoy. Get too close too fast, and the whole op would be blown. The soldier in the Humvee's top-mounted machine gun might see them and sound the alarm. Zeke's orders were to hold back until Artemis and Lancet sprang the trap.

Two minutes later, it happened. A beam of red energy slashed across the street, demolishing a fire hydrant. The beam cut into the side of the lead Humvee, spinning the vehicle in a circle. The energy blast was from Lancet; Monahan had picked up on her powers with eerie skill.

"Lancet has engaged," Zeke snapped. "Everyone, go!"

Stormcry screeched to a halt behind the rear Humvee, which was now spinning around to drive in the opposite direction. She fired two sonic blasts, striking the Humvee dead center in its grill, stopping the vehicle in its tracks and ripping the machine gun from its back.

The soldiers poured out as Torrent pulled up next to Stormcry. Torrent leaped forward and grabbed the rifle from the hands of one soldier, crumpling the barrel in his fist. Stormcry snapped out her leg in a high kick, catching the nearest soldier in the chin and knocking him back into the Humvee. Then, she extended her left hand and fired a blast of sound that caved his door in and crumpled it, trapping him inside.

A terrified shriek split the air. A stray beam of red energy ripped into the side of a building, sending debris crumbling down toward the sidewalk. But where had the scream come from? Stormcry scanned the street, using her aural detection abilities to hone in on the noise. An elderly couple knelt next to a parked car, cowering before the horrific sight of Lancet's energy blast.

Stormcry rushed to the couple. "Get out of here!"

Crack-crack-crack. Something impacted against Stormcry's back, knocking her forward. She raised her hands to fire a wild sonic blast. The soldier who shot her hurtled back and slammed into the truck. Stormcry reached around behind her, feeling the cracks in her padded suit where the bullets had struck. If not for her Kevlar armor, she would be dead. She turned back to the elderly couple, but they were already running into the nearest undamaged building.

Rage bubbled inside her. She had been trying to help the frightened elders, and that man hit her with a cheap shot. Stormcry charged toward the lead Humvee. Two soldiers remained standing. The armored car's back doors swung open, and the six navy-and-white-clad Sterling Labs security guards jumped out, rifles blazing.

Stormcry jumped for cover in front of the armored car. Her suit might resist a few shots, but a sustained barrage from multiple attackers would penetrate it. She clenched her fists and took a deep breath. Fighting angry would only get her killed. A metal bar twirled through the air and impaled one of her attackers. Torrent followed the hurtled bar, plowing into another guard.

The two soldiers from the leading Humvee peppered Torrent's mercs as they charged the truck. Stormcry blasted one of the soldiers in the back, knocking him flat on his face. Lancet grabbed the other by the collar. A bloodthirsty grin twisted across the blonde woman's face.

"Wait! Don't!" Stormcry shouted.

Lancet's eyes glowed, and she fired a beam of energy through the man's skull. Stormcry's stomach revolted. She swallowed the bile that threatened to rise. These men were just doing their jobs. There was no reason to kill them. They only needed to be taken out of commission. The driver was dead, too. From the mess of his chest, it looked like another of Monahan's blasts had cut through him. Somna stepped up to the truck and dragged the driver's corpse onto the ground.

"Let's move," Somna called.

Stormcry rounded the truck. Four of the six guards who had exited the truck lay on the ground now. Torrent wrestled with a fifth. The sixth went down as one of Torrent's mercs shot him in the back. Stormcry swallowed the bile that threatened to rise in her throat.

Torrent grabbed the last guard in a chokehold and twisted. The guard's neck snapped with a sickening crunch, and he collapsed.

Torrent straddled his motorcycle. "Mount up, Stormcry."

Stormcry nodded and walked back toward the bike, which was parked not far from the rearmost Humvee. Her eyes trailed across the jumble of bodies and destruction. Two of Torrent's mercenaries had gone down, but the rest of the bodies belonged to their enemies.

Stormcry mounted her bike and wiped away tears. Had any of the guards or soldiers survived? Between her allies' murder spree and Ashcroft's new, monstrous form, Stormcry wondered if she had been fooling herself the whole time. Was she on the right side at all? Or had Ashcroft's offer to heal her cancer blinded her to the truth of who he really was?

Stormcry gunned the bike's engine and sped after the armored truck. This wasn't over. Not by a long shot. And Stormcry wasn't sure whose side she really wanted to be on anymore.

* * *

Gideon pulled himself into another chin-up and held himself there. *One, two, three, four, five.* He dropped down and pulled up again. Amplified or not, it was important to keep himself physically fit. His martial arts training had saved him more than once, and he had to keep himself in shape in order to use those skills to maximum effectiveness.

The rest of Monday had passed with no reported sightings of Norris, Pierce, or Knight, let alone any of the escapees. After sunset, Gideon patrolled the Brooks with Carter, but they hadn't found any sign of the villains. If they hadn't left the city by now, they were idiots. But here or elsewhere, the Vindicators would catch them eventually.

Gideon dropped from the chin-up bar and squared up to a punching bag. The sooner they caught Ashcroft's lackeys, the better. With his mysterious spectral visitor and the involuntary burst of power he'd used to kill the cryptid, Gideon had enough problems in his own life without the supervillains causing trouble.

"There's been an attack in D.C.!" Dean rushed out of the ops room, looked around, and spotted Gideon. "A group of supervillains hit an armored convoy on the way to the Pentagon."

Speak of the devils. "The dispersal unit?"

"It's got to be. The emergency report went out on all Sterling channels."

"We knew it was only a matter of time."

Dean jerked his head toward the ops room, all business. "The Raptor can be in D.C. in half an hour, but we need to move now, before we lose the trail."

The last time Dean had been this focused and intense was when he discovered that his father was part of the plot to overtake Sojourn City with a criminal empire. When he got like this, he was serious, and Gideon had found it was best to go along with whatever he said. Gideon rushed into the ops room and pulled on his armor.

"Do we have time to gather the others?"

Dean slid on the plates to his own suit. "No way. Patrick's in school; Carter's at work; and I haven't heard from Wes. By the time they get to the airport, it'll be way too late."

"What about Jarrett and Hannah?"

"They're here, but—"

"Tell them to suit up." Gideon clenched his jaw. "Looks like we're giving the recruits a test run."

CHAPTER 22

Dean craned his neck to look out the Raptor's front viewscreen. "There's the truck. Looks like several motorcycles are escorting it."

Gideon pulled on his hood. Could the four of them handle this on their own? They could be outnumbered and overpowered. Jarrett wasn't amplified, and Hannah was still getting a handle on her abilities. She had a lot of potential, but most of the time, she fell back to using her guns. That might not be enough in this situation. They couldn't know how many of the Regency's amps were with the device.

Maddox would drop them off directly over the armored truck. Hopefully, that would give them the element of surprise. That, combined with Dean's teleportation, should be enough to take out at least a couple of the villains before the real fight began. That was the plan, anyway. If they could even the odds at the start, the rest of the fight might go better for them.

God, please give us victory. Gideon had played catch-up to Ashcroft for too long. It was time to get a win under the Vindicators' belts.

"Dropping in ten," Maddox called.

"All right, everyone in position." Gideon stepped toward the ramp. "You know your role. We catch them by surprise and take them out as quickly as possible. Keep an eye out for civilians. Our primary objective is saving lives, but if we can stop them from getting that device, even better."

"Don't worry, boss man." Jarrett slid an arrow into his crossbow. "We won't let you down."

Gideon slapped the control panel, and the ramp lowered. "Vindicators, move!"

He leaped off the ramp and flew parallel to the street, keeping low. The supervillains must have noticed the approaching plane, but he hoped the strafing run would make him harder to see. There were four bikes in front of the armored car, all driven by men in dark paramilitary uniform. Two more motorcycles came behind the armored car, driven by Torrent and Stormcry. The rest of the troupe must have been inside the armored truck. Gideon could not believe that Ashcroft would send only two of his amps to steal the device. There were more somewhere.

The Seraph arced around, coming at the convoy from the front. As he passed the line of lead motorcycles, he lashed out, kicking the back tire out from under the nearest bike. He tackled another mercenary from his bike. As the two bikes fell, the Seraph circled around to the back of the armored truck, unlatched the door, and yanked it open. He launched himself at Torrent's bike. He was the only one of the team equipped to take on the villain—and even that was a long shot.

By then, the green flash signaling Drifter's appearance crackled just above Knight's bike. Explosions and gunshots farther up the street indicated that Brass Bison and Yeoman had engaged the riders at the front of the group. The Seraph focused on Torrent and rocketed toward him.

Torrent pushed himself off his bike, looked up at the Seraph, and sneered. He gripped the handlebars, spun in a circle, hurled the vehicle at the Seraph, and immediately leaped after it. The Seraph blinked in surprise and dodged the bike, but Torrent attacked with full force. The

Seraph tumbled through the air and caught himself two stories up. He shoved at the super-strong villain, trying to dislodge him. Torrent clutched the Seraph's waist and squeezed. He grimaced as his breath rushed from his lungs. He had to do something—fast.

He discharged a blast of light from his body. The force of the blast hurled Torrent back to the ground. The Seraph struggled to maintain his altitude, righting himself over the road. Torrent hit a tree on the roadside, bending the trunk backwards and partially uprooting it. The Seraph soared down toward him and balled his light-enhanced fists.

"You don't have to do this, Norris! You've made some mistakes, but you don't have to be involved with these people."

Torrent climbed to his feet. "Oh, spare me."

He grabbed the tree trunk and ripped it from the ground, showering clumps of grass and dirt on his gray suit. The Seraph extended both hands and fired a light burst at Torrent's chest. He would do everything in his power to keep from engaging the villain hand-to-hand. At close range, Torrent had all the advantage. Torrent slid backward and dropped the tree on top of himself. The Seraph stepped forward.

Torrent hurled the tree like a spear, and the Seraph dropped to the ground. Leaves rustled as the tree soared over his head. The Seraph spat dirt from his mouth as he rose. *Wham.* The fist that struck his face hit like a jackhammer. The Seraph stumbled back and raised his arms defensively. Torrent swung another punch, striking Seraph in the ribs. His golden breastplate caved, and something internal cracked. The Seraph gasped, the air whooshing from his lungs, and stumbled backward.

He flailed his arms and managed to keep himself upright. He raised his left fist, and Torrent grabbed his wrist and squeezed. The Seraph screamed as the pressure increased. Something popped in his wrist, a miniature explosion of bone beneath his skin. Gritting his teeth, the Seraph raised his free hand and unleashed a beam of light into Torrent's face. Torrent cried out as he hurtled through the air.

The Seraph managed a deep, shuddering breath and looked down at his arm. It was fractured, along with at least one of his ribs. His aionium suit was bent inward from the force of Torrent's punch. Taking another, steadier breath, the Seraph faced his opponent. Torrent lay face-down on the sidewalk, unmoving.

The Seraph lifted into the air above the street. Torrent was down, at least for the moment, but there were still several threats back on the street. The Seraph rejoined the rest of his friends in securing the device.

* * *

With Yeoman engaging the mercenaries at the front of the convoy, Drifter handling Audrey Knight, and the Seraph locked in battle with Torrent, Brass Bison was left to secure the truck. She slipped her revolvers from their holsters and approached the vehicle. She felt tense in her new uniform. It was comfortable and sturdy, but she had no experience wearing it. The mask felt odd on her face. Her guns were the only source of normalcy in the situation.

Brass Bison had no way of knowing if there were others waiting inside the truck. Several supervillains were unaccounted for: the man in green, with his radioactive field; the prisoners who had escaped; more of the mercenaries. She swallowed, determined and ready to face them.

She took a cautious step toward the truck. The door hung ajar, pulled open by the Seraph in his initial descent, but it had swung closed as the vehicle screeched to a halt. Keeping her guns at the ready, she slid the barrel of her left-hand gun inside and used it to nudge the door open.

The door exploded outward. Bison conjured a paltry energy shield and grunted as the heavy metal slammed into her chest. She fell back, slamming hard into the pavement, and sucked in a breath. If not for her shield, the impact would have caved in her chest. As it was, each gasp of air sent a wave of pain through her abdomen. She crawled backward, away from the armored truck. Smoke rose from the opening. A feminine figure clad in black dropped onto the street. Her eyes glowed a cruel red, and she grinned wickedly as she approached Bison.

The woman laughed. "Do they give just anyone costumes these days? Pity. I was hoping for another chance at the Seraph—or at least, that I'd get to kill another Crusader."

"Who are you?"

"They call me Lancet."

Bison opened fire. Lancet threw herself aside, and beams of concussive red energy shot from her eyes. Bison tucked into a roll and squeezed the triggers until her revolvers clicked empty. Lancet's eye blasts disintegrated the bullets. For a moment, there was silence. The world around them seemed to close in until all that existed were the two of them, squaring off in the middle of a D.C. avenue.

Lancet waved her in. "Come on."

Bison holstered her pistols. She held her hands out to the side, and a pair of short swords, glowing bronze, appeared. Lancet's eyes widened and glowed brighter. Brass Bison somersaulted aside, and a beam of red light shot over her head. She sprung back to her feet and closed the remaining distance between them in three steps. She twirled her swords and swung them at Lancet's head. The woman ducked back, barely avoiding the energy blades. Bison continued the swing, bringing her left-hand blade in low. Lancet raised a knee, and the blade cut a thin furrow in the black cloth of her leggings.

She jabbed her fingertips at Bison's throat. Bison jerked her head to the side and ran the end of one of her swords into Lancet's shoulder. The villain recoiled at the cut, but she recovered quickly, spinning her leg into a high kick. Bison ducked under the blow, and Lancet brought her heel down on the back of Bison's head. She grunted and fell to the ground.

"Many better than you have tried to defeat me." Lancet's eyes glowed again. "What makes you think you can?"

Brass Bison jerked to the right as Lancet fired another laser beam from her eyes. The gauntlet on her left arm warmed. She reformed the energy in her palms, changing them from swords to a long staff, and swung it toward Lancet, who slapped the energy weapon aside with her palm. Bison kicked out her right leg, catching Lancet behind the left knee. Lancet stumbled forward, and Bison brought her left fist up into Lancet's face. She reeled back, and Bison advanced, driving her staff down toward Lancet's prone form. Lancet grabbed the rod of pure energy with both hands, just before the end touched her torso. She smirked, twisted the staff aside, and kicked upward. Brass Bison grunted as both heels struck her chest. Her grip on her staff loosened, and the weapon dissolved into nothingness. Bison struggled to catch her breath and brought up her hands in a ready position.

Lancet's eyes glowed again. "Impressive powers. Can you do anything without them?"

Brass Bison lunged to meet her.

* * *

Stormcry's feet touched the ground. *What?* One moment, she was riding her motorcycle behind the armored truck. The next, a pair of hands had touched her shoulders, and she was on a rooftop half a block away. She looked around for who had grabbed her and raised her hands defensively.

Drifter backflipped away from her, landed on his palms, and sprung backward, landing in a ready stance, a circular shield on either arm. Stormcry lowered her hands. If she could catch him off-guard, this fight would go easier for her.

"I know who you are." Drifter's gaze drilled into her. "I thought you were dead."

"The celebrity Audrey Knight is dead." She took a step forward. "I am Stormcry. And you, Dean Sterling, are a rebel against the Evolving."

She fired a sonic blast at him. Drifter disappeared in a flash of green light. Stormcry looked around. *Thump.* Something struck the small of her back. She tucked, rolled, came up in a crouch. Drifter stood where Stormcry had been just a moment before, his arms held casually at his sides.

"Coward." She rose and resumed a ready stance. "Stand and fight."

"Why?" Drifter shook his head. "I don't have a problem with you, Audrey. My problem is with your *boss.* Ashcroft's plan is going to hurt a lot of people. I'll fight you if I have to, but I'd prefer if you just stepped aside."

Stormcry raised an eyebrow. Was he really asking her to back down? Stormcry answered to a greater calling. He had no idea of the good they could do. If he did, he surely would have joined them. Turner's leadership had blinded Dean. She had seen the good Sterling did for Sojourn City. A man like that could not resist positive change. If only she could make him see.

"I can't do that." She extended a hand and gathered a sonic pulse in her palm, but she didn't fire it. "I don't think you are a bad person. I think you have been misguided. Please, if you could only see what we hope to achieve, you would understand."

"Ashcroft's plan isn't going to help anyone. The more people have superpowers, the more people are going to die."

Her own doubts returned to the forefront of her mind. She'd always feared collateral loss, but she had believed that Ashcroft would know how to avoid that. Only Pierce and Zeke were so callous as to find human loss acceptable. At least, that's what she had thought. But every member of the strike team had gone about murdering the soldiers and guards in the convoy. They hadn't shown any regard for their lives. And what if Ashcroft was every bit the cold killer that they were? What if she was wrong about him, about the Regency? Maybe Ashcroft's physical transformation had allowed her to finally see the man he truly was.

"People die, anyway." She tried to make the words, copied from her companions, sound convincing, but they rang false even to her own ears. "If good people have powers, they can overcome the bad."

"Even if the bad people have powers, too?" Drifter stepped forward. "Terrorists, rapists, murderers . . . You're really going to tell me it's a good idea to give those people superpowers?"

Stormcry blinked. "I—"

A pillar of energy ripped into a building nearby. *Monahan, no doubt.* "I've got to go. There will be people in there who need my help. Please, think about what I've said."

In a blink of green light, he was gone. Stormcry stared at the place he had stood a moment before. He was putting his life at risk to protect people that were in danger because of Quinn's actions. Zeke or Pierce never would have done that. And Artemis would never have told them to.

Ashcroft would have, right? Audrey wasn't so sure what he would have done. Not anymore. He had saved her life. He had cured her of cancer. He said he wanted to provide the same help to the rest of the world, but was that what he really wanted? Or were Ashcroft's motives darker than he had let on?

Audrey flew over the fight and hovered high in the air. Zeke's last two mercs had the archer pinned behind a tree. Every time the archer peeked out to fire an arrow, they peppered him with rifle fire. At the back of the truck, the Seraph and the orange-clad woman armed with revolvers were battling Zeke and Monahan.

This was madness. There was a small-scale war taking place in downtown D.C. over one piece of technology. Was it worth it?

Suddenly, the armored truck's tires screeched, and the vehicle shot forward. *Artemis!* She hadn't joined the fight; she'd only been waiting for her chance to escape. The truck plowed over the two remaining mercenaries before they saw it coming. The Seraph launched toward the truck and braced himself. He squared his shoulders and held his hands out. The truck barreled into him and pushed him forward, but he held onto the grill and pushed back.

Audrey shook her head. She didn't want to be involved in any of this. Maybe she should help Drifter with the burning building.

She flew in that direction. On the sidewalk in front of the building, several dozen people watched the fire. Audrey landed next to them.

"The man who saved you—where is he?"

There was a green blink off to her left. She found Drifter standing next to her with a teenage boy. The boy nodded to his savior, thanked him, and limped over to join the crowd. Drifter glanced at Audrey and raised an eyebrow.

"Is there anyone else in there?" she asked.

He shook his head. "He was the last one. Now, if you'll excuse me, I'm going to go help my friends."

"Wait—"

Another green flash, and he was gone.

CHAPTER 23

As he teleported back into the battle, Drifter's mind reeled. *Had Audrey Knight really come to help me save innocent people instead of joining her Regency friends in fighting to get the device back?* Maybe his words on the rooftop were more effective than he had expected them to be. He hoped she took them to heart. He could tell that she was not like the others. She was a good person who'd been misled.

But now wasn't the time to hope for her redemption. His friends still needed his help. Brass Bison was tangling with Katrina Monahan, of all people, who was firing beams of red energy from her eyes. *Carter's gonna love that.* Bison rolled aside and hurled darts of bronze energy at Monahan, while blocking the assassin's concussive blasts with a circular shield formed from the same energy. Hannah was getting better with her powers. That was good, but Monahan still had her in retreat. Drifter loosened the latch on his right-hand shield. He'd designed them to retract into his gauntlets, but they could also detach.

Drifter hurled the shield at Monahan's solar plexus. The aionium disc sliced through the air and into the villain. Monahan crumpled to the pavement. Drifter rushed in and put a hand on Bison's shoulder.

"You okay?"

"Yeah. Nice throw!"

"Thanks. Let's get to the truck."

The truck's tires spun in place, fighting against an unseen obstacle. Drifter scooped up his fallen shield, grabbed Bison, and teleported them inside the rear of the truck. The device sat in the middle of the rear compartment, strapped down with thick cords.

Through the window of the cab, Drifter glimpsed the long, curly locks of Somna's hair. Outside the truck, a glowing form pushed back against the vehicle. *Gideon!* A flicker of worry clutched at Dean's heart, but he forced himself to focus on the task at hand. Gideon had stopped a train before; he should be able to hold the truck long enough for them to reclaim the device. Drifter moved to one of the cables, raised his shield, and slashed through it.

"Help me get this loose."

Bison projected a knife, knelt next to the device, and cut at another cord. Drifter slashed another one loose. Two more to go. He raised his arm, and searing heat scorched his elbow. A red beam of light sheared through the truck and through Drifter's arm. He screamed and stumbled back, clutching his elbow, the rancid smell of scorched flesh filling his nostrils. The pain was so hot, so intense, that he nearly passed out on the spot.

"Drifter!"

Bison rushed to Drifter's side and looked at his arm. Her eyes went wide. Suddenly all Dean felt was numbness, and he knew it had to be bad. Monahan stood just outside the truck, her eyes a fiery red. They glowed brighter, and she grinned wickedly.

"Goodbye," she said.

Drifter braced himself.

A concussive blast knocked Monahan forward. She fell against the ajar truck door and crumpled to the ground. *Who?* Audrey floated into the truck and put an arm around Drifter.

"What are you doing?" Bison exclaimed.

"Saving him. Come on."

Drifter felt himself fading from consciousness. He tried to tell them that they had to get the device, that it was very important to keep it out of Ashcroft's hands, but his voice didn't work. He blinked rapidly. *Stay awake, Dean . . .*

Stay . . . awake . . .

* * *

The Seraph pushed back against the truck with all his might. The metal grill dug in around his palms. He was fully horizontal, hovering a few feet over the street and applying all the force he could to keep the truck in place. The grill bent and warped under his glowing fists. He reached up and grabbed the hood with one hand and then the other. Every muscle in his body trembled as he pushed against the truck, and it pushed back. Baring his teeth, the Seraph let out a strangled growl and surged forward, forcing the truck back. He couldn't keep this up forever. And if the truck ran him down, he was durable, not invincible. Wes could stand up to it, but Gideon would be flattened as surely as any pedestrian.

What if I disable the truck?

Holding back the vehicle's weight with his right hand, he reared back his left and drove his fist into the engine block. If he could find something essential and break it free, the truck would be worthless. He probed around, and something stronger than the truck plowed into him from his left side. He grunted as the unexpected projectile hurled him out of the street. The truck's tires squealed, and the vehicle shot away. The Seraph shook his head and tried to push himself up.

An impossibly strong fist struck his back. Ignoring the pain, the Seraph brought his arm up to block a follow-up blow. He stumbled back and raised a hand as Torrent lunged, bringing both hands down in a haymaker punch. The Seraph weaved aside and shot a burst of light into Torrent's kidneys. The villain howled and dropped to his knees. The Seraph brought a light-encased fist down on Torrent's jaw. The villain finally sunk to the ground, unconscious.

Yeoman rushed up to the Seraph. "You good?"

"Yeah." Gideon wiped a stream of blood from his lip. "They got away with the device."

"We'll catch her, but not now. Drifter's hurt. Bad."

Gideon spun, looking for his best friend. But they couldn't just leave the villains to get away. If they did, they had accomplished nothing here; they'd lost. He glanced back at the ever-shrinking truck. Dean's life was more important.

"I hate to say it, but you're right. We let them go for now."

A gust of wind tugged at Gideon's hood. He looked up at the sky. The Raptor was already descending. Gideon stepped away from Torrent.

"All right, let's—" Sirens wailed, and red-and-blue lights flashed. "Are you kidding me?"

Five black SUVs pulled up. Gideon held his hands carefully away from his sides and brought his hood down. Superheroes were legal in Sojourn City, but most of the country had yet to follow suit. As vigilantes, the Vindicators were technically just as criminal in this situation as Ashcroft's people. It would be best not to spook the authorities and instigate a crisis. A dozen armed men in black tactical suits rushed from the SUVs and trained their rifles on the heroes.

"Hands up!" one shouted. "Do not move!"

"Our friend is hurt. We don't have time for this. Feel free to take those who are unconscious into custody. But let us go."

"No one's going anywhere." The man gestured to Torrent and the other downed villains. His men moved in with handcuffs. "We're not just going to take your word for it that you're the good guys."

"Look, I'm sorry." Gideon raised his hands. "We have to."

"Not an option." His rifle zeroed on Gideon's chest. The bullet wouldn't even scratch his aionium armor, but the government agent didn't know that. "Hands up!"

Gideon glanced over his shoulder. Hannah and Audrey were loading Dean onto the Raptor. Maybe he and Jarrett should stay behind. It would look better than trying to run from federal agents, and it would give the others a chance to get medical help.

"Wait!"

Jarrett held up a hand to the black-clad government agents. "He's telling the truth."

Gideon gaped at him. *What is he doing?*

"They're on our side." Jarrett slung his crossbow over his shoulder and removed his wallet from his belt. "Agent Jarrett Mercer, CLOUD, clearance level beta."

CLOUD? Gideon furrowed his brow and stared at Jarrett.

The government agent lowered his weapon. "Sorry, sir. I didn't know. We'll—"

"Hey!"

Gideon swiveled in the direction of the shout. The agent who had been cuffing Torrent lay on his back. The villain scowled, looked up at the sky, and leaped. His jump carried him over the nearest buildings and out of sight. Gideon looked back. Monahan had disappeared, too. Only Audrey Knight remained.

There was nothing he could do about losing Torrent or Lancet, but his stomach churned at the thought of so many failures in one day. He tried to focus on the situation in front of him. Jarrett had been a government agent all this time and had failed to mention it even once. He spun on Jarrett and surged forward.

"Have you been spying on us?"

"It's not like that." Jarrett shook his head. "Gideon, you have to understand—"

"It wasn't an accident that you ran into us while we were chasing the cryptid, was it?" No wonder Gideon had sensed that Jarrett was hiding something. He felt energy building in his hands. "You were there because you had orders to be there."

Jarrett clenched his jaw. "Yes."

No wonder Jarrett had been so quick to offer his help, and no wonder he had asked to join the team. He hadn't been doing it out of the kindness of his heart; he'd been on a mission. And worse, Gideon had sensed that he was hiding something, and he'd chosen to ignore it because he believed Jarrett was a good guy. He'd let a potential threat into their base.

"Look, Gideon, it's nothing against you. Really. I actually did fully intend to help you, and I am on your side."

"Are you even really a vigilante?"

"I was . . . I am." Jarrett sighed. "CLOUD picked me up a few months ago for my vigilante activities. They were going to toss me in jail, but they offered me a chance to make a difference instead by becoming an agent. I took them up on the offer. What else could I do? But nothing I told you was a lie. I just . . . omitted details."

"We don't have time for this. We need to get Dean help. Come with us if you want; I don't care. But you've got a lot of explaining to do."

"I know." Jarrett's next words were directed at the agent. "Tell the Director that we'll handle the situation from here."

Gideon jumped into the Raptor and walked straight to Dean. His breaths were short and choppy. His face was pale, and sweat beaded on his brow and pasted his curly brown hair to his forehead and cheeks. But the worst damage, by far, was to his left arm. It had been completely severed below the elbow, the skin there burned dark. The heat of Monahan's beam had cauterized the wound, and Dean was not at risk of bleeding out. Gideon supposed that was a blessing hidden in an otherwise terrible situation. But even so, Dean was in bad shape. The shock alone could be deadly.

"Maddox!" Gideon called. "Get us back to Sojourn City—now."

He pulled a blanket from an emergency compartment and draped it over Dean, who was shivering violently. The ramp's pistons whined as it closed, and the plane ascended.

Gideon probed everyone in the plane with his mind. Jarrett had come aboard with them. Gideon sensed his presence at the back of the compartment, alone and upset. Gideon wasn't sure if he was glad or furious that the archer was there. And Audrey was there, too. Had she thrown in her lot with them? What had caused the sudden change in heart?

He focused his attention on Dean's wounded arm, and as he did, he saw a flicker of white out of the corner of his eye. He raised his head and, for a moment, saw the apparition of Wyatt Jonson sitting at the back of the plane. The Raptor rattled as it hit turbulence—and Wyatt was gone. Gideon shook his head. He had to focus. His best friend needed him.

CHAPTER 24

Red thumbtacks marked the map of Sojourn City, each representing a location that Jolie had searched for Luca Serban and come up empty. There were a lot of red thumbtacks.

Jolie stared at the map. Most of the places she'd checked were in the Brooks. She had spoken with a few informants, urging them to come to her with any rumors they might hear about Serban's return. Carter was combing rooftops and warehouses, looking for any sign of the crime lord. But the truth was, all of their efforts might wind up being for nothing. If the superhuman convicts had escaped the city without detection, it was entirely possible that Serban had, too.

But where would he go? Back to Romania? From what Jolie knew of Serban's past, he had moved to the U.S. because he was up against the glass ceiling in his own country. His Romani heritage kept him from rising to the top in any organization headed by Romanian nationals. His search for advancement led him to Sojourn City. It was unlikely he'd give up and crawl back to his old masters like a wounded dog.

More than that, Jolie's gut told her he was still in the city. She had learned a long time ago to trust her instincts. She had been right about Gideon's secret identity, even when that had seemed ridiculous. She had been right about Detective Simon Walters working for Serban's mob via Katrina Monahan. She had been right about Vince Powers hunting for Wes. Jolie's gut was rarely wrong, so she was all but certain that Serban was still around.

But where?

"You stare at that map any longer, you'll burn a hole in it."

Jolie's former partner, Paul Jordan, leaned against her cubicle, a wry smile on his face. Paul was a middle-aged beat cop, nearing retirement, but the wrinkles on his mahogany-colored skin had more to do with laugh lines than age. He was like a second father to Jolie, and she knew she could count on Paul for a laugh or a word of encouragement. He'd always had her back.

"Hey." She forced a smile. "Sorry, I'm just . . . really focused on trying to find Serban."

"I can see that. Actually, that's what brings me by. Someone's here to see you—FBI agent by the name of Ross."

"Thanks, Paul."

"You bet." He started to turn, but he looked back. "Take it from me, Jolie. Don't let this guy get in your head. Once he does, you'll never catch him."

Jolie stared down at her desk. Maybe Serban *had* gotten in her head. She was determined to catch him because she wanted to keep him from harming her loved ones. Serban was a man of means, and he had an axe to grind with most of the people in Jolie's life. If he wanted revenge, he'd find a way to get it. Maybe she was so focused on finding him that she was overthinking it. She had to be missing something. But she would have to figure out what that was later. There was a federal agent waiting for her.

She rose and weaved her way through the bullpen. Agent Ross stood near the front door of the precinct with his hands clasped in front of his waist. As Jolie approached, he removed his sunglasses and tucked them in his suit pocket. Jolie resisted the urge to roll her eyes. *So cliché.* She plastered a fake smile on her face and extended a hand.

"Agent Ross. How can I help you?"

Ross shook her hand. "I'm here to follow up on your progress with the Serban investigation."

"I don't have anything for you. And since a federal agent is asking a local detective about an investigation, you must not be doing so hot, either."

"Afraid not. Luca Serban appears to be very skilled at not being found. We hoped you might have some insight. Safehouses, old haunts . . . "

"I'm sorry, Agent Ross, I—" Jolie frowned. *Wait . . .*

Safehouses. She'd mostly checked locations in the Brooks, but Serban had holdings in other parts of the city, too, maybe including the house where Jolie had first seen Monahan—as Regina Langston. Monahan had been working for Serban at the time, so it made sense that she might stay where he could get to her easily. Maybe he had loaned the property to her.

"Actually, I have an idea." She held up a finger. "Stay here. Let me get my badge and gun, and I'll go with you."

Before Ross could respond, Jolie rushed to her desk. She had no idea if this lead would pan out, but she didn't have much else to work with. They were on a timetable, and Serban wasn't going to wait around for them to come looking. This was a long shot, but it made sense that he might hide at a property that no one knew he owned. And if she was wrong, at least no harm was done.

Jolie retrieved her badge and gun and hurried back to where Ross was waiting. She shot him a nod and moved past him to exit the precinct. Ross's dress shoes clacked on the steps as he led the way to his black SUV.

"Where are we going?" he asked.

Jolie climbed into the passenger seat. "A residential subdivision just outside the Brooks. Start driving. I'll show you where to go."

She considered calling Carter for backup—he was the closest of the Vindicators, and the most familiar with Serban with Gideon and Dean out of town—but she didn't know Ross's opinion on vigilantes, so she decided to play it safe. If she needed backup, Patrick could be there—with Carter in tow—in moments.

It only took ten minutes to reach their destination. The house was in a peaceful neighborhood that didn't see much crime. Judging from the overgrown look of the lawn, no one had lived there in some time—not since Monahan had vacated it, Jolie guessed. It was late afternoon, and there were no lights on, inside or out.

"Doesn't look like much," Ross said.

"That's the point." Jolie unbuckled her seatbelt and exited the car. "Watch your step. If Serban's here, he won't be caught by surprise."

Ross checked his gun. "No problem."

Jolie secured a bulletproof vest provided by Ross and tied her hair back in a ponytail. Drawing her sidearm, she walked up the sidewalk toward the front door.

Ross trailed her and stepped onto the porch, flanking the door from the left. Jolie stood to the right, bit her lip, and nodded to Ross. He reached for the doorknob. Jolie's heart thumped in her chest. *He's just a criminal; he's not even amplified.* One good shot would take Serban down. Still, her palms were sweaty, and every nerve was alert. Serban was one of the most dangerous men in the city, regardless of his mortality.

Ross inched the door open and peered in, poking the barrel of his gun through first. He nodded and pushed it in the rest of the way. Jolie swiveled to stand in the doorway and raised her gun. Even in the dark, Jolie could tell the living room was empty. She stepped inside and swept her weapon back and forth, scanning the room. She clicked on a flashlight and held it underneath her gun hand.

Dust coated everything—the couches, the coffee table, the TV stand. She wrinkled her nose at the musty smell. *Maybe I was wrong.* She glanced back at Ross, who withdrew his flashlight and stepped into the house behind her.

Jolie tilted her head to the left. "Hallway."

The kitchen was directly ahead and had a screen door at the back that connected it to the fenced-in backyard. It was divided from the living room by a counter, but it was open enough to see that it was empty. The hallway she'd indicated led to the rest of the house—and, hopefully, to Serban.

Ross moved toward the hallway and leaned against the wall for cover. He shone his light down the hall and peered around.

"Four doors," he whispered. "The closer one on the left is open. The others are closed."

Jolie was glad the floors were carpeted. It would muffle their footsteps. She approached the open doorway.

"Clear." It was an empty bedroom—no dressers, no beds, nowhere to hide.

Ross walked past her to the next closest door, which was on the right side of the hallway. He put his hand on the doorknob. Jolie trained her gun on the door, and Ross pushed it open.

"Clear. Bathroom. It's empty."

Jolie took a deep breath. Her heart pounded like a drum at a rock concert, and the rate increased with every room they checked. *Stay calm.* She motioned for Ross to move to the remaining door on the left. He crept toward it while Jolie covered him. He pushed it open.

Crack-crack-crack!

Ross spasmed and dropped to the floor. Jolie's eyes widened as she realized the shots had come from behind. She spun on her heel and fired. Serban stood in the doorway of the empty bedroom. Jolie's shots struck the wall next to him. Serban ducked back into the room, stuck his arm out, and fired an automatic pistol. Jolie threw herself into the bathroom as bullets shredded the wall around her. She dropped into a crouch and peered around the corner. Serban was leaning out of the doorway, firing shot after shot. Jolie raised her gun and pulled the trigger. Serban grunted and clutched his thigh.

"Luca Serban, drop your weapon!" Jolie shouted.

Serban limped into the hallway and backed toward the living room, still firing at Jolie. She pulled her head back inside the bathroom as bullets punctured the doorframe. She took a deep breath, held it for four seconds, and exhaled through her nose, a technique she had picked up from studying Gideon.

She jumped up and returned to the hallway. Serban was in the living room. Jolie snapped off a series of shots. The crime lord threw himself over the counter and into the kitchen. Jolie rushed after him. She rounded the corner and saw him running through the backyard. She trained her gun on his back.

"Freeze!"

Serban fired a wild burst. The spray of bullets shattered the glass door to Jolie's left. She threw herself back into the kitchen as he fired again. She peered back into the yard, and he was gone. He must have jumped the fence.

Jolie lowered her gun. *Ross!* Holstering her weapon, Jolie sprinted down the hall and knelt next to the FBI agent. There was no blood. His vest had taken the shots. She rolled him onto his back.

"Ross, are you okay? Agent Ross?"

She felt for a pulse, and he groaned. "Did you . . . get him?"

"No. He got away."

Ross cursed. "Back to square one."

"Not necessarily." Jolie helped him to his feet. "We can get out a BOLO. We know he's in this neighborhood. Every officer in the vicinity can be combing the streets for him. It's only a matter of time before we've got him."

"I hope you're right, Detective." Ross grimaced. "Because as long as that nut job is on the streets, nobody's safe."

CHAPTER 25

Maddox called ahead to Arianna to instruct her to prepare everything they needed to operate on Dean. By the time Gideon and Maddox, working together, carried Dean upstairs to the training room, there was an operating table, a supply cart, and surgical tools waiting for them. Carter and Patrick rushed alongside them, barraging them with questions. Gideon cut them off with a glare, and Wes grabbed the younger men by their shoulders and held them back. Gideon eased Dean onto the table. Sweat drenched Dean's clammy skin.

Gideon peeled his armor plates off. "I'm going to go wash up. Arianna, Maddox, get prepped. You're helping me. He needs fluids."

Gideon hurriedly showed them how to start an IV. He had never installed a prosthetic limb before. He could treat Dean's symptoms, clean the wound, and so on, but Arianna and Maddox would have to do most of the legwork on installing the arm.

He went to the nearest bathroom and pulled scrubs over his super suit. He washed his hands thoroughly and looked at his reflection. His eyes were bloodshot, and his hair was a mess. He had a few bruises and a blood-stained upper lip from his fight with Torrent. His body screamed at him every time he moved, and even breathing was agony.

He pulled on a mask and a pair of surgical gloves, taking extra care with the glove on his injured left hand, and he walked back into the training room. Arianna and Maddox had also scrubbed up and stood at the table next to Dean, who was already hooked to an IV.

"G-Gideon . . . " Dean muttered.

"I'm here, buddy."

Gideon checked the IV Arianna had run. She had done a good job. No surprise. The two geniuses were quick learners. Gideon set to work getting anesthetized. He had not done that since his days as a surgeon. In a strange way, it was like reliving old times. He stilled his trembling hands and calmed the stream of light that shone through his gloves. *God, please help me to save Dean.*

"Let's do this."

* * *

As Gideon, Maddox, and Arianna prepped for surgery, Wes guided Carter and Patrick down to the living room and clenched his fists. They looked as downcast as Wes would have felt if there hadn't been another emotion consuming his attention—*rage.*

They had been betrayed. Gideon had called Wes on his way in and told him the news. They trusted Jarrett enough to bring him along and let him join the team, and Jarrett had lied to their faces. He was a government agent, which meant that he'd been spying on them all along. He knew their secret identities, so the government probably had them, too. If they ever decided to round up amps and run tests on them, there would be no way for the Vindicators to hide.

Patrick and Carter walked into the kitchen, neither one speaking. Hannah sat on the couch, and Audrey Knight stood at the base of the stairway and looked up, as if waiting for news on Dean. That was one more oddity to add to everything. He wondered why this supervillain was tagging along with them.

As Jarrett walked past, Wes grabbed him by the shoulder and shoved him up against the wall. Jarrett blinked in surprise. Wes touched the brick pillar behind Jarrett's head, and his right arm took on the dark hue and rough texture. He pressed that hand against Jarrett's chest.

"You'd better have a good explanation."

"Wes!" Hannah shouted.

"Shut up. You haven't been on this team long enough to form an opinion." He looked over at Patrick and Carter. "You two stay there."

Patrick furrowed his brow. "What's going on?"

"Yeah, chill out." Carter held up his palms. "Clue us in."

Jarrett grunted. "We can talk this out. I'll explain everything, but I think we should wait for Gideon. It's only fair that he hears, too."

Wes clenched his jaw and stared at Jarrett. He was right. Gideon deserved to hear the explanation as much as the rest of them. He was the one who had brought Jarrett onto the team in the first place. Reluctantly, Wes lowered his hand and faded his skin back to flesh.

"I'm keeping an eye on you."

Patrick looked dumbfounded. "What . . . "

"You tell them, Jarrett." Wes stormed up the steps. "If you have the guts."

He walked into the ops room and stared at his suit, resting in its place on a mannequin. He should have been there with them. He could've helped, and Dean might not have been injured. Why hadn't they called him? *They took the newbies, but not me.* And they had failed the mission. What happened now? He walked back downstairs. Jarrett stood near the window, looking out at the city. He and Hannah were still in their uniforms.

"You two get comfortable. Go change. My guess is we'll be here a while."

Hannah headed upstairs first, and Jarrett finally trailed behind her. Wes took a water bottle out of the fridge. As he took a drink, he considered whether he was really angry at Jarrett or at Gideon and Dean for not calling him. Or maybe it was because they had failed to stop Ashcroft's team. He swallowed the cold water.

"Is it true?" Patrick asked. "Is Jarrett really a spy?"

"He's working for the government, and he didn't bother telling us. Seems a bit suspect, don't you think?"

Carter's jaw was working overtime. "He had to have a reason, right? I mean . . . he's been helping us out."

Patrick nodded. "Yeah. I don't think he's a bad guy."

"I can't say if he is or not." Wes slammed his water bottle down on the counter. "But he lied. How do we know we can trust anything he says?"

He looked past the two teenagers. Audrey paced across the living room. Crossing the room in five long strides, Wes drew up face-to-face with her.

"What are you doing here?"

Audrey looked up at him and blinked. "What?"

"Don't make me repeat myself. I'm already in a bad mood." Wes stepped toward her. "Why did you come with them?"

"I . . . don't know." Audrey looked down at her mask, which was cradled in her palms. "I didn't know what else to do."

"Why did you turn on the Regency?"

"Your friend Dean made me realize that Dr. Ashcroft's plans may not be as noble as he has led me to believe. And judging by the actions of my former teammates, it seems like he may be right. And your team—your friends—I've seen you all go out of your way to help people. My friends never even tried."

So, one of them had a conscience. That was nice to see. But they had already been deceived once by someone allegedly wanting to join the team and help stop Ashcroft. Wes would have preferred to leave her out of it and avoid the possibility of being lied to again. The team had been doing just fine before Jarrett and Audrey. But that would be up for Gideon to decide. His empathic powers should be able to pick up on whether Audrey was being genuine.

If she was, it would be to their advantage. Ashcroft's cronies were powerful, and they were hard to beat. Having Audrey on their side might even things up a bit, especially if they decided not to keep Jarrett around. Plus, she brought insider knowledge that might prove invaluable in stopping Ashcroft's plan before it came to fruition. Wes forced himself to relax his scowl and offer her the best smile he could muster.

"It's nice to see that someone around here can be transparent," he said. "Do you want to change out of your uniform? I'm not sure we have any extra clothes, but there might be someone I can call."

Audrey hesitated and then bobbed her head. "That would be nice."

Wes pulled out his phone and dialed Jolie. "Could you get to the lair as soon as possible? Bring a change of clothes with you, if you don't mind. We've got a lot to talk about."

CHAPTER 26

Seven years ago

The floor beneath Ashcroft's feet seemed completely solid. There was no evidence that anything other than stone was underneath. But he knew there was. There had to be. Still, there was no way for him to get down there using the supplies they had. Ashcroft and Roger returned to their tent outside the catacombs for the night, only to make the trek back to the spot early the next morning with pickaxes. Together, they chipped away at the floor.

"Are you sure this is the right spot?" Roger asked.

"It must be." Ashcroft smashed his axe into the floor. "The energy readings are strongest here. That means there must be less resistance than anywhere else in the catacombs."

He swung again. Sweat soaked his body, sticking his shirt to his back. He was not used to manual labor, but he was too close to give in now. He would chip away until his heart gave out if that was what it took. This work was too important for him to give up. He would show Mark and Adler and everyone else that he was not the buffoon they took him for. He would prove that his father was not a madman. Ashcroft was right about humanity, right about the Nephilim. They were just too scared to admit that they needed to evolve. Father had seen it. Why couldn't they?

Ashcroft's pickax came down on a notch carved in the floor.

A trap door swung open beneath Ashcroft's feet. He screamed as he fell, his stomach remaining behind in the catacombs above. *This is it; I'm going to die.*

He met the ground with a painful crash, his body racking with the impact. His ears rang, and his head spun. Grimacing, Ashcroft pushed himself to his feet. The room was dark, lit only by an artificial blue glow. It felt like being in an aquarium.

Five tanks lined the small room, three on one side and two on the other. The tanks were filled with bubbling liquid, the source of the blue light. And within each tank was a body. They looked human, but not entirely. Their mass was greater, their features otherworldly. They had to be eight feet tall, at least. Ashcroft took a tentative step toward one.

These tanks . . . The technology was beyond anything Ashcroft had ever seen. Based on the dust and cobwebs, they hadn't been disturbed for a very long time. Ashcroft laughed. He was right. Whoever invented these machines had done so at the same time these catacombs were dug. As advanced as they seemed, the tanks—and the beings they held—were ancient.

"Doctor!" Roger called. "Are you all right?"

Ashcroft looked up the shaft. "Yes! Get some rope and get down here!"

He pressed a hand against the nearest tank and shook his head in disbelief. *I found them. I found the Nephilim. We were right, Father, and now the whole world will know it.*

CHAPTER 27

Present Day

Jeremiah Ashcroft liked to think that he knew his followers better than they knew themselves. Artemis was prideful and egocentric, and she took pleasure in manipulating others. And she was marvelously easy to manipulate herself. Given the impression that she was in control, she could be made to do anything. He knew that because he knew her. He knew all of them that well. He got to know them intimately over months of experimenting and watching them learn to use their powers.

They never surprised him. Never.

But Audrey Knight's betrayal had. He had been certain the girl was in the palm of his hand. She was his most faithful follower. He was her miracle worker, her savior. She was indebted to him. Out of any of them, he would have expected her to turn on him least of all. Yes, she had the strongest conscience, but she also had the strongest faith in him. Yet here they were.

Who else do I have to watch? Artemis was ambitious, but he knew she would never betray him. She couldn't. The neural inhibitor he installed in her would fry her brain if she tried. He never told her that, of course. He only told her that he was immune to her control, and she had no idea that it was because of the inhibitor in her own brain.

The rest of them were either too loyal or too lazy. Ashcroft did not believe any of them had the gall to betray him. Maybe Monahan, the newcomer, but he had instructed Artemis to keep a close eye on her. She would not be a problem.

They would deal with Audrey's betrayal when the time came. For now, he had other matters to attend to.

He stepped into the loading bay on the back wall of his base, the tips of his new wings brushing the edges of the door. Backfire and Red Raider flanked him. A pair of guards, members of Torrent's mercenary group, looked up at him and backed away, their fear evident on their faces. He grinned. Ashcroft had always been a small, unthreatening man. Now, he was the alpha. Their fear fueled him.

When he had awakened hours before, lying on his stomach, he had struggled to see. Everything was dark and blurry. He had grabbed the edges of his bed and rolled over, and something pinched on his back. He looked back. *Are those wings?* He had jumped off his bed and craned his neck. Yes, there were large, bat-like wings protruding from his back. His wings matched the sickly orange color of the rest of his flesh, and black nails like talons protruded from his fingers.

His muscle mass had more than doubled. Perhaps more than tripled. He was almost too tall to fit through the base's doorways.

His black hair hung in tangled knots around his head. His brow had grown heavy, giving him a menacing glower. His eyes, however, contained that same spark of intellect. He was still Jeremiah Ashcroft, but he was also more.

Why had it changed him physically? Even Father's serum, completely free of Nephilim DNA, had only enhanced his muscle mass. It had not mutated his skin or caused him to sprout wings. Other than being unnaturally muscular, Solar Flare had looked human. Ashcroft did not. Had he failed?

He had looked down at his hands again, studying them as black smoke wafted up from his fingertips. He'd pointed his left hand at a table across the room. A column of smoke shot forward, wrapped around the table, and shattered it against the wall. He struggled to crush a rising swell of disappointment inside him. He wasn't like Father at all. He was nearly the antithesis. How had Gideon Turner inherited Solar Flare's powers, while Ashcroft was transformed into a monster? It should have been Ashcroft shining a golden light for the world to see. Instead, he cast shadows.

He may not have replicated his father's powers exactly, but his own powers were godlike, beyond those of any of his followers. The Vindicators would be unable to stand against him.

The armored truck pulled into the loading bay. It was almost time—at last—for the Evolving. They would see. They would understand him. The machine would require some modifications before it was ready to go, and he had to finish the synthetic serum and ensure it would work with the machine. But in that time, he had other ways that his followers could work toward their goals and distract the rebels at the same time.

Ashcroft applauded with giant hands. "Well done!"

Artemis stepped out of the truck. "Thank you, my lord."

Zeke jumped out of the back of the truck, carrying the device. Ashcroft gestured toward his lab and stepped aside so the brute had a clear path. Norris's two lackeys dropped to the ground and helped their boss carry the machine—an entirely unnecessary gesture, given Norris's strength, but a noble one done out of loyalty to their leader. As the others clambered out of the truck, Ashcroft stepped down to meet them.

"I am most pleased with your success." He frowned. "Stormcry's betrayal is unfortunate, but we can adjust."

"What is next, Lord?" Artemis asked.

"Patience, Somna." Ashcroft followed Norris out of the dock. The others fell in line behind him. "The next phase of the plan will require you to return to D.C. The others will begin preparations for other steps."

"Then we are in the final phase?"

"We are, my dear." Ashcroft smirked. "Our time is finally at hand."

"Finally." Artemis smiled. "Your plan is coming to fruition, Lord Ashcroft."

"It is indeed. But, Somna, I am Jeremiah Ashcroft no longer." He looked out over the rest of his servants in the garage and raised his voice. "Call me Nephilius."

CHAPTER 28

As he stepped out of the training room, Gideon exhaled deeply and removed his gloves. He hadn't performed surgery in a long time, and he never expected to do one on his best friend. But it had worked. Arianna and Maddox said that the connection between Dean's nerves and the prosthetic arm was promising. The medicine they had him on should reduce his fever and fight infection. God willing, Dean should pull through.

Gideon stopped before he reached the balcony, leaning against the wall with one hand. He was exhausted, physically and mentally. And he still had his own injuries to attend to. The fracture in his wrist was on the same arm he had broken only months ago stopping the runaway train. It had been difficult to use that hand for anything during the surgery. It was a good thing Arianna and Maddox had been there to help. And his rib, which was at least bruised, if not fractured, made every breath he took an agonizing struggle. All he wanted to do was crash into bed and sleep for days.

But first, there were other matters for Gideon's attention. The Regency had escaped with the device, and it was imperative that the Vindicators locate them before the next phase of Ashcroft's plan was put into motion. And then there was Jarrett, who was a government agent who may have been spying on them all along. Gideon needed to determine his true motivations. Audrey Knight had joined them unexpectedly, too. Dean was the only one who knew the reason, and he wouldn't be telling them anything anytime soon. Arianna and Maddox were still working on the potential antidote for Ashcroft's serum. Gideon was seeing visions of a dead man wearing white. All pressing issues—but even a superhero could only deal with one thing at a time.

The most immediate issue was feeling at least a little bit normal. He stepped into the bathroom and peeled off his scrubs and the armor underneath. His plainclothes lay folded in a neat pile next to the sink. He wondered who had put them there.

Gideon cleaned up, removed his bodysuit, and changed into the khaki joggers, gray t-shirt, and blue long-sleeved shirt that had been left for him. He looked at his reflection. *Just a normal guy.* If his identity had not become public knowledge, no one on the streets would never suspect he was a superhero. *Wouldn't that be nice?* He loved his powers, but he'd almost forgotten what it was like to be normal.

Would I use Arianna and Maddox's cure? He knew instantly that the answer was no. His powers were too important. As much as he might like to have a normal life, he was burdened with using his powers to protect the innocent. And he enjoyed doing it, most of the time. He wouldn't give them up. Still, it was the second time in only a few days that he wished he could have a secret identity again.

Gideon pushed the bathroom door open and walked out onto the balcony. It was quiet—surprisingly so. Usually, conversations drifted up from the living room or kitchen. Laughter and shouts of joy were not uncommon sounds. But now . . . nothing. He walked down the stairs. Wes, Jolie, and Audrey sat on the couch, deep in conversation. Hannah and Jarrett were in the kitchen.

"Where are Patrick and Carter?" Gideon asked.

Wes glanced up. "Carter went home to check on his family. Patrick is doing homework back at our place."

Gideon sensed something unspoken behind Wes's words. *Anger . . . and guilt.* He suspected Wes had told them about Jarrett's secret. No wonder the two young men had left; Patrick looked up to Jarrett, and Carter was a cautious person to begin with. Gideon pressed his lips together. Whether intentional or not on Jarrett's part, he had delivered a hit to the team. Hopefully, they could swing back from it quickly.

"How's Dean?" Jolie asked.

She rose from the couch and crossed the room to embrace Gideon. He grimaced and sucked in a sharp breath as she bumped his sore rib, driving a sharp pain through his chest. The pain passed, and he hugged her back, her warm embrace easing some of the tension in his shoulders.

"He's doing as well as can be expected. We were able to install a prosthetic hand. Arianna and Maddox say it should work as well as the original. There will hardly be a difference in its functionality. Still, the trauma . . ."

"Poor Dean." Jolie stepped back. "We were just talking with Audrey. She's got a lot of information that could be useful."

Gideon walked toward her. Audrey rose, and Gideon sensed her nervousness. He extended a hand to her. She glanced down at it, furrowed her brow, and finally reached out and shook it.

"Why don't you start from the beginning?" he suggested.

He sat next to her, and she told him the story of how she had met Ashcroft and what he had done for her. She explained why she had become a member of the Regency. Gideon understood her passion. If he had been cured of cancer in a similar way, wouldn't he want everyone to know? It was the same passion that Gideon had for telling lost souls how Jesus could save them.

"But all that changed," Audrey continued. "He used his serum on himself yesterday, and the transformation was . . . monstrous. The worst part is, he used the last of the serum to do it. Now, he has to create a synthetic serum to use on everyone else, and who knows what that will do to people? It may never work. He might commit mass genocide trying to make the population stronger. But I don't think he even cares. I know now that he's no better than Pierce or Zeke or any of the others who don't care about the people in their way. They only care about themselves."

As she talked, Gideon probed her emotions. He detected no trace of a lie in any of it. Audrey was genuine in her horror at the Regency's disregard for the lives of others and in her desire to help.

"I thought Ashcroft would help everyone, just like he helped me." She shrugged. "I was naïve."

"You're right." He didn't see any reason to sugarcoat it, but she needed to hear some encouragement, too. "But the important thing is, you realized the truth and acted on it. That's what matters in the end. What can you tell me about Ashcroft's operations? What about the beasts? What are they?"

"They're called nephiloids." Audrey bit her lip. "They're . . . abominations. When he first began his experiments, Ashcroft tested the serum on animals first. When many of them died, he began combining tissue from multiple animals to create something that could survive the serum. He succeeded."

"How many does he have?"

"Maybe a few dozen? He compartmentalizes information. Only Artemis comes close to knowing everything, and even she's in the dark about a lot, I'd bet."

"A few dozen? Why has he only released four?"

"He wanted to use them as a distraction, so Quinn and Melanie could break the others out of prison without your interference. But Ashcroft has a bigger plan for the rest of them."

"What plan?"

"I'm not supposed to know this; I overheard it several months ago. Easy to do when you have audio-kinetic powers. I think he wants to unleash them on major cities. Those who survive the attack and are injected with the nephiloids' venom will become superhuman."

The image of dozens of nephiloids rampaging through cities like Sojourn or Chicago or New York, tearing people apart and turning the survivors into superhumans, mortified him. It was a mad plan. Having seen the creatures in action, Gideon doubted there would be many survivors.

"What cities?"

"I'm not sure. I didn't hear that much."

Gideon placed a gentle hand on her shoulder. It wasn't her fault that she didn't know these things. He took a deep breath, nodded, and pushed himself off the couch.

"Can . . . can I see Dean?" she asked.

"What?"

"I'd like to see him." She rested her hands on her knees and looked up at him. "He's the reason I realized how bad Ashcroft was—the reason I'm here."

Audrey *had* blasted Monahan to save Dean. Maybe she deserved this. Gideon put his hands on his hips and studied the floor. He could feel Wes's and Jolie's gazes burning a hole in him. Jolie's emotions implored him to go easy on Audrey, while Wes felt more reserved. He was less certain of their new ally. That was fine. Someone needed to be cautious.

"When he wakes up, if he wants to see you, then you can go talk to him," Gideon said. "But for now, he needs rest."

Audrey smiled. "Thank you."

"You're welcome. It's the least I can do since you saved his life. And you're welcome to stay here for as long as you need." He glanced at the kitchen. "But if you'll excuse me, I've got another situation to deal with."

He stepped between the counter and the island, where Hannah and Jarrett were speaking. Hannah looked up, narrowed her eyes, and left the kitchen without a word. Gideon probed her. He didn't detect any animosity toward Jarrett in her. She was more upset at the rest of them than at Jarrett. That surprised him, and he wasn't sure why. Like him, she was a new addition to the team. Of course, she would stick up for him, at least until she had the whole story.

Jarrett's mouth was drawn in a thin line, and he didn't say a word. His presence felt completely calm, unconcerned. His casual stance, leaning against the island with one leg crossed in front of the other, also indicated he was relaxed.

"What is CLOUD?" Gideon asked.

"The Center for Location and Observation of Unidentified Dangers." Jarrett pursed his lips. "It's a mouthful, so we decided to be clever."

Gideon bit back the urge to tell Jarrett to cut the jokes. This would go better for them if Gideon tried to be understanding. It was how Jarrett coped. He wasn't being irreverent or flippant.

"Unidentified Dangers," Gideon said. "Like superhumans?"

Jarrett hesitated and finally nodded. "Like superhumans. CLOUD was originally formed in the early seventies, after a superhuman named Solar Flare nearly proved too difficult for the U.S. military to kill. They wiped out all traces of Solar Flare's existence, chalked it up to a media blitz for an upcoming movie. And they waited for the day when someone like Ashcroft showed up and for dangers like the cryptids. They were my mission, not you."

That lined up with what Artemis told Gideon about Ashcroft's father months ago. Gideon and Dean had tried researching the superhero, but there was no trace of him. The government had completely buried him. Gideon wondered if Dad remembered this so-called media blitz. If he asked his father about Solar Flare, would he come back with fond memories of a movie from his youth?

Gideon crossed his arms. "So, you didn't come with us out of the goodness of your heart. You needed to stay with your target."

Jarrett bit his lip and looked at the ceiling. "Yes. I had to get the cryptid, or at least a sample of its DNA, back to my superiors. I got some hairs from the field before we found the cave, but I couldn't let the beast itself slip out of my grasp without at least trying to stay with it. I'd already lost the other one I killed when it was dragged away by its mate. My coming here was nothing personal. And honestly, Gideon, I really like you guys."

"Oh, thanks." Gideon snorted. "Makes me feel better."

"Hey, I could've disabled you and Patrick and taken the cryptid from you before your plane arrived. Did you ever think of that?"

"I'm supposed to thank you for being merciful, is that it?"

"No, I—" Jarrett pushed himself off the counter and pressed his hands together in front of his mouth. "I'm sorry. It seemed like the best option at the time, and it seemed like you needed all the help you could get. And I figured my superiors wouldn't mind if I helped you bring down the escaped supervillains. They're basically the reason we formed in the first place."

"And what happens when your superiors consider me a danger, Jarrett? Or Patrick?"

"I don't—"

"What if the government decides someone that can move that fast is a danger? Are you going to shoot him with an arrow?"

"I don't know!" Jarrett smacked his palm down on the island. "I don't know. Not long ago, I would've said yes, but now . . . "

"But now, you know us. You know we're not dangerous, except to people who are trying to hurt innocents."

"Which is why I told the other agents you're on our side—because I believe that you're the good guys, and you wouldn't hurt anyone. But, Gideon, you've got to admit, we're living in a whole new world here. You were the first public superhuman in almost fifty years. You showed up less than a year ago, and you just so happen to have the same powers as Solar Flare. In the digital age, there's no putting someone like you back in the box. Now, there are dozens more amplified people out there, and a bunch of them are the bad guys. Gideon, we just had an all-out superhuman brawl in the middle of Washington, D.C. Tell me we don't need an organization like CLOUD to watch out for the little guy."

Gideon closed his eyes and took a deep breath. "You're right."

"Thank you. So, can we just agree to work together to take down Dr. Ashcroft before he makes the whole world into unidentified dangers?" He extended a hand. "Please."

Gideon stared at Jarrett's hand and mentally probed him. There was no trace of deception coming from him anymore, no hint that he was being anything other than completely genuine; he really did want to help.

Gideon shook his hand.

"If I catch even a hint that you'd turn on us, you'll regret it."

"I understand." Jarrett looked past Gideon and inclined his head toward the living room. "They're your family—some literally, others by choice. You'd do anything to protect them. I can understand that."

Gideon nodded, remembering the picture of Jarrett's wife. "I guess you can."

"And for what it's worth, I'm sorry about Dean. He's a good guy."

"The best. You might want to let your bosses know that more of the creatures—and they're called nephiloids, by the way—might be coming. And they may target major population centers."

He left Jarrett in the kitchen to ponder the revelation and headed back up the stairs. It was time to worry about the other matters. His injuries, for starters. He'd have Jolie drive him to the hospital. Once he was patched up, he could focus on finding Ashcroft before he unleashed chaos on the world.

One thing still bothered him. Jarrett had slipped it into his diatribe almost unnoticed, but Gideon caught it. Solar Flare had the same powers as Gideon. *What did that mean?* One more mystery to add to the pile.

Gideon wondered when he would start getting answers.

* * *

Patrick tried to focus on the homework that he had failed to finish over the weekend, but his mind seemed all too eager to zip back to the sight of an unconscious Dean, his arm severed below the elbow, being dragged into the Tower. And if it wasn't that, it was the hurt he felt at Jarrett's lies. Homework was the least of his concerns.

If only Lucy was there. She would know what to say. Patrick stared at the wall across the room and imagined Lucy sitting on his bed, leaning forward, and encouraging him to let it all out. He would vent and vent until he could hardly speak anymore. She would smile and say some comforting words, and somehow, it would help. They had gone through that exact scenario so many times, dealing with so many issues—his personal faith, school problems . . . She had been there through it all.

He picked up his phone and pulled up her number. His finger hovered over the call button. He'd called her countless times in the three months he'd lived in Sojourn City. He knew why he couldn't bring himself to press the little green circle. He needed to see her—and not over video chat. In person.

Patrick jumped off his bed and sprinted down the hallway. He was out the door and blasting down the street in seconds before he could talk himself out of it. He darted between cars and ran up an on-ramp to the interstate. San Francisco was a long way away. It might take him hours to get there, but he had to see her. That singular thought nestled in the center of his mind and refused to budge.

He hoped he would get back before Gideon and the others returned home. They would probably chew him out for using his powers so carelessly, practically running across the entire country while there were so many supervillains on the loose. But he didn't care. He'd take his dressing-down if it came. The central thought in his mind was that he had to see Lucy, that she was the only one who could clear up the messy weave of thoughts that threatened to overwhelm him.

The farther he ran, the faster his feet seemed to move. Cars and trucks practically stood still as Patrick darted between them or even over them. He climbed over a mountain road and crossed a long stretch of plains. All concept of time dissolved as he zoomed toward his goal.

Finally, he skidded to a halt a block away from Lucy's house. He looked around, wondering how long it had taken him to get there. He checked his phone. It had been an hour and one minute since he had left Sojourn City. *I just ran from Michigan to California in barely an hour.* He couldn't begin to calculate his speed.

He took a step forward and stumbled. He caught himself and sat down on the curb. His legs felt like Jell-O, and his head spun with the stress of stopping so abruptly. Maybe he needed to rest for a moment. He'd never run that fast before—not even close. As he sat, his vision clouded. He took a deep breath, held it for four seconds, and let it out. *I definitely can't do that too often.* He sucked in another breath through his nostrils. He needed calories and water.

Patrick pushed himself to his feet and wobbled. He just had to make it to Lucy's house. Then, he could ask for some food and water. He staggered up the steps to her front door and knocked weakly. He slumped down onto the wooden swing that hung on the porch.

"Patrick?" Lucy stepped out onto the porch. "How did you get here?"

"I ran." He leaned forward. "Can I come in? I think I'm going to pass out now."

Patrick shot up and looked around. *Where am I?* He wasn't back in his apartment; this was the living room of a house. It wasn't his parents' home, but it was familiar.

"Hey, easy there." A hand rested on his shoulder. "Relax."

He looked up. Lucy stood next to him, dressed in dark blue jeans and a red shirt. She sat down on the couch.

"You ran all the way here from Sojourn City and passed out on my porch." She extended a glass of water. "Drink this. I've got plenty more and a whole tray of food, when you're ready for it."

The memory of his sprint came rushing back. Patrick closed his eyes. He'd never felt so exhausted in his life.

"How long was I out?"

"Two hours. I was starting to worry a little."

Patrick sipped at the water. As the cool liquid washed down his throat, he tilted the cup back and downed the whole thing.

"Slow down." Lucy giggled. "You need to pace yourself. I'll get you some more, but first, why don't you tell me why you're here?"

He started from the moment he got the call that Gideon and the others were on their way to D.C. He was hurt that they had gone without him and scared that they would get hurt if he wasn't there to run backup. Word had come back about Dean's injury. Audrey Knight had betrayed the Regency. Wes had told Patrick that Jarrett was a spy. Lucy sat and listened, her piercing blue eyes never averting from Patrick's gaze. The more words spilled from his mouth, the calmer he felt.

"I knew I needed to talk to you, but a phone call just didn't seem like enough."

Lucy put a hand on Patrick's arm. "Sounds like you've had a rough day. So, your friend Dean—he's going to be okay?"

"I . . . I think so." Patrick nodded. "I didn't stick around to see if he recovered, but it was just his arm. I'm sure he'll survive; it's just—"

"Brutal?"

"Yeah."

"Are you worried that you're going to get hurt?"

Patrick shrugged. "Honestly, I hadn't thought about it until now. I know I'm not invincible, but my speed helps me stay out of reach of the bad guys. It's not myself I'm worried about, not really. Although, that monster in Kansas did land a pretty good one on me. If that thing could hit me, I guess anything else could, too."

"So, you're scared." Lucy slid closer and wrapped him in a hug. "That's normal. You're doing some totally crazy things, so of course you're going to be scared about it. Superpowers don't take away fear."

"I know."

"Now, what about this guy, Jarrett? How do you feel about him?"

"I liked him—a lot. He was a really cool guy. He was nice and funny, and he treated me the same as everyone else, not like I'm a kid. I liked that. But now, I'm confused. Why would he lie to us?"

"Come on, Patrick. You've watched as much TV as I have. You know government agents can never tell the people they're close to what they actually do. It doesn't mean Jarrett wanted to hurt you. Maybe you should talk to him and see if you can work this out."

Patrick didn't want to talk to Jarrett right then—maybe not ever again. He'd blatantly lied to their faces about who he was, and Patrick was supposed to just let that go? What if Jarrett had joined up with them because his agency had ordered him to spy on them?

"Just think about it," Lucy said. "You can't stay mad forever. You know what the Bible says about unforgiveness. You forgave the man who killed your grandfather, didn't you? You can forgive Jarrett, too."

Patrick groaned. *Why did she have to bring that up?* He knew he needed to forgive Jarrett, but being angry felt good. It felt right. He and his friends had been through a lot; that should buy him at least a few hours to sulk. But unfortunately, she was right.

"I know." He smiled. "Thank you, Lucy. I'm glad I came back."

"Me, too." She stood up. "I'll go get you some more food and water. You might want to call Gideon and tell him you won't be back for a while. I don't think it'd be a good idea to cross the country again for a few hours."

CHAPTER 29

"Help me get this loose," Dean said.

Hannah nodded, formed a blade, and cut at another cord. Dean slashed another one loose. Two more to go. He raised his arm.

Searing heat scorched his elbow. A red beam of light sheared through the truck and through Dean's arm. Dean screamed and stumbled back, clutching his elbow, the rancid smell of scorched flesh filling his nostrils.

Dean jerked upright and looked around. His breath came in choppy pants, and he struggled to calm down. He was in a familiar setting—their training room in the Tower. An IV tube trailed his right hand. He took a deep breath and brought both hands up, cradling his forehead in his palms. He didn't remember returning here. The last thing he remembered . . .

He pulled his head back and looked down at his left arm. He turned it over and stared at the palm, flipping it again to look at the back. There wasn't even a scorch mark. Not a single hint that it had been seared with a powerful energy beam. *Was it all a dream?* It couldn't have been. The intensity of the heat, the cold shock that rolled through his whole body . . . It was all too real.

He brought the fingers of his right hand up to touch the flesh. And he understood. The flesh of his left hand was cold and smooth. As he moved the fingertips of his right hand to touch the ones on his left, the sensation in his left hand felt distant, like a layer of hardened wax coated it, allowing him to feel the sensation of touch but not texture, not detail. It was like touching his fingernail to an object. He could tell he was touching something, but if he closed his eyes, he'd never be able to discern what.

His left hand was gone. As lifelike as this one looked, it wasn't. It was a fantastic prosthetic—far better than he could've ever hoped for—but it was fake, nonetheless. He struggled to keep his breaths even. His hand—his real hand—tingled, and he felt a strange pain where his other hand should have been, even though he knew it wasn't coming from the prosthetic. A cold sweat broke out across the back of his neck and his forehead, making him feel clammy.

It didn't help that he was alone on an operating table in the middle of the training room. He had to get out of here. Fingers trembling, he disconnected his IV, pushed himself off the operating table, and hurried for the door. His breaths came in short, shallow gasps. Dimly, he realized that he was wearing the interior bodysuit of his uniform, but the outer layers had been removed. The left sleeve had been slashed off above the elbow. He'd have to design a whole new bodysuit now. But that was the least of his concerns.

He scrambled through the bathroom door on his right. The mirror showed the reflection of a man limping back from death's door. He was pale, his curly hair matted and tangled. Huge bags hung beneath his eyes. Dean turned on the faucet and leaned down to splash his face with cool water, but as he bent over, a vice-like weight clenched at his chest. He filled the basin and dunked his head into it. The rush of cold water brought him back to himself, at least somewhat.

Deep breaths, deep breaths. Dean recalled Gideon's four-four-four method of breathing and tried it. Four in . . . hold for four . . . out for four. The first few were shaky, but finally, he started to feel normal again.

Okay, so . . . so my hand is gone.

The others had acted remarkably fast to get him a prosthetic. Judging by its quality, he suspected Arianna and Maddox had a hand in creating it. *Had a hand . . . real nice, Dean.* He stuck the limb under the faucet. He felt the touch of the water, but not the sensation of wetness.

They had to work on this.

Knock, knock. "Hey, Dean. You all right?"

Dean swallowed. That was Gideon. Of course. His empathic senses would have picked up Dean's panic attack from downstairs. Bile rose in Dean's throat, threatening to project itself outward. He lifted the toilet lid just in case he did lose his lunch.

"I . . . I just need a minute." Dean ran a hand through the limp strands of his soaking wet hair. "Just . . . processing."

There was silence for a moment. "You don't have to go through this alone, buddy."

"I know. I'm not. I won't."

"All right. We'll be here when you're ready."

Dean took another moment to compose himself. Gideon checking on him meant a lot, but Dean didn't want anyone, especially his best friend, to see him like this. Dean was the morale booster of the team. *What would it do to them if they saw me in this condition?* He dried his face and hair with a hand towel, forced a few deep breaths, and walked out onto the balcony. Unsurprisingly, Gideon was waiting for him.

"We don't put up a front with each other, right?" Gideon's gaze bore into Dean's soul as they spoke. "We're best friends. Even if we're not real with anyone else, we're real with each other."

"Right. This is . . . it's the worst." Dean turned his prosthetic hand over. "I've lost something I can't get back, a literal part of me. I'm a scientist. Other than my mind, my hands are my most important tool. It's going to take a while to get used to this."

"It will." Gideon stepped forward and gripped Dean's shoulder. "But we're here to get you through it."

"Thanks, bud." Dean looked over the living room. "All right, let's do this."

Jolie sat on the couch with Wes and Hannah. Jarrett was in a chair, distant from the others but still facing the television. Arianna and Maddox stood near the front door, speaking quietly.

A woman stood near the window. *Is that Audrey? What is she doing here?*

Dean mounted the stairs and walked down into the living room with Gideon at his side. Wes noticed him first. His head snapped up, and he jumped off the couch and bounded up the stairs to meet Dean halfway. Dean held up a hand to indicate that he was fine and walked the rest of the way down by himself.

"It's just my arm. I can walk."

Wes blushed. "Sorry."

Gideon glanced down at Dean's left hand. "How does it feel?"

"Different. Like . . . like there's something between my hand and everything I touch." The dark tendrils of panic played with his mind again, but he held them at bay. Dean studied the limb. "But at least, I've got a hand at all. I guess I have you to thank for it."

"Arianna and Maddox did most of the hard work."

Dean looked at his two longtime friends and coworkers. They studied him nervously and meandered toward him. He smiled and waved them over.

"Thank you." He hugged each of them. "Really."

"You're welcome." Arianna grabbed the prosthetic hand and lifted it up to inspect it. "We'll make improvements on it. In time, I'm sure you won't notice the difference anymore."

"Thanks." Dean looked at Gideon. It was best to talk, to think, about something else right now. Anything else. "What did I miss?"

Gideon gestured for Dean to sit down. Dean noted the brace on his left hand, the bruise under his eye, the split lip, and the way he microscopically cringed with every breath. *He didn't escape unscathed either.* Dean dropped onto the couch between Jolie and Wes and looked up at Gideon.

"For starters, Jarrett is working for a government organization called CLOUD."

Dean flicked his eyes to study the other man. No wonder he was so far from the rest of the group. He was lucky they hadn't thrown him out already. Jarrett didn't speak up as Gideon explained why the government agent was with them. He leaned forward, fingers interlaced and elbows resting on his knees, and watched Dean. The hope for approval in his eyes was evident—and surprising. Jarrett was a man who desperately wanted to be liked. That was unusual for a government agent.

Dean met the man's gaze. "If you're on our side, we'll take whatever help we can get. What else?"

"Audrey saved your life." Gideon nodded toward the woman. "She said you convinced her that Ashcroft's team was the wrong one to be playing for."

Dean had hoped his talk with Audrey would keep her from joining the fight, but he'd never imagined it would convince her to switch sides. She stared out at the sunset a moment longer before walking up to him.

She held out a hand awkwardly, as though unsure what to do with it, before finally resting it on his shoulder. Dean felt a rush of excitement at her touch, a glimmer of happiness shining like a pinprick through the darkness of the rest of Dean's day.

"I'm glad you're okay," she said.

"Thank you—for that and for saving my life."

"You're welcome. Enough people have died. I couldn't bear the thought of any more lives on my conscience."

Gideon continued. "Audrey told us that Ashcroft's creatures are called nephiloids. He created them himself. He may be planning to release them in highly populated cities so they can attack people at random and turn them into superhumans."

"Oh, man." Dean whistled. "We've got to stop him."

"We will." Gideon pointed at him. "But you need time to recover. If you're feeling up to it, let's get you back to the apartment and into bed. Hannah, Jarrett, and Audrey can stay here in the Tower for tonight."

Dean wondered if sleep would bring the sweet embrace of nothingness . . . or more nightmares of his injury. "Sounds fine to me."

He rose, told everyone goodbye, and headed for the door. As he did, he cast one last glance back at Audrey—the girl who had saved his life.

* * *

The apartment Gideon and his roommates lived in was less opulent than the penthouse, but not by much. Three of the walls were red brick, and the fourth was made up of floor-to-ceiling windows with a door that led out to a balcony overlooking the city. The bedrooms were large enough to be divided by a curtain, allowing for a greater level of privacy, even though the four men shared two rooms.

The door to Wes and Patrick's room was closed. Patrick must have secluded himself to finish his homework. Gideon watched Dean as he entered the bedroom they shared and closed the door. Then, he walked over to the couch, where Jolie had already settled.

"How's the search for Serban going?" he asked.

"We—Agent Ross and I—found him at the safehouse where I first saw Monahan. We got in a firefight, and Serban escaped. We set up a perimeter around a two-block radius of the house, but somehow, he managed to slip away. Again."

Gideon wrapped an arm around her shoulders. The thought of her in a shootout with Luca Serban made all his muscles go tense, but he forced himself to relax. Jolie was capable of taking care of herself.

"You'll get him. I have faith in you. Do you want me to help?"

"You've got enough on your plate, babe." She rested her left hand on his chest. "Spies and supervillains and monsters . . . "

"But Serban's a danger, too. He's the reason I became the Seraph in the first place. I'm not going to watch while he undoes the progress made in the Brooks."

"He won't." Her fingers traced Gideon's collar. "Trust me. We've got this."

"Okay. If you do need help . . . "

"I know where to find you." Jolie smiled and kissed him on the cheek. "You need dinner, and so do I. Come on, let's get some food. And while we eat, maybe we can talk about wedding plans instead of the latest crisis."

"I think that would be a nice change of pace."

CHAPTER 30

Seven years ago

Unsurprisingly, the Nephilim were dead. Through long, arduous work, Ashcroft figured out how to open the tanks and remove their occupants. When he did, he found no sign of life in any of them. Perhaps their life support systems were shorted out by the waters of the Great Flood. Or perhaps these tanks had never been meant to keep them alive, but to preserve their bodies. If that was the case, Ashcroft was grateful to them. Even without living Nephilim, he could continue his research. The bodies allowed him the opportunity for dissection and examination, the chance to learn what had made the Nephilim so spectacular. Maybe it was something he could replicate in a human being.

Humanity could reach perfection. Ashcroft was determined to get them there. For all their flaws and shortcomings, there was so much potential. Father had proven that.

"We need to get them out," Ashcroft said. "But we must be careful. If the bodies begin to decompose, I will lose everything."

Roger nodded. "Just tell me what to do."

For the next day, the two men carefully removed the Nephilim one at a time from the hidden chamber and took them back to their tent. When they at last had all five bodies, Ashcroft prepared them for transport. They would return to his lab in the States and begin his research there. It might take years of study and experimentation, but he had worked for decades already. Someday, it would bear fruit.

CHAPTER 31

Present Day

The armored truck sat in the loading dock—unguarded, unwatched. This was the perfect opportunity for Powers to leave, one he might never get again. All he had to do was sneak out to the truck, drive it a few miles from the base, ditch it on the roadside, and disappear into the woods. They would never find him. He could live his life again, do what he wanted rather than be an indentured servant to a madman whose ideas somehow worked against all odds.

But he couldn't move until he was sure everyone was in bed, or at least away from the loading dock. Artemis would doubtless be up all night with Ashcroft—or Nephilius, as he called himself—going over last-minute details of their newest plan, but they would stay near the labs. He was more worried about the others, whose locations he couldn't guess.

At two in the morning, Powers rolled out of bed and pulled on a pair of blue jeans, a gray t-shirt, and his usual brown hoodie. He zipped it up, pulled the hood over his head, and slid his bedroom door open. Quinn had the room opposite his. The door was closed, and he didn't see any lights coming from underneath it.

So far, so good. Just in case, Powers wasn't going to risk his own neck just yet. He created a doppelganger and sent it down the hall.

All the bedroom doors were shut. The light in Melanie's room was still on, but she was a teenager; it was unsurprising that she was up this late. He slipped past her room and turned the corner into the hallway leading out of the barracks.

The hall was empty. Powers pulled open the barracks door and walked out, leaving the door open so his original body could sneak through. He glanced left toward the loading dock and right toward the training room and cafeteria. Both halls were empty, although the light in the cafeteria was on.

He turned left and crept toward the loading dock. He could feel his pulse throbbing in his neck. He took a deep breath; it didn't help. The fear of being caught threatened to overwhelm him, and he nearly gave up, dissolved his doppelganger, and went back to bed. Instead, he forced himself onward.

Powers released the latch to the loading dock and tugged the heavy door open. The truck still sat in the middle of the large room, attended only by a pair of Zeke's mercenary buddies. Technically, Powers was their superior; so if he gave them some story about Ashcroft sending him to dump the armored truck, they wouldn't give him a second look. The switch to open the huge garage doors was just to his right. He reached out to flip it.

"Well, well."

Powers jumped back. Quinn leaned against the doorframe, arms crossed. He had that pretentious smirk on, as usual. He raised his right index finger, and a small flame appeared at the tip, like a match. Alerted by the voice, the two mercenaries walked from the truck toward the door. They kept their guns casually at their sides. Powers hoped to keep it that way.

"Kinda dark in here," Quinn said in that posh British accent. "Need a light?"

"Quinn—"

"It's Red Raider. What are you doing here, Fragment? Thought you could slip away, did you?"

"No, I just—"

"Oh, you did." Quinn pointed his lit finger at Powers like a gun. "Now, you just stay there a moment." He lifted his free hand to his ear. "This is Red Raider. I've got Fragment here, trying to steal away in the armored truck."

The two mercenaries raised their guns, training them on Powers. Powers's heart stopped. There was no way out of this. If only he hadn't been there as a doppelganger. If his original body were there, he could duplicate himself and overwhelm Quinn and the mercenaries. If he tried to replicate from his real body's location, it would take the doppelgangers far too long to reach Quinn. And worse, Quinn was between the real Powers and his only escape route.

"Kill him?" Quinn lowered his hand from his ear. "With pleasure."

A column of fire shot from Quinn's hand.

Powers stumbled back and gasped. What was he going to do? He had no way out, and Quinn had ratted on him. There was no way he could play this off. Sending a doppelganger was the most condemning evidence. Any lie he tried to make up—that he'd just been doing a security check, that he'd just gone for a late-night stroll—would be useless.

He slammed his door shut and grabbed his uniform off the wall. If it came down to a fight, he would be more protected in this than his hoodie. He stripped his clothes off and pulled the white-and-red costume on.

Someone pounded on the door. "Open up, *amigo*."

Powers faced the door and created four copies of himself. Maybe he could escape by sheer force of numbers. The door glowed and reddened. Powers ducked behind his bed. The door exploded inward, crushing one of the doppelgangers.

Powers leaped up, and his three duplicates charged the door. If they could just hold off Mendez, Powers could slip past and create more duplicates to fight whomever he encountered on his way out. He pushed his way past Mendez as the muscular soldier battled the clones. Two of Mendez's guerrillas were with him; Powers sent another two duplicates to fight them. He kept his eyes on his escape route and ran. Several doors squeaked open. *No, no, no.* The explosion must've alerted the others who had been sleeping. Even with dozens of himself, Powers didn't think he could take on all of his former comrades.

Around the corner, Powers saw that the door leading out of the barracks was still open. He had a shot. Creating two more duplicates of himself, he sent them to guard his back and kept running toward the doorway. Behind him, a sound like a rushing tidal wave was joined by two identical screams.

Powers ran through the doorway and turned left. Quinn stood ahead, blocking the way to the loading dock, backed by Zeke's mercenaries. There was that self-righteous sneer again, all over Quinn's face. Powers growled, stopped in the middle of the hallway, and closed his eyes. He concentrated, gathering all the reserve power he could.

"Giving up?" Quinn asked. "Pity. I'd enjoy a fight. I've never liked you, Fragment. You are pathetic—nothing. You don't belong with us."

"Bold words coming from a war profiteer." Powers opened his eyes. "Move."

"I think not." Quinn formed a fireball in his right hand and tossed it up casually, as if it were a baseball. "Come on, Fragment; make things interesting for me."

"Whatever you say."

Powers shouted in exertion and pushed out a dozen copies of himself. They charged at Quinn and the mercenaries, filling the hallway and shielding the real Powers from Quinn's line of sight.

Powers's legs wobbled a bit, and he leaned on the wall for support. He created another two doppelgangers and sent them back toward the barracks. Melanie would be catching up any second now.

"Stay back, lads," Quinn told the mercenaries. "I'll handle this."

Sheets of fire consumed the doppelgangers. Powers staggered forward, creating a new duplicate with each step. They mobbed Quinn, pushing him to the ground so the real Powers could pass.

Powers smirked. "You wanted a challenge."

"This . . . is . . . nothing."

Quinn growled, and a halo of fire surrounded him, blasting away all the doppelgangers on top of him. The two mercenaries shielded their eyes and stepped back. Powers's eyes widened, and he froze in place. *No, it can't end like this.* Quinn, his body cloaked in fire, stormed toward Powers and raised his hands. Powers brought his hands up to shield himself.

"Stop!"

Quinn's footsteps silenced. Powers opened his eyes. The flaming man stood just feet away, but he made no move to end Powers's life. Powers lowered his arms and turned around. Nephilius and Artemis stood behind him. Powers swallowed. Maybe if he created another wave of doppelgangers and had them rush the two newcomers . . .

But if he did that, Quinn would just incinerate him. He was trapped.

"Of all my followers." Nephilius clucked his tongue. "I would've thought you too cowardly to try to escape."

"I'm tired of being under other people's thumbs," Powers growled. "It was worth it to try and escape."

"Was it? You failed—dramatically."

"So, what are you going to do? Order Flame Boy here to burn me to a crisp? Or maybe you'll have your little siren there hypnotize me."

Nephilius smirked. "I could kill you myself. But I would prefer, my friend, to follow a less violent course. You're of no use to me dead, and a hypnotized servant is one who cannot think for himself. I want you on my side. Willingly."

"That ship has sailed, Doctor." Powers snorted. "I tried that already, remember? All it got me was some jail time, and I was headed for that even before I met up with you."

"My boy, our time is coming." Nephilius stepped forward, his massive foot causing the hallway to rumble, and extended a clawed hand. "We are in the final phases of my plan, and when it is complete, you will stand by my side as one of my top lieutenants. Regency Inc. will rule the world. Just give me a little more of your time, and I will more than repay it."

Powers wasn't ready to die, and he didn't want to be Artemis's puppet. He pressed his lips together and nodded.

"I'm with you."

"Excellent, my boy. Excellent."

CHAPTER 32

It was nearly midnight when Patrick stepped out onto Lucy's porch. She closed the door behind them, walked out next to him, and took his hand. Patrick looked up at the stars. *I miss this place. This is home.*

His phone buzzed. He removed it from his pocket and checked the screen. The message from Wes said, "Where are you?" He grimaced. It was almost two a.m. in Sojourn City. He also had a text from Raina, wondering why he hadn't been at school that day. He pocketed his phone and looked at Lucy.

"I should go. If I pace myself, it's going to be four a.m. by the time I make it home, and I've got school tomorrow."

She wrapped him in a hug. "Thank you for coming to visit. Take care of yourself."

"I will. And . . . do me a favor and don't tell my parents that I was here today."

"I won't. But, Patrick, I think you need to talk to them. Soon."

That wouldn't be easy. His dad had kicked him out over his faith. Talking to them and acting like everything was normal would be one of the hardest things he had ever done. But he knew it was what he needed to do.

"I will. There's just too much going on in Sojourn right now. I'll try to come back soon."

"Run safe." Lucy smiled. "Good night, Patrick."

"Good night."

Patrick hugged her one more time, backed down her porch to the sidewalk, and waved goodbye as she stepped back inside her house. When she closed the door, he took out his phone and texted Wes, "On my way home now."

He hesitated over the word "home." Sojourn City was a great place, and he loved his friends and teammates. But it was not Patrick's home. He felt like a visitor there. In the few hours he had been back in San Francisco with Lucy, he felt more comfortable than he had in three months in Sojourn. One day, he would have to move back to San Francisco. He would have to face his parents, tell them he was coming home, and find somewhere to live if they would not accept him. San Francisco needed a superhero, too.

Patrick couldn't leave the Vindicators now. They still needed him. With the threat of the Regency's big move on the horizon, a speedster might be the key to victory. Until Ashcroft was defeated, Patrick was committed to the team.

He ran toward Sojourn City.

* * *

With chaos threatening to overwhelm Gideon from all sides, the last thing he wanted to think about was going into work. Gideon wanted to get paid, so he had to show up. Especially with no crisis on the news. He weaved through the lobby of Sterling Labs to the elevator and rode it up to the biology lab.

It would be a miracle if he got any work done that day. He had so many different things on his mind—Ashcroft, wedding planning, mysterious white-clad apparitions, Patrick's strange late-night return,

Jarrett's allegiance, Solar Flare—that he could barely focus on walking straight. Some of those problems had easier solutions than others. A quick conversation with Patrick would resolve Gideon's questions about his absence. Time would heal the wounds Jarrett opened in the team. The wedding would come. Planning would be over. The other problems were not so easy.

The elevator doors slid open. Gideon strode through them, walked straight to his desk, and slumped down in his chair. Once Ashcroft was dealt with and Gideon and Jolie were married, he intended to take a long vacation. He wanted to stay away from Sojourn City, superhumans, and secret agents for as long as possible.

"Gideon!"

He craned his head around. Arianna approached from the elevator, her blonde ponytail bobbing behind her. He couldn't tell by her expression if she was excited or disappointed. Probing her with his powers revealed that she was feeling a mixture of both emotions. That couldn't be good. Gideon rose from his seat and walked to meet her. She led him down the hallway and into a quiet corner.

"We've made a breakthrough with the antidote."

Arianna and Maddox had once shared their lab with Dean. Now, with him serving as the company's CEO, it belonged to the two scientists alone. It was neat and orderly, with designs and sketches hung on the walls and technology secured in labeled containers. Most, if not all, of the Vindicators' tools had come out of this lab. Maddox stood at a desk, typing furiously on its holographic tabletop. Arianna guided Gideon to him and leaned against the desk.

Gideon looked down at the screen. Maddox was typing notes in a small window in the top right corner, while the majority of the computer's screen space ran a simulation. Most of the graphics cycling through the simulator represented DNA.

"What do you have?" Gideon asked.

"We've got good news and bad news," Maddox said.

"Good news first," Arianna jumped in. "We can make an antidote. Based on simulations using the DNA of the nephiloid, it has a 99.5 percent chance of success. It'll attack Nephilim DNA like a cancer and kill it. If you can find Ashcroft's store of the serum and inject the antidote into it, the whole serum will be rendered inert."

"And the bad news?" Gideon asked.

Maddox pressed his lips together. "It won't work on someone who's already been amplified. When the serum is injected into a human, it alters their DNA. Take a look."

He flicked his wrists, and two holographic strands of DNA rose into the air from the tabletop. One was unremarkable, like any other human strand Gideon had ever seen modeled. The other, however, was slightly different. It had replaced a few of the horizontal strands with what looked like beams of golden-white light.

"If we tried to give the antidote to someone who already had superpowers, it would kill them," Arianna explained. "Your DNA changes when the serum is infused. It absorbs the Nephilim DNA and recodes your own genetic structure; you're basically half-angel now. Assuming that the Nephilim actually were half-angels."

Gideon clenched his jaw and stared at the screen. "So, it won't work because the antidote attacks Nephilim DNA . . . "

"But a person who's been affected by Ashcroft's serum has basically become a Nephilim. The antidote would attack their own DNA, killing them."

Maddox shook his head helplessly. "There's no scientific precedent for this. We've never seen anything like it."

"Because it's supernatural." Gideon scratched behind his ear. "Develop the antidote. If we find Ashcroft's serum before he uses the device he stole, we can render it inert before he disperses it. We're on a clock, guys. Don't let me down."

* * *

Accepted.

Wes stared at the word displayed on his phone screen. A surge of excitement rose in his chest, threatening to bubble out into a cheer. He muted the exclamation when he realized that his acceptance meant his time with the Vindicators was coming to a close. That was it. His decision was made. He was going to enroll in Juncture City School of Law at the beginning of the year. Now that his second application had been accepted, it was an easy choice to make. And yet, it wasn't. His family was here—all his friends, too. Sure, he wouldn't stay in Juncture City forever, but he would miss them. He had been close to home his whole life, and leaving now was going to be difficult. But it was the right move.

He would go ahead and enroll in classes. In the meantime, he had several months to help Gideon and the others wrap up this Ashcroft situation. Plenty of time.

Who should he tell first? Obviously, his parents and Gideon deserved to hear it before the rest of the team. They were his family. But they would also be the hardest to tell—especially Gideon. The two of them had always been close, but since they had started working together, their bond had only grown stronger.

Wes walked upstairs to the ops room. The room was empty, save for the mannequins that held the team's uniforms. Wes walked up to his suit and stared at it. The black-and-light-blue gear with its multi-textured tile belt made him smile. He had lived the dream; he had become a superhero and fought alongside a team of people like him. But now, it was time to find out who he was on his own. Rampart had to have his own identity outside the Vindicators.

As busy as he was bound to be in law school, he was still determined to bring his suit with him. Every city had crime. Juncture City could use Rampart. Of course, if anyone found out, he would probably be expelled from school for illegal vigilantism and subsequently arrested. Mayor Crowe may have made superheroes legal in Sojourn City, but that didn't apply everywhere.

Wes had time to work out the details. It was still close to four months before classes at Juncture would start. He needed to focus on bringing down the Regency. Then he could leave with a clear conscience.

* * *

Hannah didn't know Jarrett any better than any of the rest of the team did. Nor did she know any of them better than she knew him. That gave her the benefit of perspective. The Vindicators had been working as a unit for a long time, so to have a newcomer lie to them must have felt awful. Jarrett had lied to her, too, but she understood that you shouldn't tell your biggest secret to new people. And on the flipside, she could understand why they would mistrust him. She was not overly fond of government agents herself. Jarrett was an enigma, and she intended to figure him out.

The two of them stood in the center of the training room and circled each other, both poised in combat-ready stances. Now that the operating table and holding cell were gone, the room could be used for its original purpose. Hannah's muscles were tight. She crouched low and kept her arms close, ready to move at a moment's notice. Jarrett, by contrast, was interestingly loose. He kept his feet spread and his arms up, but he was not tense.

Hannah lunged first, snapping a kick with her left leg up at Jarrett's head. He moved his upper body backward so that her foot missed, but otherwise, he remained stationary. She planted her foot back on the ground and swung with her right hand, forming a baton with her energy powers. Jarrett moved to the right, behind her arm, and pushed her hand aside.

He still made no effort to strike back.

She used her momentum to spin in a complete circle and, as she came back around, kicked her right foot up. The kick struck Jarrett in the ribs. He wrapped his left arm around her leg, yanked her forward and upward, and dropped her on the ground. Hannah grunted as her back slapped against the mat. Jarrett released her leg and backed up.

"Not bad. That spin was good. You just didn't pull your foot back fast enough."

Hannah scrunched her nose in frustration and jumped to her feet. Jarrett backed away and rolled his shoulders, loosening up again. Her face warmed. Jarrett was infuriatingly passive. He behaved like this was a joke to him. She stepped in and punched with her left hand. Jarrett blocked her hand with the back of his own and jabbed at her neck. She moved aside, but his fingers still dug into her shoulder. She grimaced and brought her left hand up, catching his extended arm and twisting it.

"Ow. Not bad." He grinned and yanked his hand free of her grip. "Not bad at all."

They settled into a rhythm, matching punches and kicks as they circled the mat. Hannah struggled to keep up with him. He was well-trained. She understood now why he had been recruited to Special Forces. After a few minutes of sparring, Jarrett stepped back, lowered his hands, and nodded. For a moment, Hannah remained tense. He was already so relaxed. Was he really signaling the fight was over, or was this just a ploy?

Jarrett grinned. "We're done, okay?"

"You read my mind." Hannah chuckled. "I thought you didn't have superpowers."

"I don't. I read your body language." Jarrett picked up a towel and wiped sweat from his face. "I know my style tends to throw people off. But, hey, whatever works, right?"

"Tell me about how you were recruited by the government."

"It's not that interesting of a story. When I got back from overseas, I decided to do something about the crime in Wichita. Became Yeoman. Someone in CLOUD must've noticed, because not long after, I got scooped up. They said that they needed skilled people like me to deal with the extranormal threats in the world. If I agreed, I'd be allowed to continue my vigilante work in Wichita, so long as I followed orders whenever they called." He shrugged. "It was better than going to jail."

"I understand why you made the choice. I don't blame you for not telling Gideon and the others. But for what it's worth, I wouldn't keep secrets from them anymore. And decide which side you're really on. The government and the heroes may have the same agenda right now, but that may not always be the case. And when it comes down to that, you're going to have to make a choice."

Jarrett pursed his lips. "I know."

"Good. Just making sure." Hannah headed for the door. "I want to know who I have to watch my back around—and who I can trust to watch it for me."

* * *

Carter tossed the broken-down cardboard boxes into a shopping cart. Working at a grocery store was far from the most exciting experience of his life. It was worth it, though; it helped his mom stay on her feet. She still had to care for his siblings, after all. When he had come home from the Tower the previous night, he had found her in the living room, poring over bills and holding back tears. He sat down next to her, hugged her, and told her everything was going to be okay.

If only his dad was still alive. His job at Sterling Enterprises had paid a lot better than Carter's job—or even Mom's. There were rough times when Dad was around, but somehow, they always pulled through.

Carter pushed the cart toward the dumpster. As he threw the cardboard into the trash, he thought about his dad's old job. Carter was nineteen years old and physically fit. He knew how to fight and how to take a punch. He had even fired a gun before, albeit only for practice. He was just as capable as his father had been, and he knew the CEO of Sterling Enterprises personally. He could ask Dean for a job in security, and he was all but guaranteed to get it. Why was he still working in the stock room of a grocery store?

He smacked his forehead. "I'm such a dummy."

How had he never thought of this before? He finished throwing the cardboard away and wheeled the cart back inside. Silas Rockwell,

Carter's coworker and one of the few people who knew he was the Crusader, looked up as he approached.

"What's up, kid?"

"Just getting some clarity."

Silas smiled. "Good for you, Carter. I saw your friends on the news last night. All the way in D.C., fighting some supervillains? That's crazy stuff."

"Yeah. Crazy."

Crazy almost got Dean killed, and it lost him his arm.

"I can't tell you what to do, but I can give you some advice, if you'll let me." Silas patted him on the shoulder. "You have a lot of amplified friends. Let them handle the stuff farther from home. It's not that you can't do it because you're clearly capable. But what if something were to happen here while you were all gone? Sojourn City would be defenseless. Your mom, brother, and sister would be defenseless."

Carter nodded. "Yeah . . . "

"I'm not saying never leave, never go help. I'm just saying, you need to know your priorities. You've got a lot on your plate for a guy your age. Don't overwork yourself."

"Thanks, Silas. If I'm ever away and something does happen . . . "

"I'll be here." Silas winked. "Your family will be just fine."

"I know. Thank you."

Carter pushed through the door to the front of the store. Suddenly, the little grocery store seemed claustrophobic, restricting. He had a destiny outside of this place. All he had to do was work for it.

I'm going to make you proud, Dad. I promise.

CHAPTER 33

Four years ago

Learning how to extract the Nephilim blood and DNA and put it into a living creature had been a long process. Ashcroft's first experiments had been on animals—first rats and goats and then on to larger species. Most of them had died. Combining the DNA of multiple animals helped. Finally, he had a few living subjects, but they were nothing more than monsters. They had great power but no sapience to control them. They were good only for tests. He hoped to someday find another use for these creatures, which he had branded nephiloids. But until then, he'd have to keep them locked away for their own safety and the safety of anyone who came into Ashcroft's lab. They exhibited some modicum of intelligence, but far more prominent was a feral hunger that would be difficult to sate. A problem for a later date. He had bigger goals.

At last, Ashcroft was ready for his first human experiment.

Roger lay on the table in the laboratory. He had been Solar Flare's faithful accomplice in decades past, helping Father with his experiments. He had helped Ashcroft carry that legacy into the future. Now, he would be a part of the process himself.

"Are you ready?" Ashcroft asked.

"I am." Roger took a long breath through his nose. "Your father would've been proud of you for making it this far, my boy. His own experiments, cutting-edge as they were for the time, don't come close to what you're building here."

"I hope you're right."

Ashcroft strapped Roger to the table to keep him from flailing about. He inserted IVs and a few other needles and tubes into Roger's arms and lowered a big helmet over his head to monitor brainwave activity during the Evolving.

Roger grabbed his arm. "There is something you should know. This comes from your friend and guardian, not your lab assistant. Your father's experiments were dangerous. I've protected you from the truth for so long, but I believe you have earned the truth. In the end, it was your father's serum that drove him mad. I saw it myself. He became paranoid, obsessed with power. He thought the government wanted to take it from him."

They probably did. That would be typical. Ashcroft thought back to how the scientists had treated him at Stanford. When they saw his success, he was sure they would come crawling back. Maybe Father was not as mad as Roger thought. Maybe he had seen things more clearly than anyone else.

"In the end, Solar Flare attacked first." Roger stared up at Ashcroft, tears gleaming in his eyes. "I couldn't stop him. He attacked the Pentagon. A horrific battle followed. They killed your father, but it was the only way to stop him. I'm sorry."

Ashcroft scowled. "Why didn't you tell me this before?"

"Because . . . " Roger swallowed. "Because I believe you have what it takes to perfect your father's serum. You found the Nephilim. You advanced science. I still believe in you. I would not volunteer for this if I wasn't sure. I just wanted you to know so . . . so that if I go as mad as he did, you will stop me before it's too late. Don't let me become a monster."

Ashcroft pressed his lips together, unsure of how to respond. He wished he could say that he would honor Roger's wishes. Part of him knew that he wouldn't, and he didn't want to lie to Roger. If this experiment succeeded, he could not kill a successful subject, no matter how insane he might become. Stepping over to the console across the room, Ashcroft spared one more glance at Roger. Then he threw the switch.

Serum flowed through the tubes and into Roger's body. His heart rate and brainwaves rose in activity. Ashcroft stepped to his side.

"Are you all right?"

Roger nodded. "Yes. Yes, continue."

So far, so good. He returned to the console, his eyes dancing over the readings. Just a few more moments.

Roger's heart rate spiked. Ashcroft's eyes widened. He looked back at his assistant, who was seizing on the table, convulsing so strongly that the leather straps were strained. Ashcroft rushed to Roger's side. The older man's eyes rolled up into the back of his head. His arms tensed, and his muscles bulged. Fists clenched, Roger jerked his arms, and the restraints tore free.

Ashcroft backed away as Roger stood. His assistant reached down, tugged the IVs and tubes from his body, and removed the helmet. He wasn't seizing any longer. Roger looked at Ashcroft.

"I'm—"

He collapsed. Ashcroft crossed to the fallen body. It had worked. Roger had become superhuman. His body had resisted the change, but perhaps . . . Ashcroft put his finger to Roger's neck. He found no pulse.

Ashcroft growled between his teeth, scooped up the helmet, and threw it across the room. He pounded his fists on the empty operating table. That did not satiate his rage. Screaming, Ashcroft kicked his computer console. He had been so close. So close! Why hadn't Roger survived?

He looked down at the body. Calm washed through Ashcroft. He unclenched his fists and knelt again next to his deceased assistant. The answer was simple. Roger died because he was weak. His body had been unable to survive the changes. If Ashcroft was to succeed, he needed stronger subjects.

"Sorry, Roger." Ashcroft closed the older man's eyes. "Sometimes, sacrifices must be made in the name of progress. You made Solar Flare proud."

CHAPTER 34

Present Day

Artemis Wayans did not know where Nephilius acquired the uniform of a military colonel, nor how he managed to forge an I.D. for her. She could hazard a guess: Quinn had been involved somehow. Quinn was a former member of the British Army, dishonorably discharged for selling military supplies on the black market. If anyone could get their hands on a uniform and forged credentials, he was the man.

She didn't care how he'd done it, just that he had. Artemis's new mission was not going to be easy with the uniform. Without it, it would have been all but impossible, even with her hypnotic abilities. Nephilius had worked with her the previous night, teaching her to hone her psychic control. Before, she could only control a handful of people at a time. The most she had ever attempted was four. But now, she was confident that she could control an entire room of people if she had time to focus, and that was exactly what Nephilius wanted her to do.

A soldier on duty held up a hand. "Identification, ma'am."

Artemis withdrew the papers and I.D. that Ashcroft had given her and extended them to the soldier. *These had better work* . . . Breaking into a nuclear launch site would lead to a lot more than just a relatively cozy jail cell in Stone Gate. She would be lucky if she got locked up in Guantanamo Bay for that. As the soldier scrutinized her credentials,

Artemis focused on his mind, preparing to hypnotize him if he didn't buy it.

"Thank you, Colonel." He saluted. "Carry on."

Nice job, Quinn. The arrogant prig wasn't so useless, after all. Artemis saluted back, tucked the papers back into her pocket, and proceeded inside the base, holding her briefcase close to her side.

"Where am I going?" she said softly.

"Take a right ahead," Quinn said in her earbud. "Then you'll take the second left, and it'll be the fourth door on the right."

"Right. Good work on the credentials, by the way."

"My, my. A compliment from the great Somna?"

"The only one you'll ever receive, so don't let it go to your head." Artemis rounded the corner. "I'll call back when I've reached the objective. Out."

She tapped her earbud, silencing it before Quinn could retort. He always had a comeback.

Artemis took the second left and walked down the hall, counting the doors on her right. The fourth door was guarded by two armed soldiers. Artemis hoped she could get by them, too. If not, a little hypnotism would do the trick.

One of the soldiers shifted toward her as she approached. "Can I help you, ma'am?"

She extended the briefcase. "I need to get inside. I have a message for the general."

"We'll have to verify, ma'am."

That wouldn't do. She stretched out mentally, sending a burst of psychic static to cloud their minds and reaching past it to take control of them.

"You will let me pass."

"Yes, ma'am." The soldier entered a passcode to unlock the door. "Go right ahead."

Artemis stepped past him. The room she entered was full of technicians manning consoles. The officer on duty stood in the center of the room, watching a monitor that took up the entire wall to Artemis's right. *This is it. The nuclear control station.*

The technicians and officer didn't notice her at first. She reached throughout the space, touching the mind of each man and woman in the control room. She gently implanted a hypnotic suggestion into each of them: *obey.* One by one, the technicians straightened in their seats, ceasing their work. The officer frowned for a moment before he joined his companions in a ramrod straight posture.

"You." Artemis gestured to the closest technician. "Come here."

The technician rose and walked toward her. Artemis extended the briefcase to him, and he took it.

"You will deliver this to the missile platform. Have it installed in a missile in place of its normal payload. Return here when it's done."

"Yes, ma'am."

The technician scurried from the room. Artemis climbed the steps to the platform where the officer stood and clasped her hands behind her back. There was so much power in this room, all of it under her control. It was intoxicating. Now all she had to do was wait. Time was her ally—and Gideon Turner and his rebels had no idea.

* * *

Audrey couldn't remember the last time she'd been shopping. It had been years. When she was a celebrity, most of her clothes had been custom-made. She'd had contracts with many modeling agencies to represent their brands. She'd never had to shop; they just sent her the clothes they wanted her to wear that week. So, when Jolie offered to take her—with Hannah in tow—to the mall to find some clothes of her own, Audrey jumped at the chance.

Audrey was glad that Zeke hadn't hurt Jolie the night they saw her in Wally's Diner. It would have been one more thing to add to Audrey's guilty conscience, and she didn't need that. She needed to absolve herself of her sins—make up for the things she helped Ashcroft do.

"What style do you like?" Jolie asked as they entered the mall. "Denim? Flannel? Winter is coming, so you're going to want some jackets. But you've got literally nothing, so you'll need a bit of everything, I guess."

"How are we going to afford that?"

Jolie held up a credit card. "This is Dean's. He said to get whatever you want. Don't worry. He's a billionaire. He can handle it."

Audrey grinned. "Let's do it."

Jolie led Audrey through the mall. There wasn't much of a crowd. It was early afternoon on a Tuesday when most young people were still in school. That was probably good because Audrey also couldn't remember the last time she was in a crowd of people. She had been used to it once; performing concerts in front of thousands had numbed her to large groups. But it had been years, and she had been cloistered in Ashcroft's lair for most of that time.

She followed Jolie into a clothing store.

Jolie took a few items from a rack and handed them to Audrey. "Try these on."

Audrey spent the next hour trying on dozens of outfits. When she was satisfied with her selection, they checked out and moved on to the next store.

"I think it was brave of you to turn on the Regency," Jolie said. "It couldn't have been easy to realize you were on the wrong side."

"It wasn't, but once I did, I knew I had to do something about it. Wouldn't you do the same if you knew you were doing more harm than good?"

"Good point." Jolie smiled. "In any case, it's good to have some girls around. I wasn't the only one. Arianna was around. But she spends most of her time in the lab."

The three women laughed in unison, though Hannah's was more of a polite chuckle. Warmth filled Audrey's chest. She hadn't realized what she was missing out on. These people were friends—real friends. And it was reassuring to know that they would be there for her. She would do her best to always be there for them, too.

But maybe that started by being honest.

Audrey took a deep breath. "Jolie, there's something I need to tell you."

Jolie raised an eyebrow. "What's up?"

"Do you remember the night, a few nights ago, when you went to Wally's for a late-night shake?"

"Yeah, I—" Her brow furrowed. "Wait. I didn't know you then."

"I was at Wally's with Zeke and Pierce—um, Torrent and Tetra-Hazard. We had been staking out the Tower, and we decided to get out of the hotel for a while. We had no idea you would be there, but when we realized you were Gideon's girlfriend, I sent Zeke to follow you."

"So that's what I saw that night."

"I'm sorry, Jolie, I—"

Jolie put a hand on her shoulder. "It's in the past. There's nothing to be sorry for."

"But now Zeke knows where you live."

"I think the Regency has bigger things to worry about than a local detective. And I can take care of myself."

Audrey forced a smile. "So, we're cool?"

"Of course. Thank you for telling me." Jolie's phone rang. "I'd better get that."

Hannah frowned. "Mine, too."

She reached into her pocket and pulled out her phone. Jolie stepped away to take her call, and Hannah raised the phone to her ear.

"*What?*" Hannah exclaimed. "We're on our way."

Jolie rushed back. "I just got a tip on Serban's location. I've got to go."

Hannah nodded. "We need to go, too."

"We do?" Audrey asked.

"Yeah. Someone just launched a nuke—and it's angling for Sojourn City."

CHAPTER 35

Jarrett's government connections had come in handy. An alarmed Jarrett had called Gideon, warning him that a nuke had just been launched and was aimed at Sojourn City. If not for CLOUD, the city might have been dusted before any of them realized the danger. Gideon rushed to the terrace outside the lair. Jarrett was already scanning the sky with a pair of binoculars.

"No sign of it yet."

"How do I stop it?" Gideon asked.

"Best guess? Cut its propulsion. Destroy the rocket guiding the bomb and guide it into the lake."

"Won't the nuke blowing up in the lake be a bad thing?"

"That's why you're going to guide it down very, very carefully."

"Doesn't the Air Force have jets that can intercept it?"

"The Pentagon's in chaos. They're trying to figure out how this nuke got launched in the first place. They're saying that some kind of mind control is involved."

Gideon clenched his jaw. "Somna."

Jarrett scanned the horizon again. "You'd better get moving. If I see this thing before you get to it, we're going to be in a lot of trouble."

The air whooshed to Gideon's left. Audrey dropped Hannah on the terrace next to them. The former supervillain was wearing civilian clothes, and she wouldn't have time to change into her uniform. It looked like she would have to fly up in her civvies; but as soon as she touched down, she pulled her button-up flannel free, revealing her super suit beneath. She pulled off her jeans, put on her mask, and nodded.

Gideon pulled his hood up. "Let's go."

It was time to see how dedicated she was. As the only other flyer on the team, Audrey was their alternate if Gideon failed.

"Good luck," Jarrett said.

"Don't die," Hannah added.

The Seraph blasted off toward the east. Stormcry paced him, her expression locked in grim determination. He searched the horizon for the missile, but there was nothing so far.

Wait. A plume of smoke traced the sky in the distance. The Seraph angled toward it and focused the light energy emanating from his body into his fists. He hoped he would be strong enough to guide the missile once its thrusters were destroyed; but if not, he had Audrey there to help him.

"What's the plan?" she shouted.

"I'm going to blow the thrusters off! Then we divert the missile into the lake!"

The Seraph closed in on the rocket and hovered just above it. He aimed his hands down toward the thruster. *God, please don't let this blow us up.* The light energy surrounding his fists increased.

"Wait!" Stormcry exclaimed. "I recognize the make of that payload. It's one of Ashcroft's. He must've replaced the normal nuclear warhead with an explosive containing his serum!"

The bombs Ashcroft had detonated in Phoenix, Raven City, and elsewhere had spread the serum across a city block. Gideon mentally recalculated. If the serum was in the nuke, and if the bomb went into Lake Superior, the serum could seep into the water. Countless people would be affected and get superpowers. Or the water might dilute the serum past the point of effectiveness.

"If it only contains the serum, does that mean it's harmless to us?"

Stormcry hesitated. "Hypothetically. I can't say for sure."

"Good enough for me. Move away!"

She dropped back behind the missile. The Seraph flew forward, hovering above the payload rather than the thrusters.

"Catch the warhead!" he called to Stormcry.

He aimed his hands at the seam between the rocket and the warhead and fired a beam of light into it. The missile cracked, and the warhead dropped out of sight. The Seraph aimed at the remnants of the missile and blasted it to pieces. He arced away and scanned for any sight of Stormcry. He spotted her black-and-white form a moment later, cutting through the clouds. She floated back up toward him at a leisurely drift and held out the warhead in both hands.

She smiled weakly. "Mission accomplished."

* * *

Artemis ground her jaw as she strode out of the Pentagon and toward the waiting van across the street. The rebels had managed to destroy the missile, but it was irrelevant. This mission had only been a distraction. However, Nephilius certainly wouldn't have complained if the missile detonated in Sojourn City. Yet again, Gideon Turner and his band had made her look like a fool in front of her master.

This time, Audrey had been involved, too. Watching the missile's flight through the camera installed on the hull, Artemis had had a clear view of the younger woman and her distinctive silver-streaked hair as she flew alongside the Seraph. She had thrown in her lot with the Vindicators. Artemis grabbed the handle to the passenger side door, yanked it open, and climbed inside. She slammed the door. Quinn leaned against the steering wheel and smirked at her.

She scowled. “Drive.”

“Aye, ma’am.”

The van roared down the road. Artemis leaned back in her seat and closed her eyes. Manipulating that many people had taken a toll on her. Her mind was fatigued, and she struggled to stay awake. But now was not the time for rest. Nephilius’s plan had to be carried out now, while the Vindicators were still distracted. The rest of the Regency should be ready. Once Artemis and Quinn were in position, the final phase could begin. At last, the Vindicators would be destroyed. With Artemis at his side, Nephilius could ascend to his rightful position. Godhood.

* * *

The call from The Broken Glass’s bartender had been unexpected. Jolie figured Serban would be smart enough to avoid going back there, now that the police were on his trail. But maybe he had something stashed there—money, a passport, or weapons. In any case, Jolie wasn’t likely to get a chance like this again.

She jumped out of her Camry, secured her bulletproof vest, and checked her gun. There was no sign of Agent Ross’s vehicle yet, but if she waited for him, Serban might slip out. He might have already. She didn’t have time; she needed to move in immediately. She marched toward the bar, putting aside the thought that a nuclear bomb might descend on the city at any moment. They had the Vindicators to take care of that.

Jolie kept her gun in her right hand, pressed against her hip. With her left hand, she opened the door to the bar and stepped inside. It took her eyes a moment to adjust to the dim lighting. There were few patrons; most people were still at work. The bartender looked up as she entered and waved her over.

"He went into the back. I tried to stop him, but he just pushed past like he owned the place."

"Thank you." Jolie clenched both hands around her gun. "Get everyone out of here. Go."

The bartender scurried off, moving around the bar to the few patrons who were there and ushering them out. Jolie crept toward the swinging door that led to the back of the bar and peered through a wide, circular window.

No sign of Serban. She wondered if he had already come and gone, perhaps slipping through the back door. She pushed the door open and stepped into the back room, keeping her gun up. She scanned the room left to right. He wasn't there. She walked toward the door at the back of the room, which led to the alley.

A baton crashed down onto her elbows. Jolie cried out, and her gun slipped out of her grasp. She jerked her head back as the baton swung in again, this time at her jaw. It swept by with a *whoosh* of air. Serban stepped out from behind a rack of wine bottles and sneered.

"Detective, isn't this game getting old?"

"So, give it up."

"Sorry. Not in the mood."

He lunged, swinging his baton toward her head. Jolie stepped aside and grabbed his wrist. She kicked his knee and used her free hand to punch his face. Serban dropped to his knees, and Jolie twisted his wrist. He growled and struggled against her, intent on keeping a grip on his weapon. *Almost . . . there . . .*

Serban reached up with his other hand, clasped it over Jolie's, and pulled himself up. He jerked his head forward into Jolie's nose. A bomb detonated inside her skull. She cried out and staggered back, releasing Serban's wrist.

The mobster bared his teeth. "Should've left me alone. Now, I have to kill you."

Focus, Jolie.

Serban swung. Jolie ducked under the swipe, danced around behind him, and drove her elbow between his shoulder blades. She locked him in an armbar and twisted. Serban screamed and dropped his baton. He swung his muscular frame, driving his shoulder up under Jolie's ribs. She struggled to hang on, but another shove dislodged her.

Jolie scrambled backward. There was murder in his eyes. She looked for her gun and spotted it off to her right, near the back door. She glanced back at Serban. He reached around to the small of his back, withdrew a gun, and stepped toward her.

"Goodbye, Detective."

Jolie threw herself across the floor. *Bang.* She didn't feel the pain of a bullet; he must've fired as she moved. She grabbed her pistol, rolled onto her back, and squeezed the trigger. Blood spurted from Serban's shoulder. The crime lord grunted, clutched at the wound, and fired again. Jolie scrambled back behind the wine racks he had used for cover earlier. Serban continued to fire. A moment later, the gunshots stopped and were replaced by the sound of the swinging door. Jolie peered around the rack.

Gone.

She rushed out the door into the bar. The front door was already ajar. Jolie sprinted through it. The sunlight pierced her eyes, and she grimaced and looked around. No sign of the big man. She growled and kicked the sidewalk. A moment later, a black SUV pulled up. Jolie holstered her gun and walked toward Agent Ross, furious that Serban had escaped her again.

CHAPTER 36

Dean rushed into the lair. *Did I really miss a nuclear bomb?* Of all the days to have a meeting at Sterling Enterprises, of course it had been today. He bounded upstairs to the training room—which had been used as a lab far more often than as a training room lately—and found Arianna and Maddox studying the warhead. Gideon, Jarrett, Audrey, and Hannah stood at a distance. He moved to Gideon's side.

"What. In. The. World?"

Gideon's expression was grim. "The warhead had been replaced with Ashcroft's serum. We think he was trying to spread it across the city."

"With this detonator, he could've infected the majority of Lakeside," Maddox said. "Proper wind patterns might have blown traces all the way to the Brooks. Theoretically, the bomb's reach would allow inoculation of up to three-quarters of Sojourn City."

"Injecting one person at a time with a liquid-based serum is one thing," Arianna added. "Using the serum in aerosol like he did with the small explosions is another. But if he figured out a way to spread his serum farther than a city block at a time . . . "

Gideon hung his head. "He can infect anyone he wants."

"But why a nuclear strike?" Jarrett frowned and ran a hand through his hair. "He had to know we'd see it coming. It wasn't exactly subtle. And we know he has that dispersal unit from Sterling Labs. Why not use that?"

"Everything Ashcroft does has an ulterior motive." Audrey stepped forward. "If the bomb had detonated successfully, he would have been thrilled, but he has redundancies built into every plan. There had to have been more to it. Why bother stealing the dispersal unit if he was just going to use the nuke instead? No, this doesn't fit with what I knew of his plan."

"A distraction?" Dean asked.

Gideon reached the same conclusion as Dean. "He's getting ready to make a move. That's why he didn't use the dispersal unit; he has bigger plans for it. If he's planning to release the rest of his nephiloids on major cities, maybe the dispersal unit is for another location. He wants to maximize his reach."

"My thoughts exactly."

"We need to find him before he succeeds." Gideon glanced at Audrey. "You know where his base is, right? Can you take us there?"

Jarrett nodded in agreement. "If we could find the Regency's base now and attack it before Ashcroft can prepare, we might be able to end this a lot sooner."

Audrey hesitated. Dean didn't need Gideon's empathic abilities to tell that she was conflicted about leading her new friends to attack the base where her old friends lived. Stockholm Syndrome must have set in hard on her. Even if she knew they were in the wrong, it was clear that turning them over would be difficult for her. Dean put a hand on her upper arm and nodded reassuringly. He made sure it was his flesh-and-blood appendage. She put one of her hands over his and smiled.

"Okay. But . . . I'm not sure he'll actually be there."

"Why is that?" Gideon asked.

"He could already be in position to make his move. Keep in mind, he was close to his endgame before he got the dispersal device. Now that he has it, there's no reason for him to wait, other than to finish his synthetic serum. If he's done that—and based on this bomb, he has—he's ready to move."

Dean grimaced and lowered his hand. She was right. They might show up at Ashcroft's base to find that there was no one there, and then they'd have to play catch-up to stop him from enacting his plan.

Gideon was undeterred. "Arianna, Maddox, what's the status of the antidote?"

Maddox scratched his head. "Should be done in the next day or two."

That was another problem. Even if they did stop Ashcroft's plan, without the antidote, there was no guarantee that they could stop any backup plans he had in place.

"We'll wait as long as we can," Gideon said. "There's no reason to attack his base if we can't neutralize the serum. But if the antidote isn't ready by this time tomorrow, we'll have to move, with or without it. There's too much risk in waiting."

"Understood. We'll get to work."

Dean gestured for Audrey to follow him out of the lab. There was nothing more they could do there, and he could use this time to get to know her better.

"I wanted to thank you again for saving my life," he said. "I would be roast billionaire if not for you."

"I couldn't just let Monahan kill you. Speaking of being a billionaire, thanks for my new wardrobe. It would've been, uh, difficult if my super suit was the only outfit I owned."

Maybe it wasn't a subtle look, but Dean thought she looked great in it. The white-and-black uniform was snug and flattered her figure, and the blue highlights complimented her skin tone. But he didn't think that would be the best thing to say, at least right then. He didn't want to come off like he was flirting.

"My pleasure. It was the least I could do to repay you. I'll design a new suit for you, if you want. One that doesn't remind you so much of your past. I could even throw in a new name if you think Stormcry sounds too villainous."

"That would be great." Audrey laced her fingers in front of her and backed away. "I'm going to go change now."

"Okay." Dean waved. "See you downstairs!"

See you downstairs. Dean groaned inwardly and resisted the urge to facepalm as she picked up a shopping bag. He quickly walked down the stairs and into the kitchen. He remembered watching the Silver Siren's shows and dreaming of meeting her in person. He'd been infatuated. She was beautiful, and her voice was entrancing. But as much as he had fantasized about meeting her, he never thought it would happen, let alone that she would save his life. He still wasn't sure what had led her to do it.

What he did know was that she probably needed a friend. From what he saw before he left for home the previous night, she didn't feel welcome. Dean could change that. He was good at making people feel welcome. Maybe the others were just being cautious because she had worked with Ashcroft, but he was willing to give her the benefit of the doubt—and not just because she was gorgeous or because she had saved his life. He saw in his brief conversation with her on that rooftop in D.C. that there was good in her, an innate kindness. She had a moral core—something none of Ashcroft's other lackeys seemed to possess. That was something worth cultivating. Now that they had seen her help stop a nuclear bomb, hopefully the others would be equally forgiving.

But at least they could use their words, unlike him. *See you downstairs.*

"Stupid, stupid." He leaned his head against the refrigerator. "Talk much, Sterling?"

"You've got it bad, man."

Dean jerked his head up. Gideon stood at the entrance to the kitchen, leaning against the counter and grinning. Dean lowered his head, opened the fridge, and pulled out a Mountain Dew. He popped the can open and glanced back at Gideon.

"So?"

"It's cute." Gideon laughed. "You haven't been on a date in . . . well, at least since I've been back from Venezuela. Maybe it's time."

"Yeah." Dean sipped the fizzy drink. "Maybe."

"Just relax." He laughed. "She likes you, too. At least, that's the sense I'm getting. She may not be crushing, but she definitely feels something for you that she's not feeling for the rest of us right now."

"Really?"

"Yeah. You don't want to die alone, Sterling. Get it together. When all this is over, ask that girl out."

"She's a former pop star, Gid. She's so far out of my league, we're not even playing the same game. And what about my faith?"

"See what she believes in." Gideon shrugged. "She's clearly looking for something. Maybe before you see her as a potential girlfriend, you need to look at her and see someone who needs the love of God in her life."

"Yeah, maybe. Thanks, Gid."

"What are best friends for? Think about it, man."

That wouldn't be a problem. Dean didn't imagine it would be easy for him to think of much else for a while.

* * *

Artemis jumped out of the van and ran across the street toward the warehouse. She grabbed the big, metal door, lifting it just enough to slide underneath with Quinn. Quinn came in after her, and Artemis lowered the door back to the ground. She checked her watch. *Just after sundown*. It wasn't the ideal time to strike; too many people would already be back in their homes.

They'd wait for morning rush hour. When the city's inhabitants had flooded the streets, they would release the nephiloids, causing the maximum amount of chaos possible. She pulled her cell phone from her pocket and called Zeke.

"Somna and Red Raider are in position. We will strike at six a.m."

"Roger that. Torrent and Fragment are in position; we'll sync our attack to coincide with yours. And I've heard from Backfire and Lancet and Deluge and Tetra-Hazard. They're all ready and waiting. I'll pass on the time of attack, so we all launch in unison."

"Good." Somna smirked. "The time is at hand, Torrent. Do your job—and when we are done, our lord will rise to conquer the Vindicators for good."

"Yeah. Not if I kill 'em first."

Artemis hung up and stuffed her phone back in her pocket. They'd best get ready; the fight was about to begin.

* * *

Gideon walked down the street hand-in-hand with Jolie as the sun drifted below the horizon. He could feel her disappointment and frustration, and he knew it was because Serban had escaped her again. He resisted the urge to offer his help a second time. He knew that he could take Serban. His powers had grown since he'd faced—and defeated—Serban on the rooftop of Sterling Enterprises. But Jolie seemed determined to handle this on her own, so he would respect her wishes. He squeezed her hand, and when she looked up at him, he gave her a reassuring smile.

Her dark hair was curled into waves that framed her beautiful face. She wore a red top with a white jacket over it. She looked as beautiful as she ever had. Gideon was thankful he had the privilege of marrying her.

She smiled back. "I'm sorry. It's just . . . "

"It's okay. Remember, not that long ago, I was on a personal manhunt for Serban, too. I know how frustrating it is."

"Yeah, but I shouldn't be thinking about it right now. We've both got so much going on. We really need to take this time for us. I want to talk about our wedding or our future—anything but Serban or Ashcroft."

"Right. You're right. So, speaking of our future, we can probably start moving some of my stuff, the things I won't need between now and the wedding, into your place. That way, when I do move in after the wedding, we won't have to move it all at once."

"Okay. Whenever you have time . . . "

"Of course." He leaned over and kissed her forehead. "I love you, and I can't wait to start our life together."

"Neither can I, my love."

But is part of that life being a superhero? Once they took down Ashcroft and his followers, would there be any reason for him to be the Seraph anymore? The police, combined with the other heroes' help, had completely turned Sojourn City around in the last few months. It was perhaps safer than it had ever been. Maybe it was time for Gideon to step away from the cape for a while and just live his life with Jolie.

He pulled her to a stop as they reached an intersection. As they stood, waiting for the green walk symbol to appear, Gideon scanned the sidewalk on the other side of the street. A figure in white walked perpendicular to them, crossing to Gideon's left. His eyes widened. *It can't be . . .*

Gideon closed his eyes for a moment. When he reopened them, the man in white had disappeared.

"Something wrong?" Jolie asked.

"Hmm? No." The light switched. "Let's go."

They walked the rest of the way to her apartment and stopped outside her door. Gideon held Jolie's hands in his and looked down at her. The closer they came to their wedding day, the harder it was to part from her. Had it really been mere months since she'd been all but hostile toward him for his acts of vigilantism? God had worked in their relationship, and Gideon could not have been more thankful. He pulled her into a hug and kissed her on top of her head, running his left hand through her soft, raven hair. *How did I get so lucky?*

"I love you," he said.

"I love you, too." Jolie kissed his neck before moving up to his lips. "See you tomorrow."

He stepped back. "Get some rest. And try to relax. You're going to get Serban; I know it."

"Thank you. Good night, Gideon."

"Good night."

He stepped down off her porch and tucked his hands in the pockets of his army-green jacket. It was only a couple miles back home. He could have easily flown there in under a minute, but the walk would do him good. He prayed as he walked.

Lord, I don't know why I'm seeing Wyatt Jonson. I don't know if I'm crazy or if it means something, but if it does, please reveal it to me.

If he'd seen Wyatt in the heat of battle, he might have pushed it aside as fog of war or his imagination. But Wyatt had appeared four times now, and two of his visits were when Gideon was at rest, walking with Jolie and searching for the nephiloid in Kansas. Maybe Wyatt's appearances meant something, or maybe Artemis had planted something in his mind before she was imprisoned to make him go crazy. But why was he only seeing it now?

He turned left at an intersection. His phone vibrated, and he reached into his pants pocket for it. *Maddox.* He answered the phone and brought it to his ear.

"Hello?"

"Good news. We've got a working sample of the counteragent, and we're replicating it now. It's a good thing Audrey managed to catch that bomb intact; it was the key to our breakthrough."

Gideon smiled. "Good work. You should get some rest. You and Arianna both. You've done more than we've had any right to ask of you."

Gideon told Maddox goodbye and tucked his phone away. A weight lifted from his chest. *One step closer to finally ending this. Now if only I could get rid of these visions . . .*

As if on cue, a white-clad figure crossed the street ahead of him. Gideon stopped in his tracks as the figure disappeared behind a building. *I've had enough of this.* He rushed across the street and rounded the corner.

The man in white was half a block ahead, walking away from him. Gideon broke into a jog, following the man with Wyatt's face.

The man broke off into an alley. Gideon ran around the corner and clenched his fists, light radiating from them. "Wyatt" had stopped in the middle of the alley. As Gideon closed in, he turned to face him. It was Wyatt, all right. Gideon would recognize his face anywhere.

"How are you here?" he asked.

"'Be strong and of a good courage,'" Wyatt said.

"What?"

"'Greater love hath no man than this, that a man lay down his life for his friends.'"

He's quoting Scripture. Gideon took another step toward Wyatt. The white-clad man made no move to back away.

"Wyatt, how are you alive?"

"'With God, all things are possible.'"

"What do you want?"

"'The weapons of our warfare are not carnal, but mighty through God to the pulling down of strongholds.'"

What is Wyatt trying to tell me? This has to be a message, right? If Gideon was imagining this, he was truly delusional. Maybe he needed to see a shrink. He held out his hand. If he touched Wyatt, felt that he was there, maybe that would convince him that this was real.

"'And lo, I am with you always, even unto the ends of the earth.'"

Wyatt stepped back and vanished. Gideon dropped to his knees and stared at the spot where Wyatt had been standing moments before. There was no sign of him, not even disturbed dirt or a footprint. Had he ever been there at all? Gideon struggled to control his breaths, which came in choppy gasps.

Just breathe. In . . . two, three, four. Out . . . two, three, four.

He used the martial arts breathing technique he'd learned to calm himself. His heart rate slowed, and his mind cleared. It couldn't have been a coincidence that he had seen Wyatt only moments after praying for God to reveal the purpose of these visits. They meant something.

But what?

He'd mentioned laying down his life for another. Gideon wondered if he was referring to his own death at the hands of Katrina Monahan. And when Wyatt mentioned the weapons of their warfare not being carnal, it could have been a reference to Gideon's powers, rather than physical weaponry. *Or is there some other meaning to it all?*

In any case, he had a partial answer. He wasn't delusional. These visits were real, and they meant something. He would still puzzle over what until he figured it out, but as long as he knew he wasn't crazy, he could relax—at least a little bit. He pushed himself up from the ground and left the alley.

God, just please let this all be over soon.

CHAPTER 37

Patrick darted his head back and forth between his textbook and his laptop as he typed out the homework assignment due in the morning. He struggled to stay focused on the work. He'd had almost no energy all day, likely because of his run to San Francisco and back. It was all he could do to keep his eyes open.

It didn't help that the lair was unusually quiet. From his position on a stool at the kitchen island, he could hear the others watching TV, but it was turned down low. No one was talking. They all seemed as exhausted as he felt. Maybe it was because they had dealt with the stress of a nuclear bomb. Patrick still couldn't believe he missed that. *So, I was at school. That means I can't be in the loop?*

But it wasn't like he could have done anything to help. If the bomb had been close enough for Patrick to do something about it, it would have been way too late.

Footsteps clunked at the entrance to the kitchen. Patrick glanced up. Jarrett stepped into the room, smiled, and nodded at Patrick. He tossed a handful of empty soda cans and used paper plates into the trash can. *He seems so . . . normal. Why am I struggling to forgive him?*

"Hey, I've been meaning to talk to you."

Jarrett walked around the island and leaned against it. "I want you to know that even though I didn't tell you who I was, I never meant you or any of your friends any harm. It's just my job. I can't go around telling people I belong to a government organization that most people don't even know exists."

Patrick bit his lip and nodded. "I know. But . . . would you have ever told us?"

Jarrett stared across the room. "Probably not. But I'm sure there are people in your life who don't know your secret, right? It's like that. If you told everyone that you're Spright, it would probably cause some problems."

"Everyone knows Gideon is the Seraph."

"Yeah, and he's urged everyone else to keep their identities as secret as possible, hasn't he? Gideon understands that sometimes, to protect people, you have to keep secrets."

Patrick thought back to when Backfire had kidnapped his parents and nearly killed them. If he hadn't known Patrick's identity, he never would've done that. But keeping a secret identity from the bad guys and keeping it from loved ones was different. *But didn't I do that, too?* He hadn't told his parents he had superpowers for months.

"I hope you'll forgive me." Jarrett put a hand on Patrick's shoulder. "I like you, kid. You've got a good heart."

"Thanks. So . . . everything else you told us was true, right? Being in Special Forces, your wife, being a vigilante . . . "

Jarrett's gaze went distant again, and his lips tightened. "All true. My wife was only a few blocks away from us when we were fighting Ashcroft's people in D.C."

"Is she okay?"

"Yeah, she's fine. It's just . . . that was too close."

"Don't worry. We're going to stop these guys."

"I know. That's why I'm still with you. I believe your team has a better chance of stopping Ashcroft and the Regency than anyone else—even CLOUD."

"Thanks for the vote of confidence." Patrick grinned. "I should probably get back to my homework."

"Oh. Yeah." Jarrett headed out of the kitchen. "Good talk, kid."

Patrick watched him go and felt a flood of relief. That resolved one of the issues Patrick had been conflicted over. If only the rest could be fixed that easily.

* * *

Hannah leaned against the railing on the terrace and looked out at the lights of the city. It was beautiful in its own way but so different from her home. She could barely make out more than a handful of stars in the sky, overpowered as they were by the artificial light of skyscrapers and streetlights. But the city made up for the lack of starlight with the variance of colors. Blues, reds, yellows . . . It was a cacophony of light.

In her brief time with the Vindicators, she had grown to like them, but this place was not for her. She was committed to helping them put an end to Ashcroft and his machinations, but after that, her reservation needed her. She even missed Axel, as unusual as he was.

"Penny for your thoughts."

Wes leaned against the glass doorframe leading back into the lair. She hadn't seen him around much lately. Since his spat with Jarrett, Wes had kept his distance from the Tower. He smiled and stepped up next to her, resting his forearms against the railing and clasping his hands in front of him.

"I was just thinking how different this city is from the reservation," she offered. "The sounds of animals and nature—they aren't here."

"Heh." Wes grinned and looked out at the city. "Nope, just the sounds of car horns and sirens. Not quite as peaceful."

"And the sights, too. It's all so different—almost claustrophobic."

"Yeah, but for me, it's home. That's what you're really thinking, isn't it? You miss your home."

"I thought Gideon was the empath."

"He is." Wes offered a small smile. "But I know a thing or two about people. I know what homesickness looks like. I see it in Patrick, too."

"Don't worry. I'm here until this is over."

"I'm glad." Wes pushed himself away from the balcony. "You're good with a gun. A little bit more practice with your powers, and they'll come in handy, too. And for what it's worth, you're not bad company, either."

Hannah studied Wes for a long moment. The city lights reflected from the deep blue of his eyes. She took a cautious step closer. She was not here to make friends, but she was glad he enjoyed her company. She knew she could come off as unfriendly and overly serious.

Wes lowered his head and smiled sheepishly. "I'm about to head home and get some rest. No telling when everything's going to go sideways. Might as well be rested when it happens."

As he backed into the lair, Hannah looked out over the city for another moment before going back inside after him. He was right—a little rest would do them all some good.

* * *

Powers shifted onto his side. The threadbare sleeping bag scratched his skin in response. He grunted and rolled over to lie on his stomach, but that was somehow worse. Every individual fiber of the rough fabric seemed to find purchase on his skin and dig in if he moved, even microscopically. He rolled back onto his side and clenched his jaw.

He shouldn't be there in the musty, abandoned apartment complex in Chicago, waiting for Zeke to give the word that it was time to launch their attack. Downstairs, the nephiloids hibernated in their specialized stasis pods. Six of the beasts were ready to charge into the city and rampage in the streets. On the other side of town, Pierce, Monahan, and the remaining members of Zeke's mercenary team had set up the distributor from the D.C. job. As the nephiloids wreaked havoc, those two would activate the distributor and spread the serum across the city.

But Powers didn't have to be with them when they did. He unzipped his bag and eased out onto the cold, concrete floor.

Zeke was sleeping; he would never know if Powers left a doppelganger in the sleeping bag, climbed out the window, and disappeared into the Windy City. Powers looked back and forth between the super-strong man and the window. Golden rays from nearby streetlights beckoned for him to slip out to them. Of course, if Zeke wasn't asleep and caught Powers trying to escape, the bruiser would probably kill him.

Powers clenched his fists, digging his fingernails into his palms. *Just do it, coward.* This was his chance—maybe his last one—to get free of this life, to be who he wanted to be. He took a step toward the window. But what if Ashcroft's plan succeeded? What if he really could come through on his promises? Did Powers really care?

If Ashcroft does succeed, there will be nothing to stop him from coming to look for you.

And if he succeeded, Powers would be one of the most powerful people in the world. But if he left right now, even if Ashcroft failed and Powers got to live out the life he wanted, he'd never be at the top of the heap. At best, he would rule his own little criminal empire, but he'd still effectively live in hiding.

"Not trying to run again, are you?" Zeke mumbled.

Well, there goes my chance. "Just restless is all."

"Take it from me. It's best to just lie there until you fall asleep. Otherwise, you'll go into battle sleep-deprived, and you won't be of any use to anyone."

"Right." Powers climbed back into his sleeping bag. "Whatever you say."

CHAPTER 38

One year ago

Unfortunate as Roger's sacrifice had been, it had led Ashcroft to redouble his efforts to understand Nephilim physiology. That was the focal point of the experiment. Father's serum may have driven him insane, but it had been a wholly scientific concoction. With the supernatural DNA of the Nephilim spliced with the serum, Ashcroft was confident that he could overcome that problem. However, the more immediate challenge was keeping a subject alive. With his assistant's death, he needed more test subjects—people who were expendable and would not be missed should they turn up dead.

Ashcroft began his search in Romania. A mobster named Luca Serban provided Ashcroft with several test subjects, most of whom died. But one survived—a man named Randal Quinn, who developed the power of pyrokinesis. Serban made no secret of his distaste for Ashcroft, so the scientist took Quinn and left Romania.

After that, Ashcroft had found others in the United States. A woman named Artemis Wayans volunteered of her own free will. A mortally ill superstar named Audrey Knight. A former soldier, Zeke Norris. Kenton Pierce, a career criminal. Others came, and more of them survived the Evolving as Ashcroft came closer to perfecting his serum. He hired them all as employees of the Regency's shell corporations to provide them with cover identities.

From there, Ashcroft had gone to Venezuela, where he had conducted a successful experiment on a man named Joshua Omer. Interestingly, Omer survived the Evolving but did not initially display any powers. Ashcroft kept him in a cage for observation. His following experiments were all failures until the guerrillas brought him a young man named Gideon Turner. Turner was a doctor, a Christian missionary captured while trying to defend a clinic from the guerrillas.

Like Omer, he survived the Evolving. And like Omer, his powers did not manifest right away. Ashcroft kept the two of them together for monitoring. He brought Omer back to his lab only once. He learned then that Omer did display the physiology of the Nephilim and that there was vast potential for power within him. It was just waiting to be unlocked.

No matter. What mattered was that his serum was effective. It was time to prepare to spread it across the world. *Humanity is weak.* Roger had proved that. The poor man had died trying to help Ashcroft, but his death had only proven his frailty. Ashcroft had realized something that day—Darwin had been right. It really was about survival of the fittest. Ashcroft saw the world for what it was, and he was going to change it. Weakness dragged the strong down. If he spread his serum across the world, only the strong would survive. All weakness would be purged.

And at last, humanity could become what it was meant to be.

"Doctor!" a guerrilla called. "The prisoners have attempted another escape!"

"Follow them!"

"The older one is dead, sir. Captain Mendez killed him." The guerrilla lowered his head. "My men are pursuing the younger one into the jungle."

Ashcroft waved his hand. "Bring him back or kill him. It doesn't matter."

Turner was inconsequential now. What could one boy, whose powers had not manifested, do against Ashcroft's grand plan? Even if Turner's Evolving was discovered, no one could tie it back to Ashcroft.

He had done all he could in the jungle, and it was time to return home. "Prepare me a plane," Ashcroft said. "And bring me Captain Mendez. It is time for the next step of my plan to commence."

CHAPTER 39

Present Day

It was time.

Clad in her green jumpsuit and black cape, Somna stood on an overpass and looked down over the crowded interstate. There were hundreds—perhaps thousands—of civilians, crammed in rush-hour traffic as they headed to work. In moments, they would be swarmed by a dozen nephiloids, unable to escape as the creatures cut a swath through them. Across town, Deluge and Backfire—supported by Backfire's guerrilla allies—had set up a reverse-engineered duplicate of the Sterling Enterprises dispersal device. The city would be filled with newly created superhumans going through the Evolving. And not just in Washington, D.C. Torrent's team was set up in Chicago, and his mercenaries had placed the last of Ashcroft's gas bombs in major cities all across the United States. There were even a few on planes headed to foreign countries.

Somna raised her left wrist, pulled back her glove, and touched a command key on her wristband. A light next to the button glowed blue. In unison with the light, an explosion erupted to Somna's left as the warehouse she and Red Raider had occupied the previous night blew open. Seconds later, a shrill howl ripped through the air.

Artemis smiled. A dozen nephiloids poured from the side of the warehouse and onto the interstate. They tore into cars, smashing their hoods and reaching through their windshields to get to the occupants.

Precise footsteps clapped against the sidewalk next to Artemis. She glanced over at dark-haired Red Raider, who was wearing his red-and-orange jumpsuit and mask that concealed his face from the nose down.

"Permission to join in?" he asked.

"Granted."

The corners of his eyes turned up—the only hint of the smile hidden by his mask. He extended his hands, and a fireball formed between his palms. And then Somna watched as the world descended into chaos.

* * *

The nephiloids tore through downtown Chicago like a chainsaw through paper. Powers's stomach twisted as he watched one of the six gray-skinned beasts hoist a white sedan into the air, trapping its occupants inside. One of the sedan doors popped open, and the passenger screamed and clutched the seatbelt for dear life.

It was too late to back out now. Torrent had his eye on Powers, especially after last night. If he tried to slip away, he was sure the muscle-bound man would tear him apart. So, he stood in the middle of a park and watched a nightmare unfold.

"Keep the people contained, Fragment," Torrent ordered. "Form a perimeter. Let no one escape."

You've got to be kidding me. Powers hadn't signed up to massacre innocent people. The nephiloids wouldn't kill everyone, but the body count would be in the hundreds, at least. Those who survived would be infected with their venom, which would lead to them developing superpowers. Powers hoped that the Seraph and his friends had found a way to stop them. Even returning to prison would be preferable to this abomination.

* * *

Jarrett's gaze tore away from the computers as Gideon entered the ops room. "We're getting reports of unidentified creatures rampaging through Washington, D.C. and Chicago. Gas bombs have detonated in Dallas, Seattle, Juncture City, Miami, and half a dozen other densely populated areas. CLOUD is scrambling agents to respond, but they've got no idea what we're up against."

"We do." Gideon rushed for his armor. "Everyone, suit up."

Half an hour before, Gideon's phone had woken him with a bombardment of notifications. Jarrett and Dean simultaneously contacted Gideon with reports of the attacks. Scrambling to make it to the lair, Gideon had ordered them to get in contact with the rest of the team.

When they were all there, they gathered in the ops room and watched in horror as several different monitors showed news footage of the chaos. Police and SWAT teams had been deployed in each city, but the nephiloids Ashcroft released were stronger than the ones the Vindicators had fought so far—and they were backed up by the Regency.

They all knew what had to be done. Chicago and D.C. were the centerpieces of the action. The other cities were experiencing transformations, but the Vindicators couldn't be everywhere at once. Fighting off one nephiloid had taken the whole team. They had to focus their efforts on those two cities and pray that law enforcement could handle whatever amps evolved in the others.

Jarrett adjusted his blue-tinted goggles. "I've got to go to D.C. My wife's there."

"I understand," Gideon said. "Take Dean, Audrey, and Patrick with you. I'll take Carter, Hannah, and Wes to Chicago. This is it. This has to be the beginning of Ashcroft's endgame. There are going to be dozens of people already infected with nephiloid venom; we need to inject the creatures with Arianna and Maddox's counteragent as soon as we arrive on the scene."

"We've installed the agent in darts which can be loaded into these guns." Arianna handed a rifle to Dean, and Maddox passed them out amongst the others. "They should be sufficient to penetrate the nephiloids' hides. The counteragent will nullify the creatures' venom and likely kill them."

"What about Ashcroft?" Audrey asked. "He's got to be doing something with the distributor."

It was a good point. He used more gas bombs, even though he had the distributor, which could cover a far greater distance. Perhaps the simplest answer was the obvious one: Ashcroft didn't have time to mass produce the distributor, but random bombings could get the same job done. He had to be saving the distributor for a big target.

"We can't worry about that while so many civilians are in danger," Gideon said. "They come first."

Dean's face was pale. "The Raptor's fast, but there will be a lot of carnage by the time we get there."

"We'll do the best we can." Gideon finished pulling on his suit. "All right, everyone. Let's move."

* * *

Wes adjusted his vambraces as the Raptor descended toward Chicago. Since it was the closer of the two hotspots, Chicago's team was hitting the ground first to contain the damage as quickly as possible. Wes didn't want to imagine what D.C. would look like by the time

Jarrett's team arrived. It would be a warzone. There was nothing he could do for them, though. Wes's focus had to be here on Chicago.

Unfortunately, his mind kept drifting back to telling Gideon that he was moving to Juncture City. It was far from relevant at that moment, and yet it was at the forefront of his mind. He drove it back as he placed his domino mask over his eyes and took a step closer to the ramp.

"You okay?" Gideon asked. "You seem . . . off."

Stupid empathic powers. "There's something I need to talk to you about, but it can wait until we clean up this mess. What's the plan?"

"From the look of things, a lot of the fighting is centered in the tourist hotspots—downtown, parks, and so on. Carter will focus on crowd control, getting people out of the way of danger. You, Hannah, and I will deal with the nephiloids and the Regency."

Carter flicked his batons' electrified ends to life. "Save some bad guys for me."

"No promises." Gideon smiled. "Just get those people out of there."

"Will do."

"Ramp down in five," Maddox called.

Wes checked his rifle, loaded with several antidote-laden darts. It was odd to be using a firearm instead of his bare fists, but he was sure he would have plenty of opportunities to punch things. Slinging the weapon over his shoulder, he grabbed the nearest handhold and clenched his fist around it as the plane descended. He spared another glance at Gideon. His brother's wrist was still in a brace from his fight with Torrent in D.C., and his ribs were no doubt still feeling the effects, too. Wes wasn't sure Gideon should be fighting, team leader or no.

"Ready, Vindicators?" Gideon asked.

Wes clenched his jaw and nodded. The ramp hissed as the cabin decompressed, and the light of Chicago's early morning sky pierced the relative darkness.

"Move!"

CHAPTER 40

Team D.C.

Sheets of torrential rain slapped the side of the plane as the Raptor's ramp lowered to let Drifter leap out. Drifter hung in midair for a moment, focused on a street corner below, and teleported to the ground. As soon as his feet touched the pavement, he dropped into a crouch. Audrey soared down and hovered above the intersection. She wore the new costume he had designed for her—a white, skirted outfit with a blue musical note emblazoned on the chest and matching blue boots, vambraces, mask, and cape.

"Hey, I've been thinking. New name for the new costume." He had dialed his comm to a private frequency only she could hear. "What do you think about Aria?"

Audrey glanced down at him from the sky. "Aria . . . I like it."

"Great. Let's kick some butt, Aria."

Drifter flexed his left hand. *Still not at one hundred percent.* He could fight with it, though, and it packed a bigger punch—literally—than his real, flesh-and-blood hand.

The question was—was he ready? Last time Dean had gone into a fight, he had lost that very limb. *Should I really be fighting again so soon?* What if he froze up, panicked? He did not want to be a hindrance to his team.

No. They needed him. He would do this.

He pulled the dart-loaded rifle to his shoulder. A trio of nephiloids rampaged through the streets ahead as a SWAT team peppered them with gunfire to no avail. They needed to aim for the eyes, but the cops focused their shots on the beasts' center mass.

Drifter tapped an earbud to open the comm line to the whole team. "Spright, Yeoman, handle the nephiloids on the interstate. Audrey and I will take care of these three."

"I'm one of you now," Audrey said. "Call me Aria."

Spright disappeared in a flash of purple, and Yeoman set after him on a motorcycle.

Aria swooped down toward the street. "I'll draw their attention. You hit them with the serum."

Drifter teleported half-a-block down the street. Aria flew by and fired a soundwave from her hands. One of the nephiloids roared, stumbled back, and looked up to the sky. Aria hit it with another blast. The beast swatted at her, but Aria darted aside. Drifter brought his rifle up, looked through the scope, and trained it on the nephiloid's neck.

Raindrops clouded the scope. Dean scowled, lowered the weapon, and wiped away the water with his glove. He raised the rifle again and found a sheet of water barricading the street between him and the nephiloids. *The water girl. What had Audrey called her? Deluge. Great; we're fighting a water manipulator in the middle of a downpour.* The girl stood in the middle of the street, hands held out to both sides and spheres of water forming around her. She grinned wickedly. *Teenagers.* Dean slung the rifle over his shoulder and dropped into a fighting stance.

"Stand aside!"

Deluge didn't respond. She extended her hands, and the water spheres shot forward. Drifter threw himself aside and teleported, landing on the sidewalk behind a brown sedan. His opponent looked around for a moment, spotted him, and thrust out her hands again. Drifter teleported right behind her and brought his elbow down on the back of her head. She dropped to her hands and knees.

"No need to get hurt, kid." Drifter rotated out his aionium shield.

"The only one who's going to get hurt is you!"

"Good comeback. Very original. How long did it take you to—whoa!"

Drifter jerked his head back as Deluge swung a sword made of water. He brought up his shield and blocked as the weapon came back around. The watery blade sluiced over the aionium. Deluge pulled the weapon back and thrusted it at Drifter's abdomen. Drifter knocked it aside with the edge of his shield, blinking water droplets from his eyes as he did.

Deluge growled and swept the blade at Drifter's throat. He ducked and blocked her attacks, occasionally teleporting behind her to get in a blow of his own. Finally, when she swung her water sword wide, Drifter stepped in, grabbed her wrist, and used his other arm to smash his shield into her face. Deluge slumped over, and the wall of water splashed to the ground. Drifter turned his attention back to the nephiloids.

Aria flew in circles as the creatures did everything they could to reach her. One climbed the side of a building, reaching out with its long, gangly arms to pull her out of the sky. Drifter unslung his rifle and trained it on that nephiloid. He squeezed the trigger.

The beast howled and waved its arms frantically, releasing its purchase on the building in the process. It fell to the pavement three stories below. Its body spasmed for a moment, and finally, it lay still.

"Got one!" Drifter shouted.

The other two nephiloids roared at him and charged. *Oops.* Drifter teleported to the nearest rooftop and prayed he was fast enough to drop them both before they reached him.

* * *

Spright weaved through D.C. traffic, grabbing as many civilians as he could and taking them off the interstate. The nephiloids' rampage had spread into other districts, but D.C. police and even the military were converging. However, several men in dark camouflage cut the authorities off, pinning them down with heavy weaponry. They had to be some of Mendez's guerrillas, and if that was the case, Backfire was probably somewhere in the city, calling the shots. Spright's gut churned with the thought of finding his grandfather's killer. Backfire wasn't going to escape again. But before Spright could focus on him, he had to get the innocents to safety.

He glanced up at a nearby overpass as he dropped off another civilian. Yeoman stood on the overpass, completely still, head tilted to look through the scope of his crossbow. He elected to put the counteragent in syringe-tipped arrows rather than use a rifle, and so far, he had dropped two of the six nephiloids. It was an impressive show.

Spright dropped another civilian off in a shopping mall parking lot and darted back to Yeoman's side. The older man lowered his crossbow.

"Heard from your wife?" Spright asked.

Yeoman shook his head. "She's down here somewhere. She was on her way to the conference center when the attack started."

"We'll find her. Get me a location, and I'll get her out."

Yeoman pulled out his phone and dialed. "Jan, you there? I need you to tell me the nearest exit to you. I'm sending someone to get you."

Spright watched the interstate below. There was no sign of a live nephiloid nearby. They must have moved on. In the distance, rapid pops of automatic gunfire echoed over the torrential rain.

"Thirty-first Street exit!" Yeoman called.

"I'm on it. You find whoever's pulling the nephiloids' strings."

"Will do." Yeoman grabbed his shoulder. "Patrick, please keep her safe."

Spright nodded soberly and darted down the freeway. He weaved between stopped cars and chunks of debris. How many people would survive the nephiloids' onslaught, only to develop superpowers in the coming days? Between these attacks and the bombings in other cities, there could be dozens or hundreds of new amps. He had a feeling the world was about to change—a lot.

Spright bounded over a wrecked Prius and skidded to a stop next to the off-ramp. Where was she? He tapped his earbud.

"Yeoman, what kind of car is she driving?"

There was a pause. "A green Fusion!"

Spright scanned the interstate around him. *Fusion . . . Fusion . . . Where is it?* Raindrops clouded Spright's goggles. He reached up and yanked his mask off his head to clear his vision. If someone saw his face, so be it. No one in D.C. knew him, anyway, and there were no news cameras nearby. Finally, he spotted the vehicle halfway up the off-ramp, sandwiched between two other cars. He sped up the ramp and stopped next to the car.

The passenger's side door was jammed shut against the car, and the driver's side door appeared crumpled, its window smashed out. A blonde woman about Jarrett's age leaned back in the driver's seat, grimacing and clutching at her left shoulder. Blood stained her blouse and her right hand. Patrick vibrated his hand rapidly and punched out the windshield.

The woman whimpered. "Who are you?"

"I'm Spright. I'm here with your husband. You're Janet Mercer, right?"

"Y-yes."

"Jarrett sent me to get you." Spright reached through the opening. "Can you climb out?"

"I . . . I think so."

Spright took her hand and helped her out of the car. She wobbled a little bit as she touched the ground. He looped himself under her injured arm and helped her stand. She looked at him, and the concerned look on her face cleared. Taking off the mask had been a good idea. All she saw was a red-headed teenage boy. He gave her a reassuring smile and helped her limp away from the car. He studied her arm as they walked.

"What happened to your shoulder?"

"S-some giant creature." She gestured up the off-ramp. "It attacked me, but something drew its attention away."

"Did it bite you or scratch you?"

"It . . . b-bit me."

"I'm going to get you to the nearest hospital. Hold onto me."

He hoisted her up so he was holding her in both arms and darted down the road. As he ran, he wondered how he was going to tell Jarrett that his wife was very likely going to develop superhuman powers.

* * *

Aria flew down toward the rooftop where Drifter was frantically trying to keep away from the nephiloids. Every time they took a swipe at him, he teleported a few yards away and took another shot at them, but the beasts were so fast that it was almost impossible for him to get a bead on them before they charged him again.

She dropped toward the roof and turned so her legs faced downward. She struck one of the beasts in the back with both feet, pushed with all her might, and propelled herself back into the air. The force of the impact knocked the nephiloid flat.

Drifter teleported next to the fallen nephiloid, jammed the rifle barrel against its neck, and fired. The beast howled and flailed, and Drifter teleported away again. The second nephiloid stopped for a moment, as if sizing up the situation. Aria extended a hand and fired a sonic blast at the creature. The nephiloid shrieked at her and gathered itself to leap. Aria's eyes widened, and she soared backward, out of reach of the nephiloid.

A wave of heat washed over her, turning the raindrops around her to steam. Shielding herself with her arms, Aria soared up and away from the heat, scanning the street below for its source. Red Raider stood next to Deluge's unconscious form, orange flames dancing around his hands.

"Come down here and face me, traitor!" Raider shouted.

"I've never liked you, Quinn!" Clenching her jaw, Aria soared down toward her opponent as a wall of fire rose to meet her.

CHAPTER 41

Team D.C.

Drifter shot the last nephiloid as Aria flew over to battle Red Raider—the only member of the Regency the Vindicators hadn't faced before. As the nephiloid howled and died, Drifter lowered his weapon and looked around. This plan didn't make sense. The nephiloids had caused some chaos, and some civilians were bound to have been affected by their venom, but it was an incomplete plan at best. Unless . . .

Unless there was more to the plan. Ashcroft was an intelligent man, and everything they had seen from him indicated he was a strategist. He wouldn't have unleashed these nephiloids and all his followers at once unless he was certain that his endgame was going to work. If they failed, it would leave Ashcroft alone; and no matter how powerful he was, he couldn't take on the Vindicators without the Regency.

What does he want? The same thing he'd always wanted, no doubt—to reshape the world to fit his image, to make everyone superhuman. The nephiloids partially accomplished that goal, as did the gas bombs in the other cities. Both methods had limited range, though, so there was no way they could ever turn everyone in one city, let alone the world. But if they were just a distraction . . .

The distributor had to be somewhere in one of the two cities, set up on a timer or a remote detonator to spread Ashcroft's serum across Washington, D.C. or Chicago. He wouldn't commit all of his forces unless those cities were his primary targets. The question was, which city? Was it possible that he could reach both? In the time since Ashcroft had stolen the dispersal unit, he could have reverse-engineered a duplicate machine. If that was the case, how many of them were there? There was no guarantee Chicago and D.C. were the only cities with dispersal devices.

But they were the only two the Vindicators could save. They would have to do their best and trust God.

Turning toward the interstate, Drifter teleported. He reappeared on a building overlooking an on-ramp. Above that ramp, Yeoman stood in the middle of an overpass and fired down at a pair of nephiloids in the middle of the road. Drifter teleported to his side and hurled his shield at one nephiloid.

"How are things over here?" He caught his shield on its return. "Everything handled?"

"Spright took my wife to a hospital. She's been bitten by one of these things. But these are the last two in this area."

"I need you to do something." Drifter ducked as the nephiloid swiped at him. He jammed his shield into its thigh and backflipped away from it. "Get in contact with your buddies at CLOUD. I think Ashcroft set up the distributor somewhere in the city. They need to find it before it goes off."

Yeoman shot the nephiloid attacking Drifter and finished off the last one just moments later.

"You trust us to do that?"

"What choice do I have?" Drifter backed away. "I need to check on Aria. Just find that distributor before it's too late!"

* * *

Spright raced back from the hospital toward Yeoman's last position. He tapped his earbud as he ran. No doubt Yeoman had moved on by then to find the rest of the nephiloids. He needed to catch up to him and finish this before any more innocents were hurt. The hospital had been flooded with injuries, more than Spright had ever seen.

"Yeoman, it's Spright. Your wife is safe. I'm on my way back to you. Where are you now?"

"Half a mile north from where we talked last. Drifter has me on a new mission, but I've got two more nephiloids in my sights. And the guy with the explosives has me pinned!"

Mendez. "On my way. Where are your CLOUD buddies?"

"Helping with Drifter's request—trying to find Ashcroft's distribution device before he sets it off in the city."

Spright shuddered. If that device went off, hundreds of thousands of people might be transformed into superhumans. It would be chaos.

"I'll be at your location in ten seconds."

He weaved up the ramp to the overpass Yeoman had occupied earlier and ran north from there. Ahead, an explosion ripped through the street. Spright clenched his jaw. Time to take this guy down once and for all. Sprinting past Yeoman, he aimed straight for Backfire. The villain was clad in his shell-like crimson armor, his square jaw and heavy brow exposed. The sight of his face ignited a fire in Spright's soul.

As he approached Backfire, Spright dropped into a slide. The villain's legs were spread wide; Spright slid underneath them, coming up behind Backfire. Transferring the force of his momentum into his arm, he smashed his fist into his enemy's back. Backfire stumbled forward, his armor cracking from the force of the impact. Spright stepped forward and looped his arm under Backfire's armpit. Normally, the villain's weight would've been too much for Patrick to lift, but leverage and momentum allowed him to hoist Backfire from the ground. In one smooth motion, Spright hurled the villain over his shoulder.

The rest of the world returned to normal speed as Spright stood over Backfire. The villain, his expression frozen in shock and pain, looked up at him. Spright reached up to bat away a soaked lock of red hair that had fallen in his eyes. He stepped toward Backfire, his hands vibrating. Last time he had faced Backfire, he had nearly killed him with a series of speed-enhanced punches. He saw the fear in the merciless villain's eyes, and for a moment, Spright considered ending him. He had faced that temptation before, but he was better than that. This time, he kept his rage in check.

"What's wrong, *niño?*" Backfire sneered. "Don't have the guts to kill me?"

Spright reached for a pair of power-dampening cuffs in his utility belt. His grandfather would have been proud of him. "I'm not like you, Mendez. I'm not a murderer."

Backfire clenched his fist, extended it, and opened his fingers. A ball bearing, charged by Backfire's powers, hurtled through the air. Spright threw himself aside as the projectile spun. His shoulder struck the ground, but the ball bearing flew harmlessly past and detonated against a streetlight. An arrow struck Backfire's chest, wedging into a gap in his armor.

Spright froze, staring at the arrow protruding from the villain's body. Backfire looked up at him, confusion on his face. *No, no, no.* He wasn't supposed to die. He was supposed to get justice, to rot in prison for life for killing Patrick's grandfather. Patrick dropped to his knees next to the supervillain. Backfire stared at him, rage burning in his eye, and slumped back, staring lifelessly at the sky.

A hand fell on his shoulder. "You all right?"

Spright looked up. Yeoman's crossbow dangled from his free hand. Spright clenched his jaw and stood, staring down Yeoman. The older man pushed his blue-tinted goggles up onto his forehead. Concern was evident in his eyes.

"You killed him."

"He almost killed you first."

"We . . . we don't kill."

"I'm glad you have that option." Yeoman took his hand off his shoulder. "But as hard as I try, I don't always have the luxury. I'm sorry. I was just trying to protect you."

Some of the weight in Spright's stomach lightened. "I know."

"Come on." Yeoman jerked his finger over his shoulder. "CLOUD has located the device, but they need help. Some guerrillas are holding up their progress."

Spright gave Mendez's body one last look. For all the pain the villain had caused him, he regretted that the man was eternally lost. "Let's go."

* * *

Drifter kept his eyes on Red Raider, ready to make a move as soon as he had an opening. Deluge was still down for the count. The nephiloids were dead. Drifter and Aria only needed to finish with Red Raider so they could join Yeoman and Spright in searching for the device. They were wasting time—time that was precious and dwindling. Aria circled the roof, firing sonic blasts at the villain, who retaliated with columns of flame. *Time to finish this guy.*

Drifter ran forward, jumped, and teleported onto the roof behind Raider. He came down in a crouch behind the villain. The air in the vicinity was unnaturally hot and muggy, warmed by Raider's flames and the evaporating rain. No wonder Aria was still floating in the air at a distance, rather than coming down to engage him. Drifter shook his head, blinked, and backed away. Red Raider hadn't seen him yet.

Aria fired another sonic blast. Raider grunted and fell backward. Drifter backed away and clenched his fist. Aria pounded the villain with another blast, but he just growled, climbed to his feet, and shot another pillar of fire. Drifter ejected his shield and gripped the edge, ready to hurl it like a discus as soon as he saw an opening. He needed Red Raider to stand still and not notice him for a few more seconds . . .

Aria fired a constant pulse wave at the rooftop. Red Raider raised an arm as if to ward off the attack, but the focused beam of sound wasn't something that could be deflected. The villain growled and clutched at his ears. Drifter jumped and used the momentum of his midair spin to add force to his throw. The aionium disk flew across the roof and struck Raider on the back of the head. The wiry man crumpled. Drifter ran to him and clapped him in dampening cuffs. Aria landed on the roof next to him and smiled.

"Good throw."

"Thanks, but it looked like you had him handled to me." He grinned. "A few more seconds of that blast, and he probably would've been unconscious, anyway."

Aria smiled and tucked her silver lock of hair behind her ear. "Thank you."

"You're welcome." He nodded down to the street. "We should probably cuff the girl before she awakens."

Drifter handed her another pair of cuffs. She soared down to the street. He watched her go. Maybe Gideon had been right—about him and about his feelings for her. And from the look of things, and if the other Vindicators had had as much luck on their missions, his schedule might be open soon.

But first, they had to disarm that dispersal device. Then he could worry about dating.

* * *

Spright ducked next to Yeoman in the alleyway as a hail of gunfire peppered the buildings around them. They rendezvoused with Yeoman's CLOUD friends, only to discover that Somna was also there and had hypnotized all of the CLOUD agents searching for the device. The two heroes had a dozen feds—and the rest of the guerrillas—spraying them with gunfire.

"Nice friends you've got," Spright muttered.

"Not their fault." Yeoman peered around the corner. "I can't shoot back. I'm not going to kill them for being hypnotized."

Spright nodded. "I think I can handle this, but you'll have to cover me. Take care of the guerrillas."

Drifter had given each of them neural inhibitors that could resist Somna's hypnotic powers. If Spright knocked her out, her control over the CLOUD agents should be broken. Then, they could shut off the device and go home.

Yeoman took a deep breath and checked his crossbow. "Ready when you are."

Spright closed his eyes. He imagined the world around him moving in slow motion—the CLOUD agents, Somna, even Yeoman. Everything crawled, seconds turning to minutes, while Spright remained constant. When he opened his eyes, Yeoman was still looking down at his bow.

Spright broke from the alley and sprinted into the street. Bullets, seemingly suspended in midair, hung all around him. He weaved his way through them and ran toward the federal agents. When he reached the first one, he turned his gun to the side so he'd be firing at a brick wall. He yanked the gun of another straight from his fingers. He redirected or pulled weapons away from each one, aiming away from Yeoman.

He darted between the guerrillas to where Somna stood in the middle of an intersection, her expression a mask of intense concentration. Spright drove his fist into her face. He halted his momentum next to her, and the world resumed its normal speed. The guerrillas dropped, one at a time, as arrows struck their shoulders. Yeoman was a good shot. The federal agents who still held their guns fired wildly into the ground or the wall, and a moment later, they stopped. They looked around in confusion.

"Impressive," Yeoman said over comms.

"Not as impressive as your shooting." Spright knelt next to Somna and cuffed her. "Let's find the device and go home. I'm *really* tired."

CHAPTER 42

The wiry young man handcuffed to the table looked friendly at first glance, but his pretty-boy appearance belied that he had been a high-ranking member of Serban's mob. His name was Costin, and he held no love for Jolie. There were plenty of other Romanians still in prison, but Costin was closer to Serban; Jolie had dealt with him before; and he spoke English.

"Are you sure this is going to work?" Ross asked.

Jolie shrugged. "We've already looked everywhere that Serban might run to, and we've found him twice. Do you know the odds of him showing up anywhere else we can connect him to?"

"Right. Not good." Ross gestured to the door. "Do your thing."

Jolie opened the door to the visiting room. Costin hadn't been informed who was coming to see him, only that he had a visitor. Ross stayed near the door while Jolie sat at the bolted-down steel table across from the prisoner.

Costin's frown deepened as recognition lit in his eyes.

"You?"

Jolie leaned forward. "Hello, Costin."

"Got a promotion, I see. Congratulations, Detective. But what could you possibly want with me? It couldn't have anything to do with my boss being on the lam, could it?"

Jolie scowled. "No, I just thought I'd pay a friendly visit. Why else would I be here?"

"Yeah, pretty obvious." Costin looked around. "Don't see your buddy, the Seraph, anywhere. You two on the outs? Why don't you get him to track Serban down?"

"Look, Costin, I'm sure you'd love to show me the door right now, but I can make your life a lot easier if you'll just talk to me. I can get you more yard time and even a chance at early parole, but it's a one-time offer that expires as soon as I step out that door."

"All those things will mean nothing if Serban finds out I sold him out. If you recapture him—doubtful—and he's thrown back in here, I'd be toast."

"We'll make sure Serban's in maximum security. He'd never get to you."

"He wouldn't have to. Don't you get it? Serban runs things in here. Every prisoner and a lot of the guards are in his pocket. All he'd have to do is say the word, and I'd be dead."

"Edgar Sterling isn't dead. If Serban wanted to kill anyone, it'd be him."

"Sterling's rich. He's paid off some of the guards to keep him safe."

Jolie grimaced. She wondered if Dean knew that—and what he'd think about it. It was technically wrong, but she wondered if she wouldn't have done the same thing in his situation. He wasn't paying them to do anything illegal, just to protect him. She decided not to mention it to Dean.

"Costin, what if I could guarantee your safety? I'll get Serban transferred to another prison entirely—a supermax, even."

Costin bit his lip. "Look, lady, I appreciate the offer, but I don't have a death wish. And even if I did, I don't know where Serban would go."

"You don't have the slightest idea? Really?"

"Look, I . . . ugh." Costin rubbed his forehead. "Serban had a contact at the docks. If he was trying to get out of town on the downlow, he might try there instead of the airport. Since, you know, his airport contact is locked up here with me."

"All right. I'll see what I can do on my part."

"Remember, you didn't hear it from me, understand?"

"I know. Thanks, Costin."

Jolie stood and backed away from the table. Ross crossed his arms and studied her. She rubbed the bridge of her nose as she stepped from the interrogation room into the hallway. Ross closed the door behind them.

"We've already combed the docks, Anderson."

"We can try again. Serban may not have wanted to show up there until he was sure that his contact could get him on a boat. Maybe he's got something lined up by now. Or maybe he's already slipped out of the city, and we'll never find him again." Jolie clenched her fists. "We're running in circles. He's one man, Ross. How hard can it be to find one man?"

"When that man doesn't want to be found, it can be very hard. Especially a man as powerful as Serban."

Jolie took in a deep breath through her nose. "The docks, then. We'll stake them out until we see something."

"Sounds like a plan."

Jolie stomped down the hallway. *I'm going to get this guy if it's the death of me.* Serban wasn't going to escape justice for the pain he'd brought on her city—not if Jolie Anderson had something to say about it.

* * *

Nephilius watched the battles unfolding in both cities from the safety of his lair, anticipation building with every moment. The dispersal units were nearly charged. The time was coming at last.

Turner's alliance of so-called heroes—his Vindicators—were faring as well as could be expected, but they hardly had the upper hand. They seemed to have concocted an antidote or counteragent to his serum and were using it to kill his nephiloids, but their reserves were limited. They could not hold out forever. And even if they managed to defeat his forces, they would still be diverted for long enough for the dispersal units to go off. Already, Nephilius' last stash of gas bombs had detonated. Dozens of new superhumans were born. A few more minutes, and those dozens would be joined by thousands more.

"Just a little more time, my servants," he rumbled. "Just keep them busy a little longer."

CHAPTER 43

Team Chicago

The sounds of battle met the Crusader as he leaped out of the Raptor. Police officers and SWAT teams fired on the nephiloids, which seemed unfazed by the hail of bullets and continued their rampage. A series of gunshots echoed behind him as Brass Bison opened fire on the creatures. The Seraph soared overhead, flying straight toward one nephiloid and blasting it with beams of light. Another of the creatures spotted the Crusader, roared, and charged at him.

The Crusader swung his staff in a tight circle, an arc of electricity trailing behind it. The nephiloid he was facing roared and swiped a hand at him. He rolled to the side, and the large, clawed hand swept through the air above him. He pushed off with his left foot and sprang off his hand into a front-flip. The flip gained him a few feet from the beast. It stood its ground and bellowed at him.

The Crusader reached over his shoulder for his dart rifle, and an arm snaked around his neck. The forearm pressed against his throat, cutting off his air supply. He struggled to suck in a breath, but whoever had a hold of him wasn't letting up. The Crusader jabbed his staff backward, and the tip found purchase. The arm loosened. He kicked out, catching his assailant full in the chest. He glanced over his shoulder. The nephiloid had lost interest and had resumed its rampage through the streets.

The Crusader's assailant stood and clutched his side. Immediately, the Crusader recognized the black-and-red uniform and the messy hair.

"Hey there, Powers."

"Little Crusader. You shouldn't be here, kid. Go home."

"And let you parade your ugly pets through the city? I don't think so."

"You can't stop it." Fragment straightened and clenched his fists. "I don't like this any more than you do. I just wanted to feel like I was in control of my own life. I didn't want to be the lowest common denominator, y'know?"

"I get it, man, but you chose the wrong side. Besides, you didn't seem to have a problem hurting innocents a few months ago. Starting that apartment fire? Attacking Silas Rockwell at the school?"

"I was doing what I had to do to protect my interests." Fragment's expression darkened. "But Ashcroft is insane. His ambitions are going to destroy us all."

The Crusader lowered his staff. "If you really believe that, stand down. Surrender now, so we have a better chance of stopping him."

"Can't. Ashcroft's already caught me trying to run once. Happens again, I'm a dead man. I hate all this, but I understand self-preservation. I'll keep ahead no matter what, kid. Sorry."

"Me, too."

Fragment lunged. The Crusader stepped aside and swung his staff upward into Fragment's chest. The older man grunted, crumpled to his knees, and vanished. Crusader scowled. Where was the real Vince Powers?

Footsteps shuffled behind the Crusader. Two more Fragments stepped toward him. *Aw, man, not again . . .*

* * *

The Seraph lunged forward to grab Torrent by his shoulders. Torrent raised both arms and slapped the Seraph's grasp aside. He kicked the Seraph in the gut. Gideon stumbled back, his injured ribs jarred by the closeness of the blow. He barely raised his left forearm in time to block a downward punch. He screamed between clenched teeth as the fractured limb took the force of Torrent's blow. The villain took advantage of the injury, stepping in and swinging again. Torrent's left fist shot forward and smacked the Seraph across the cheek.

Gideon had just managed to take out one nephiloid—saving a civilian in the process—when Torrent found him. Since then, they had been locked in an endless battle.

The super-strong villain surged forward, not letting up. The Seraph blindly fired a burst of light, the energy striking Torrent's fist. The attack halted the brute's advance for a moment. The Seraph took advantage of the pause to pivot so his left flank faced forward, raised his left hand, and fired a stronger burst into Torrent's chest. Torrent slid backward, his boots digging into the concrete and tearing it up. The Seraph lunged forward and uppercut Torrent's chin with a light-encased fist. Torrent flew off the ground a few feet and fell back down with a crash. The Seraph advanced on him.

A leg snaked out and struck the Seraph's ankles. He tucked into a forward roll and kept his balance, but the attack gave Torrent time to recover. Gideon glanced over his shoulder. Fragment, or one of his doppelgangers, stood behind him. The Seraph turned to face him, and Torrent grabbed his shoulder and jerked him backward. He struggled for balance and tried to take off, but Torrent yanked him back to the ground. The Seraph grunted as he struck the pavement. Torrent stood over him, raised a boot, and stomped down onto the Seraph's chest, caving in the already-dented suit. The breath left his lungs in a *whoosh* of air, and he felt his already damaged ribs break. Tears streamed from the Seraph's eyes, and he clenched his jaw so tightly, he thought his teeth would break.

A scream escaped his lips as Torrent raised his boot again. The Seraph discharged a blast of light from his body that knocked the villain away.

Three fights with Torrent, and Gideon ended up maimed after each one. Not only that, but the super-strong villain had damaged the supposedly indestructible aionium armor. He would be glad when Zeke Norris was behind bars for good.

Four more Fragments joined the one that had tripped the Seraph, and the five of them flanked him while Torrent advanced straight toward him. The Seraph reached out with his senses, trying to gauge when they would attack. He felt a hint of anticipation from the Fragment behind him to his left. He jerked his elbow backward as the doppelganger advanced, smashing it into the man's rib cage.

The remaining four Fragments charged in. The Seraph roundhouse kicked the one in front of him and used the momentum to wheel about and jab his fist into another's jaw. Light energy flared at the point of impact. One of the doppelgangers brought a foot up into his gut. The Seraph grunted and reeled back. Another Fragment jumped onto his back and wrapped his arms around his neck.

The Seraph grabbed Fragment's arms and jerked his body forward, using his own momentum to flip Fragment over him. The doppelganger landed flat on his back. The Seraph slammed his fist down into Fragment's chest, and the doppelganger disappeared. Immediately, two more of them were on him.

A steel hand shot out, knocking one of the Fragments to the side, and was joined a moment later by a matching steel foot. As the two Fragment doppelgangers recoiled and vanished, Rampart stepped up to the Seraph's side and put a hand on his shoulder. Gideon forced a weak smile and nodded his thanks.

Rampart smiled. "You look awful."

The Seraph struggled to catch his breath. "Thanks."

He looked past his brother. A dozen more Fragments approached, and Torrent stood among them. Clutching his wounded ribs, the Seraph glanced at Rampart.

"Prism?"

Rampart nodded. "Prism."

He reached down to his belt and touched a glass tile, his skin shifting into transparency. Without another word, Rampart blitzed the group of Fragments. The Seraph gathered all the energy reserves he had within him, charging his hands with light. As the Fragments descended on Rampart, the Seraph fired. The beam of light diffused through Rampart's glass body, refracting off him and discharging in every direction. The Fragment doppelgangers vanished, and Torrent flew backward. Rampart shifted back to his fleshly self and staggered back toward the Seraph.

"Good . . . thinking."

"I'll handle Torrent." Gideon stepped past Wes. "You get the rest of the nephiloids."

"You sure?"

"Yeah." *Not really.* "Sure."

Rampart rushed down the street. Torrent rose from where he'd fallen, spread his legs, and gestured to the Seraph.

"Let's finish this," the villain rumbled.

The Seraph didn't respond. He lunged in, light pulsing around him.

* * *

The Crusader couldn't count the number of Fragments assaulting him anymore, but he had to deal with them fast. Crowd control was hard enough without Fragment distracting him, and there were still nephiloids rampaging through the streets. This had gone on long enough. The Crusader flicked on the electrified ends of his *jo* staff and rammed it into one doppelganger's head.

All of this could end if he could find the real Powers, but for all the Crusader knew, the coward could have slipped out of the city while his doppelgangers distracted the heroes. He could be long gone—and the Crusader would have to take out each of these duplicates individually. It was hard to focus amid the swinging and blocking, punching and kicking. His brain was in full fight mode, darting from one moment to the next as he struggled to keep the doppelgangers from landing blows on him. Gideon had trained his mind to focus during a fight, but Carter was still learning how to do that.

He reached into his belt and grabbed an adhesive bead and a shock bead. One of the doppelgangers kicked him in the back. The Crusader stumbled forward and nearly dropped the beads, but he squeezed it in his palm.

A fist struck his face. Pain exploded behind his nose, and a hot stream of blood trickled down his lip. He raised his staff and waved it wildly to ward off further attacks. One of the Fragments grabbed his right arm and pinned it to his side.

"No!" the Crusader growled.

He swung his left fist, knocking his accoster loose. Then, he backflipped away from the mob of doppelgangers and hurled the adhesive bead on the ground. It exploded and spread its green goo across their feet. The doppelgangers exclaimed in protest and tried to free themselves.

Time to find out if this stuff conducts electricity.

He tossed the shock bead into the midst of the goop. The Fragments spasmed and twitched, and one by one, they disappeared. Finally, all that remained was a puddle of the blue-green substance.

The Crusader twirled his staff and rested it on his shoulder. "Get shocked."

CHAPTER 44

Team Chicago

Rampart spun in the air, kicking Tetra-Hazard in the chest and knocking him away from the truck he'd been about to detonate. Fighting Tetra-Hazard was a challenge. As long as he emitted radiation from his body, Rampart couldn't change into any form but rubber, and his rubber form wasn't strong enough to take the villain in a hand-to-hand fight. He had to get creative to win this one.

Rampart jerked his head to the left to avoid a punch and swiveled on his right foot, kicking with his left. His rubber foot struck Tetra-Hazard behind the knee. He snapped his right fist forward into the villain's jaw. Neither blow had much effect. Tetra-Hazard extended a hand and fired a stream of acid. Rampart threw himself aside. The substance would eat through his rubber form with ease.

He came to his feet and raised his hands, ready to block a blow; but as Tetra-Hazard turned toward him, gunshots punctured the air. Tetra-Hazard stumbled forward, dropping to his knees. Reaching over his shoulder, Rampart grabbed his dart rifle, gripped the barrel in both hands, and smashed the butt of the weapon across Tetra-Hazard's head. The rifle shattered, but the villain crumpled to the ground. Tossing the broken weapon aside, Rampart pulled a pair of dampening cuffs from his belt and clapped them on Tetra-Hazard's wrists. He rolled him onto his chest. Four bullets were lodged in the armor on his back but hadn't punched through. Rampart looked up as Brass Bison rushed in.

"Thanks." Wes huffed. "How'd you know that wouldn't kill him?"

"I didn't." Bison scrunched her nose. "I was kind of hoping it would."

Rampart grinned—and he lunged forward, shifting from rubber to steel and tackling Bison as a nephiloid dropped from a rooftop. The creature slapped him in the chest. Rampart hurtled across the street and into a car, denting the vehicle. He groaned and pulled himself to his feet. The nephiloid crouched down and roared at him.

"Yeah, hello to you, too."

He grabbed one of the counteragent darts from his belt as Bison holstered her revolvers and generated an automatic rifle out of her energy field. Rampart's dart rifle was useless, but he hadn't loaded all the darts into the weapon—he still had two left. Hopefully, that would be all he needed. Rampart ran toward the nephiloid, touching the aionium tile on his belt as he did. His skin shifted to a shinier shade of silver, and he leaped forward. The nephiloid swiped its claws at him but missed as Rampart fell toward it and landed on its shoulders. He brought his metal fist down on the top of the nephiloid's head. The beast howled and bucked. Energy bullets struck its neck and chest, and one pinged off Rampart's shoulder. Rampart stumbled and reached out to catch himself. He found purchase grabbing the beast's ear, hanging in front of the nephiloid's gaping maw.

"Hi, there." Rampart used his free hand to jab the dart into the nephiloid's throat. "Sleep tight, ugly!"

The creature shrieked and bashed Rampart aside. He hit the ground and backed away as the nephiloid flailed through its death throes.

"You all right?" Bison asked.

Rampart nodded. "You?"

"Yes. But Drifter just called from D.C. He thinks that Ashcroft's people may have set up the serum distributor there and that they may have another one here."

"We need to find that device. I'll get to work on that." Rampart pointed down the street. "Go find Crusader. Hopefully, between the four of us, we'll be able to find that device before it goes off."

* * *

The Seraph smashed through the wall and into the lobby of the business center. His back struck a pillar, and he crashed to the ground. Everything hurt, and Torrent would not go down. Every time Seraph hit the guy, he got up and hit back harder. Gideon hoped the others had been able to take down the rest of the nephiloids because the longer this fight went on, the more people those beasts were going to kill, injure, or turn superhuman.

He groaned and pushed himself up. Torrent stormed through the newly formed hole in the wall and toward the Seraph. And behind him, once again, was the now-familiar, white-clad apparition of Wyatt Jonson. The man—or ghost, or whatever he was—stared at the Seraph with a fiery intensity. If he was real, why didn't he intervene?

"'*Be strong and of a good courage.*'" It was Wyatt's voice, but it spoke directly into Gideon's mind, echoing around inside his skull. "'*The Lord thy God is with thee.*'"

"Lord, help me . . . "

He steadied himself against the pillar with his right hand. He glanced at Torrent and back at the hole. Wyatt was gone. Torrent stomped toward him, raised a fist, and swung. The Seraph pushed himself off the pillar, rolled away from Torrent, and fired a blast of light from both hands that struck Torrent full in the back. He didn't stop with a single burst; he kept up the beam of light, burning into the villain's back.

Torrent lay flat on the ground and struggled to push himself up against the force of the beam. The Seraph took a step forward and continued to pour light from his fingers. Torrent screamed and pushed with all his might. *Unbelievable*! He didn't know how the villain still found the strength to get up, but somehow, he did. Still taking the full brunt of the Seraph's blast, he held up a hand to block the beam. The Seraph growled and pushed harder. His growl stretched into a drawn-out shout of exertion as Torrent continued to advance. The Seraph's arms glowed as more energy pulsed from his body into his hands and out of his fingertips. The beam of golden light intensified.

Torrent's hand lowered, and the beam struck him in the chest. Torrent flew backward, carried by the beam, and smashed through the wall behind him and into the next room. The Seraph stepped forward and continued to pour light into his opponent. Finally, Torrent stopped moving.

The Seraph cut off the beam and lowered his hands. His arms were numb, and his legs felt like noodles. He took a step forward, wobbled, and leaned against a pillar for support. He'd never fired a blast that intense for that long before. He felt nearly as exhausted as he had when he'd stopped a train with his bare hands. But Torrent was finally down. *Thank You, Lord.*

He staggered to the opening to the next room and looked down at Torrent. He could still feel him mentally, so he wasn't dead—but he was unconscious. The Seraph half-knelt, half-fell on the ground next to the villain and put him in cuffs. *Now, to take care of those nephiloids.* He left Torrent where he was for the moment and walked unsteadily through the lobby and out into the sunlight. *If I can even stay on my feet, that is.*

Off to the Seraph's left, something exploded. He walked in that direction, scanning the street for the source. The Crusader and Brass Bison rushed down the street, and a red laser beam sliced through the air behind them. The Seraph flew forward, grabbed them both, and tackled them to the ground as the beam ripped through the air, tearing through the buildings behind them.

Carter sighed. "Thanks. You all right?"

"Just . . . tired. It took about everything I had to drop Torrent. Status?"

"We took down the last of the nephiloids, but we think the distribution device is in the city somewhere. Rampart's looking for it, but . . . " Carter jerked his thumb behind him. "We ran into Monahan."

"She's not our priority right now. We've got to find the distributor."

"I know, but someone's gotta draw her attention. I can do it, Gideon."

Another beam of red tore through the air. "Normally, I'd disagree, but I'm in no condition to face her. All right. You take her, and I'll help Rampart find the device." He looked at Bison. "You stay with Crusader. Help him with Monahan."

"I will."

"Okay." The Seraph pushed himself up. "Go!"

* * *

Carter wouldn't let this fight end with Monahan's escape. Justice for his father's death had been a long time coming, and now Monahan would face it. He glanced at Brass Bison. The woman seemed to understand what Carter needed. She formed a pair of energy weapons but kept her distance. Monahan stood directly ahead. The Crusader's heart pounded at the sight of her. With his left hand, he reached down to his belt and grabbed the blade he kept with him at all times—the blade given to him by Gideon back when he had first become the Seraph, the blade that Gideon had snapped off of Monahan's gauntlet not long after she tried to kill Carter.

"Little Crusader, Jr." Monahan sneered. "So glad we finally get to have a rematch."

"There's nowhere for you to run." The Crusader took the blade in one hand and his staff in the other, dropping into a ready stance. "Surrender now or stand and fight. Either way, it's over, Monahan."

Monahan's eyes glowed red, and the Crusader threw himself into a sideways roll as she fired intense blasts of heat at him. Grimacing at the warmth, the Crusader came up in a crouch, hurled the blade at Monahan, and rushed toward her. She batted the blade aside with her forearm. By then, the Crusader was on top of her. He brought his staff down vertically, driving it toward her head. She blocked with her forearms, stepped to the side, and shoved his staff to the ground. Out of his peripheral, the Crusader saw her leg snake up. He ducked as she kicked at his head, and her foot went over him.

He brought his staff up behind her, striking her in the back. Monahan stumbled forward, and the Crusader delivered another blow to the soft spot between her shoulder and neck. Monahan tensed, dropping flat on the ground, and quickly rolled onto her back. Her eyes glowed. The Crusader dropped back as a beam of red split the air.

Brass Bison stepped in, firing bursts of energy from the pistols she'd generated. Monahan cut off her eye blasts, leaped out of the way of the simulated gunfire, and closed in on Bison. Bison trained her weapons on the assassin-turned-supervillain.

Monahan clenched her fists. "You should've stayed out of this."

"Your boss brought me into this when he unleashed the wendigos on my people."

She fired three times in rapid succession. Monahan dropped back to avoid the shots, but a small spurt of red from her shoulder indicated that Bison had at least grazed her. This was Carter's shot. He knelt and picked up the blade he'd thrown earlier. He caught Bison's gaze and nodded. The red light around Monahan's eyes intensified so greatly that Crusader could see the glow even from behind her.

Bison's eyes widened, and she changed her energy pistols into a circular force field. Monahan fired, and the energy slammed into the shield. Bison ducked back behind the car. Crusader crept toward Monahan, clutching the blade.

"Neat trick!" Monahan said. "But you're outmatched. I could shred that car like paper. Come face your death like a warrior."

Bison stood, still shielding herself with one arm, and used the other to draw a bead on Monahan with a revolver. "A warrior never gives in to death. She fights it to the end."

Monahan's eyes glowed, and with her attention on Bison, the Crusader stepped in. He jabbed the blade into the back of Monahan's left thigh. The assassin screamed, and the Crusader grabbed her by the back of the head and rammed her forward, smashing her forehead into the car Bison had been hiding behind. Monahan crumpled.

Bison grinned. "Nice move."

"Thanks." The Crusader cuffed Monahan. "Let's round up the bad guys we've taken out. Hopefully, Gideon and Wes can find the device on their own."

CHAPTER 45

Gideon's heart thumped in his chest as he weaved between skyscrapers, scanning for any sign of the dispersal unit. In a city this large, there was no telling where it might be. He was looking for one microbe in a multi-cell organism, and he was running out of time. This was an organism that would cause more damage to its host than Gideon was willing to allow.

As he flew, he tapped his earbud. "Arianna, Maddox, we could use a little help here. Any advice you could give on narrowing down our search would be great."

"Ashcroft would want a central location," Maddox replied.

"And somewhere up high," Arianna added. "The higher, the better. The way the dispersal unit works, it would spread the gas upward into an expanding mushroom cloud which would descend on the surrounding area. The higher the device is when it activates, the greater the spread by the time the gas reaches the ground."

"Search rooftops in the city center." Maddox's voice was level, but it sounded like he was rushing around. Gideon wondered if he was checking Sterling Enterprises satellite feeds for evidence. "Skyscrapers in particular."

Gideon tightened his jaw. That was where he was already searching, but he could narrow the search to the rooftops. He ascended further, above the highest towers, and swung his head back and forth as he swept over the buildings. Any sign of activity would be enough. He just needed something to go on.

Six men, clad in matching dark blue outfits and armed with assault rifles, milled about the rooftop of Willis Tower, formerly known as Sears Tower. Police had evacuated the building when the fighting started. The building's height made it the ideal location to activate the distributor. Based on the height of the building and the armed men occupying its roof, Gideon was sure this was the spot. Calling the team to notify them of the device's location, the Seraph descended toward the gunmen.

"I'm right across the street," Rampart said. "Heading up now."

The Seraph circled twice more, giving Rampart time to get there, and swept down. As he approached, the mercenaries spotted him and raised their weapons. The Seraph landed in a crouch and generated an aura of light around himself as the men opened fire. Their bullets disintegrated as soon as they touched his shielded form. Smirking, he stepped toward one, grabbed the barrel of his rifle, and twisted it aside. With his other hand, he punched the man in the jaw.

As the man crumpled, the Seraph extended his left hand and fired a burst of light, which struck the next man square in the chest, dropping him flat. The door to the interior of the tower burst open, and Rampart rushed out. Two of the remaining gunmen turned to face him, their bullets bouncing harmlessly off his steel skin. The Seraph lunged at one of the shooters guarding the device. With a quick elbow to the jaw, he dropped one. The other withdrew a collapsible baton from his belt.

The Seraph shook his head. "Come on. What do you really think that's going to do?"

The man furrowed his brow, studying the Seraph, and glanced at Rampart. The steel-skinned hero made short work of the two mercenaries who had attacked him. Turning back to the Seraph, the man dropped his baton, shrugged, and got down on his knees, placing his hands on the back of his head.

"Good choice." The Seraph stepped past him. "How do we disable this thing?"

"I've got Drifter on the line," Rampart said. "They've located the device in D.C., and they're trying to figure out the same thing."

"I don't suppose it's as simple as flipping a switch."

The device, which was shaped roughly like an inverted cone, had a simple control panel on one side. The Seraph knelt next to it. Above the panel was a small screen displaying a countdown. The device was set to go off in one minute.

"Drifter said we can't touch anything because we would risk quickening the detonation, but if we destroy it, the serum will still be released—albeit over a smaller area."

"What options do we have left?" The Seraph watched the timer tick down. "We're running out of time."

* * *

Drifter knelt next to the distributor, surrounded by a handful of CLOUD agents. They had located the device in a warehouse, where Ashcroft's mercenaries were loading it onto the back of a truck. At least, the device hadn't made it to its intended destination yet. If it detonated here, the warehouse's walls would keep it contained. Only the CLOUD agents would be affected. He supposed it would be futile to ask them to leave him alone with the device, but their presence was distracting him. Yeoman and Spright had gone to round up the villains that had been cuffed, but Aria knelt by Drifter's side, her hand on his shoulder. He clenched his jaw and pulled his rain-matted hair back out of his face.

This was his device. His company had produced it. If anyone could figure out the solution, it was him. *No pressure there.* Unfortunately, he had no idea what kind of modifications Ashcroft might have made since stealing it. With so many people around, disarming or destroying the device was out of the question. Any tampering might trigger a failsafe that would detonate the device prematurely. There had to be another way. Maybe stopping the device wasn't the answer. By itself, the dispersal unit was not dangerous. It was the serum loaded within the device that was the problem.

He voiced the conundrum to Arianna and Maddox. "Any ideas?"

"Maybe . . . " Arianna hesitated. "It's possible that our counteragent would have the same effect on Ashcroft's serum as it did on the nephiloids. You might be able to inject the counteragent into the distributor and nullify the serum. Hypothetically, whatever the device did release would be harmless."

Maddox cleared his throat. "There is a risk. It's possible the device might release the counteragent instead. Any superhumans in the vicinity, yourself included, could be in danger. The counteragent could kill you."

Dean swallowed. That was less than ideal. Maybe they should just evacuate the warehouse, seal it off, and wait for the device to detonate. But it was a big building, and they did not have much time until detonation. What if there were homeless squatters somewhere in the building or people hiding from the battle? There was no guarantee they could evacuate everyone in time, even if the CLOUD agents did get out. And evacuating the warehouse did not solve the problem in Chicago. That device was still going to go off.

He looked at Audrey. He didn't want to die, and he certainly didn't want her to die. *But what choice do I have?* Meeting his gaze without flinching, Audrey nodded.

Dean tapped his earbud. "Rampart, look for a receptacle on the device. It would be the place where Ashcroft injected the serum."

About a fourth of the way up the side of the device, on the opposite side from the control panel, was a small access port where a syringe could be inserted. If Dean remembered the schematics for the device correctly, that was the receptacle. He removed the last syringe of the counteragent he had. He hoped that amount would be enough to counter Ashcroft's serum.

"Do you see it?" he asked. "It's on the bottom quarter."

"Yeah, we've got it!" Rampart said. "What do we do?"

"Do you have any of our counteragent left?"

"A little."

"Insert it into the receptacle and inject the full contents into the device. It should be enough to render the serum inside inert."

"Are you sure about this? If the device releases the counteragent, it would be lethal to . . . well . . . us."

"I don't see what other choice we have." Dean swallowed. "Besides, I'm hoping that the serums canceling each other out will result in the device releasing a harmless fog."

Wes laughed grimly. "Hoping?"

"Hey, we're all about faith, right? These people are counting on us."

Wes's voice dropped to a whisper. "God, please don't let us die . . . "

Drifter's heart pounded in his chest. He pressed the syringe against the receptacle and looked up at Aria. Her brow was furrowed, but she gave him another calm nod and patted his shoulder. Pursing his lips,

Drifter nodded back, placed his thumb on the depressor, and pressed it down. The counteragent flowed out of the syringe and into the device.

The device beeped out a shrill warning alarm. Drifter crossed back to the control panel. The timer continued to count down. Drifter clenched his jaw. Now for the moment of truth. If this didn't work, either all the CLOUD agents around them were about to develop powers, or Dean and Audrey would fall down dead.

Three . . . two . . . one

A fine mist seeped into the air. He heard a sharp gasp over his earbud. *God, please don't let Wes die.* Drifter held his breath, waiting. The mist coagulated on his skin and armor . . . and nothing happened. *Thank You, God.* Drifter slumped to the floor and rested his head in his hands.

"Rampart?"

"We're good."

"Fantastic." Dean cracked a smile and looked at Audrey. "Let's go home."

CHAPTER 46

Stakeouts had never been Jolie's favorite part of the job. The first hour wasn't bad—the setting was still fresh; the temptation to drift off to sleep hadn't set in; and the body hadn't decided it was a good time to void all the contents of its stomach yet. But after that, it became miserable.

She groaned and rested her head against her palm, her elbow awkwardly balanced on the edge of the car window. Agent Ross was less fidgety, but as a federal agent, he'd probably done this a lot more than she had. That was good for him, but Jolie couldn't have cared less if she never had to do a stakeout again.

"We can't sit here forever," she grumbled. "We have no idea if he'll come to the docks today. That's assuming he hasn't come already, or he's even planning on coming at all. What if his contact doesn't work here anymore?"

"It's the only lead we've got," Ross said. "We'll stay for another hour, and then we'll swap out with another team."

"Mm."

"Look, we can talk to pass the time."

She glanced over at Ross. "What do you want to talk about?"

"Your boyfriend's a superhero." Ross grinned. "What's that like?"

Jolie bit her lip. She had to admit, part of her restlessness was not knowing how Gideon and the others were doing. She'd heard snippets of news reports about the battles in Chicago and Washington, D.C., but there had been no word from Gideon directly. He more than held his own against Ashcroft's followers whenever they fought, but she couldn't help but worry. The team was split this time.

God, bring him back safe. They had less than three months to go until their wedding day. She couldn't lose him now. She hoped that he could find a way to finish all this before then. What if Ashcroft launched an attack on their wedding day or on the honeymoon? Gideon would feel obligated to help, and Jolie wouldn't blame him. He was one of the few people who could. He'd be selfish not to. But if Ashcroft had already been dealt with by then, it would be a moot point.

Either way, the world was about to change. Reports poured in of new amps showing up in cities all around the U.S. and even a few overseas. Ashcroft's choice in targets had been strategic. Even if the Vindicators won in Chicago and D.C., he had still made a world-shattering impact. Gideon and the others would have their work cut out for them. Jolie's only consolation was that many of those who were amplified by Ashcroft's serum might become superheroes. Maybe the Vindicators wouldn't have to bear the burden of protecting the whole world with eight people anymore.

How had they come this far in less than a year? Last Christmas, Jolie had pondered whether or not she believed Gideon was a vigilante. She had been staunchly against anyone who would put on a mask and fight crime outside the law. Now, he was a public superhero. He didn't even wear a mask underneath that hood. Back then, their biggest concern had been Serban, a powerful crime lord but a completely human one. Their only responsibility had been Sojourn City. Now, they fought supervillains and monsters in cities around the country, and hundreds of superhumans were about to join their ranks.

"Detective?" Ross probed.

Jolie shook herself from her thoughts. "It's . . . interesting. I mean, think about it. Imagine your significant other turned out to be a vigilante, illegally fighting crime. That's bad enough, but then you find out she's got superpowers she hasn't even told you about. But when she saves the whole city, you realize maybe she's been a hero all along. How would you feel?"

Ross shook his head. "It'd be a rollercoaster."

"You're telling me. After that, it only gets *crazier.* Supervillains, monsters—"

"Monsters?"

"You have no idea. I'm so proud of him but also constantly worried because who knows when he's going to go up against something that he can't handle?"

"Yeah." Ross smiled. "That's how my wife feels about me being an FBI agent, actually."

Jolie supposed, in some way, there were a lot of similarities. If Gideon had never developed powers and remained a doctor and Jolie had still become a cop, she was sure he would've worried for her the same way she worried for him now. Her job, in its own way, was no less dangerous than what he did. She faced things that could kill her on a regular basis, and she didn't have powers to protect her. He was doing the same; the stakes were just higher.

They passed the next hour in relative silence, watching the docks for any new arrivals. Unless he'd stolen a car or borrowed one from a contact, Serban would likely be on foot, but Jolie suspected he was too smart to walk up to the docks. He would've acquired a car somehow. But the docks remained void of either foot or vehicle traffic.

"Let's switch out," Ross said. "My partner can sit here with another cop for a while."

Jolie nodded. She was eager to get back to the lair and find out the status of the team. She put the car in reverse, backed out of their hiding spot, and pulled onto the street. Serban would have to wait for another day. She had other priorities.

* * *

When the Raptor settled down in D.C., Gideon was surprised to find Patrick, Dean, and Audrey standing in the street by themselves. There was no sign of Jarrett, CLOUD agents, or any villains the team had captured. As Gideon stepped down the ramp toward them, Patrick looked up. Gideon realized he wasn't wearing his mask. The boy's face was drawn; he looked as exhausted as Gideon felt.

"What happened?" Gideon asked.

"Jarrett said to tell you goodbye," Patrick said. "He's going to care for his wife. She was bitten by a nephiloid. He feels like his place is with her. He said to wish you good luck in finding Ashcroft, and if we need any help in the future, we can call. But right now, he wants to be with her."

An unexpected pang of sadness gripped him. Gideon was going to miss the agent and his dry sense of humor. Jarrett had grounded the team, in a way, but Gideon understood why he would stay. If Jolie had been a bite victim, Gideon would have done the same. Jarrett had never planned to be a permanent fixture, and they had Carter to keep them grounded.

Still, Gideon would have liked to probe Jarrett further for information about Solar Flare. It bothered Gideon for reasons he couldn't quite explain that his powers matched those of Ashcroft's father. Was there a deeper meaning to that? If Solar Flare went insane and had to be put down, was that Gideon's destiny? The thought frightened him, and he banished it from his mind. There were more pressing things to worry about, like why Patrick and the others were there, but there was no sign of the supervillains they were sent to fight. Had they all escaped?

"What about the Regency?" Gideon asked.

"CLOUD took them into custody. Most of them. Mendez died."

"What? What happened?"

"Jarrett killed him." Patrick shrugged. "Come on. I just want to go home."

Patrick walked up into the Raptor and sat next to Carter. Gideon followed and looked around the compartment as the ramp raised behind him. They had Torrent, Lancet, and Tetra-Hazard in custody; and CLOUD had Somna, Red Raider, and Deluge. Other than Ashcroft himself, that left only Powers unaccounted for. Gideon wasn't surprised the slippery weasel had managed to escape again.

"Not a bad day's work," he muttered.

The plane lifted off the ground. Gideon settled in the seat next to Dean. His friend fiddled with his new prosthetic hand, touching it and wiggling its fingers. It must've been so different from a flesh-and-blood hand. Gideon probed Dean's emotions, but what he felt had nothing to do with the hand. All Dean's attention was on the woman in white across the plane.

Gideon smirked. Dean had it bad for Audrey. He had called it, and Dean seemed more certain of it, too. Gideon hoped it worked out for him. Dean deserved to have someone. He'd been waiting long enough.

"What's your take on Jarrett?" Gideon asked.

Dean shrugged. "Can't say I blame him. Hate to see him go. He was a nice guy. Never seemed to realize that I'm the team funny guy, though. That position is filled."

"Yeah." Gideon grinned. "Yeah, it is."

CHAPTER 47

Four months ago

Ashcroft sat in his lab and watched the news reports from Sojourn City. Several months before, he had received word of a man fighting crime in the city, firing beams of light from his hands. Drawn by the similarities to Solar Flare's powers, Ashcroft researched the situation. Gideon Turner, the man Ashcroft experimented on in Venezuela, had been a resident of Sojourn City before his kidnapping. Ashcroft was not a believer in coincidences. Turner was this vigilante. The report playing out before him confirmed as much, showing the so-called Seraph unmasked, revealing Turner's visage. He had at last developed his powers.

And I let him go. Ashcroft had finally recreated his father's powers. A new Solar Flare was out there and using his powers for the same purpose, no less. It was just Ashcroft's luck it would happen in a subject who had escaped. Given his captivity and the violence of his escape, Turner would likely work against Ashcroft if he ever discovered the Regency's agenda. But he was just one man, and Ashcroft had more than enough superhumans on his side. If Turner tried to find him, they would be ready for him.

Pity. He would have been a great asset to the Regency. And it would've been a comfort to have a reminder of Father around.

"Do you want me to find him, my lord?" Artemis asked.

Ashcroft glanced back at her. "No, Somna. You have a new task. My old friend, Mark Garvin, has a gene splicer that we may be able to use to perfect the serum. Go to him in San Francisco and see if you can persuade him to help us. But do not use your powers. The world is not ready to see what we have become. But with Turner in the open, it won't be long until we can move forward at last."

CHAPTER 48

Present Day

Nephilius hurled a workbench across his lab. His screams echoed off the walls. He had been so close! How had the Vindicators managed to stop his lieutenants again? Clearly, he had chosen the wrong people to give powers. If the Regency was worth anything, Gideon Turner and his rebellious cohorts would have been dead a long time ago. Nephilius dug his clawed fingers into the screen of his television and slashed it in half. His shoulders rose and fell as he panted. No one was there to witness his fury; he could unleash it in peace. Black smoke stretched from his palms and ripped light fixtures from their mountings. Finally, his rage sated, Nephilius took a deep breath and stared at the remnants of his TV.

"Turner," Nephilius rumbled.

The man who could've been Ashcroft's greatest success was instead a thorn in his flesh, one Nephilius just couldn't seem to pick out. He caught a glimpse of his own reflection. Was it mere chance, or was it fate that Gideon Turner, not Jeremiah Ashcroft, had inherited Solar Flare's powers? One day, Nephilius would tear the Seraph apart and study his remains. He would learn the truth. To do that, he needed backup, and he had precious little of that.

It was surprising that Fragment, out of all of them, had reported that he was on his way back to base. He had calculated that Fragment would use the heat of the battle to slip away. His loyalty was unexpected. It was unfortunate that he was the only follower Nephilius had left, but it did not matter. Nephilius' own powers were far more powerful than any of theirs. Fragment's presence alone would not turn the tide of the battle.

Once Nephilius defeated Turner's Vindicators, he could easily free the rest of his people from whatever cage Turner would lock them in. As powerful as he would be, he still needed their help. This had been a bump in the road—losing his distributors and his nephiloids put a dent in his plans. But through his own power, he would show the rest of the world that he'd been right. There were still multitudes of new superhumans out there. The bombs in Juncture City, Dallas, and the other cities had detonated successfully, even if the distributors did not. Nephilius could recruit new members to the Regency. Together, they would conquer the Vindicators and take the world for themselves.

They had called him and his father insane. They said making superhumans was immoral at best. But he had known all along that for peace to come, a man with the power of a god would have to be in charge. No one lesser would be able to bend others to his will. Father had trusted in a spiritual God above the world. Nephilius would become a physical god *over* the world.

When they saw that those under his rule were prospering, that crime and hunger had been eliminated by the might of their benevolent ruler, perhaps they would change their tune. Perhaps they would ask him for his power. They would beg him to lead them into a golden era of peace. But for those who resisted . . . They would taste the wrath of a god. A wrath that would begin with Sojourn City.

* * *

Carter could have slept for a week after all the fighting in Chicago. His muscles were sore; his eyes barely stayed open; and his brain struggled to free itself from the daze of combat. He wasn't thinking so much as perceiving one moment at a time in staggered dissonance. He focused on putting one foot in front of the other until he could drop onto the nearest comfortable surface.

The Vindicators trudged back into the lair. Carter made a beeline for the couch and slumped onto it face-first. He had always said that the couch was one of the most comfortable he'd ever sat on. It felt like heaven. He groaned loudly into a throw pillow until he was out of breath and buried his face in it.

Gideon chuckled. "Adrenaline comedown is the worst."

"Uh-huh," Carter grumbled.

He heard the others' footsteps as they went up the stairs to the ops room, but he made no move to join them. He wanted to sleep for a week. *I'm the only normal person on the team, guys. Remember?*

I should really get out of this armor. As comfortable as the couch was, the Sterling Labs suit was not meant to be slept in. He was bound to wake up sore all over if he fell asleep wearing it. He cringed, pushed himself off the couch, and wobbled up the stairs, leaning on the railing for support. Powers had gotten in a few good licks—not to mention the hits Monahan dealt him. The bruises would serve as a reminder for Carter that he had come up against his father's killer and won.

The others were in the ops room, and Dean and Wes had already changed out of their suits. Gideon and the others still wore theirs. Jolie was there, too, with an arm tight around Gideon's waist.

"What's up?" Carter asked.

"Just surveying the results of the attacks," Dean said. "It's grim. Hundreds injured and dozens dead in Chicago and D.C. alone. Other cities are reporting superhuman transformations in droves. It could've been a lot worse. I'm trying to get hospital records on which patients in the two major cities were checked in with bite wounds. From there, we may be able to monitor the ones who develop superpowers."

Carter removed his mask and walked to his mannequin. He placed the mask on its head and tugged off his gauntlets and boots.

"They're in for a surprise," Carter muttered.

"There will probably be too many for us to handle ourselves. Do you think we should pass this information on to CLOUD, Gid?"

Carter watched Gideon, waiting for the team leader's answer. Personally, he wouldn't have cared that much. Government agents were way better suited to take care of these new superhumans than they were. But it wasn't his call. It was Gideon's.

"Based on what we know of Jarrett and CLOUD's actions in D.C., I think we can trust them to evaluate and treat the victims properly," Gideon said. "I'll reach out to Jarrett once we have a complete list."

"Are you sure that's a good idea?" Audrey asked. "What if CLOUD decides to take them all in, stick them in cells?"

"She's right." Wes crossed his arms. "Government agencies aren't exactly known for their passivity."

Hannah stepped forward. "I trust Jarrett, but I won't speak for whom he works. I agree with Audrey. What if the victims are apprehended and subjected to tests? I was the first bite victim. I can only imagine how I would have felt if the feds had broken down my door and stuck me in a cell."

Jolie shook her head. “They wouldn’t do that. They would only apprehend any who appeared to be a threat.”

Carter didn’t care what decision they made. He just wanted to get some sleep. He finished removing his uniform except the black bodysuit, caught Patrick’s eye, and jerked his head toward the door. Patrick followed him out.

“You as tired as I am?” Carter asked.

Patrick nodded. “And I’m also missing another day’s homework now. Raina will be even more suspicious of me not being at school today. Sooner or later, she’s going to see a pattern.”

“Don’t worry. Your identity is the most secure out of any of ours. You wear a full-face mask.”

“Not today I didn’t. I just hope no one caught me without it on video, or my secret identity is down the tubes.”

“As fast as you were moving?” Carter walked to the closet where many of them kept a spare set of plainclothes. “You’re set, man. If anything, the school will just think you’re playing hooky.”

He pulled out a t-shirt, a button-down shirt, a pair of jeans, and black sneakers. After changing in the bathroom, he walked back out into the hallway and nodded at Patrick, who had apparently used his superspeed to change right where he was.

“Let’s get out of here.”

* * *

“Look, I want to protect them all as much as everyone else,” Gideon said, “but we’re stretched thin as it is. What if there are dozens of new superhumans? We can’t possibly watch them all.”

Wes understood his brother's point, but he was still concerned. CLOUD might be every bit as upright as Jarrett said they were, and it would be a relief to let someone else handle everyone who had been amplified. But what if Jarrett was wrong? What if CLOUD had ulterior motives?

Why does this matter to me? Wes wouldn't be there for much longer, and with Hannah likely returning to Arizona, the Vindicators would be down a few hands. They couldn't keep track of a bunch of new superhumans on their own. They probably needed the help, even if it was from the government.

But Wes knew from experience what it was like to suddenly have powers. It was exciting, but it could also be scary—especially if you couldn't control them. In a perverse way, Wes had been blessed that Somna had hypnotized him into being able to control his abilities. He hadn't gone through the terrifying new-powers stage. Most of these people would have to experience that.

"You're the team leader," he said. "We all trust you. Just make sure it's the right call before you make it."

"I will." Gideon nodded. "I'll talk to Jarrett at length before I give him any information. This won't be an act of blind faith."

That made Wes feel a little better. He uncrossed his arms. "I'm going home to get some rest. Call me when we're ready to make our next move."

CHAPTER 49

Gideon's phone call with Jarrett reassured him. Jarrett promised that if the Vindicators gave Dean's list of bite victims to CLOUD, the agency would observe from a distance to see if they developed powers. If they did, CLOUD would only get involved if the amps used their powers in a way that endangered themselves or others.

"Dangerous to themselves" could mean getting involved in vigilante activities; but since Jarrett himself was a vigilante, Gideon had a feeling that CLOUD might be lenient if the vigilantes acted under CLOUD supervision.

Jarrett offered to send Gideon some archived footage of Solar Flare as a thank you for all he had done to prevent a worldwide disaster. When Gideon asked why Jarrett's superiors were suddenly open to sharing the footage, Jarrett didn't respond. Even over the phone, Gideon could sense Jarrett's wry amusement. He suspected CLOUD had no idea that Gideon had the footage now. The possibility of finally getting answers brought both a sense of relief and dread. He might learn the truth, but it might not be what he wanted to see.

Gideon slumped down to the floor of Jolie's living room and leaned the back of his head on her couch. Jolie sat next to him and wrapped her arms around his neck.

"Great work today."

"Thanks." He leaned his head on her shoulder. "I'm exhausted."

"I bet." She ran her fingers through his hair. "The past few weeks have been brutal on you. I'll be glad when Ashcroft is dealt with just so you can get some rest."

"Me, too. Did I do the right thing, giving those names to Jarrett?"

"I think so. Babe, you'd never be able to handle all of them, even with your team. And let's be honest. It's a team that may not be together for that much longer, anyway. The more of them leave, the more you'll feel responsible for; and you can't live like that."

Gideon straightened to look her in the eye. "You really think they're going to leave?"

"Jarrett's already gone, and who knows if he's ever coming back? Hannah's going to go home sooner than later. Patrick, too. You must be able to tell that he's homesick."

"Yeah. And he did disappear for hours a few nights ago. I have a feeling he might've run back to San Francisco."

"That already puts you down three people. We have no idea if Audrey wants to be here long-term, either. And Carter . . . Gideon, Carter's a good fighter, but he's more at home defending the Brooks from criminals than he ever will be fighting monsters."

Gideon had noticed Carter's odd detachment when they returned to the Tower. Maybe Jolie was right. That left Gideon with Dean and Wes to handle large-scale problems. That wasn't a lot to work with. The three of them couldn't protect the whole country by themselves. It was possible that the Vindicators would be a very short-lived alliance.

And Gideon was about to get married, too. He owed Jolie his time and attention. How could he be a proper husband and spiritual leader if he was running off to fight supervillains in other cities all the time?

It wouldn't be fair to her. Not to mention the ghostly visits of Wyatt Jonson, which he still hadn't told her about.

"You're right." He forced a smile. "I know turning the names over was the right thing to do. It's just that so many of them protested, and I wasn't expecting that."

"That's part of being a leader—making the tough calls. And you're great at that."

"Thanks. How's the search for Serban going?"

"It's not. He's a ghost. Costin—you remember, the guy we interrogated on the roof back before the Uprising—said Serban has a contact at the docks. Agent Ross and I staked them out, and we didn't see anything. We've got people there now, but . . . "

"Serban is smart and driven. What would he want more than getting away from the city?"

Jolie lapsed into silence, pondering. Gideon remembered his final fight with Serban, battling on the rooftop of Sterling Enterprises. The brutish thug gave as good as he got. He had been there to kill Edgar Sterling and solidify his hold on Sojourn City. Gideon blinked, sat up, and felt Jolie's emotions light up as she came to the same realization.

"Revenge," she said.

"Why didn't he kill Edgar Sterling when he escaped prison?"

"Sterling paid off guards to protect him from Serban. Maybe he didn't have a chance to get near him."

"The guards were so busy with the escapees, there's no way they were paying attention to Sterling." Gideon shook his head. "If Serban wanted to kill Sterling, he would've done it then and there."

"What about you? You're the one who stopped him, put him in prison."

Gideon nodded. "And he knows my identity and where I live—or used to . . ."

"He only knew about your home in the Tower, but that's your lair now. Maybe he's been lying low not because he's waiting to escape the city but because he's trying to find out where you live. And by now—"

"By now, he might know exactly where my apartment is." Gideon jumped to his feet. "I've got to warn Wes and the others before—"

Gideon's senses lit up like a firework show. He threw Jolie to the ground and shielded her with his body as the window exploded, sending shards of glass and wood framing flying into the living room. Shrapnel cut through the fabric of Gideon's jacket and shirt and into his back. He grimaced and belatedly generated an aura of light around himself. Nearby chunks of wood and glass disintegrated, as did the shards in his back—but the damage had been done. Luca Serban dropped through the window, a knife in one hand and a pistol in the other. A wicked smirk crossed his face.

"Hey there, Seraph." His smirk transformed into a deadly-serious line. "Remember me?"

"Go!" Gideon snapped.

Jolie sprinted for her bedroom as Gideon extended his left hand and fired a blast of light. Serban was already in motion, throwing himself out of the way of the blast and firing a series of shots. Gideon's halo of light incinerated the bullets before they landed, and he stormed forward to engage the crime lord. He blasted the gun out of Serban's hand and dropped the light shield. As tired as he was, he couldn't fight and keep the shield up at the same time.

Serban swiped the knife at Gideon's throat. Gideon raised his left arm to block the strike and crosscut a blow across Serban's jaw. He jabbed his left palm forward, knocking Serban back a step, grabbed

Serban's wrist, and twisted the knife free. He advanced on the Romanian and spun into a roundhouse kick. Serban ducked under his foot and swung a punch up under Gideon's arm, striking him in the ribs. Gideon grunted and staggered back. Serban's elbow snapped forward and struck Gideon in the jaw. His teeth clacked together, and he felt blood pool inside his lip. Serban knelt to pick up his weapon.

"What's the matter, superhero?" Serban thrust with his knife, and Gideon slapped the blade away. "You seem tired."

"I beat you last time we fought, Serban, and I've only improved since then."

"Serban!" Jolie had returned from her bedroom with her pistol. "Hands up!"

Serban chuckled. "I'm starting to get déjà vu, Detective. I thought this game of cat and mouse was done."

"Hands. Up."

Gideon stayed in a defensive stance, ready to move if Serban tried anything. He might decide suicide by cop was the best way to go and try to at least take Gideon with him.

"This isn't over. I'll be back."

Serban hurled his knife at Jolie. Gideon snapped a hand up and blasted the weapon out of the air, but the beam of light also intercepted the bullet Jolie fired at Serban. The crime lord rushed for the window and leaped out. Gideon and Jolie hurried to the edge and looked out. He was gone.

* * *

Jolie shuddered as the FBI combed her apartment. The shivers that swept over her arms, leaving gooseflesh behind, had nothing to do with the chill wind that blew in from the smashed window. It had everything to do with Luca Serban watching her apartment—perhaps for a long time—unbeknownst to her. She had been hunting him for days, and all along, he was the one on her tail. She wondered if she would ever feel safe again.

It seemed obvious now that he wasn't after her. He was after Gideon. That was why he had waited until that night to attack. Serban must have been watching him, waiting for the right time to strike. Gideon's own apartment was occupied by three other superheroes, so it was no wonder Serban wouldn't strike there. He must have seen Gideon enter her building, exhausted from the fighting in Chicago.

Agent Ross scooped a few shell casings into a bag and handed them to a CSI.

"You all right?" he asked, looking at Jolie.

"Yeah. Fine."

Gideon stood next to the smashed window, glowering out at the streets. She was surprised he hadn't already gone out to track down Serban. Even with all that was going on with Ashcroft, he'd managed to retain a lighter demeanor lately. *Not tonight.* She hadn't seen him this intense since he had first started fighting crime. He was back in vigilante mode.

Ross followed her gaze, pursed his lips, and looked back at Jolie. He quirked an eyebrow and jerked his head at her kitchen. She nodded and followed him in.

"What happened?" he asked. "I've seen footage of your boyfriend steamrolling guys much tougher than Serban."

"He's exhausted. Fighting monsters and supervillains really takes it out of you, I guess. He did his best, but Serban caught us off guard."

"Everyone's got their off days. I'm glad you're okay—both of you. Don't worry. We're going to catch that scum."

"I know." Jolie smiled. "That's my job, too. Remember?"

She led Ross back to the living room and left him with the other agents. She stepped next to Gideon and wrapped an arm around his waist. He rubbed her shoulder and continued to stare out into the night. She could tell he was disturbed, probably blaming himself for not being more aware.

"We're okay," Jolie said. "Neither one of us got hurt."

"How long has he been watching us?" Gideon asked. "I should have noticed. And I should have been able to take him down."

"You're exhausted, babe. It's not your fault."

"I should've gotten involved sooner. If I'd just dedicated myself to searching for him, I could've caught him by now. You never would've been in danger."

"Maybe but I was the one who told you to let me handle it, remember? I wanted you to focus on Ashcroft. And if we're being honest, I really wanted to prove I could catch this guy myself."

Gideon rubbed her arm. "I don't blame you. This is your case, and it's your call. If you don't want me to get involved, I won't."

"He's made it personal now. I wouldn't try to keep you from getting involved after he tried to kill both of us. But I still think you've got bigger things to worry about. The Regency may be in shambles, but Ashcroft is still out there. He could make a move any day. I'm not going to ask you to stay out of the search, but I think your time would be better spent protecting us all from Ashcroft. Agent Ross and I can handle Serban."

At this point, Jolie would've felt safer with Gideon at her side. But in the past few weeks, Ashcroft had launched multiple supervillain attacks all over the country, had one of his lackeys fire a nuke at Sojourn City, and released rabid monsters in rural and urban areas. Who knew what he had planned next? Serban might be nothing in comparison.

Gideon kissed the top of Jolie's head before walking over to Ross. "Agent Ross. Good to see you again."

"Mr. Turner." Ross smiled. "You've come a long way from where I found you in Venezuela."

"I wouldn't be here without you."

"Just doing my job."

"I appreciate it, and I also appreciate you being here tonight. I know Serban is slippery, but I hope that after this, you'll be hot on his trail."

"He's our top priority. Don't worry, sir. His days as a free man are numbered. We'll stick him in a box so small, he'll need a straw to breathe."

Jolie wished she had Ross's confidence. At this point, she wasn't sure Serban was ever going to see the inside of a prison again. And with everything he'd done, she would be just as content if the next box he was stuffed in was a coffin.

CHAPTER 50

“He came in her window?” Dean exclaimed.

Gideon nodded as he rushed up the stairs toward the ops room. He respected Jolie’s opinions on why he should focus his attention on Ashcroft. He fully intended to let her take care of Serban herself, but there was no reason he couldn’t give her access to the resources at their disposal.

After the police and FBI cleared Jolie’s apartment, the two of them had returned to Gideon’s place. Gideon slept on the couch and spent the rest of the night reacting to every little noise and movement, sure that Serban was back for round two. First thing in the morning, he had awakened Dean, and the two had returned to the Tower.

“He’s been watching us.” Gideon typed in the code to unlock the ops room. “Probably ever since he got out of prison. He’s just been waiting for me to be vulnerable.”

“There’s got to be others on his hit list. Like Dad—or me. I was there the night he was arrested. He knows I was involved in helping you take him down. Carter, too.”

“Yeah, but I was the one who beat him. He’ll come for all of you, too, but he’ll be gunning for me first.”

“Do you think he knows I have superpowers? Or Wes?”

“I think we can’t ignore the possibility. If he’s been observing me, he has to have noticed that you and Wes look an awful lot like Drifter and Rampart.”

Gideon turned on the computers. Dean had connected their monitors to Sojourn City's traffic cameras and CCTV. They had a complete view of the city at any given moment. If anyone could find Serban, it would be them. Once they had the location, he'd give it to Jolie and let her take a strike team to bring in the crime lord.

He was tempted to join them himself. The only thing stopping him was the damage Torrent had done to his Seraph suit. The breastplate was bent beyond recognition. A shame. He had grown to like the aionium armor. It would have been invaluable against Serban. Without it, there was too great a chance Gideon might be overwhelmed due to his injuries.

"Serban might be able to avoid the traffic cameras," Dean said. "He's a smart guy, and I'm sure the police have already thought of using them, anyway."

"He can slip up." Gideon stepped aside. "You'll have to do this part."

Dean sat down and typed the necessary commands. "I'm going to visit my dad. It's been a while since I've seen him. Maybe he'll have some insight on where Serban might go next."

"All right, facial rec is set up, and I've tasked Sterling Enterprises' satellites to scan the city, too. They'll have a more complete view than the traffic cams."

"Thanks, Dean."

"You bet. You and I both invested too much time locking Serban away to have him out on the streets now." Dean rose. "I'll go see Dad now and let you know if he gives me anything we can use. In the meantime, you may want to talk to Audrey about setting up a raid on Ashcroft's base. He's still a priority, too."

Gideon followed Dean out of the ops room and back downstairs. Logically, he knew Dean was right. With Ashcroft's plans crumbling, the leader of the Regency might be more deadly than ever. Who knew what he would do as he became more desperate? Serban was a problem, but Ashcroft could cause a catastrophe.

* * *

Dean fidgeted as he waited for his father to be brought in. It had been a long time since he'd been to visit Dad. He had long ago forgiven his father for his actions, but it was still strange to visit him in prison. Strange, and a little disturbing. Dean's mother had left them when Dean was a child, so Dad was the only parent Dean had ever known. Edgar Sterling had done his best under the circumstances, but their relationship had never been ideal. Now it was like they were cut off completely.

Never too late to mend that. Dean knew his father had carried the city's best intentions in his heart and even believed that he was doing God's will. Although he had been wrong, he was still a good man. When he got out of prison, he would need Dean's support. Maybe he needed it even more right now.

Across the glass that separated the prisoners from their visitors, a door opened. A guard ushered Dad inside. He sat down across from Dean, smiled, and picked up the phone. He still had the same full beard that he'd had for years. His hair was graying around the temples, more so than before his prison days. His orange jumpsuit was rumpled, but he didn't look hurt. Just tired.

"Hello, Dean. How are you, son?"

"I'm . . . busy. The company recently had a big theft in D.C., and we're running damage control here. Other than that, things are good. After the success of the maglev, four other cities have signed contracts with Sterling Enterprises to have one built."

"Good. But how are you? Personally?"

"I'm fine. Still living with Gideon. His brother Wes moved in with us. There's a girl. A girl I like, I mean." He realized he hadn't said that last part out loud yet. "We've just met, and we're just friends right now. But I . . . I have feelings for her. She's special. I can feel it."

Dad grinned. "What's her name?"

"Audrey." Dean exhaled. "Look, are you okay? After that prison break, I was worried Serban might have hurt you."

Dean's father grew serious. "Has he approached you? He told me he wouldn't hurt me because his best revenge would be coming after you. I thought he would never get past Sterling Enterprises' security, but the man has his ways."

"I'm fine. He hasn't come anywhere near me. But Gideon . . . He's trying to find Serban, and so is Jolie . . . uh, Detective Anderson."

"Of course. Well, son, I'm afraid I've no idea where Luca Serban might go, other than to hurt you. Keep an eye out, my boy. He will come for you if the police do not get to him first. Do not be caught off guard."

"I won't." Dean nodded. "Thanks, Dad. I'll try to visit again soon. I'm sorry that I haven't been around more often. I've been . . . "

"Busy. I know. It's all right. Live your life. I'll be here whenever you have time."

"I love you, Dad."

"Love you, too."

Dean hung up the phone and backed away. He gave Dad one last nod. If Serban had promised to come for Dean to make Dad suffer, then he'd likely show up at either Sterling Labs or Sterling Enterprises sooner or later. And if he did, it would be the last mistake he made.

* * *

Powers leaned against the back wall of the lab and watched Nephilius work. Even when the scientist first brought Powers in, Ashcroft had been off his rocker. Now, whatever his transformation had done to him, it had him dangerously close to altogether snapping, and it had only gotten worse since the Chicago and D.C. teams were defeated. His Regency was crumbling before his eyes. Powers wasn't sure he wanted to be around to see it when Nephilius finally lost it.

Why did I come back? He kept asking himself that question, and he couldn't come up with a valid answer. He could have let Nephilius believe that he had died or had been captured by the heroes. He could have disappeared into the underbelly of Chicago and never had to worry about the mad scientist tracking him down. But something had stopped him. He couldn't say what it was, and it was bothering him.

Maybe I'm just that much of a coward. Too scared to stand and fight, but too scared to run away. Nephilius was terrifying. If he won, the first thing he would do once his rule was consolidated was execute those who betrayed him. Powers would be at the top of this list. Maybe that was it. He came back to the only place he might be remotely safe, no matter how much he hated it, because as long as he stood with Nephilius, at least he didn't have enemies on both sides.

Nephilius muttered to himself as he walked around to the cryogenic tanks where he stored the husks of the Nephilim. *If that's what they really are.* The idea that these corpses belonged to half-angels mentioned in the Bible seemed too crazy to believe. But then, so did the possibility of a man creating duplicates of himself.

"I don't have enough to make more synthetic serum," Nephilius said. "I'll need to draw a sample from a live superhuman. One of Turner's? Yes, it will work." He turned abruptly to face Powers. "You will be rewarded for coming back. Yes. When the dust settles, you will be a god with me."

Gods. The man really had lost it. *So, why am I here?* The question lingered in the back of his mind. Ever since he had watched the nephiloids tearing up the city, hurting and killing people for no other reason than to provide a convenient distraction, he had known he couldn't keep working for Ashcroft.

Maybe it was more than cowardice. Maybe Powers still had a part to play in all this. When it came down to it, he might be needed to help take Nephilius down. Vince Powers was no hero, but he wasn't a monster. A selfish, cowardly criminal, yes. A killer, even. But everyone he had ever killed deserved it. Powers wasn't about mass slaughter. He couldn't sit by and let a man with a god complex destroy everything Powers knew. Nephilius would wreck the world trying to fix it.

That could not happen. Powers wasn't going to stand and fight with the heroes. He didn't want any part of their little squad. Even if he did, they would never have him. He wasn't like Audrey. He didn't have the benefits of charisma and good looks. He was a loser, through and through. Worse, he had history with the Vindicators. Wes Turner hated him, even if none of the others did. But he could help in his own way. Maybe at the right moment, a misplaced lab tool or an inconvenient power outage would slow Nephilius enough for the Vindicators to bring him down for good. Whatever Powers's role was in the coming conflict, he was ready to play it—on his terms. He wasn't throwing his life away, not even to save the world.

CHAPTER 51

Carter tapped his foot against the marble-tile floor of the balcony as he waited for Dean to return. It was Carter's day off, so it was the perfect time to ask Dean for a job as a security officer at Sterling Enterprises. With all the chaos of the past few days—nukes and monsters and supervillains—he had completely forgotten to ask. Now that life was somewhat returning to normal, he didn't want to miss his opportunity. Working in a grocery store was not his life's ambition. At least, guarding a corporate high rise would be a little more fulfilling.

He thought about the previous night's conversation with Patrick and his own ponderings about his role as the Crusader. The Vindicators' mission to stop Ashcroft was important, and he was determined to tough it out until the end. But after that? Carter's heart was with Sojourn City, specifically the Brooks. He could do his best work there, protecting the city from rapists and drug dealers and gangs. That was his role. That was how he could best honor his father's legacy. Someone had to look out for the little guy. Compared to the rest of the Vindicators, Carter *was* the little guy.

Protect Sterling Enterprises by day and the Brooks by night. That sounded like the life he wanted. Stay close to home, provide for his mother and siblings, be there for them, and honor the mantle of the Crusader all at the same time. That was his calling. It was his mission. But first, they had to finish off Ashcroft. Carter had already managed to bring down Monahan. That satisfied the personal nature of this mission. But he had dedicated himself to helping the others stop Ashcroft, and that was what he intended to do.

Footsteps pounded on the stairs. Carter straightened.

It was Gideon. His hair was combed and his clothes straight, but he was tense, jumpy. His head snapped up as Carter took a step toward him. That was unusual.

"What's up?" Carter asked.

"I'm coming to check on the search for Serban. Dean's running facial rec on our computers."

Carter fell in behind Gideon as he walked into the ops room. *Serban? Weren't the police supposed to be on that case?* "What happened?" Carter asked.

"Serban hit Jolie's apartment last night while I was there." Gideon dropped down into a chair in front of the computers. "He got away, and we're trying to find him before he disappears again."

Another criminal Carter would love to bring in himself. While Serban hadn't been the one to murder Carter's dad, he pulled Monahan's strings. That made him partially responsible.

"Can I help?" Carter asked.

"We're just tracking him. Jolie wants to make the arrest herself." Gideon glanced at him. "I wouldn't mind if you shadowed her team, just to make sure they stay safe. It's not that I don't trust her. I do. I just don't trust Serban to play fair."

Carter nodded. "I can do that."

More footsteps clicked on the hallway floor. "I'm back!"

Dean stepped into the room and dropped into a chair next to Gideon.

"Got anything?" Dean asked.

"Not yet." Gideon sighed. "Looks like he's covering his tracks pretty well."

"Hey, Dean," Carter said. "Can I talk to you for a minute?"

"Sure thing, kid."

Carter stepped back out into the hallway. Dean followed him and leaned against the door frame.

"What can I do for you?" he asked.

"I want a job. Specifically, my dad's job. I want to work security at Sterling Enterprises."

Dean nodded. "I'll set up an interview."

"It's got to pay more than my minimum wage grocery store job, and it would mean a lot to me. I'd be dedicated, on time, attentive—wait. You said yes? Just like that?"

"Yeah, I can pull some strings." Dean put his hand on Carter's shoulder. "It's all yours, bud."

"Really?" Carter grinned. "Thank you!"

"You bet. I'm going to get back to the search for Serban, but if you show up at Sterling Enterprises on Monday for an interview with our head of security, I can pretty much guarantee the job's yours."

"Will do. Thanks again!"

Dean stepped back into the ops room. Carter pumped his fist and let out a whoop of excitement. That had been easier than he had hoped.

* * *

Spright blasted through the streets of Sojourn City as fast as his feet would carry him. The run felt good. Somehow, with the world around him moving in slow motion, the wind blowing against his face, and the surging energy he felt flowing through his body, everything fell into perspective.

His teachers—and Raina—were curious why he'd missed another day of school. Curious and, in the teachers' cases, annoyed. It was getting more difficult to come up with excuses. How much longer could he keep this up? He had planned to finish the semester at Sojourn High, but his conversation with Lucy a few nights before had him even more eager to get back to San Francisco. That was where he belonged.

Spright was ready to be home. As soon as Ashcroft was dealt with, he was out. He had spent enough time hiding from his parents just because they were angry about his faith. His time had come. He was going home, and he was going to face them. He was going to ask Lucy on a date. He was going to finish high school in San Francisco and go to college there.

Maybe there was a silver lining to Jarrett killing Mendez—not because the guerrilla was dead, but because it severed Patrick's last real personal motivation to stay. Stopping Ashcroft had always been Gideon's mission. Patrick was dedicated to seeing it through, but it never felt as raw and as personal as catching the man who had murdered Patrick's grandfather. That chapter of Patrick's life was closed, and he could move on.

Satisfied with his decision, he circled around toward the lair. He would miss Carter most of all, but even his friendship with the fellow young hero couldn't keep him there forever—not when he had so much pulling him back home.

He screeched to a halt outside the lair and took a deep breath. Removing his mask and goggles, he stepped inside. Audrey and Hannah stood in the kitchen, talking quietly.

"Do you miss home?" Audrey asked.

"I do. I'm ready to take out your old boss so I can go back."

Her, too, huh? Patrick slipped through the living room and up the stairs before they could see him. How would the others feel about both him and Hannah leaving the team? It was sad to see the end of an era, but it had always been a temporary setup. No matter how cool it was, it had to come to an end eventually. Better this way than some tragic failure. Patrick was determined to see all of them come out of this alive.

* * *

The following days passed uneventfully. Gideon was eager to move on Ashcroft, and he could sense the restlessness everyone else was feeling, particularly Hannah. But they were all still recovering from the strain of the fights earlier in the week. They needed some rest. None of the others had sustained serious injuries, but Gideon's ribs and left arm acted up anytime he did anything too strenuous. He still felt light-headed and weak when he tried to fly. The others were exhausted, too, even if they wouldn't admit it. Charging to Ashcroft's base would be foolish because none of them were at one hundred percent.

Still, not knowing Ashcroft's next step kept Gideon from being able to relax completely, so he wasn't sure how much the rest was helping. He devoted most of his time to tracking Serban, rather than actually resting. And then there was the footage of Solar Flare, which Gideon had not yet brought himself to watch.

It was time to talk to Audrey. Not only did she know where Ashcroft's base was, but she also knew his mind better than anyone else. With his plans in Chicago and D.C. foiled and most of his followers imprisoned, Ashcroft might make a desperate move. If anyone knew what that move would be, it was Audrey.

He found her on the exterior terrace with Dean, looking out at the city lights. Gideon took a step back. Mentally, he groaned. All this time pushing Dean to talk to Audrey, and now he had nearly interrupted a quiet moment. His questions could wait for a few minutes. He backed inside the penthouse as quietly as he could. Audrey stirred and looked over her shoulder.

Oh, right. Super-hearing.

"You don't have to go," she said.

Sorry, Dean . . . "I didn't mean to intrude."

"You're not. Dean was just talking to me about visiting church with you all in the morning."

"I think you should."

"Told you," Dean said.

Audrey shrugged. "I just didn't really grow up a church person, you know? I'm not sure I've ever been in a church in my life, except for my best friend's wedding, and that doesn't really count."

"Doesn't matter." Dean put a hand on hers—his real, flesh-and-blood hand. "Never a better time to start than now. I'm in the worship band, so it's not like you'll be looking at a bunch of strangers on stage."

Audrey raised her eyebrows. "You're in a band?"

"I play a little electric guitar."

"A little?" Gideon grinned. "He's been in the church worship band since he was fourteen. I'll leave you guys alone. Whenever you get a chance, come find me, Audrey. It's no rush."

"Okay."

Dean nodded his thanks. Gideon walked back inside and downstairs to the living room. As important as finding Ashcroft was, getting Audrey into church was far more important. Besides, if God had chosen them to be the instrument of stopping Ashcroft, as Gideon believed He had, they would get it done. It was only a matter of time.

CHAPTER 52

Audrey didn't know what she had expected from church, but it wasn't this. The friendly, loving atmosphere and the reverent spirit of worship opened her eyes to a world she hadn't realized she was missing. She feared that she would feel out of place, but she felt nothing but love as one church member after another welcomed her with handshakes and hugs. But it was the compassionate message delivered by Gideon's father that really spoke to her. *If what he says about God is true, it changes everything.*

She had seen Ashcroft as her savior. He had cured her of cancer and given her powers and a new purpose. After that, Dean had saved her from making more terrible mistakes in Ashcroft's service, but he was only human. A good human—better than Ashcroft—but human, nonetheless.

What these people were saying about Jesus struck her to her core. He was a true Savior, not a man clawing at power in a vain attempt to become a god. Audrey had felt incomplete her whole life, even as a rich, beloved pop star and model. When she left the Regency, she was consumed with guilt. She felt like she had to help the Vindicators to atone for her actions. Yet no matter how many lives she saved, she still felt that guilt. Listening to Gideon's father speak, she knew in her heart what she really needed.

"If you're feeling lost here today," Turner said, "and you know that you need Jesus to rescue you and forgive you of your sin and guilt, we have staff members who can show you how that can be a reality."

"Dean," she whispered.

He leaned over to her. "Hmm?"

"I . . . I'm guilty. I need Jesus to forgive me."

Dean's eyes widened, and he nodded rapidly. He grabbed her hand and bowed his head forward. She followed him down, and he leaned in close to whisper in her ear.

"Audrey, if you know that you need Jesus to forgive your sins and that you can never overcome your guilt and shame on your own, all you have to do is believe that He died for your sins and rose again. Turn away from those sins by asking Him to be the Lord of your life, and you'll be saved."

"But . . . how?"

"It's simple. You believe in your heart, and you can ask Him to be your Lord in prayer."

"I've never prayed before."

"Just talk to God like you're talking to me."

Audrey squeezed her eyes shut. "God . . . I need You. I've been looking for a Savior all my life. Please be the one I'm seeking." With each word that left her mouth, Audrey felt a marvelous sense of peace enfolding her like a warm blanket. A supernatural assurance that she was forgiven settled in her heart. "I dedicate my life to Your service. Amen."

* * *

After a meal that turned into a celebration once Audrey announced her conversion, everyone dispersed to do their own thing. Gideon was looking forward to taking a nap, but Jarrett's footage of Solar Flare was calling his name. He had put it off long enough. Whatever history that video held, it was time to know the truth. Was Gideon a bizarre extension of Solar Flare's legacy? How had Ashcroft recreated his father's powers in Gideon—and not just Gideon, but Joshua Omer?

Alone in the ops room, Gideon settled into a comfortable leather chair and opened the video file on one of Dean's computers. The footage that appeared was grainy, obviously from a decades-old camera. It showed a downtown street of an unidentifiable city. A '50s-model car screeched down the street. A pair of men leaned out the back seat, firing guns into the air. The car swerved abruptly and crashed into a fire hydrant.

A muscular man in a skin-tight, caped costume landed behind the car. A halo of energy surrounded him. As he approached the car, the men in the back seat continued firing. Solar Flare pressed on undaunted. *He's dissolving their bullets—just like I do.* Solar Flare ripped the car door free, yanked the men out, and knocked each out with a quick punch. The driver took off running. Solar Flare extended his right hand, and a beam of energy lanced out and struck the man in the back, sending him sprawling.

More clips in the video showed similar scenarios. Solar Flare fought criminals, saved innocents, and even put out a fire by carrying a fireman's hose high into the air to spray it down on the burning building. As the film progressed, Solar Flare became more violent with criminals. He burned one into submission. He hurled another through a storefront window. Finally, the superhero took a man in a chokehold and snapped his neck.

The video cut to different footage, looking down on the Pentagon. Solar Flare dropped from the sky and landed in a three-point crouch. Even from the distant camera, Gideon could see the bright glow of Solar Flare's eyes. A squad of soldiers rushed out to meet him. Gideon's heart sank. He knew where this was going. The battle that played out was short but brutal, and it ended with Solar Flare lying dead on the lawn in front of the Pentagon.

Gideon stared at the blank screen. He wasn't sure what answers he had hoped to glean from the footage, but it had not provided any. It confirmed that he shared abilities with Solar Flare, and it lined up with Jarrett and Artemis's stories of an old-time superhero. But it did not tell him why they had powers in common. Nor did it reassure him that he wouldn't follow the same path as Solar Flare.

But I haven't devolved into murdering my enemies. He had blasted clean through that nephiloid just blocks from the Tower without meaning to, though. *Is that where it starts? What about the Scripture-quoting Wyatt Jonson?* Maybe Gideon was going mad.

"God, please don't let that be my fate," he whispered.

Jolie would know what to say. She always did. Gideon leaned back in the chair and stared up at the ceiling. Why hadn't he told her yet? He should have opened up as soon as he saw Wyatt for the second time. He knew what she would say. *Gid, you are not insane.* She would reassure him that he was levelheaded and competent, even if he did have a temper at times. And he would believe her. Still, some part of him needed answers. Answers he could get from Ashcroft.

But first, he should be honest with his fiancée. They were about to start sharing their lives. She deserved his complete honesty.

"Ahem."

Arianna and Maddox stood in the doorway to the ops room, the latter holding a box. He frowned, rose from the chair, and stepped toward them.

"What's going on?" he asked.

"Your suit is trashed," Arianna said. "I didn't think aionium could bend that way, but Torrent found a way to do it. You'll obviously need something to wear, though, so we found something."

Maddox held out the box. "Go ahead. Open it."

Gideon took the box from them, set it down on the workbench, and pulled the lid open. Resting on a folded dark blue cape was a familiar navy, gold, and midnight blue costume. Gideon's first Seraph suit, the one Dean had designed for him back in the early days of his career as a vigilante.

"Figured you might need it if you're going to raid Ashcroft's base soon," Maddox said. "We didn't have time to design a new one, so we pulled this out of mothballs and repaired some of the damage to it. Everyone's got to be at a hundred percent, right?"

Gideon removed the suit from the box. "Thank you, both. Not just for this—for all the hard work you've put into helping us. From the start, this has been my mission, but as soon as I needed help, you were there."

Arianna smiled. "It started out as a favor to Dean, but now, it's our mission, too. This world is a safer place with the Seraph in it, Gideon."

"Thank you."

Gideon refolded the cape and suit. He found himself suddenly and unexpectedly emotional. This all really could be coming to an end soon. Not his career as a hero, but the mission that had driven him for months. If they took Ashcroft down and CLOUD got a handle on the new amps, Gideon would have effectively accomplished his goal. His crusade was coming to an end. With the others doing their part, Gideon didn't feel the pressure of being the only protector of Sojourn City. Even the police had become more effective since the corruption was rooted out. The city didn't need vigilantes or superheroes as much as it had when he started.

He took a deep breath. He could feel his strength returning; the constant exhaustion he had felt since Chicago was abating. His injuries weren't healed, but they were on the mend. He felt like himself again. If the rest of the team felt similarly, it might be time to launch their assault on Ashcroft and finally stop his insane experiments for good.

Gideon looked down at his suit. For now, maybe he owed it to his city to be the Seraph they remembered.

* * *

Patrick decided to tell Gideon. He wasn't going to wait until Ashcroft's defeat to drop that he was going home in Gideon's lap. It was better to give him a heads-up now so he would be prepared for it. Especially with some of the others planning to leave, he didn't want to burden Gideon with too much at once. It would be a two weeks' notice of sorts. He thought it was the courteous thing to do.

It seemed as good a time as any to tell Gideon. The air was buzzing with excitement. Everyone seemed to have recovered from the stress and exhaustion of defeating the nephiloids, and Audrey's conversion added another layer of happiness to the day. With Gideon's spirits up, he might accept Patrick's departure more readily. The lair was also almost empty. The only others there at the moment were Arianna, Maddox, and Hannah.

Footsteps rapped on the stairway. Patrick jumped to his feet and walked to the base of the stairway. He found Gideon standing in his Seraph suit—not his bright blue armor with its bold, golden-winged emblem, but the suit Patrick had first seen him in on television, the dark blue costume of a vigilante. With the domino mask covering his eyes, the hood draped over his head, and the cape flowing behind him, it was a terrifying look.

"Wow." Patrick swallowed. "Feeling nostalgic today, huh?"

"My armor was trashed in Chicago. Arianna and Maddox gave this back until they could make a new set. I just got back from patrolling the Brooks. It was . . . I'm not sure there's a better word for it than nostalgic."

"It suits you." Patrick cleared his throat. "Hey, can I talk to you for a second?"

"Sure."

"Out on the terrace."

Patrick walked up the steps, and Gideon turned to trail him. Patrick stepped out onto the terrace. It was nearing October, and a chilly wind brushed Patrick's face. Patrick wasn't used to temperatures like this. San Francisco had always been temperate. One more reason to go back as soon as possible.

Gideon lowered his hood and draped his domino mask around his neck. "What's up?"

"I'm ready to go home." Patrick puffed out a breath. "Whew. I said it. Look, I'm going to stick around until we defeat Ashcroft, but after that, I just think it's time for me to head back to San Francisco. My family and friends are there, and Sojourn City's got plenty of superheroes. I just feel like it's time."

Gideon nodded slowly. "We always knew that having you here would be temporary. I understand. I'm going to miss you, and I really appreciate all the help you've given to the team. You've grown a lot in the four months since I've met you, and I'm not just talking about your powers."

"Thanks." That meant a lot coming from Gideon. He was Patrick's hero, in more ways than one. "I appreciate it. And don't worry. I'll still come around. I mean, I can run here in just a few hours. Of course, I'll have to nap for a while once I get here, but . . . "

Gideon grinned and patted him on the shoulder. "I know you won't be a stranger. I wish you the best of luck in all y—" He froze.

"What's wrong?"

"Get down!"

As soon as the first word left Gideon's mouth, Patrick's body tensed. The world slowed around him, Gideon's mouth frozen mid-shout. Patrick pushed him back into the lair, and something grabbed Patrick's ankle and tugged him backward and upward. Even the nephiloids, fast as they were, couldn't have grabbed him while he was in motion. Swatted, maybe, but not grabbed. This had to be something else.

The world returned to normal speed as Patrick was jerked up off the balcony. The penthouse windows flashed by, and suddenly, Patrick was hanging over the Tower. He cried out and looked around. What was he supposed to do from up there? Even if he could free himself from his attacker, he had no way to stop himself from falling. He craned his neck up to get a look at his attacker. Whoever or whatever it was, it had waxy skin, covered only by tattered black pants. It held Patrick's ankle in a massive, clawed hand. Huge, bat-like wings protruded from its back and flapped madly, forcing gusts of wind downward into Patrick's face. He couldn't get a good look at the creature's head, but he spotted strands of wispy black hair sprouting from it.

The beast flew down toward the Tower's rooftop and dropped Patrick on his back. *What do I do?* Clearly, this thing was fast enough to counter whatever move Patrick made, so he needed help. With any luck, Gideon would already be on his way.

A beam of light slashed through the air and struck the hovering creature full in the chest. Gideon flew onto the roof, landed next to Patrick, and extended a glowing hand toward the beast.

"Who are you?" Gideon demanded.

"Don't you mean what?" Patrick exclaimed.

Gideon shook his head. "I can sense it; it's human. Or was."

The beast cackled. "Perceptive, Turner. I was human. You don't recognize me? After months of hunting me, that must be disappointing."

Patrick shuddered. Ashcroft? What had he done to himself? He'd never met the man before, but Gideon had, and Patrick was fairly sure he would've mentioned him having huge wings and talons. Whatever he had done with the splicer Backfire had stolen months ago, it must have worked. Ashcroft had made himself into the most frightening image of a Nephilim Patrick could imagine.

"Ashcroft." Gideon clenched his jaw. "What do you mean you *were* human?"

"I have outgrown that name as I have outgrown humanity." Ashcroft held up his hands, and clouds of black smoke floated around them. "I am Nephilius."

Somehow, Gideon's voice remained calm, level. "I know who you were. Artemis told me your father was a superhero, that his serum drove him insane. I saw the footage myself. I'm sorry that happened, but this is not the way to go about making it right."

"What do you know about it?" Ashcroft snarled. "You weren't there."

Patrick took a deep breath. He needed to strategize before Ashcroft—or Nephilius—made a move. The guy seemed too strong and too fast to take out with a speedster punch, and he and Gideon were the only two around. Gideon's light blast had stunned Ashcroft for a moment. Patrick could be down in the lair in seconds, send out a distress call, and even change into his uniform in time to get back before Gideon and Nephilius had exchanged a few blows. Maybe Gideon could keep stalling him.

That was the only option. They had no idea what they were up against, and they didn't want to test Nephilius's skills alone. Patrick sprinted toward the stairwell door. He grabbed the handle.

A black cloud surrounded Patrick, smashed the door to splinters, and yanked him backward. He cried out as he tumbled through the air. Panicked, he flailed with both arms, trying to find purchase. His right hand clasped down on the edge of the roof. He sucked in a trembling breath and looked down. His feet dangled in the air. The balcony was perhaps two dozen meters below him—a hard fall—and if he missed it, he'd plummet all the way to the street. His only choice was to climb. He threw his left hand up and grabbed the edge of the roof.

Gold beams flashed from above, shadowy clouds mixing with them. Those clouds around Nephilius' hands must've been the source of whatever had grabbed Patrick and whatever was trading shots with Gideon. *Gotta get up!* He ignored the pain burning in his chest and pulled with all his might. He scraped over the edge of the roof and crawled back up.

His chest felt like it had been hit with a fireball. There was no visible damage to his clothing, but touching the skin underneath confirmed it was blistered. He was also short of breath, which rarely happened to him. But it could have been much worse if not for his speed healing.

Another cloud shot toward Gideon, flung from Nephilius' clawed hands. Gideon pirouetted out of the way of the beam, extended his hand, and fired back with a golden blast. Nephilius grunted as the blast struck him, stumbled back, and fired a column of smoke from each hand.

With Nephilius distracted, Patrick rushed toward the shattered remnants of the door and sprinted down the stairwell. He rounded the corner and found Fragment, frozen mid-step, pounding up the stairs. Powers was clad in his black-and-red uniform, a look of confusion and conflict on his face. As Patrick ran past, he stuck his foot out to trip the villain. Fragment fell, and Patrick sped down the hallway and rushed into the lair.

Hannah looked up. "What's going on?"

"Trouble on the roof! It's Ashcroft!"

He didn't wait for her response. He blasted upstairs into the ops room, palmed the brand-new alarm button Dean had installed that would send a red alert signal to each team member's phone, and grabbed his uniform. It was time to end Ashcroft's threat, once and for all. *God, keep us safe. Amen.*

CHAPTER 53

Powers didn't know what to do. Witnessing the full extent of Nephilius's power in person, he saw that the monstrous leader of the Regency was impossibly close to unstoppable—fast enough to surprise Spright and strong enough to resist a direct blast from the Seraph. The pillars of cloudlike blackness that fired from his hands did not give way when they met with Turner's beams of light. Yet Nephilius was not able to break through the light to hit Turner, so he wasn't all-powerful. Just terrifyingly strong.

But Turner was outmatched. Powers had considered lying in the stairwell where Spright flattened him, but something inside urged him on. If nothing else, he had to watch this fight. It was like witnessing a battle between two forces of nature, light and dark incarnate.

Turner terminated his beam of light and rolled aside as Nephilius' cloud advanced. He was good. It was like he sensed when Nephilius was going to make a move a split second before he did it and acted in advance. As far as Powers could tell, that was the only thing keeping the Seraph alive. If Powers duplicated himself and swarmed Turner, the hero was as good as done for.

Powers stood just outside the stairwell entrance, unable to pick a side. He didn't want Nephilius to win. Turner was the last thing standing in Nephilus's way. This fight could be the deciding moment in the future of the world, and Powers did not want to see Nephilius's world. If he tried to help Turner, he was likely to end up dead, if not now, then once Nephilius recovered enough to exact his revenge. But if he attacked Turner and helped Nephilius win, Powers was doomed to a life of servitude to an evil monster.

Coward. He thought back to his moment of clarity in the lair. *I'm a coward. I'll always do whatever it takes to preserve my own skin.*

A black pillar slammed into the ground where the Seraph had been standing a moment before. Another cloud shot out at him, and he flew sideways to avoid it. The cloud cut off and reappeared, assailing Turner. The Seraph dropped to the ground, grimacing and clutching the wound. Nephilius flapped his wings, launched himself high in the air, and gathered a massive cloud of black energy between his hands. The attack was sure to kill Turner, and neither Spright nor any of the other heroes had returned yet.

I can't believe I'm doing this.

Powers clenched his fists, focused, and created four duplicates of himself. He was a loser, a selfish criminal. He had been his whole life. He never did anything daring or selfless because he was afraid of getting hurt. But if he didn't do something now, lots more people were going to suffer because of it, and he would be doomed, anyway. It was time to own up to his mistakes.

Three of his doppelgangers leaped up toward Nephilius. Two of them caught the monster's feet and dragged him down. The third wrapped his arms around Nephilius's waist. Powers and his fourth doppelganger stood back for the moment, watching the fray. Howling in rage, Nephilius bucked his elbows, sending the doppelganger around his waist tumbling to the rooftop. The final doppelganger rushed in to help. Turner climbed to his feet. He looked weak and pale, and he was still clutching his chest. If he died, Powers was truly dead.

The Fragment holding on to Nephilius' left foot pulled as hard as he could, struggling to bring the monster down to the ground. If they could pin him just for a moment, they could overwhelm him with doppelgangers, and the Seraph could finish him off.

The monster roared and kicked his right foot. The Fragment on that foot slipped off and fell to the roof below. Fragment grunted and held on to Nephilius's left foot more tightly. He just had to keep him distracted.

Nephilius looked down at him, malice and hatred burning in his golden eyes. He extended both hands and fired black pillars to strike Fragment. The clouds pushed him down to the rooftop and pinned him there. Everywhere the black energy touched his body, agony ripped through his flesh and dug down into his skin.

"I never should've trusted you," Nephilius rumbled.

Fragment screamed.

Powers panted and stumbled back, his body trembling. He'd never felt pain like that; none of his doppelgangers' deaths had compared. He leaned against the doorframe for support. Nephilius turned back toward Turner and gathered a cloud in his hands again.

"No—"

Bang.

Pain ripped through his chest. Powers stared numbly at the bullet hole and the blood blossoming on the front of his uniform. He stumbled forward.

A black cloud enveloped him. Powers screamed. Agony dug into every nerve-ending in his body. Compared to this, the bullet he'd just taken was nothing. Powers's vision blurred. He cast his mind about, searching for one of his remaining doppelgangers. *There.* The one Nephilius dropped to the roof earlier had survived the fall. *Maybe if I move my mind there...*

The doppelganger struggled to his feet and dragged himself closer to the door. A few meters away, the original Powers stood in the middle of the rooftop, a black cloud enveloping him. He was between Nephilius and Turner. The attack that was draining him must have been intended for the hero. At the doorway stood one of the new members of Turner's team, the Bison girl. Her revolver was still smoking. So, she was the one who had shot him—the one who had killed him. Did she realize Powers had been trying to help? Probably not.

She seemed distracted by Nephilius's attack. She didn't notice the doppelganger, the last vestige of Vince Powers. Maybe he could still get away; maybe he could survive in this body. Maybe he didn't need his original body to live on. He stood and stumbled. He looked down at his hands. They were fading.

"No," he muttered. "No . . . "

He could feel his power slipping away. His life was ebbing, too, but his powers were going faster.

Fragment dropped back to his knees. His arms were almost completely gone, and the rest of him was quickly following. This is what he got for trying to be a hero, but it was probably better than living under Nephilius's rule. He closed his eyes and waited for the darkness to take him.

* * *

Gideon thought he was hallucinating when Powers attacked Nephilius. Had the villain switched sides? Hope blossomed inside the Seraph. Maybe with Powers's help, they could win this. He pushed himself to his feet and tried to build up a reserve of light energy in his left fist. With his right hand, he clutched the wound on his chest. It was bad, but hopefully treatable if he got help soon. He had to deal with his enemy first.

Nephilius kicked the first Fragment off his leg and hit the other with his dark energy. The Seraph staggered forward a step to help.

Bang. The Seraph spotted the real Powers standing in the stairwell doorway, a circle of blood growing on the front of his uniform. Malice filled the Seraph's senses. A cloud of black power hurtled toward him, and he raised his hand in a feeble attempt to block it.

But the cloud didn't reach him. Powers stumbled forward into the pillar of darkness. The malice Gideon sensed from Nephilius was overwhelmed by the intense pain and fear that now enveloped Powers. The Seraph grimaced and clutched at his head. He'd never felt anything that dark and oppressive.

Powers screamed as the cloud surrounded him. The remaining Fragment doppelgangers disappeared one by one. Hannah stepped out of the stairwell and trained her gun on Nephilius. The Seraph looked over at the last Fragment, kneeling next to the door. The doppelganger began to fade out. The Seraph's heart ached for him. *He made the right decision, in the end.* If only Hannah had realized that.

Patrick reappeared on the rooftop next to Hannah, dressed as Spright. The Seraph backed toward his friends. Together, they might stand a chance.

"What a waste," Nephilius growled.

He ended his assault on Powers and floated down to the rooftop. The former villain lay still. The Seraph probed him with his empathic powers and sensed nothing. Nephilius lumbered toward the three Vindicators.

"You see? You cannot defeat me." Nephilius smirked. "Bow to me now, and I will be merciful. I need new servants. If you surrender to me, you can be at the top of the chain. If you do not, then you will die."

Hannah cocked back the hammer on her gun. "You're insane."

"Everyone says that, but look! I succeeded. I created superhumans." Nephilius spread his hands. "I made you. All of you!"

Whatever madness had taken Solar Flare, it was clearly working in Nephilius, too. That gave Gideon an ember of hope. *Maybe it isn't the powers.*

Gideon shook his head. "You used us as pawns to achieve your own ambitions. All you care about is vengeance for your father and completing his mission, and you'd raze the world to do it. But that's not what he would've wanted. Stop this while you have a chance, Ashcroft. We won't give you another chance."

The Seraph sensed Spright's intention a split second before the teenager bolted forward. *No*! The teenager could not match Nephilius's power. With a twitch of his hand, the Seraph fired a bolt of light at the ground in front of Spright's feet. He froze for a moment, and the Seraph seized the opportunity to leap toward Nephilius, his fists glowing.

"Gideon, no!" Spright shouted.

The Seraph swung his fists at Nephilius. The hulking monster stepped out of the way of the blows and grabbed the Seraph by the throat, hoisting him in the air. The Seraph gathered the light within him for a powerful blast, and Nephilius slammed him into the ground. The air rushed from Gideon's lungs.

Nephilius frowned. "I can feel Fragment's power coursing through me. Interesting."

Nephilius' dark energy must have drained Fragment of his Nephilim DNA. If Nephilius grew stronger every time he absorbed a superhuman's power . . .

"You're coming with me. If any of you follow me, Turner dies."

He brought a huge fist forward and struck the Seraph on the side of the head. Stars exploded in Gideon's vision, and the world drifted away.

CHAPTER 54

Patrick pulled his mask off and threw it to the ground as Nephilius soared away, carrying Gideon's limp form with him. *This can't be happening. Not now.* He looked over at Hannah, who lowered her gun and reluctantly tucked it away in her holster. Patrick shifted his gaze to Powers's unmoving body.

A flash of green light lit the roof, and Dean appeared. He rushed to Patrick's side and looked down at Powers.

"What happened?" he asked.

"Ashcroft attacked," Hannah said. "At least, Gideon called that thing Ashcroft, but it didn't look human to me."

Patrick could barely meet Dean's gaze. "He took him. He took Gideon."

Dean's face fell. Without Gideon, how were they going to go up against the monster that Ashcroft had become? On the bright side, the madman was on his own. Powers had been the last member of the Regency. Maybe the Vindicators could take Nephilius down on the sheer advantage of numbers alone.

"What happened to Powers?" Dean asked.

Hannah pursed her lips. "I shot him. I think it might've been a mistake. He might have been helping fight Ashcroft, and I didn't realize it until too late."

Dean nodded and vanished in another flash of green. Patrick picked up his mask, took Hannah by the arm, and sped her down to the lair. Audrey was there, a look of concern on her face.

Dean put a hand on her shoulder.

"You were right about Ashcroft turning himself into a monster," Dean said. "Where are the others?"

"I haven't seen them. Is there anything I can do to help?"

Dean shook his head. "It's over. We just need to get Powers's body off the roof."

"He's dead?" Audrey swallowed. "All right. I'll go get his body. We can't leave him there."

Patrick watched her go. Where were the others? They should have received the alert, like Dean and Audrey had; but they didn't have the benefit of speed, flight, or teleportation. If they had all been there, maybe Ashcroft wouldn't have escaped. There was nothing to be done about it except to regroup and find Ashcroft before he killed Gideon.

* * *

Wes paced the living room, clenching and unclenching his fists. He'd returned to the lair to find that the emergency had already passed. Gideon was gone, and Vince Powers had been killed. He could see in the guilty looks on their faces; Carter, Jolie, and the others felt, as he did, that they should've been there to help. Dean walked downstairs. Wes stopped pacing and looked at Gideon's best friend. Everyone else turned their attention to him, too.

Dean shook his head. "I can't find him. He was wearing his old suit. I hadn't installed a tracking device in it like I did the others."

"That's our fault." Arianna wiped her eyes. "We should've tried to fix his aionium suit instead of sticking him with the old one."

"No, you couldn't have known. Besides, we can find him easily enough; Audrey knows where Ashcroft's base is. Right now, we need to decide how to stop him."

"I've been reviewing security footage of the fight," Maddox said. "Although Hannah did shoot Powers, it looks like Ashcroft's smoke quickened his death. It's like it just sapped the life out of him."

Wes finally found his voice. "We need to go after him."

"We need to keep a cool head." Dean rested a hand on Wes's shoulder. "Strategize."

Hannah snorted. "Strategize? Every second we wait, Gideon could die. I may be able to fend off Ashcroft's smoke with my powers, create a force field or something that can block him out. If I can, the rest of you should be able to take him."

"That's a big maybe," Audrey noted. "What if you try and the smoke blasts right through your force field and kills you?"

"Guys!" Wes punched the nearest wall. "We've got to do this. Every second we waste, Gideon's chances get smaller."

They could take Ashcroft together—he was sure of it. If they could catch him by surprise and Audrey could disable him with her sonic powers, Wes and the others could take him down before he could recover.

"I think you're forgetting one very important thing," Maddox said.

"What's that?" Wes asked.

"Ashcroft's physical changes," Arianna replied. "Unlike the rest of you, Ashcroft underwent physical mutation when he took the serum. Even if you put power-dampening cuffs on him, he's still got wings and an enhanced muscle mass. You may not be able to restrain him."

Wes pursed his lips. They were right. Even if the cuffs took away Ashcroft's smoke powers, his mass alone would make him a threat. If they captured him and he broke out of his cuffs while they were on the Raptor, they would all be as good as dead.

"What option do we have?" Carter asked. "Whether Gideon's with us or not, we may not be able to restrain him."

"You may only have one choice," Arianna said.

"The counteragent," Maddox continued for her. "It did the job for the nephiloids; no reason to assume it wouldn't for Ashcroft, too."

"You're talking about killing him." It was the first time Jolie had spoken up. Her throat bobbed, and unshed tears glistened in her eyes. Behind them, though, there was a deadly fire. "Gideon told me about what the counteragent would do to a superhuman."

"Is there another choice?" Hannah asked. "If no one else wants to do it, I will. I've already killed one of his people. It's not going to hurt my conscience to take out a monster like him."

"Gideon wouldn't want us to kill unless absolutely necessary," Dean said. "That's never been our policy."

"We killed the nephiloids," Hannah pressed.

"Non-sapient, mutated animals that Ashcroft Frankensteined. That's different than killing a human being."

Hannah shook her head. "Is he even human anymore?"

"I think Dean's right," Carter said. "Gideon's never killed before. Dad didn't, either. We don't have to."

Wes scratched the back of his neck. This was ridiculous. They were discussing the morality of killing Ashcroft when they hadn't even found him yet. This was a waste of time.

"If it comes down to Gideon's life or Ashcroft's, wouldn't you choose Gideon's?" he asked. "I'm not condoning murder, but this is killing to protect a friend. In my opinion, that's different."

"Audrey?" Dean looked at the newest member of the team. "What do you think?"

"I don't want to kill anybody," she said softly. "But Ashcroft is a monster, and he might kill not just Gideon but also a lot of other innocent people. His actions have already led to *so much* death and destruction. If the options are killing him or leaving him out there, I think our choice is clear."

"But we need to move now," Wes urged.

"Jolie?" Dean asked.

Everyone turned to her. Wes understood; Gideon was their leader, and as his fiancée, Jolie was naturally to whom they would look for a decision. But it stung a little, too. He was Gideon's brother. Didn't they trust him to make that choice? He swallowed his pride. She was older and more experienced than he was. It only made sense to listen to her.

Finally, she nodded. "Go. If it comes down to killing Ashcroft to save Gideon, do it."

Good. He expected she would understand the gravity of the situation. Wes didn't like the idea of going into battle without Gideon, but Ashcroft had forced their hand.

"All right." Wes rushed toward the stairs. "Let's suit up and—"

Knock, knock. Wes froze. Who would knock on the door to their lair? Who would even have access to this floor? The others tensed, and Hannah reached for her guns. Wes walked toward the door, reached for the knob, and peered out the peephole. On the other side of the door stood Jarrett Mercer. Wes frowned and opened the door.

"Jarrett?"

"What are you doing here?" Dean asked.

"I, uh . . . " Jarrett ran a hand through his unkempt hair. "I felt guilty about leaving a job unfinished. I promised to help take Ashcroft down, and that's what I intend to do."

"You came to help us?" Wes asked.

"That, and my wife has been shooting lasers from her toes nonstop. It was getting kind of old." He didn't so much as crack a smile. "So, yeah, I came to help. What's going on?"

"Come on in. We've got a lot to talk about."

* * *

Gideon stood on the Tower rooftop. Night had fallen. Lightning flashed in the distance. Gideon scanned the sky for any sign of Nephilius. Save for the clouds that were rapidly moving toward Sojourn City, there was no sign of movement in the sky. Where had that madman gone?

Oh. Right. He had taken Gideon and flown away. This had to be a dream. Gideon wasn't on the rooftop. Vince Powers's body lay at Gideon's feet, his expression frozen in a rictus of horror. Blood stained the front of his costume, but it was the black lines running down his neck and face that drew Gideon's attention. He knelt next to Powers to examine them. They were veins—darkened and protruding and crawling toward the crown of Powers's skull. What had Nephilius done to him?

"You must stop him."

Gideon closed his eyes. The voice belonged to the familiar apparition of Wyatt Jonson. Gideon stood and looked out to the horizon. He didn't want to look at the ghost, not right now. He'd seen too many dead men as it was. Looking at this one would only confirm the fragility of Gideon's mental state.

"I don't know how."

"Your light was beating back his darkness," Wyatt noted. "You only need to push harder. Light can always overcome darkness."

"But he seems so strong."

"'Greater is He that is in you, than he that is in the world.'"

Gideon nodded. When he needed it most, it seemed that God had amplified his powers to stop Torrent. Surely, He would do it again when Gideon faced Nephilius.

"I was right. Stopping Ashcroft—Nephilius—is God's purpose for my life. That's why He allowed me to be captured in Venezuela. That's why He's led me to this point."

*"'*For I know the thoughts that I think toward you*, saith the Lord.'" Wyatt smiled. "Often, we cannot see His plans until they are already in motion, or even past. All we can do is follow Him and do what we know is right."*

"I've always tried. I don't know if I've succeeded."

"No one succeeds all the time. What matters is a genuine desire to serve and a genuine effort to follow through with that desire."

"Stopping Ashcroft . . . It's going to be the hardest thing I've ever done."

"The Lord goes with you." Wyatt nodded and backed away. "Trust Him and push on. He will deliver you."

Gideon reached out. "Wyatt . . . "

It felt odd to say the name. Wyatt Jonson had been dead for months. This apparition, whether a figment of Gideon's imagination or supernatural presence, was not Carter's father. It couldn't be. But what else could Gideon call him?

"Am I going insane?"

Wyatt laughed gently. "What makes you say that?"

"Solar Flare did. I have his powers. And right now, I'm talking to a dead man." Gideon resisted the urge to drop into the fetal position and clutch at his head. "I don't want to be like him. Solar Flare became a murderer. His fall led to Ashcroft's bitterness and evil. I don't want my legacy to be that way."

"It won't be. Trust the Father. Your shining moment is yet to come."

CHAPTER 55

Gideon's head swam as he struggled back to consciousness. His brains felt like they had been stuck in a blender and poured back in his skull. He tried to raise a hand to rub his head, but his hands were bound to . . . something. The floor? A chair? He wasn't sure. He tried to open his eyes, and his head revolted violently. He moaned and sank back onto whatever uncomfortable surface he was resting on.

The spinning in his head and the queasiness when he tried to move told him he had a concussion, probably from Ashcroft throwing him around. He kept his eyes squeezed shut and tried to relax. Not an easy thing to do when he didn't know where he was.

God, please help me get out of this.

He charged his hands with light—maybe the force of the energy would allow him to break the restraints—but as he did, a new wave of nausea washed over him.

"You're awake."

The raspy growl sent shivers down Gideon's spine. In the confines of the lab, it was unmistakably the voice of the man he remembered from Venezuela. But now, it sounded . . . other. It wasn't entirely human. There was something ominous and otherworldly about it. He resisted the urge to open his eyes again, knowing the assault of light on his optical nerves would send fresh waves of pain and dizziness to his head.

"Where am I?"

"My home. Ironic, isn't it? This all started when I created you in Venezuela. Now it ends with you in my grasp. It all comes full circle."

"What do you want from me?"

"I want your obedience—or your power. It's your choice. Stripping away Fragment's power killed him and strengthened me in the process. I can do the same to you." There was a pause before Nephilius's voice came again, closer. "I don't seem to have taken Fragment's actual abilities, though. Pity. Self-replication would be useful. Perhaps I should practice before I try on you. I would love to have your powers. Call it sentimentality. Of course, you could just surrender them to me willingly."

"You're insane if you think I'd ever work with you, Ashcroft."

"Nephilius."

Gideon opened his eyes. He winced as his head threatened to crack open, but his eyes adjusted to the light. Nephilius stood before him, a monstrous form with sickly, wax-colored skin and massive wings.

"Call yourself whatever you want. You'll always be the same pathetic, insane man you've always been."

Nephilius spread his arms. "Look at me. I am a god."

"No. You're a man playing god, and the real God doesn't like that much. You're going to lose, Ashcroft, because when you challenge God, He doesn't sit idly by."

Nephilius sneered. "My father thought as you do. Where was his God when he was shot dead in front of the Pentagon? We'll see how arrogant you are once your body has been sucked dry of the power I've given you. A quick blood sample so I can recreate my serum, and then I will drain you. And as you die, you will know that your power will fuel my ascension."

* * *

The rumble of the Raptor's engines was strangely calming to Audrey, almost the way the gentle patter of rainfall against the roof calmed her as she tried to sleep. It was a soft, constant sound that lulled her into a state of rest and preparation. She took a deep breath, closed her eyes, and focused on gathering her power.

The others shifted restlessly around her, but Audrey tuned them out and focused inwardly. She reached out to God in a silent prayer that they would all make it out of this alive. She had been a believer for less than a day, and already, her faith was being tried. *Why would God allow this to happen?* He must have a purpose for it. She was determined to see it through.

She wished Gideon was with them. His leadership and cool head during intense situations were reassuring. Dean and Wes were doing their best to fill that gap. But Wes was nervous and angry, and Dean was scared. Audrey didn't mind that; they all were. Dean refusing to hide his fear made her respect him even more.

"Coming up on the base," Maddox called. "Get ready."

Ashcroft's compound rested in a clearing in a wooded area a few hours from D.C. The lab was the original property of Regency Inc., the company owned by Ashcroft's father, but Ashcroft had wiped it from any records that would lead back to him. Now it was an anonymous cube of concrete and steel, nestled away from prying eyes.

"The lab is protected by motion-tracking guns," Audrey said. "We'll have to get past them to make it inside. And the doors are all reinforced aionium."

"How did he get his hands on that?" Dean asked.

"Beats me. But in any case, we'll have to find a way to open them or get inside by some other means. Nothing can cut through aionium."

"I can teleport inside and open the doors from there. Patrick should be fast enough to draw the guns' fire without getting hit. While he does that, the rest of you take them out. I'll use the distraction to get inside."

"That could work. Once we're inside the doors, we should be able to make our way to Ashcroft's lab; I'm sure that's where he'll be."

"What about security cameras?" Jarrett asked. "Won't he see us coming?"

Cameras were one thing Ashcroft's lair had in abundance. "Probably. But he'll know as soon as the automated guns start firing. They'll trigger an interior alarm that will alert him to our presence. But it's not like we have much of a choice, right?"

"Yeah, guess not." Jarrett loaded arrow after arrow into his quiver. "I have CLOUD agents on standby if we can't finish him off. You should know—if we fail, they've been ordered to bomb the lab."

"What?" Wes exclaimed.

Jarrett barely looked up. "If we fail, we're all probably going to be dead, anyway. We can't risk a threat as big as Ashcroft getting away."

Audrey tried to push the conversation out of her mind. She couldn't entertain the possibility of failure, not if she wanted to stay focused. Their only option was success. Even if CLOUD managed to kill Ashcroft, the world would be much darker if the Vindicators were wiped out, too.

The sound of the engine shifted so subtly that only Audrey's enhanced aural senses could detect it. The plane was descending. Audrey stared down at her blue domino mask for a moment before she pulled it over her eyes. The suit Dean had made for her was much more her style than her old one. The rest of the team put on their masks and checked their gear. Dean, Patrick, and Jarrett each had a syringe of the counteragent; they were the most likely to be able to hit Ashcroft with it.

"Touching down in five," Maddox called.

Dean exhaled shakily. "Here we go."

"You okay?" Audrey asked.

"I will be." Dean massaged his prosthetic hand. "Once we've got Gideon back."

"God protect us," Carter whispered.

The plane touched ground, and the ramp descended. Audrey jumped from her seat, clenched her fists, and soared out into the night.

* * *

Nephilius reached out with his right hand and hurled a column of smoke at a nearby workbench. The smoke wrapped around the workbench, and Nephilius tugged it into the air. The workbench flew across the lab and smashed into the wall. As the smoke dissipated, Nephilius clenched his fists and laughed.

"I knew I would become godlike, but this . . . this is more than I could've dreamed."

"A god doesn't have to reassure himself that he is a god every five minutes," Turner said. "And doesn't seek only personal gain and vengeance through the use of his power."

"Personal gain?" Nephilius spun to face Turner. "I will remake the world! Hunger, pain, and war will vanish under my rule."

"Sounds like dictatorship to me. Never works. Never will. Superpowered or not, people like you will always meet the same end." Turner's stare bored into Nephilius's eyes. "You might as well kill me now, Ashcroft. I will never serve you."

Nephilius shook his head, snarled, and turned away. *How could he not see? How could none of them see?* With the power they all possessed, they could become an unstoppable force. Working under Nephilius, they could free his followers and rebuild the Regency. As one, they would become lords over the whole world, remaking it into whatever they wanted.

"What is it, Ashcroft?" Gideon pressed. "Why do you hate me so much? I can sense it. You've got a lot of anger built up inside you, but so much of it is directed at me. What did I do? What makes me special?"

"My question exactly." Nephilius whirled. "What makes you so special, Turner? Why did you, of all people, get his powers? Why you and not me? Why—"

A shrieking klaxon snapped Nephilius from his tirade. He scowled. "It seems your time is up."

CHAPTER 56

Drifter sprinted forward and rolled behind a tree as one of the automated machine guns lining the perimeter of the lab opened fire. Bullets peppered the tree, sending chunks of bark flying. He grimaced and pressed himself closer to the tree, clenched his fist, and unfolded his aionium shield.

"Cover!" he shouted.

Spright darted through the field and toward the compound. Alerted by his movement, the guns swiveled to face him. Their heavy rounds exploded into the ground, sending dirt spewing in the air like a geyser. Aria soared overhead and fired a sonic pulse at the gun firing on Drifter. The turret exploded, and another gun spun to track her movement. Drifter leaped out from cover and hurled his shield. The silver disc slashed through the air and severed the gun's fragile base. Drifter clenched his fist, activating the magnetic sensor in his gauntlet, and the shield returned to his hand. A third gun fired on him. Drifter raised his shield, and the bullets bounced off the aionium surface.

Yeoman and Brass Bison rushed in, firing their respective weapons. Arrows and bullets struck the remaining perimeter turrets, making short work of them. Yeoman fired an arrow at the gun that was blasting Drifter. The arrow's explosive tip detonated the turret.

"Rooftop!" Rampart shouted.

Drifter looked up. Four more guns were mounted on the roof, directly over a dilapidated sign reading "Regency Inc." They turned, tracking the heroes, and opened fire. Drifter blocked the hail of fire directed at him and dug his feet into the sod as the barrage pushed him back. Yeoman and Bison ducked for cover. Rampart charged forward, his skin matching the surface of Drifter's shield, and drew their fire, the bullets bouncing harmlessly from his aionium flesh. A purple blur, barely visible in the dim moonlight, appeared on the roof. One of the guns shorted out, electricity sparking from the wires that powered it. As the few remaining turrets turned to face Spright, Aria came back around and unleashed a prolonged sonic wave as she flew across the rooftop. Each of the guns exploded in turn. Dean lowered his shield as the onslaught ceased and breathed a sigh of relief.

"Move in!"

He rushed toward the massive door at the front of the lab. Aria landed beside him.

"What's on the other side of the door?" Drifter asked. "I need to picture it in my mind. Otherwise, I might teleport into the middle of a wall or something, and this mission would be over real fast."

"If you teleport about four feet directly in front of your current position, you should come out right in the middle of the hallway." Aria cringed. "But you may want to teleport a bit high in the air in case there's something sitting on the floor."

"Great." Drifter closed his eyes. "Wish me luck."

He imagined reappearing where Aria had described—four feet forward and a few yards in the air. He opened his eyes as he felt his body shift in location and looked down to see the floor rising to meet him. He landed in a crouch. The hallway was dimly lit, with brownish walls and concrete flooring. Another corridor intersected it about halfway down, and this hall continued for some distance until it branched right. But most importantly, it was empty. Drifter walked over to the touch-screen control panel next to the door. It wasn't locked from this side; there was a blue "open" button in the middle of the screen. Drifter tapped it; the screen flashed green; and the door rumbled and slid ponderously open.

Aria smiled. "Nice work."

"Thanks." Drifter clenched his fists. "Now, let's go find Gideon."

* * *

Gideon tightened his jaw and focused all his energy into his hands and forearms. Nephilius was facing away from him, watching the Vindicators on a security feed as they fought their way into the compound. With any luck, he would remain distracted long enough for Gideon to snap free of his restraints.

He tugged on them with all his might, his left arm screaming in protest as the fractured bone met more resistance than it was ready for. Gideon ignored the pain and shot as much golden energy through his arms as he could. The straps around his wrists glowed red with the heat. Sweat beaded on his forehead. *Come on. Come . . . on!* He jerked his hands free. The restraints snapped in half and clattered to the floor.

Gideon jumped to his feet while Nephilius was distracted. He unloaded his store of energy straight into Nephilius's chest. The impact hurled the monster backward, and he smashed through the wall into the next room. Gideon staggered past the new hole in the wall and out the lab door. He was in no condition to face Nephilius alone, but if he could meet up with the others, they might stand a chance.

Heavy footsteps thudded in the hallway behind him. *He's coming.* That blast hadn't bought Gideon nearly as much time as he had hoped. Refusing to look back, Gideon pressed forward and turned right at the next intersection. He could sense the vague presence of his friends in that direction; he hoped he was in the right hallway and that he wouldn't end up doubling back.

The thumping footsteps stopped, replaced seconds later by the loud flapping of giant wings. Gideon increased his pace. He would never be able to outrun Nephilius when the villain was flying, but the narrow corridors gave him some advantage. Ahead, the corridor ended at a right angle. Gideon pushed himself toward the corner. He glanced over his shoulder. The huge, winged form of Nephilius appeared in the hallway behind him, bearing down relentlessly.

Gideon pressed forward, fighting the urge to look back again. He had to do this with his senses alone. Reaching out with his empathic abilities, he waited for them to alert him to imminent danger.

Now!

Gideon threw himself to the right. A heavy crash sounded behind him. He looked back. Nephilius had smashed into the wall at the end of the corridor, unable to change the vector of his flight in time. The monstrous supervillain growled and leaped forward.

"Gideon, down!"

Rampart's silver form battered against Nephilius, knocking him back against the wall. Gideon leaned against the wall and backed away as Rampart slammed one metal fist and then the other into Nephilius's jaw. Nephilius roared and backhanded Rampart. The hero backed up a step, squared his shoulders, and stepped in again, bringing his knee up into Nephilius's gut. He balled his fists together and brought them down on top of Nephilius's head.

Gideon looked around for the others. Yeoman and Bison rushed around the corner with their weapons trained on Nephilius. Gideon did a double take at seeing the archer. Jarrett spared a glance at Gideon, smiled, and nodded. Gideon nodded back and returned his attention to the fight. Rampart and Nephilius were locked in an all-out brawl, fists, feet, and wings flying as they battled. Drifter appeared at Gideon's side.

"You all right, buddy?" Dean asked.

"I'll be fine. Thanks for coming." Gideon straightened. "Let's finish this thing for good."

"Thought you'd never ask." Drifter extended his shield. "Vindicators, move!"

* * *

Catching Nephilius off guard worked to Rampart's advantage. The villain had barely managed to recover from the initial blow before Rampart was raining down strikes on him, and now that the others were there, they had an opportunity. Rampart leaped, snap-kicked Nephilius in the jaw, landed, and rammed his shoulder into the monster's chest.

"Drifter, now!"

Drifter materialized over Nephilius and dropped onto his back. The villain growled, bucked, and flapped his wings. Rampart drilled punches into Nephilius's chest. Nephilius roared and grabbed Rampart's hand. Bison opened fire with her revolvers. The bullets didn't do much damage to Nephilius's chest and arms, but they drove him back. Rampart surged forward and grabbed Nephilius's right arm. If he could just hold him for a few seconds . . .

He looked up at Drifter, who removed the syringe from his belt, popped the cap off, and raised it to drive it into Nephilius's back. Nephilius swept his left arm toward Rampart. Rampart braced himself, but the blow didn't land. Rampart glanced over at the hand. It was frozen midair, lassoed by a bronze strand of energy.

"Hurry!" Brass Bison gasped. "Can't . . . hold this . . . long!"

"No!" Nephilius roared.

Clouds of black smoke exploded from his hands. Rampart grunted and flew back, carried by the force of the cloud. He smashed against the far wall and grimaced as the cloud wrapped around him. It had weight to it—and not just physical. He could feel the dark energy burning beneath his skin and into his very being. The aionium that shielded his body began to dissolve away, his skin returning to flesh form.

Drifter had been bucked free, too. He was lying on his back behind Nephilius, pinned by another column of smoke. Rampart yelled incoherently and pushed himself forward against the black pillar. A beam of light exploded across Nephilius's back, sending the villain stumbling. The smoke dissipated. Rampart rushed forward, dropped into a slide, and drove his fist into Nephilius's kneecap.

Yeoman poked his head around the corner. *Come on, Jarrett. Shoot him!* Yeoman ducked back around the corner for a moment and reappeared, his crossbow leveled. Rampart leaped up and grabbed one of Nephilius's wings, pulling him down while he was still off balance. Seraph fired a stream of light into the villain's back, keeping him unsteady.

Yeoman fired. The villain tore himself free from Rampart's grasp and slapped the arrow aside, snapping it in half. He brought his foot down on the syringe tip, crushing it. Raising a hand to shield himself from the stream of light from Seraph, Nephilius wrapped a massive hand around Rampart's chest and hurled him aside. Out of the corner of his eye, he saw a flash of green as Drifter teleported away. A moment later, he reappeared at Rampart's side.

"What now?" Drifter asked.

"What happened to your syringe?"

"I fell on it when he threw me off. It's crushed."

It was up to Spright. He was the only one with the counteragent, and Nephilius had already proven that he could match the speedster.

Rampart struggled to catch his breath. "We have to regroup. We need a new plan."

"Not necessarily," Drifter said. "Maybe Aria can—"

Thud. Wes froze. The sound repeated. Nephilius's heavy footfalls echoed down the corridor as he approached. Wes saw the same realization in Dean's eyes. They had to move fast, or they would be trapped again. But where could they go? Even if they ran down the hall, this place was a maze that Nephilius knew like the back of his hand. They would be lost and trapped in no time.

Their only option was to surprise him again, hitting him as he came around the corner, and not let up on their assault. Maybe between the two of them, him with his aionium fists and Drifter with his shield, they could stun him long enough for the others to get back outside. Then, Drifter could teleport them out to the plane. But he wasn't confident that CLOUD would be able to take Nephilius down if they left.

Thud.

"Ready?" Rampart asked.

"As I'll ever be."

Rampart touched the aionium tile on his belt, restoring the segments that had faded. *That was weird.* It was like Nephilius's smoke had been draining his power. He couldn't let Nephilius get a hold of him like that again. Once again armored in aionium, Rampart nodded to Drifter, and they crept down the hallway toward the thudding footsteps.

* * *

Spright clenched his jaw as Nephilius stomped down the hallway toward Drifter and Rampart. The villain had manhandled the Seraph into the wall, stunning the Vindicators' leader. Without a distraction, Spright wasn't confident that he could hit Nephilius with the serum. Even if he could, he wasn't sure he wanted to. He hadn't even been able to kill Mendez, the man who murdered his grandfather. Could he really kill Nephilius, even to save his friends' lives?

As the villain disappeared around the corner, Spright rushed to the Seraph's side. Gideon stirred, his eyes fluttering with the effort of maintaining consciousness. Spright tucked his arm under the Seraph's shoulder and hoisted him up. Together, they limped back down the hall to where the rest of the Vindicators had gathered.

"We need to go help them now," Aria said.

"How do we do that?" Bison asked. "My bullets are having about as much effect on him as Nerf darts. I can try energy projections, but I can't keep it up for long."

The Crusader turned to Spright and the Seraph. "Gideon, your powers are doing the most damage to Nephilius. If we give you an opening, can you take him out?"

"I'm not sure Gideon's in much position to do anything," Spright said.

The Seraph put his hand on Spright's shoulder. "I'll be fine. Just give me a minute."

"Dean and Wes don't have a minute," Aria urged. "If we don't get in there now, they're both dead."

Drifter could attempt to teleport them out of there, but it would be risky with Nephilius right on top of them. If Nephilius grabbed either one of them while Drifter was teleporting, he'd go with them, and then they'd be farther from help. But if Spright could go in and distract Nephilius long enough for them to teleport away . . .

He adjusted his goggles. "I've got this."

"No." Gideon stepped away from Patrick and straightened. "We have to do this together. All of us, as a team. Hold him off long enough for me to gather my strength. I can't do this by myself. If we're going to beat him, we need to work in unison."

Yeoman nodded. "Maybe an explosive arrow would stun him long enough for Dean and Wes to get out of his way."

"That seems like our best option," Aria said. "Yeoman, you hit him with an explosive arrow, and I'll let out the biggest sonic blast I can manage. Between the two of us, we should be able to distract him, at least long enough for Dean to get Wes out and come back for the rest of us."

"Let's do it."

Spright helped the Seraph sit down on the hallway floor. He hoped it didn't take Gideon too long to gather his strength. Bison holstered her guns, formed a pair of energy swords, and jerked her head toward the hallway. Aria stepped out first. Spright stood and followed her. The world slowed around him. The cacophony of battle rang from around the corner that Drifter and Rampart had rounded—

Nephilius roared and stumbled back into the hallway. Drifter and Rampart were on him like savages, striking him repeatedly with limbs and shields. Nephilius waved his arms to ward them off, but the suddenness and ferocity of their attack seemed to have taken him aback. Spright gathered himself and rushed in. As he approached Nephilius, he leaped through the air and clambered onto the villain's back. He reached for the syringe in his belt. This was his chance. He could end this now. But he couldn't kill someone, even Nephilius.

"Drifter, Rampart—move!" Yeoman shouted.

Aria unleashed a high-pitched soundwave. Nephilius roared and clutched at his ears. Drifter grabbed Rampart and teleported away. Spright kicked Nephilius in the back, flipping through the air away from the monster and landing in a crouch. An arrow shot past him and struck Nephilius in the chest. It exploded, and the hulking monster stumbled back. A split second later, Drifter and Rampart reappeared next to Aria. Spright sped back to their side. Nephilius, his shoulders heaving up and down with rage, turned to face them.

"Run!" Bison shouted.

Spright understood. If they drew Nephilius away, it would give the Seraph more time to gather his energy. They couldn't go toe-to-toe with the villain, so they'd have to play cat and mouse. Rampart, Bison, and Yeoman sprinted down the hallway and out of sight. Aria continued to pour sonic waves at Nephilius. He roared and flailed, clutching at his ears and stomping toward her. Drifter put a hand on her shoulder.

"Let's go!" he said.

Aria backed toward the hallway, continuing to emit as high-pitched a blast as she could maintain. She took another step back. Nephilius removed his hands from his ears and extended his hands. Pillars of smoke shot forward. Spright tucked into a ball and rolled out of the way of the pillar, but Aria cried out as one of them struck her in the chest and carried her back into the wall. Her soundwave died as her concentration broke. Drifter hit the wall next to her and grunted. Nephilius stomped toward them. Spright ducked back into the hallway, waiting for an opening.

"You should never have left me," Nephilius rumbled. "Now you'll pay for your betrayal, just like Powers."

“What do we do?” Aria cried.

Drifter shook his head helplessly. “I . . . I don’t . . . ”

Spright surged forward, ramming his shoulder into Nephilius’s side. For a split second, the smoke evaporated. Spright glanced at his friends.

Go, he mouthed.

Drifter clutched Aria’s hand, and with a flash of green light, they were gone. Spright withdrew the syringe from his belt—not to use it, but to show Nephilius he had it. It was just the two of them now. The monstrous supervillain loomed over Spright, a death glare in his eyes. Patrick swallowed the lump in his throat. *Be not afraid of their faces: for I am with thee to deliver thee, saith the Lord.*

“Come on, ugly.” Spright backed away. “Come and get me!”

Nephilius stepped forward, and a glowing figure carried him down the hall and out of sight. Relief flooded through Patrick’s body.

Gideon.

CHAPTER 57

The Seraph plowed into Nephilius's body fists-first, between the monster's wings, and discharged the maelstrom of light energy he had gathered, sending Nephilius flying down the corridor. Nephilius struck the hatch at the far end of the hall and smashed through it. The Seraph landed in the middle of the hall, gathering his energy for another attack. Spright darted next to him.

"You okay?" Gideon asked.

"I'm fine." Patrick held up a syringe. "I had the chance to kill him, but I couldn't."

"I'm proud of you. Go on; get out of here. I'll take care of Nephilius."

"Alone?"

The Seraph gathered light energy into his fists. "Trust me."

"But—"

The Seraph reached out into Spright's mind. His mental abilities were limited, but he planted a single feeling in his young friend's mind: *gather the others.* The speedster bobbed his head in understanding, and a tendril of black smoke struck Spright in the chest. He stumbled back and screamed as the black energy surrounded him. The Seraph charged up as much light as he could in his hands and jumped in front of Spright. The tendril retreated slightly, wavering in the luminescence of Gideon's fists. But the shadow advanced nonetheless, pressing in toward him.

"Go!" he shouted.

He didn't wait to see if Spright complied. He stepped toward Nephilius, expanding the light energy in his hands around the rest of his body and pushing back the dark aura with a halo of light. The darkness pushed back at him, encircling him and squeezing him, threatening to extinguish his light. He gritted his teeth and pressed forward.

"I can't wait to be rid of you!" Nephilius roared. "You've taken everything from me. My followers, my mission—even my father's powers. You have no right to them, and yet you wield them more effortlessly than he ever did. Those powers should be mine!"

Gideon ignored Ashcroft's tirade and focused on drawing from the wellspring of light within. He had to do this—for all his loved ones. For Patrick, so he could go home and be with his family and protect his city. For Dean, so he could have a chance to cultivate a relationship with Audrey. For Wes, so he could live out his dreams. For Carter, so he could grow even more into a man his father would be proud of. For his parents, so they could live in a world safe from the evil Nephilius would bring. For Jolie. Because he loved her with all his heart, and he would never let anyone, or anything, harm her. For the family they could have one day, so that they could grow up never seeing this kind of darkness.

It didn't matter that Solar Flare went insane. Gideon was not Solar Flare. He was the Seraph. His destiny was not set in stone by another man's fate. He made his choice. He would stand in the gap and beat back the enemies of the light. Ashcroft's darkness would not consume the world—not while Gideon was there.

The light bursting from his body brightened from gold to nearly white. Still the tendril—which had grown to form a massive column of smoke—pressed in around him. He glimpsed Nephilius through the cloud, stomping forward and snarling with the effort of his continued assault. At least, it was as taxing on him as it was on Gideon.

The Seraph grunted as darkness oppressed him from all sides. His knees buckled, and his shield of light flickered. The clouds pressed in around him. The Seraph's breath left his lungs as the dark energy's touch brought impossible pain. It seeped into every pore and, even worse, into his mind. He struggled to revitalize his aura of light, but the darkness was too close.

God, help me!

Consciousness flickered, and he screamed with the effort of producing even a spark of light. But the darkness was all-encompassing. He couldn't see through it. Seraph dropped onto his back and blinked rapidly, trying to keep his eyes open.

Back in the alley, the ghostly apparition of Wyatt Jonson had said that there was no greater love than to lay down one's life for a friend. Maybe this was what he meant.

* * *

Nephilius took another step forward and poured all the darkness he could muster into Turner's unmoving form. The last vestiges of light were fading from his nemesis's body. Nephilius sneered at him. The Seraph had at last been snuffed out. He maintained the assault for another five seconds and lowered his hands. The dark clouds dissipated, and Turner's body lay in the middle of the corridor, lifeless.

Though it was a pity to lose someone so powerful, Nephilius felt a measure of satisfaction. The insignificant missionary boy from Venezuela had not earned the power that Solar Flare wielded, yet he had taken to it with ease. At least, he had served to fuel Nephilius's power. A renewed energy coursed through his body, just as when he had killed Fragment. But the ability to wield light had likely been lost to Nephilius forever. *So be it. If I can't have the light, I'll settle for darkness.*

If the other Vindicators had any sense, they would've already taken their plane and left the compound. He would hunt them down in time, after he'd freed his servants from whatever prison they'd been locked in. The Regency would have one last chance to serve him; now that he was all-powerful, perhaps they would be more properly motivated.

He stormed past Turner's body.

"Yah!"

Nephilius turned toward the grunt, and a silvery disk slammed into his brow. He staggered back and clutched his head. Blood oozed between his fingers. He looked around, searching for where it had come from.

A sonic blast struck him in the back, sending him stumbling forward. As he stepped, a metal rod struck his kneecap. Nephilius staggered toward the ground. As he fell, a rapidly moving fist clad in purple appeared in front of his face and smashed into his jaw. The arc of his fall changed. Nephilius rolled onto his side and landed badly on his left wing. He cried out as cartilage popped and bone cracked.

A hail of bronze energy bullets struck his chest, and although they did not penetrate, he felt the force of each impact keenly. He raised his right hand to ward off further shots and pushed himself into a crouch. Something sharp sliced into his palm. An arrow protruded from his hand. He roared and stomped forward.

A heavy form landed on his back and wrapped an arm around his throat. Nephilius bucked and roared, but the arm was made of something sturdier than human flesh.

"Enough!" Nephilius shouted.

He expelled dark energy from every inch of his body, propelling each of his opponents away from him. He pinned them—all seven of them—to the walls around him with smoke columns.

"You couldn't stop me before. Now that I have your friend's power in me, how can you hope to compare?" Nephilius clenched his fists. "Imagine how unstoppable I'll become once I've drained all of you."

* * *

"Gideon."

The voice echoed oddly. Gideon opened his eyes and looked around. He was surrounded by golden-white light, similar to that which he shone from his own body, but somehow brighter. There was nothing else around him—only the light. Where had that voice come from?

A figure appeared, shining even more brightly than all the radiant light around them. Gideon felt his insides turn, and he dropped to his knees. Was he standing before God?

He bowed his head. "My Lord."

"Rise. I am not the Lord your God. I am only a messenger."

If a mere angel was this glorious, how unspeakable must God be? Every fiber of his being urged him to remain on his knees, but he ignored the feeling and stood.

"Am I dead?"

"Yes."

Tears welled in his eyes. He had come so close to stopping Ashcroft. So close to surviving. So close to saving the world from a terrible fate. So close to a beautiful life with Jolie in a world free of Nephilius. He mourned for that missed opportunity, even more for Jolie's sake, because she was left behind. She would be crushed, but she was strong. With time, she would recover.

Along with that sorrow, though, and quickly overpowering it, came a wellspring of joy. All the pain he had endured, all the suffering in the past few years—could it really be over? He was about to enter Heaven. His eternal rest was coming sooner than he had expected, but was that such a bad thing? He was about to meet his Savior. Maybe that made it all worth it. Gideon was just a man, after all. God could still use the other Vindicators to stop Nephilius. They didn't need him.

"Yet there is still hope," the angel said. "There is still time. God is not finished with you yet. You have not fulfilled your purpose."

"My purpose to stop Ashcroft . . . Nephilius?"

"Indeed."

"Who are you?"

The light faded from the figure, revealing a familiar form—a dark-skinned man dressed all in white. Gideon stepped back in surprise.

"Wyatt?"

"No. I have taken this form for your sake." The angel extended his hand. "I am Michael, commander of the Lord's legions."

Gideon shook his head. "Why come to me?"

"You have branded yourself the Seraph." Michael grinned crookedly. "That makes you one of mine, doesn't it?"

"I guess so." Gideon laughed. "So, if I'm dead, how do I stop Nephilius?"

"'And ye shall know that I am the Lord, when I have opened your graves, O my people, and brought you up out of your graves.'"

"You're going to bring me back?"

"Not me. Only One has that power. But there is a cost, Gideon, one you must count if you are to do this. Defeating Nephilius will drain you of your powers—permanently."

"Is that possible?" Gideon frowned. "Maddox said the Nephilim DNA had fused with mine. It would be impossible to remove it without killing me."

"'With men this is impossible; but with God all things are possible.'"

His powers? Gone forever? Gideon felt a heaviness in his chest. As much as he'd first considered his powers a curse, he now considered them a blessing. He loved his powers, and he was grateful for the good he'd been able to do with them. Why would God take them away? He could still do so much good, even after Nephilius was vanquished.

"Why?" Gideon asked.

"'The Lord gave, and the Lord hath taken away; blessed be the name of the Lord.'"

It wasn't for him to know. So be it. If it came down to his powers or his life, of course he would choose his life, a life with Jolie. He'd lived a normal life before he'd been given his powers; he could do it again. He would have to wait a little longer to experience Heaven; but now he had glimpsed just a taste of what waited for him when death did come.

"I understand. But Michael?"

"Yes, Gideon?"

"Why did I get Solar Flare's powers? If I kept the powers, would I be doomed to insanity like he was?"

Michael smiled gently. "No, you would not. Solar Flare's madness was thrust upon him by enemies, those who were jealous of his power. His serum was never the cause. Losing such a servant of the light was a tragedy, but we knew you would rise in his place."

"That's why I inherited his powers? Because I was chosen as his heir?"

"You were chosen because you exhibited similar traits: nobility, selflessness, leadership, heroism. Traits also found in Joshua Omer. Had he survived, he would have been a hero of the ages." Michael shrugged. The gesture seemed heavy with

sorrow. "But on a fallen earth, all is not always as it could be. You have fulfilled the role God would have chosen for Solar Flare and for Joshua Omer."

Gideon swallowed and nodded. "Thank you."

"Go in peace," Michael said. "Fulfill your calling."

Screams filled the air around him. Gideon gasped and sat up. Nephilius stood with his back to Gideon; seven dark tendrils extended from his body, pinning the other Vindicators to the wall. The Seraph pushed himself to his feet, clenched his fists, and allowed light energy to course freely through him.

"*Let them go*!"

Nephilius spun around but continued to drain the others. "Impossible!"

"I'm not finished with you."

The Seraph took two steps, leaped into the air, and soared toward Nephilius. He struck him in the chest and carried him to the far wall, smashing through it and continuing into the next room. He swung Nephilius around and slammed him into a stack of supply crates. The villain smashed his right hand against the side of Seraph's head. The blow rang the Seraph's ears, but he pushed on and kicked Nephilius in the chest.

"You want to know why I got these powers instead of you, Ashcroft?" Gideon leveraged his weight and hurled his opponent into the wall. "Because our powers are derived from who we are. Artemis is a manipulator. Mendez was destructive. Wes is a bulwark supporting his friends and loved ones. Your father started his mission with a noble goal and only went insane after he acquired his powers. You, Nephilius? There's no nobility, no light, in you. It's all corruption, all dark, petty vengeance. That's why you look like this now. You're more of a monster inside than you'll ever be on the outside."

"You will not stop me!" Nephilius cried. "I am a god!"

He extended his hands, and clouds of smoke surrounded the Seraph and closed in on him. The Seraph closed his eyes and held out his hands to either side, pouring out light energy so bright that he could see it through his eyelids. He let the power stream through every cell in his body.

When he opened his eyes, white light had obliterated every trace of shadow in the room. Nephilius shielded his eyes and cried out. The Seraph reached forward and grabbed his opponent's chest. Waxy flesh burned instantly at his touch. Nephilius screamed and tried to shove the Seraph away. Black smoke surrounded the Seraph's body just as pure light surrounded Nephilius's. The smoke burned Gideon. He ignored it.

"The Nephilim weren't gods, Ashcroft. There's only one God, and in trying to usurp Him, you have earned His wrath."

The Seraph concentrated all his energy into his hands and, with a mighty effort, expelled it through his palms and into Nephilius. In turn, the intensity of the smoke around the Seraph increased, and the burning in his body raised to excruciating levels. His scream matched Nephilius's. The villain flailed his arms, but Gideon held fast. Slowly, Nephilius's bulging muscles shrank. His orange skin took on a paler hue. The wings on his back withered like dead leaves until they fell from his back and crumbled on the ground.

Finally, Nephilius collapsed. The smoke and the light dissipated as one. The Seraph stepped back and looked down at him. Whatever he had once been, Nephilius was just a man once more—the man Gideon had seen all that time ago in Venezuela. He was, once again, Jeremiah Ashcroft. Breathing heavily, Ashcroft stared up at the ceiling. Gideon lowered his hood, removed his mask, and knelt next to the scientist.

He took a deep breath and glanced at his hands. He concentrated on creating a ball of light. Not even a glimmer.

It's done. The combination of Gideon's light and Nephilius's darkness had snuffed the powers from each other's bodies without killing them. Perhaps it had returned their physical forms to some metaphysical balance or sent their Nephilim DNA into an inert state. It didn't matter how; their powers were gone.

"Gideon?"

Dean stood in the hole that had been punched through the wall. He stepped inside, and the rest of the Vindicators followed him. They looked down at him, eyes wide. Gideon wondered what they were feeling. For the first time in a long time, he couldn't tell.

Dean ran a hand through his hair. "You were . . . dead."

"I was. Now, I'm not."

"Impossible," Jarrett said. "How?"

They would never understand; even those who had been believers for many years, like Dean, wouldn't believe it if he told them. What he had just been through was an impossible experience, one that even Gideon would have doubted if he hadn't been the one to whom it happened. But it had been real—real and very personal.

"I guess God wasn't done with me yet. Is everyone all right?"

Dean nodded. "A little shook up, but it looks like we're all safe now."

"Good."

Audrey looked down at Ashcroft. "Nephilius. Is he . . . "

"Not Nephilius anymore. But he's alive and ready to be taken into CLOUD custody. Come on. There's no reason to stay here. Let's go home."

CHAPTER 58

"So, your powers are gone?" Dean asked.

Gideon nodded. "Haven't been able to produce so much as a spark. And I haven't sensed any emotion from any of you."

Dean shook his head in disbelief. When Gideon had pulled him aside as the team debarked from the Raptor, he expected some explanation for how Gideon had survived. This was more intense than Dean had imagined. It was a lot to swallow, but he knew as well as Gideon did the kind of miracles God could do. This one was just more overt.

He wondered what it meant for the future of the team. Gideon had started it all, brought them together, and led them through everything. Without him . . . They could still function—they'd proven that when they'd come to save him—but it would be different.

"I'm sorry, man."

"Don't be." Gideon smiled. "I had them for a purpose, and I fulfilled it. Now, I can marry Jolie, and we can have a normal life together. And don't worry. If any of you need any vigilante advice, I'm here for you. But between you and me, I have a feeling this team might not be long for the world, anyway."

Dean raised his eyebrows. "Really?"

"Yeah. Patrick's already told me he's ready to go back to San Francisco, and we know Hannah and Jarrett are probably as good as gone, too."

"And there's nothing keeping Audrey here, either."

"Isn't there?" Gideon chuckled and slapped Dean's arm. "Get with the program, man. Make a move."

He walked down the ramp to where Jolie was patiently waiting for him. Dean followed him and wove around the couple. Audrey stood nearby, talking to Hannah and Wes. She glanced over at Dean, smiled, and waved. Dean waved back. Gideon was right; it was long past time for Dean to make a move. How many guys got to ask out their pop star crush?

* * *

Jolie squeezed Gideon into a crushing hug and kissed him. She had been so worried he wouldn't come back, and she had spent the whole time he'd been in Ashcroft's clutches pacing, praying, and trying not to fear. But he was safe, and from the look of things, they had won. Everyone was smiling and slapping one another on the back. There was a sense of relief and victory in the air that Jolie hadn't felt in a long time.

"Welcome back," she said.

Gideon smiled. "Thanks. I'm glad to be back."

She studied him. He seemed different, somehow. Sober, despite the smile. He was happy and somehow sad at the same time. Everyone had come out unscathed, so why was he off? He had matured almost a decade in the hours he'd been gone.

"What happened?" she asked.

"I'll explain on the way back. It's a long story."

"You all right?"

"I am." He rubbed her shoulder and stepped back. "Come on. I'm exhausted. Let's get out of here. We need to stop by the lair before we go home."

Jolie took Gideon's hand and walked back toward her car. Finally, Gideon's quest seemed to be at an end. If only Serban wasn't still on the loose, maybe she could relax. But that would be a problem for another day.

* * *

The team gathered in the lair's living room, bringing in chairs from the kitchen and the ops room to have enough seats for everyone. Gideon dropped into a kitchen chair next to Jolie and watched the others. It was the first time they'd all gathered like this, and it might be the last.

He leaned forward to speak. "I just wanted to let you all know how proud I am of you. You rallied together to save me, even when I wasn't here to take charge. You worked as a team, and you acted like real heroes."

"We were just following your example," Patrick said.

Gideon smiled and glanced at Jolie. Tears welled in her eyes, but she smiled and nodded. He'd told her that he had lost his powers on the way there, and she had sobbed when she heard that he had been dead for a few minutes. He assured her that he was fine and that his life as a superhero was over. They were going to get married and live their lives together.

"That's something you're going to have to keep doing," Gideon said. "Because when I came back to life to stop Nephilius, there was a catch."

"What catch?" Jarrett asked.

"My powers are gone, just like his are. Something about our powers mixed together like that . . . They're just gone." He inhaled and watched their expressions. "I'm officially out of the superhero game. I know some of you will leave soon, and I wish you the best of luck. Whether you stay or go, I'm always here for all of you, for advice, support, or a friend who understands." He looked at Jarrett, Hannah, and Patrick in turn. "I hope you all know I'm just a call away."

Gideon was simultaneously grateful and regretful that he couldn't feel their emotions anymore. Patrick wiped tears from his cheeks. Jarrett clasped his hands in front of him and rested his elbows on his knees while staring at the floor. Wes swallowed and stared off into the distance.

Carter stood. "Thank you, Gideon. For everything. You've been a friend, a mentor, a hero. I couldn't have asked for a better man to train me after my father died."

A lump formed in Gideon's throat. He nodded.

"I'm going to honor you—my father and you," Carter continued. "I'm going to keep on being the Crusader, but I'm going to focus my attention on this city. I'm not a superhero like the rest of you. My talent lies in fighting street crime. I'll do it to the best of my ability, but I can't do that as a Vindicator. It's time for the Crusader to find out who he really is on his own."

"Me, too." Patrick sniffled and wiped his eyes. "I'll honor you, I mean. I guess now's as good a time as any to tell you all. I'm going home to San Francisco. I've been here long enough, and I feel like it's time."

Carter's face fell at that. Gideon smiled sympathetically. The boy had come to consider Patrick one of his best friends, the way Dean was to Gideon. This would be hard for him.

"Well." Wes shifted from foot to foot. "While we're all sharing . . . "

Gideon blinked. He'd known about Patrick, and Carter's revelation hadn't surprised him. He was counting on Jarrett and Hannah to return home. But Wes? Gideon remembered Wes's distraction as they'd approached Chicago, his off-handed comment that he needed to tell Gideon something later. This must've been it.

"I'm going to law school in Juncture City. I've been thinking about it for a while. Rampart's done his part for Sojourn City. It's time for Wes Turner to make his mark."

Gideon glanced at Jolie. Tears streamed down her face. Gideon took her hand, stood, and walked over to Wes. Wes stood up into the middle of their hug. Gideon squeezed his brother as tightly as he could. He couldn't imagine being prouder of him.

"Love you, Wes."

More arms wrapped around Gideon. He looked up. Dean had moved in to join the hug. Patrick and Carter rose, too, and wrapped their arms around Wes and Gideon. The others shuffled and moved in.

"I love you all," Gideon said. "More than words can say."

Dean patted Gideon's back. "We love you, too. All of us."

* * *

Ashcroft sat in a featureless gray cell in a government holding site far from civilization. He stared at the wall across from his bunk, trying to make sense of everything that he had experienced. He had wielded so much power that he had been practically invincible. For one glorious moment, he could've done it. His goal to dominate the world and remake it in his image under the Regency was within reach. Weakness and terror would have been things of the past.

And then, Turner. How he had returned to life, Ashcroft did not know. Maybe he had been playing dead somehow, hiding his life essence from Ashcroft. It seemed impossible; on Turner's passing,

Ashcroft had felt the hero's power flowing into him. But moments later, there he had been, standing stubbornly in Ashcroft's way once again.

How did he take my powers? His light had burned its way into Ashcroft's very cells, stripping away the shadowy power in them. Ashcroft shifted in his seat, his shoulder blades aching with the phantom pains of his severed wings.

It was over. The last of Ashcroft's serum, real or synthetic, had either been destroyed or confiscated by the clandestine government agency that now held him prisoner. Ashcroft's plan had failed. But perhaps, in a way, it hadn't. He'd set out to honor Father, who had only wanted to make the world safer. Ashcroft may not have gotten his vengeance, but he'd done something else. Foolish and naïve as they were, the Vindicators did protect the world. Maybe they had been the solution all along. If so, Ashcroft was content in knowing he had, in some small way, succeeded. Maybe Father would've been proud of that.

He reclined in his cot, careful not to put too much pressure on the scars where his wings had been. *One day, I'll be useful again. One day, this government agency will need my expertise.* It was only a matter of time.

CHAPTER 59

Carter adjusted the collar of his polo shirt. It was the nicest shirt he had, and his mother had insisted he wear it for his job interview. He smoothed out the wrinkles in the gray fabric. *I'm not tucking my shirt in, though. Not even an option.*

He checked the time on his phone and bounded up the stairs toward Sterling Enterprises. He was ten minutes early, and he figured that would help his chances. Not that he was worried. He was friends with the CEO, so the job was as good as his. He tucked his phone back in his pocket, pulled open the glass door to the lobby, and stepped inside.

He had almost asked Dean to reschedule the interview. After everything that had happened the day before, it would have been nice to take a day off. The fight with Nephilius had been enough, but afterwards, the goodbyes in the lair had just about drained Carter altogether. It had been a lot of emotions for one night.

Carter glanced over his shoulder. Gideon's sweet navy-blue Mustang was parked on the curb. He'd picked Carter up for the interview that morning. It was strange to see him so normal. He was adjusting well, or so it seemed. But for Carter, it would take some getting used to. The Brooks would feel a lot less safe without the Seraph there to back him up. How would the local criminals react once they found out that the Seraph was retired?

A guard stepped up to Carter. "Can I help you?"

"Yeah, Mr. Sterling told me to report today for an interview with the security chief."

"May I see your I.D.?"

Carter handed over his driver's license and glanced around the lobby. It was surprisingly bustling. He expected a few men and women in lab coats and others in business suits, plus a handful of security officers, but there was also a pack of teenagers huddled near one of the elevators, listening to a woman in a lab coat.

A field trip? Carter scanned the teens. Patrick and Raina stood among them. Carter ducked his head to conceal a smile. He would miss working with Raina at the grocery store, even if there was nothing about the job itself worth missing. Patrick had hinted that Raina had feelings for Carter. If that was true, Carter should make his move before his two weeks were up.

"Wait here," the guard said.

He handed Carter his driver's license and walked to a door marked "authorized personnel only." Carter rolled his shoulders, tucked his hands in his pockets, and waited. The woman in the lab coat pressed the elevator call button and gestured for the teens to prepare to step aboard. A few businessmen shifted restlessly, probably waiting to be admitted for a big meeting. Carter sympathized.

A brawny shoulder bumped Carter, and a muscular man in a greatcoat stepped past him. Carter furrowed his brow and started to say something. He bit his tongue. There was no reason to start something; the guy hadn't done any harm. Carter started to turn away.

The man in the greatcoat glanced to the right, giving Carter a profile view of his face. Carter's heart dropped. He would know that face anywhere. *Luca Serban.* He reached into his pocket, subtly removed his phone, and tapped the alert button that would notify the rest of the team that he was in danger.

The elevator door opened. The tour guide motioned for the teens to enter, and Serban reached into his greatcoat, withdrew a submachine gun, and fired it into the air.

"Nobody move!"

The businessmen who'd been shuffling around jumped to their feet and drew Uzis and pistols, and one of them fired wildly to add to the mayhem. Carter frowned. *How did they get past security? Come to think of it, how had Serban? Unless . . .*

He'd paid the guards off. That was why the guy who'd checked Carter's I.D. had left; he was going to find cover.

Serban brandished his weapon. "Bring me Dean Sterling, or I start dropping bodies."

* * *

Gideon leaned his head back against the headrest of the comfortable leather chair and drummed Dean's desk. He was glad he had the chance to bring Carter in for his interview. It was something to do. He had his job, but he had asked Dean if he could take a few days off to process everything. It was almost as big of an adjustment losing his powers as it had been getting them in the first place.

Waking up that morning felt so different. No more going out for early morning flights, no strategizing with the team about their next move to track down Ashcroft, no waiting to hear about a bank robbery so the Seraph could jump in and stop it. Maddox had run a DNA test on Gideon that morning. He still had all the genetic markers of a Nephilim, but those cells were dormant, as Gideon had suspected.

Almost like a cancer, his powers had gone into remission. Maddox was baffled, but Gideon knew the truth. It was an act of God. There was no other answer.

At least, it provided him more time to plan the wedding with Jolie. Unfortunately, she still had to work. The police hadn't tracked down Serban, and they were losing hope that he was still in the city. Not Jolie. She was as sure as ever that he was still there, and Gideon was inclined to believe her.

He wished he had helped her while he'd had the chance. She had wanted to let him focus on finding Ashcroft, but with his powers, he would've been able to bring Serban in easily enough. Now, he didn't have anything more than his martial arts skills. Good for vigilantism, but those days were long over.

Mostly, he was just ready to be married to Jolie. They'd had a long road to get there, and they'd almost reached the end of one journey and the start of a new one. It was exciting and scary all at once.

"We should celebrate tonight," Dean said. "I know losing your powers doesn't seem like an occasion to celebrate, but we won. Patrick, Hannah, and Wes are all leaving soon. This may be the last chance we have to get the whole crew together."

Gideon nodded. "You're right. I think it's a good idea. What if—"

Dean's phone buzzed, and Gideon's did, too. That was never a good sign. Gideon withdrew his phone from his pocket. An alert had gone out on the team's frequency, and it was from Gideon's location. He glanced at Dean and raised an eyebrow. He hadn't hit the alarm, and neither had Dean.

Dean studied his phone. "I just got another alert—a hit on our facial recognition program. It spotted Serban."

"Where?"

Dean looked up at him. "Here."

Gideon shut off the phone's alert system and called Jolie. "Get to Sterling Enterprises now. Serban's here. He just walked in the front door!"

* * *

Patrick covered his head with his arms and ducked as gunfire split the chattering din of noise in Sterling Enterprises' lobby. Someone screamed. Patrick grabbed Raina and pulled her down next to him. His powers kicked in instinctively, slowing the world around him. He looked up at another girl and saw a row of slow-moving bullets drilling through the air toward her. There was no way he could use his super speed without being noticed, but if he didn't, she would die. He had microseconds.

Patrick darted forward, grabbed the girl, and pulled her to the ground. The bullets arced overhead and struck the far wall. The world resumed its normal pace. He glanced back at Raina to see if she noticed. Judging from her wide-eyed expression, she had.

"Bring me Dean Sterling, or I start dropping bodies."

Patrick glanced past their chaperone. The man who had initially fired into the air stood in the middle of the lobby, a short submachine gun pointed in the air. Three men in suits had drawn guns and were moving around the lobby to round up people. The shots that had nearly killed Patrick's classmate must have been from one of them. He glanced toward the front desk. *Carter!* He was crouched down next to the desk, eyes focused on the lead shooter.

Carter's eyes tracked across the room, and he met Patrick's gaze. He shook his head subtly. It was a little late for a warning not to use his powers, but Patrick understood. They'd have to wait for backup to arrive. If it was necessary to save someone's life again, Patrick would make a move. But if he could wait the shooters out, and the police or another one of the team—even Carter—could defuse the situation, there was no reason for Patrick to act yet.

"Cell phones!" the leader snapped. "Put 'em on the floor and kick 'em to the center of the room."

The man had a hint of a foreign accent. *Serban*? Patrick had never seen the famed crime lord before, but he knew he was still on the loose. It must've been him. That would explain why he was calling out for Dean. He wanted to kill him to get revenge on his father, who had betrayed Serban. At least, that was the way Patrick had heard it. And if this was Luca Serban, then Patrick knew he wouldn't stop at three guys with guns. There had to be more to his plan. This guy had backups within backups.

"Phones!" one of Serban's cronies snapped.

Patrick yanked his phone from his pocket, put it on the floor, and kicked it across the room. He looked at Raina and nodded. Hands trembling, she reached into her own pocket and withdrew her phone. One by one, the other teens sent their phones skidding into the middle of the room.

"Lock the doors," Serban said.

Patrick looked around for anything he could use for a distraction, but he was cloistered between too many of his classmates to do anything. If Serban or his men shot at Patrick, one or more of the other teens might be hit. Patrick couldn't risk it. He'd have to do the thing that was hardest for someone with super speed—wait.

CHAPTER 60

Jolie floored the gas pedal and weaved through traffic over the bridge to the Platform. Three police cruisers and Agent Ross's SUV paced her. How had Serban gotten into Sterling Enterprises at all, let alone armed? He must've paid someone off or replaced a guard with one of his own men.

Either way, he wasn't going to get away with it. He was out in public, maybe the first real mistake he'd made since he'd escaped. No way she was going to let him slip away again. She tightened her fingers around the steering wheel and pulled off the exit ramp onto the Platform.

"Gideon, update?"

Gideon's voice echoed from her car's speakers. "We have the security footage pulled up in Dean's office. Serban's men just locked the doors. I see four of them, counting Serban."

"Carter's inside?"

"Yeah. He's behind the front desk. He moved out of sight of the guy who went to lock the door."

"You don't think he'll try to make a move, do you?"

Gideon paused. "No. He's too smart for that. He's biding his time."

"We're minutes away. Just stay where you are."

"They're lining up the captives against a wall."

"Where's Dean?"

"He's here with me, but he can't use his powers without revealing to everyone here that he's Drifter. If he goes downstairs, Serban's likely to shoot him where he stands."

"If it comes down to using his powers or people dying—"

"I know."

"What about the rest of the team?"

"We sent out another message for them to hold back. If a bunch of superheroes come blasting into this situation, Serban will open fire. People will die."

Despite herself, Jolie felt a swell of pride. Nearly a year ago, Gideon would've leaped into the middle of the situation without a second thought, truncheons twirling and light blasts flying as he recklessly took out Serban and all his men, regardless of the consequences. She'd been worried about his impulsiveness then. She didn't now.

She rounded the corner and saw Sterling Enterprises ahead. She squealed to a halt behind Gideon's Mustang and leaped out of her car. The other police vehicles came in behind her. Agent Ross jumped out of his SUV and began gearing up. Jolie went to her trunk and took out her bulletproof vest and sidearm. She placed her phone inside the trunk and put it on speaker so Gideon could hear everything.

"Hostages in the lobby," she said. "Four gunmen, counting Serban. He's got them lined up against a wall."

"What's his goal?" Ross asked.

"Revenge. He wants to kill Dean Sterling for his father's betrayal."

"Great. That'll make this fun." Ross strapped on his vest and grabbed a bullhorn. "You want to handle negotiations?"

"I think you're a bit better trained for that than I am."

Ross turned to the others. "All right, everyone. Fan out and find alternate entrances to the lobby. Anderson, with me."

Jolie retrieved her phone and followed Ross up the steps. They huddled behind a pillar near the glass doors, where they could peer inside without being obvious. Ross took a deep breath, nodded to Jolie, and stepped out from behind the pillar. He raised his bullhorn. Jolie drew her sidearm and trained it on the glass door.

"Luca Serban, this is Agent Timothy Ross, FBI! We've got the building surrounded. Come out now, and no one gets hurt."

Gunshots and shattered glass filled the air. Jolie pressed herself behind the pillar. A moment later, the gunfire stopped. Ross lay on his back, gasping, but it looked like his vest had taken most of the shots. He had a bloody wound on one shoulder.

"I'm . . . really tired of . . . that guy shooting me." He grunted.

He crawled behind the pillar and slumped over next to Jolie. She knelt next to him and checked the wound. It was a clean through-and-through.

Ross hissed as Jolie's fingers probed his shoulder. "He's not coming quietly."

"No," Jolie replied. "I think this is going to get messy."

She clenched her jaw. There was only one option she could think of, and it was risky. She reached into her belt and withdrew a Crybaby, one of the sonic grenades Sterling Labs had created for police riot control. The shrill cry it emitted might be enough to disable Serban and his cronies, but it would also affect everyone else inside. It was better than watching them die.

"Get down to the other cops and tell them to get their earbuds in. Have them get ready to breach. It's our only move."

Ross eased up to his feet and hurried down the steps. Jolie put her own noise-canceling earbuds in and gripped the Crybaby in her left hand. If this didn't work, a lot of people would die, and it would be on her conscience. But there were few other options. It would have to do. Jolie hung up her phone and tucked it away.

Her strike team rushed up the stairs, armed to the teeth. Thumbing the activator on the Crybaby, Jolie faced the lobby. Serban and his lackeys had turned away, their attention focused on the hostages. Jolie took a breath, released the activator, and hurled the sonic grenade. The silver sphere touched the ground, and everyone in the lobby clutched their ears and screamed.

Jolie rushed in, pistol raised. Across the vast room, Paul led the other officers in through the side door. Serban's three cronies pressed their palms to their ears and screamed along with the lobby's other occupants. Jolie ignored them and rushed up to the first gunman. She took him by the wrist and slapped cuffs on him.

The other officers quickly disabled the remaining gunmen. The Crybaby fizzled out, its timer expired.

"I apologize for any harm you may have sustained. It had to be done to stop the men holding you hostage." Jolie looked around the lobby. "Where's Serban?"

No way had he slipped out again. Maybe he'd ducked into one of the clusters of people to hide. She scanned the faces, hoping to catch a glimpse of his grim, square features. A hand rested on her shoulder.

Patrick pointed behind Jolie. "He ran down that hallway. Took off as soon as our ears started tingling. Carter rushed after him. I would've gone too, but—"

"Your secret identity, I know. I'm going after them. Tell Gideon."

Jolie shoved the man she'd cuffed toward Paul and ran down the hallway Patrick had indicated, not waiting for a response. Serban wasn't going to get away this time. She'd run him to ground no matter what it took.

* * *

With Dean at his side, Gideon stepped off the elevator and into the lobby, clutching the nightstick he'd appropriated from one of Dean's guards. It didn't look like he'd need it; the situation was well in hand. He stepped past Agent Ross, patting the man on the shoulder as he went, and into the lobby. Patrick rushed up to him.

"Where's Jolie?" Gideon asked.

"Serban ran. Jolie and Carter went after him."

"Which way?"

Patrick pointed to a hallway.

"Catch up to them," Dean said. "I'll make sure everything's all right here."

Gideon sprinted in that direction. He couldn't be more than a few seconds behind. Between him, Jolie, and Carter, they had a chance to take Serban down for good. He rushed into the hallway, looking for any sign of the others. The hall intersected with another. Gideon stopped and listened. The dull thump of footsteps sounded like it was coming from the left. Gideon ran that way.

He spotted Jolie ahead, rounding another corner to the right. He sprinted faster and came around the corner after her. The hall ahead ended with a door, the sun shining through a narrow window. Serban must've already made it outside. Jolie pushed through, and Gideon stopped the door from closing and stepped out after her.

She stopped to scan the area. "Where'd they go?"

If Gideon were Serban, he would've made for the edge of the Platform. He might've even had a boat there, waiting to pick him up. The nearest edge was to their left.

He stepped around a dumpster and looked out. The alley between Sterling Enterprises and its neighboring building led out into a small park. On the other side was a boardwalk that sat just above the water. Gideon scanned the park.

"There!"

Serban dashed across the grass with Carter hot on his heels. Gideon nodded to Jolie, and they took off in pursuit. There were no civilians in sight for Serban to use as hostages to ensure his escape. Carter reached the boardwalk first and threw himself behind a hot dog stand as Serban fired on him. Gideon clenched his jaw and pushed himself harder. Jolie paced him step for step. They sprang off the grass, over the sidewalk, and onto the boardwalk. Gideon dropped down next to Carter.

"You all right?"

Carter nodded. "He didn't get me."

Gideon glanced around the edge of the hot dog stand. Jolie had continued after Serban, who had reached the end of the boardwalk. Gideon offered Carter his hand. The younger man took it, and Gideon pulled him to his feet. Together, they rushed after the escaping crime lord.

* * *

Jolie raised her pistol as Serban reached the edge of the boardwalk. The burly man stopped, looked over the edge, and swung around. His jaw was set, a fiery rage smoldering behind his dark eyes. He tightened his grip on his gun.

"Don't move, Serban! Drop the weapon."

"Why can't you just let it go?" Serban shouted. "The game is over, Detective. You're never going to catch me."

"Looks like I just did." Jolie took a step forward, keeping her gun trained on him. "Put your gun down. Right now."

Footsteps clacked on the wooden surface behind her. Jolie didn't take her eyes off Serban. He backed toward the edge. Jolie tightened her finger on the trigger.

"Don't move!"

"Just give up, Serban." Gideon's voice, coming from behind her, was surprisingly calm. "You know it's over."

The crime lord shook his head. "I didn't rise to the top for some scruffy vigilante and his wannabe-cop girlfriend to bring me down."

"The top, Serban?" Gideon asked. "Is that where you are? Constantly looking over your shoulder, only coming out of the shadows long enough to hurt someone who's wronged you and disappear again? Is that what the top looks like to you?"

"I can rebuild. I'm patient. It may take a year or five or more, but I'll get back what you all took from me." Serban took another step back.

Jolie clenched her jaw. She didn't focus on his words, or even Gideon's. Her aim never wavered. Serban had hurt too many people, caused too many deaths, for her to feel any sympathy for him.

"Not one more step!" she yelled.

"What are you gonna do, Detective? You're no killer; you'd have done it by now." Serban's heel brushed the edge of the boardwalk. "Goodbye."

Serban raised his gun.

Jolie fired.

Once, twice, three times. Serban toppled off the edge of the boardwalk. Jolie rushed over and looked down. A boat sat in the water below. Serban lay in the back, blood pooling on the white surface around him. A driver at the front of the boat stared at his boss's body for a moment before cranking the engine. Jolie fired as the boat sped away, but her bullets struck water.

She dropped to her knees. Her shots had been accurate. They all had struck Serban's center mass. Based on the blood in the boat and the flecks on the planks beneath her knees, she surmised that he hadn't been wearing a vest. Luca Serban was dead. One boat-driving crony wouldn't cause them problems.

Gideon sat on the edge of the boardwalk and wrapped an arm around her shoulders. Jolie shifted her legs so she was sitting beside him rather than kneeling, her feet dangling above the water. Carter sat down on her other side.

"He didn't give me a choice," she whispered.

"I know." Gideon kissed her forehead. "You did the right thing. He's gone now. He won't bother us or this city again."

Jolie leaned her head against Gideon's shoulder and cried. She'd taken lives before, but it had always been under fire. The only other time she'd so directly and intentionally shot someone who hadn't been shooting back was when Katrina Monahan had killed Carter's father. Even then, Monahan had survived. But Serban was dead, and Jolie had to live with the knowledge that she was the one who'd killed him.

But the city was safer. She'd have to sit through hours of paperwork, IA investigations, and debriefs from her superiors and Agent Ross's, but at least the end was in sight. That was all that mattered. It was over.

CHAPTER 61

One month later

Patrick grinned as he walked through the church auditorium toward Carter, who was talking and laughing with Raina. They had gotten together shortly after the Sterling Enterprises debacle, after Patrick returned to San Francisco. He and Carter had talked over the phone many times since then, and from the sound of things, he and Raina had hit it off.

Patrick missed it there, but it was different from the homesickness he had felt for San Francisco. It was more nostalgic, a bittersweet feeling, knowing he was where he belonged back home but missing the friends he'd made here.

Wes intercepted Patrick and enfolded him in a backslapping hug. Patrick grinned and hugged him back. Patrick had returned at the beginning of the week, but all the preparations for the wedding had kept him from really getting reacquainted with anyone.

"How's life on the coast?" Wes asked.

"Couldn't be better. Honestly, I was surprised I was even welcome at home. But it turns out Mom and Dad had been reading my Bible while I was gone. They had a lot of questions for me, and I was able to lead both of them to Christ! We started attending church with my . . . friend Lucy's family."

"That's great!" Wes smirked. "Did I sense a bit of hesitation before the word 'friend'?"

Patrick rolled his eyes. He and Lucy had gone out on a few group dates since he had returned to San Francisco. Their relationship was growing, and so was Patrick's confidence that he loved her. Speedster or not, he knew that there were some things that he'd have to move a bit slower on.

"We're getting there."

"Congrats, man." Wes ruffled Patrick's hair. "It's good to have you back. We'd better head back; it's almost time to start."

"Be right there."

Patrick continued his path toward Carter and Raina. He made it a few more feet when something pressed into his lower back.

"Freeze; federal agent."

Patrick rolled his eyes. "Hey, Jarrett."

The older man gave Patrick that contagious half-smirk, lowered his extended finger-gun, and gestured for him to sit down. Patrick dropped down in the chair next to Jarrett. On the other side of him sat his wife, a kind-looking blonde woman with ice blue eyes. She wore a formal dress that matched her eyes. Whatever powers she had developed—and Patrick doubted it was toe-lasers, as Jarrett insisted—she seemed to have them under control.

"How's CLOUD?" Patrick asked.

"Got a lot of cataloguing to do," Jarrett said. "Early estimates indicate as many as a few hundred people might've received powers from a nephiloid bite, and there's no way of knowing if we've caught them all. Some might not have checked into a hospital, and that's the only way we can track them. But it's coming along."

"Good." Patrick glanced at Jan. "And you?"

"I'm . . . adjusting."

"I've been there. It gets better." Patrick smiled. "Good to see you guys. I'd better get into position. See you at the reception?"

Jarrett pointed the finger-gun at him. "You know it."

Patrick rose from his chair and subtly sped through the crowd to get to Carter and Raina before anyone else could accost him.

"Well, well. Am I a matchmaker, or what?"

Carter rolled his eyes. "You do pretty good."

"I'll say." Raina smiled up at him. "We miss you at school, Patrick. You sure you won't consider coming back?"

After the hostage situation at Sterling Enterprises, Raina had confronted Patrick. She had seen him use his powers and put two and two together. That made things easier on him. She understood why he had missed school so many times, and it made it easy for Carter to admit that he was the Crusader.

"I've thought about it, believe me," Patrick said. "But no. I'm where I belong."

"Don't be a stranger. Drop in whenever you feel like hanging out."

"Will do." Patrick grabbed Carter's shoulder. "We'd better get moving, bud."

"Oh. Right." Carter rose. "See you in a little bit, Raina."

Patrick and Carter moved toward the front of the church, where Wes pushed the side door open and led them into a hallway. Patrick smiled. He might not be back for good, but while he was there, he at least intended to enjoy every possible moment with the friends who had become his second family.

* * *

Gideon adjusted the knot on his bowtie and studied his reflection. Hair—freshly cut and combed to the side. Beard—immaculately trimmed. Trousers and jacket—so perfectly ironed that no wrinkle dared come near them. Now if only he could get the stupid bowtie into place. The stubborn thing refused to give in.

"Monsters, crime lords, and supervillains, I can handle," he grumbled. "But the Seraph is brought low by a measly length of fabric."

"Need a hand?"

Gideon tilted his head so he could see behind him in the mirror. Dean stood in the doorway, arms crossed, grinning just like the carefree guy Gideon had always known. Gideon turned as Dean entered the room. He, too, was dressed up, though not in a tux, as Gideon was. Slacks and a tie were as far as Gideon could nudge him and the other groomsmen to go.

Dean wiggled the fingers of his prosthetic extremity. "I've only got one real one now, but this one will do in a pinch."

Dean grabbed the knot and tugged it into place. Gideon shook his head helplessly. How had he done that?

"Go to enough black-tie events, you learn a thing or two." Dean rolled his eyes. "Not that those ever get more fun."

Shortly after Ashcroft's defeat, Jarrett had contacted Dean and told him that the government, specifically CLOUD, wanted to contract Sterling Enterprises to build superpower-dampening prison cells, like the ones Arianna and Maddox had developed for Stone Gate. The downside was that Dean had to move to Washington, D.C. while the details of the contract were pounded out. He'd taken Arianna and Maddox—and Audrey—with him two weeks ago, and they had only come back for the wedding.

At least, Dean was coping with his injury. Making a joke about the prosthetic was a good sign that he was healing from his trauma. That made Gideon happier than Dean would ever know.

"You look good," Dean said.

"Thanks." Gideon grinned. "You, too."

"Everyone else is ready, all lined up in the hall and waiting for you."

"What are we waiting for? Let's go."

He followed Dean into the hallway and looked at the row of groomsmen that had assembled. Wes was his best man; and Dean, Carter, and Patrick comprised the rest of the group. If there had been more time, Gideon might have even asked Jarrett to be a groomsman, but those plans had already been made before he met the archer. Jarrett was there, though, and Gideon was glad. He hadn't seen him or Patrick in the month leading up to their return at the beginning of the week.

The four men gathered around Gideon, hugging him and giving last-minute words of encouragement. Gideon smiled and nodded but couldn't begin to process what they were saying. *It's my wedding day.*

"It's time," Wes said.

"Let's do it." Gideon beamed. "Thank you all for being here. I wouldn't want to do this with anyone else standing with me."

"Hey, we've had your back against the worst of the worst," Dean said. "This is nothing."

The others laughed. Dean patted Gideon on the shoulder and nodded toward the door to the sanctuary. Gideon swallowed. He stepped forward and pushed his way in. Roughly two hundred of his and Jolie's relatives and friends were gathered in Refuge Church's sanctuary. As he stepped out, some of those closer to the door smiled and extended their hands. Gideon shook them but did not stay to converse. He pressed toward the stage.

Gideon's father stepped up from the front row. "You ready, son?"

"Definitely."

"After you." Dad gestured to the stage.

Gideon stepped up onto the platform, and the groomsmen lined up beside him. Dad, as the officiant, took his place at center stage. Gideon took a deep breath, swallowed the lump in his throat, and watched the door at the back of the sanctuary, waiting for the moment when his bride would walk through.

The past three months had passed with surprising peace. With Ashcroft in CLOUD custody and Serban dead, Gideon's and Jolie's lives had settled down. They had more free time to be together and to plan the wedding and their future. Not having Patrick, Jarrett, or Hannah around had been the downside to the otherwise-blissful time. Finally, the wedding day had come. Gideon clasped his hands in front of him to keep them from shaking.

Across the sanctuary, the doors parted, and the ushers brought in Jolie's mother, Gideon's mother, and both his and Jolie's grandparents, followed by the bridesmaids. Jolie's sister Rachel was her maid of honor, and the other bridesmaids were some of Jolie's coworkers on the police force and college friends. Jolie had confessed recently that she would have loved to have Hannah and Audrey up there with her, but as with Jarrett, things had already been in motion. Instead, both of the amplified women—along with Jarrett and his wife—sat near the front of the room, immediately behind the families. Gideon tapped his foot as the women made their way down the aisle. Finally, Gideon's white-clad bride appeared in the doorway. He grinned and swallowed the massive lump that instantly formed in his throat.

She was beautiful. He took in the trim white dress and her dark, braided hair, but it was her smile as she saw Gideon that made her truly beautiful to him. Through it all, the guerilla kidnapping and the vigilantism and the supervillains and the sieges, they had remained determined to stay together. He had always known that he was meant to be with her, and he had never wavered in that. Neither had she, even though she must've had her doubts. She had stayed strong, and at last, their time had come. And it was worth it all.

Gideon only heard the pounding of his own heart as Jolie's father gave her away and Dad went through the opening statements of the ceremony. He wished he could still read people's emotions. He would've loved to sense exactly what Jolie was feeling. If her smile was anything to go by, it was the same overwhelming joy Gideon felt.

"At this time, Gideon and Jolie will exchange vows, which they have written."

Gideon swallowed. "Jolie, from our first date, I knew that you were the one for me. I never doubted it as we went through college together and as you moved on to the police force while I started medical school. I never doubted it as I sat in a dirty cage in Venezuela, although I did doubt whether I'd ever actually see you again. But by God's grace, I did make it back, and I did see you again. And through the hard times we've faced—including some very stubborn decisions on my part—my love for you has never faltered. It's only grown. I can't imagine going forward in life without you.

"So, I vow to always protect you, to always love you, to always provide for you. I may not be a superhero anymore, but I vow to be your hero always. I vow to trust you to take care of yourself when I can't. I vow to be the man—to be the leader—that God has called me to be."

Jolie laughed nervously, wiped her eyes, and grinned. Gideon smiled back. That had been hard enough to get through; he couldn't imagine how tough it was going to be for him to listen to her vows without crying.

"You stole my line." Jolie laughed. "Because through it all, I never doubted our love, either. There were times when I was so afraid of what was going to happen because I thought you might be gone or might be drifting away from me. But I never doubted that I loved you or that you loved me."

Gideon smiled sadly. The early days of his vigilante career had been hard for her; she'd considered his actions those of a criminal and had to reconcile that with her love for him. He regretted putting her through that but never what had come from it. It was because of those days that he'd been able to become the Seraph, and the time of difficulty in their relationship had only strengthened their love.

"Watching you fly away to fight evil was never easy," Jolie continued, "but I always knew you'd come back. Not because you were so tough or so invincible but because you were so faithful. You trusted God to get you through every moment, so I did the same. I knew God would bring you back to me because I know He has great plans for our life together.

"So, Gideon Turner, I vow to remain faithful to you always, to be your strongest supporter and your loudest cheerleader, to encourage you when you're down and point you to God when you're struggling. I vow to stand by your side and fight whatever struggles we face together. Forever."

Gideon brushed a tear from the corner of his eye with his thumb and bobbed his head gratefully. Dad stepped to the side to retrieve their rings and handed them to Gideon. They exchanged their rings and the words that went along with them, but Gideon's focus was on the joy he saw in Jolie's eyes—the same joy he felt bubbling in his heart.

"By the power invested in me as a minister of God's Word and this church," Dad said, "I pronounce these two husband and wife. You may kiss the bride."

Gideon stepped forward, pulled Jolie into his arms, and kissed her. Applause filled the sanctuary. Gideon held the kiss for a few more seconds, stepped back, and grinned.

"It is my distinct honor to present to you Mr. and Mrs. Gideon Turner!"

EPILOGUE

Gideon stepped into the dark living room of the old lair in the Tower and looked around. This place, which held so many memories—some good, some bad—was about to leave their lives forever. With him out of the superhero business and everyone else but Carter gone or leaving, they didn't need it anymore. Dean had sold the lair. To whom and for what, Gideon didn't know, but it was done.

He reached over and flipped on the light switch. Jolie stepped behind him and wrapped her arms around his waist as he scanned the room. To his left, where the couch had been, he had tended to Wyatt Jonson's wounds and learned that he was the Crusader. It was also the spot where Gideon had told Dean he was a vigilante, ironically at a time when Gideon himself had been injured. Just in front of him, in the middle of the living room floor, he had stood and fought Katrina Monahan when Jolie walked in and discovered he was the Seraph.

This was my home. So much had happened there. It hurt Gideon's heart to leave it behind, but it was just a place. He would still have the memories with him.

"We should get going," Jolie said.

Gideon had promised to keep the stop brief. He'd just wanted to see it one more time before it was gone forever. They had to get to the airport soon. He turned, slipping out of her arms, and smiled at her. In her eyes, he saw his future.

"Not gonna leave without saying goodbye, are you?" a familiar voice called.

Gideon looked up. Dean stood on the balcony overlooking the living room, leaning against the guardrail and smiling.

"Hey. Didn't know you were here."

"Yeah, but I figured you would be. You're such a sap." Dean walked toward the stairs. "You're a little bit later than I expected."

Gideon blushed. They had made a brief stopover at Jolie's apartment before heading there. He glanced at her, and she gave him a mischievous smirk and a wink.

Dean didn't press the matter. "As busy as the reception was, we didn't really get a chance to get everyone together again."

"Everyone?"

A gust of air blew past Gideon, and Patrick stood next to him, leaning against one of the pillars that supported the balcony.

"Couldn't go back to San Francisco without telling you guys goodbye."

Dean made it to the bottom of the steps and held out his arms. Gideon hugged his best friend and looked around. Audrey, Hannah, and Jarrett walked down from the balcony. Footsteps from the doorway signaled more arrivals. Gideon turned to see Carter and Wes enter.

"Gang's all here." Dean winked. "One last time."

Gideon blinked back tears. "Thank you all for coming."

"We wouldn't have missed it," Patrick said.

Carter pressed his lips together. "You started this. My dad may have been a vigilante first, but you were the first superhero of our age."

"If it hadn't been for you, none of us would be here." Wes stepped forward and wrapped an arm around Gideon's shoulder. "And I do mean that."

"You're an inspiration," Audrey said.

"And a leader," Hannah added.

Jarrett inclined his head. "We'd follow you anywhere."

Gideon smiled, his heart threatening to explode with the array of emotions he felt. He hugged each of them in turn.

"I couldn't have done any of it without all of you," he said. "Dean, you saved my life more than once, back when this all started, and you've been an unconditional supporter since. Carter, Patrick, Wes, you've all stuck by my side and believed in me. Jarrett, Hannah, Audrey, we couldn't have brought down Ashcroft without you three on the team. Thank you all for the kind words, but without you, I'd probably be lying dead in an alley somewhere. So, thank you."

"Group hug?" Dean asked.

Hannah rolled her eyes. "Maybe this once."

Gideon took Jolie's hand and pulled her into the group. The others gathered in and wrapped their arms around one another. Gideon closed his eyes, and tears rolled down his cheeks. *God, thank You for my friends.*

"Okay, Vindicators." Dean smiled through his own tears. "Break."

"I should get back home," Hannah said. "The reservation will not protect itself."

"Same here." Patrick tossed a two-fingered salute. "Love you guys."

Jarrett backed toward the door. "And my wife's waiting up, so I'd better go, or she's going to shoot me with her toe lasers."

"Will you give it up with the toe lasers?" Patrick rolled his eyes. "We all know that's not what she does."

The three of them disappeared through the door. Dean took Audrey's hand and followed.

"Love you guys," Dean said. "And congrats again."

Audrey smiled. "I wish you the best in everything. Bye."

Gideon fought the new wave of tears that threatened to come. With everything going on, he had barely had time to process that Dean's departure was long-term. He was grateful for his fresh start with Jolie, but life without Dean was going to be an adjustment.

Carter patted him on the back and shuffled toward the door. "I'll watch over the city until you get back from your honeymoon. Promise."

"Me, too," Wes added as he ducked out. "I've got a few more months until I leave for law school. I'll make the best of 'em."

Gideon nodded. "I couldn't ask for better successors."

Gideon and Jolie stood alone once again. Gideon exhaled shakily and interlaced his fingers with Jolie's. Together, they walked hand-in-hand toward the door. His eyes scanned the familiar room, soaking it in one last time. Then, reaching for the switch beside the door, he flipped the lights off. They stepped into the hallway and closed the door behind them.

The mischievous light flickered in Jolie's eyes again. "Come on, you. We've got a wedding to celebrate."

"Right behind you."

For more information about

Jake Tyson

&

Heroes' Might

please visit:

www.creatingforcreator.wordpress.com
www.facebook.com/jaketysonauthor96

For more information about
AMBASSADOR INTERNATIONAL
please visit:

www.ambassador-international.com
@AmbassadorIntl
www.facebook.com/AmbassadorIntl

If you enjoyed this book, please consider leaving us a review on Amazon, Goodreads, or our website.

www.ingramcontent.com/pod-product-compliance
Lightning Source LLC
Chambersburg PA
CBHW070611310726
48982CB00001B/51

* 9 7 8 1 6 4 9 6 0 4 4 6 0 *